WILD TEXAS HEARTS

♠

BY

TRACY GARRETT

Tracy Garrett (signature)

Wild Texas Hearts
Copyright© 2017 Tracy Garrett
Cover Design Livia Reasoner
Prairie Rose Publications
www.prairierosepublications.com

DEDICATION

For Jo Davis, my dearest friend, my confidant, my "partner in crime." Who would have thought two empty chairs at the same table would be the start of such an amazing and treasured friendship? You encouraged, badgered and sympathized in equal measure. And you never gave up on this story.

Wolf is for you.

PROLOGUE

The Texas Panhandle, September 1889

Some days a man got so tired of being on the trail he couldn't even stand the company of his own horse.

Cain Richards trudged up the hill, the reins of his mount loose in his fist. Scarlett would probably follow, but he didn't want to chase the big mare if she decided otherwise. He just didn't have the energy. Even his pack horse, a sturdy little mustang mix that could usually go for weeks without tiring, lagged behind, foot sore and all but done in. It'd been a hard couple of months.

He stopped at the top of the rise to wipe the sweat from his face with the sleeve of his dusty shirt and look over the patch of earth he called home. A swell of pride straightened his weary shoulders. The house was situated close to the rocky stream that bisected the land. The corral was off to the right, its whitewashed fencing gleaming in the late afternoon sun. The enclosed area was big enough for a dozen horses, with several large trees shading nearly all of one side. Last spring, he'd finished installing the pump to pull water into the troughs. Now that he didn't have to carry water, he could add to his herd.

To the north of the house sat a decent sized barn, and in its shadow, the chicken house he'd finished for Emily the day before he left to go hunting.

Everything else, for as far as he could see, was wide open prairie, perfect for grazing the horses he planned to have someday. The first time he'd ridden through this valley, hunting buffalo for the Army, he'd known he was meant to live right here, between these hills.

That was the summer he'd earned his nickname. The soldiers in the hunting party started calling him *Wolf* for his ability to find their quarry when no one else could. His skill had served him well, earning enough money to buy this spread and plan for the future. And it had brought him his wife.

He was eighteen when he signed the papers to buy the land he now called home. He remembered that rainy spring morning like it happened yesterday. By the first winter, he'd dug a well for the dry times—which turned out to be nearly every summer—put up a small corral for the horses, and built a one-room cabin. Then, he met Emily.

Wolf grinned, thinking of his wife of eight years—or almost eight. When he'd led that small group of worn-down, dusty soldiers past the gatehouse of Fort Elliott that cold October afternoon in 1881, he never dreamed his life was about to change forever. He thanked God every single day that he'd gotten that assignment.

Leading the horses, Wolf trudged down the hill to the stream, humming Emily's favorite tune. He wanted to wash the dust and sweat from his face and neck. The last two days had been high-summer hot, unusual for September, even here in the Texas plains. But the aspen trees were gilding the higher elevations with golden leaves, meaning fall was coming on fast. Wolf was looking forward to some cool mornings for a change.

He glanced toward the house, but didn't see any movement. The silence was unusual, but he was late coming home. He'd planned to be back mid-morning. Maybe that's why the kids hadn't come squealing out of the house to greet him. They'd probably grown tired of watching for him.

It had been a hell of a trip, but worth every sweaty, dusty mile. He'd been gone for a little more than two weeks. The meat he brought would feed them well this winter, and the otter and beaver pelts tied across the packhorse should bring in enough money to purchase all the other supplies they needed.

Wolf shook the water from his hands and knocked the dust from his hat. Right now, he was looking forward to enjoying a good meal and spending time with Emily, making up for the thirteen nights he'd spent alone. He pushed to his feet and studied the cabin again.

Nothing moved. Not even the chickens were pecking in the grass for feed they might have missed. And the wash was still hanging on the line beside the house. Emily never left it out past noon. A wave of foreboding scratched down the length of his spine and stabbed into his gut. He took two steps forward, studying the little house.

No smoke. There was no fire burning in the hearth, no smoke staining the brilliant blue sky behind the house.

Something was wrong.

Wolf picked up his pace. "Emily?" He called for his wife, then his two children. "Calvin? Amanda!" The corral was empty. The barn door stood open. Feathers were strewn around the coop.

He took the last two hundred yards at a run. Vaulting over the stairs, he slammed through the half-open door, then skidded to a halt. Chairs were overturned, dishes were smashed, clothes were strewn in a trail leading from the children's bedroom. Dark puddles of jam dripped from the kitchen table to the floor. Where the hell was his family?

"Cain?"

Wolf spun toward the sighing sound and spotted his wife on the floor beside their bed. Throwing furniture out of his way, he dove to his knees beside her. He didn't need to ask what happened. The torn bodice of her dress, the scratches and bruises on her exposed breasts, the blood on her skirt. An animal cry of pain ground its way from deep in his soul. His hands shook as he smoothed her honey blond hair off her battered face.

"Honey, who did this?"

"Took them. My babies," she panted.

Wolf couldn't breathe. His children. Someone had stolen his children. "When?"

"Morning," was all she could manage. Her body began to shake. Wolf tried to gather her close. Her moan stopped him.

Dread and grief warred in his mind. Raw fury eclipsed them both.

"Who?"

"Don't know." Emily tried to moisten her lips. Wolf kissed her gently, doing it for her. "Six. Seven. Men. Went south." She coughed, the sound rasping from her lungs.

"Easy, honey. Let me go for the doc and—"

She shook her head, once. It was all she had strength for.

He pressed a kiss to her forehead, brushing away the tears that fell onto her skin as he cried. "You have to hold on, Emily. You can't leave me."

"Love. You. Find my...babies." Her breath eased out on the word.

Emily was dead.

CHAPTER ONE

Doan's Crossing, Texas, December 1889

Wolf sat at the far end of the saloon, such as it was, with his back against a rough-sawn pillar. The narrow block of splinter-edged wood wouldn't offer much protection to a man his size if bullets started flying, but it was better than the walls. They looked flimsy enough for the winter winds howling outside to knock them over and blow them clear to Missouri.

Sitting in a saloon of any kind went against the grain. Wolf was an alone kind of man now, and the last months riding a hard trail hunting for the Harrison gang had hammered that into his bones. But tonight, he needed more than his own company.

He rubbed a tired hand across the thick growth of beard edging his jaw. The wind had kicked up just after sundown, moaning through the walls of his rented room like a woman's screams, making him itchy, jumpy. This two-bit watering hole in a town teeming with cowboys, peddlers and thieves was just across the street from his boarding house. Besides, whiskey was whiskey, and the amber liquid in his glass was less watered down than most would serve.

Wolf downed the contents in one swallow, felt it sear a path to his gut. He'd had worse in the three months he'd been hunting the Harrison gang. Eighty-seven days, three hours and a handful of minutes since he'd come home to find his wife dying, and his son and daughter gone.

Emily.

His beautiful, fragile, perfect wife. Grief sliced under his tough hide to knife him in the heart again. He made himself focus on the hate burning in his belly, demanding revenge, and fed the blaze with the memories that haunted him every second of every day. He would find his children. Then the men who'd defiled and murdered a defenseless woman would die like the animals they were.

Wolf glanced around the saloon. The establishment was little more than four plain walls and a white-washed ceiling. Four kerosene lamps that would have been more at home on a sailing ship were suspended from the low ceiling, and the lack of illumination gave the bar a dingy, seedy appearance. At least, it smelled clean. Evidently, the saloon-keeper preferred the scent of lye soap to sour mash.

He'd expected it to be busier on a Saturday night, but there were only four of them in the place, counting the bartender. The other two patrons, drunken cowboys whose smell alone would have driven him to the back of the room, sat at the same table, arguing across the three feet of scarred, stained wood that separated them.

Wolf studied the woman behind the bar—at least, he thought it was a woman. She wore stained buckskin pants that were thin from years of wearing and a baggy homespun shirt that looked equally well-used. The only clean things about her were the matching pearl handled revolvers she wore at her waist, stuck into mismatched holsters, held up by a wide leather belt.

No real curves showed beneath the ill-fitting garb, but she didn't look like any man he'd ever seen. Her dark brown hair looked like it had been hacked off at her shoulders with a dull knife. What was left was held out of her eyes with a colorful beaded band. If she truly was a female, she made sure few would realize it. She didn't seem to take much notice of it herself.

As if he'd drawn her attention by wondering, she grabbed a bottle of whiskey and headed his way. The gentle sway of her hips brought his body to painful attention. Definitely a woman.

"Want another?" She gestured with the half-full bottle.

He nodded toward his empty glass and looked back to the cards spread out in front of him. Solitaire wasn't really his game, but he refused to suffer through the stench of the other two just for a game of poker.

"Queen of hearts."

Wolf glanced at the finger pointing to his card game. Her clothes might look stained and dirty, but she wasn't. When he inhaled, the clean scent of soap surrounded him. His gaze traced her arm, past the bulky shirt that, up close, hinted at some interesting curves, into an amazing pair of dark blue eyes, edged with gold, and fringed with black lashes that curved nearly to her eyebrows. Eyes a man could lose himself in. "What?"

"You missed a play. Red queen to black king."

She moved the card for him, filled his glass and turned back to the bar. For the time it took her to cross the room, Wolf didn't look away. He couldn't. His whole body hummed with need. There was a time, back when he was young and foolish, when he would have tossed down a few coins and satisfied the need.

Then he met Emily James, daughter of Major Reginald & Ophelia James, of the United States Army, in command at Fort Elliot, and the darling of every soldier there. Only seventeen, she was so tiny. The top of her head, even with her hair piled on her head in some fancy style, barely reached the middle of his chest. And he could span her waist with both hands with the better part of one left over.

When he married her, took her to his bed, Emily was far too delicate to bear even a small part of his real need. So he learned to control his desires, deny his body's pounding want.

Now, Emily was dead. And it had been so long.

Disgusted with himself, he threw down the cards and tossed back the whiskey. He had to get out of here. He was losing his mind if the sight of a woman in men's clothes had him wanting to change his plans for the night.

A shout rang out.

"Now, see here, ya yeller bellied low-life. I say I can."

"Ain't possible," the other bellowed. "Yer too dang short!"

The bartender waded into the middle of the argument. "Cletus! Rufus! Stop this right now. I have other customers."

Wolf glanced around to be sure he hadn't missed anyone in the room. She must be referring to him.

"Don't you fret, Miss Lizzie. We can solve this right quick." The cowboy tried to pat her arm, but he was so soused he had to grab her shoulder to keep from toppling over.

Wolf was half out of his seat before he realized she didn't seem concerned. He settled back to see how she handled them, but kept a hand on the well-worn handle of his Colt revolver.

"Rufus," she leaned away from the man, waving at the air beneath her nose. "You're drunk." She lifted his hand from her shoulder and gave him a shove that landed him back in a chair.

"Well, o' course I am," he cackled. "It's Fri-dee!"

"Today is Saturday, and since when did the day of the week matter?" She planted her hands on her decidedly shapely hips and scowled at the men. "If you two spent half as much time riding herd as you do in here, you'd be retired and back in Tennessee with your wives by now."

The other cowhand hooted with laughter. "Yer probably right, Miss Lizzie. Rufus, let's settle this so I can go git rich and git home."

"Sure, but *I'll* be the one t' get rich, not you." Rufus surged to his feet and reached for Lizzie to steady himself again. When he stopped swaying, he swept his hat from his head. "Thank you kindly, barkeep."

Even from where he sat, Wolf could see Lizzie turn her head and stifle a gag. But it didn't slow down her talking.

"Just what do you two have to settle?"

"I say I can spit farther than Cletus, here, and—"

"I say he's too short," the other finished.

"Hold on." Her hands went back to her hips, causing an interesting gap to open between the buttons up the front of her shirt. Wolf settled his attention on the exposed curve of pale skin while she berated the cowboys.

"You know I don't allow spittin' in this establishment." She pointed toward the door. "Take it outside."

"Well, hell," Cletus grumbled. "You can take the first shot, Rufus."

Wolf's gaze snapped to the men. He hoped they meant shots of whiskey, but both drew their revolvers. He shot to his feet. "Put them away before someone gets hurt."

Lizzie and both men turned to stare at him, or rather at the Colt he held steady in his hand.

"It's all right, mister. They ain't hit it yet." She winked at him and turned away.

Wolf frowned, confused. What the hell was going on? Two men were threatening to shoot up the saloon and she just winked like a floozy on a work night?

He watched in disbelief, as first one, then the other, took a bead on the fancy mirror above the bar and fired. Neither bullet hit the target.

"That's enough now. You've had your fun. Out!" With a hand on a shoulder of each man, Lizzie aimed them toward the street.

To Wolf's amazement, the men holstered their pistols, tipped their hats and stumbled out the door, weaving together in perfect synchronization. Lizzie watched them climb on their identical roans before turning back to him.

"Sorry about that. I suppose I should have warned you." She carried their empty glasses, and the half bottle they'd been too drunk to finish, to the bar.

Wolf slipped his revolver back into the holster at his waist and strode to the bar. "What the hell was that all about?"

"Rufus and Cletus are brothers. They were sailors who got too old for the sea. When no captain would sign them on, they used their shooting abilities to protect a wagon train heading west from Tennessee. When they got to Texas, they fashioned themselves into cowboys and joined up with an outfit moving cows to Dodge City. Late last fall, the herd came through Doan's Crossing. Rufus and Cletus dropped in here on their night off, decided they liked it, and never left town.

"They come in here every night, get stumbling drunk, and start arguing. Been at it for almost a year, or so I've been told." She shook her head, remembering. "When they get to the part about which one can spit the farthest, I throw them out. They each take one shot at my mirror and leave. It's become a—well, a ritual of sorts." She glanced at the garish gilded object on the wall. "They always miss."

"Why let it continue?"

She glanced toward the sound of the two men singing a sea-shanty at the top of their lungs as they rode out of town. "They always pay for their whiskey." She pinned him with her night-dark stare. "Well, hell. Look around you. It isn't as if they're chasing away customers." She wiped at the bar with a damp rag, smearing around a year's worth of old liquor and sweaty customers. "Besides, they used to be sailors."

Sadness lingered after the statement, but Wolf chose not to pursue it. "They had to hit something. These walls are too thin to stop a bullet."

"That's why the mirror is hanging where it is. It used to be over there." She waved the grimy rag at the opposite wall where a haphazard patch had been nailed onto the smoke-darkened wood. "The first time, they missed and put two holes through the preacher's parlor wall while he was sitting in the room, reading the Bible—the Book of Revelation, I think. Evidently, the good reverend thought the end time had finally come and was not too pleased to discover he was mistaken."

Her lips curved in a wicked grin, snagging his attention. "Thought he'd finally been delivered from this hell on earth." She snickered. "After that, the sheriff said I had to move the mirror, so I moved it over here to keep the peace. There's nothing on the other side of this wall but dirt. The boys can have their fun and nobody gets hurt."

Wolf glanced at the mirror. Why anyone would want such a fancy piece of wood and glass was beyond him. "What will you do if they hit it?"

"Make 'em take a bath."

Her statement was so matter-of-fact, he laughed. The sound surprised him. He hadn't laughed since Emily...

The smile froze on his face. He could feel his lips grow stiff, ugly. Raw grief snuck up and cleaved him down the middle, left him wide open, bleeding.

The woman's eyes rounded until he could see his own reflection in their remarkable blue depths, a portrait of loss edged in gold. "Uh—I mean—they'd better not break it." She eased away until she bumped up against the wall. "It isn't mine."

Wolf stared at the woman who could face down two armed drunks, but got spooked when a man stopped smiling. Hell. He tossed down a couple of coins. "Thanks for not watering down the whiskey."

He strode across the street to the boarding house, hesitating as he reached for the door. He couldn't go inside. The thought of being trapped under a roof made his lungs seize. He headed for the livery to check on his horses, instead. He could watch for the men he hunted from there.

• ♥ •

Lizzie Sutter watched the intimidating stranger until he was swallowed up by the darkness. She could barely pick out his footsteps on the boards of the sidewalk. He was real quiet for such a big man.

There was silence for a moment as he crossed the bare dirt beyond the bank to the steps in front of the general store. She counted the soft thud of boots on the wood as he went the length of the walk. Silence again, then a flash of light as he opened the door to Hank's livery. When the glow disappeared, she slumped against the wall and hauled in a deep breath.

Even with his heavy beard and trail-worn clothes, he'd seemed to be a good man. Then he'd looked at her like she crawled on her belly instead of walking upright. As long as she lived, she hoped never to see that look aimed at her again. What had she done to bring such a look of anger, of pure despair into his eyes?

She went to get his glass and dropped into the chair he'd vacated. Leaning forward on her elbows, she moved the cards around without really looking at them. He sure was a good-looking cuss. Tall, broad through the shoulders, lean in the hips, with eyes like hammered pewter. His hair was black as a moonless night, shot through with silver. She didn't think he was all that old, but he looked worn out, like he'd been carrying a heavy load on his shoulders for a long time. The stranger's laugh was nice, though. Real warm. It made you want to find out what he thought was funny just so you could hear it some more.

Then, without warning, those silvery gray eyes had changed to the color of steel, like a winter sky right before a thunderstorm. A shiver ran down her spine. She hated storms.

It was a shame, really. He was a lot more handsome than she was used to seeing. When he came into the saloon, she'd had to look up to see his face and she was a far cry from dainty. His shoulders were wide enough to cast a shadow she could hide in on a hot summer afternoon.

Lizzie had to admit, at least to herself, that she'd looked more than twice. A lot more. Her fingers were still itching to sink into all that long dark hair.

What was it about him? Lots of the men who wandered into her saloon were big and strong, a few were more handsome, but none of them made her wish they'd stick around a while longer.

Lizzie tossed down the card she held. "Foolishness," she spat out as she straightened the deck. It was pure foolishness to want to snuggle close and let him keep all her troubles at bay. But dang it, she did.

Staring at the scarred table top, Lizzie sighed. Why couldn't a man like him be interested in her? She could shoot as well, drink as much and spit as far as any man, she could make a living playing poker, but she didn't know the first thing about making a man want to stick around for dinner.

She wandered across the stained wood floor to stand in front of the ornate convex mirror, the only token that remained from her childhood aboard her grandfather's ship. The reflection that stared back was the same as before the stranger came into her saloon, but now she felt restless, unsatisfied. "What is it, Grandpa? What's wrong with me?"

A deep ache in her chest accompanied the memories of the man she'd spent most of her growing-up years with. She missed the old Captain. The only other person who remembered those days was her brother, Will, and he was all the way out in California. She'd started west more than a year ago, intending to join him, but she stopped for a spell in Texas and couldn't seem to get going again. Maybe it was finally time to move on.

She gathered the cards and empty glass and carried them back to the bar, blowing out lamps as she went. Stains from years of patrons decorated the wood-plank surface. Dunking the glasses into hot soapy water, she scrubbed them out and reached for a clean towel. If only she could have made him a little bit interested. She slapped the first dried glass onto the bar, disgusted with her silly wishes. If a man didn't want her the way she was, to hell with him. To hell with the whole danged lot of them.

She yanked the heavy canvas curtain across the front window, and slammed the big door hard enough to have it bouncing open again. Muttering at her foolishness, she stepped outside to grab the wooden latch. Something made her stop. A tiny sound, out of place even in this rough part of town. Listening carefully, she waited. There it came again. A muffled scream. She latched the big door, ran behind the bar and fumbled for her rifle. That wasn't the voice of a woman begging a man to go easy with her.

It was the plea of a terrified child.

Lizzie doused the remaining lights and slipped out the back door. There wasn't much of a moon and she wasted precious seconds waiting for her eyes to adjust. Panic bubbled just beneath the surface of her control. She couldn't be too late. Turning in the direction she thought the sound came from, she did her best to move in silence. Peeking around each corner she came to, Lizzie finally spotted the shape of a man stretched out on the ground near the back of the livery. His weight held a struggling little girl pressed into the dirt.

The man raised a hand and light from the livery window glinted off the knife he held, threatening, stealing a childhood.

Lizzie would die before she let that happen. The click when she pulled back the hammer of her rifle stilled the monster.

"Get off her. Now!"

The man moved and the knife flashed again as he threw it at Lizzie. Time slowed. She should duck, but that would give the monster time to use the child as a shield. She pulled the trigger an instant before the knife buried deep in her thigh. Sheer force of will kept her on her feet as the man collapsed with a third eye blooming in the middle of his forehead.

Pinned down by the dead weight, the little girl screamed and screamed. Lizzie swore like the sailor she used to be. "Hush now, baby. He won't hurt you anymore." She had to work had at making her voice gentle. Her leg hurt like a son of a bitch. "I'll get you out from under there, but you have to give me a minute, here." Thankfully, the child's screams subsided to terrified sobs. Lizzie wasn't sure that was an improvement.

Leaning on her rifle for support, Lizzie murmured a prayer for courage and yanked the knife from her leg. She couldn't stop the gasp of pain, though she snapped it short. *Damn, that hurt!* Tying off the wound with her handkerchief, she limped to the little girl, dropping to the ground beside her. The girl who stared up at Lizzie from under the dead man was even younger than she'd guessed. The sight of her torn nightdress and the bloody scratches on her arms and chest made Lizzie want to kill the son of Satan again, but slower, so he'd really feel it.

When Lizzie pushed at the heavy body, the girl whimpered. "Easy, sweetheart. You're safe now." Lizzie tried to move the body again. The man weighed more than a horse and the child was going beyond panic to shock. "We'll have you home in no time." She leaned closer and put her shoulder against the man's. "Here we go now, honey. Just. Let. Me…" On the third shove, the body moved enough for the girl to scramble free. Sobbing, calling over and over for her mama in a choked voice, the child fled down the alley and disappeared into the darkness.

Lizzie collapsed into the dust, her leg hurting like fury. Just lying still for a while sounded wonderful, but she couldn't stay here. Someone had to have heard the shot, and if they paid it any mind, they'd run for the law. She couldn't be found with the body. She wasn't sorry the devil's spawn was dead, but she didn't want to be connected to his demise, either.

Lizzie tried to stand, but couldn't get her legs under her. A small sound warned her she wasn't alone. She lunged for the rifle, but a huge hand snagged it before she could. Terror pounded through her as she rocked back onto her backside and looked way up into a pair of storm-gray eyes.

The man who'd been in her saloon earlier that evening racked the lever action to flip out the spent shell then held out a hand. She hesitated before accepting his help. Once on her feet, she worked at holding herself together.

Damnation! Her heart thudded in a rapid tattoo and she could feel every beat in her leg.

Glancing around, the man scooped up the spent casing and offered if to her along with the rifle. "Get out of here before someone sees you."

"I'm not leaving you to take the blame for this. I did it, and I'm not sorry. He deserved to die for doing what he was to that baby."

The man nodded. "That may be, but he wasn't in town alone, and you don't want his friends to find out it was you who pulled the trigger."

"Who the hell was he?" She gritted her teeth against a wave of nausea.

"One of the Harrison gang."

Lizzie searched her memory for any rumor she'd heard. "Don't know them."

"Pray hard you can keep it that way. Now, get going. I won't be blamed because no one will know I was here. If I'm seen, the marshal can check my rifle. It hasn't been fired."

He turned his head, listening, then nudged her toward the saloon. "Someone's coming. Get moving. I'll catch up to you." Leaning over, he scooped up the dead man's knife and cleaned it with several quick stabs into the dry ground, covering each mark with a slide of his boot. Then he dropped the lethal blade close to the body, where no one could tell it had been thrown with near-deadly accuracy.

"Thanks, mister." Lizzie limped away, working hard not to drag her leg. No need to leave a trail that a blind man could follow. Even rushing, she couldn't move very fast. A short minute later, the stranger loomed behind her, swept her off her feet and strode into the thick shadows behind the buildings.

Too shocked to struggle, Lizzie lay still in his arms. What a strange feeling, being carried like a princess in those books her mother once read to her. She should protest. Self-preservation kept her silent. He carried her faster than she could walk.

Voices. Someone was coming on fast. They had to get out of sight. With a tug on his sleeve, Lizzie directed him to the back of the saloon, expecting to be spotted any second, but he shouldered the door open and they slipped inside without being challenged.

While he barred the door and covered the window with an old, grimy curtain, Lizzie limped to the bed. Her leg was on fire, every step agony. Stifling a groan, she collapsed onto the thin, hard mattress. "Thanks for getting me this far. I can take care of myself, now. You should get out of here, in case someone saw us leave. Go out the front. Everyone else will be in the back."

Ignoring her, the stranger stoked the fire and set a large pot of water over the flames to heat. "Take off your pants," he ordered without turning around.

"What?!" Lizzie blushed. She could feel the heat in her cheeks. She'd grown up surrounded by men. How could four little words turn her into such a—a woman?

He glanced over one wide shoulder. "Take it easy," he chided. One eyebrow arched when she still didn't move. Somehow, it made him less frightening. "I want to get a look at that knife wound."

"Sorry, but I don't know you well enough to undress with you in the room." She tried for humor, anything to keep from whimpering like a girl. "You look like an outlaw."

"Sometimes your eyes tell you the truth." He waited for her to make a choice.

"I don't even know your name."

He didn't smile, just reached for the waistband of her trousers. She batted his hands away and snagged the knife she always kept hidden beneath the mattress. Brandishing it, she motioned him back.

"Cain Richards." The exasperation in his voice would have made her smile, if her leg didn't hurt so darn much. He only stared at the knife. "Most folks call me Wolf."

"It fits." Lizzie took a deep breath. She had to calm down. Grandfather always said her instincts were darned good when it came to sizing up strangers. She stared at Wolf, waiting for her heart to slow and her insides to tell her what to do. Finally, she laid the knife aside and relinquished her hold on her buckskin pants. "Do your worst, Wolf Richards," she muttered.

Lizzie stood up long enough for him to get the well-worn hide past her hips, then dropped back to the mattress, clenching her teeth against the pain as he slid the blood-stained cloth the rest of the way down her legs. Her blush returned full force when she remembered she wasn't wearing much beneath the pants. She tugged at the hem of the shirt she had on, praying it was long enough to hide her modesty.

Wolf didn't seem to notice. He held the lantern close and leaned over her leg. "The knife was sharp, at least," he mumbled. "Went in deep, though." He poked at the puffed and red edges around the wound, causing blood to flow again.

"Damned outlaw." She chewed back a little more nausea. "Probably gave me blood poisoning."

One corner of Wolf's mustache twitched, but she couldn't say he was smiling. He set the lamp on the floor. "It needs to be cleaned up, and I'm going to have to sew this some. Do you have a needle and thread?"

Bile soured her throat at the thought of what came next. Lizzie pointed, not trusting the stew she'd eaten for dinner to stay where it belonged if she opened her mouth and gave it a clear path of escape. Wolf rummaged in her sewing box and dumped his choices into the boiling water.

He washed up and came at her with a pan of steaming water, a rag, and a hunk of lye soap. Sitting on his heels beside the bed, he thoroughly cleaned the wound, digging deep to get out any dirt and cloth that was in there.

Lizzie leaned back on both elbows and breathed through her mouth against a wave of nausea. Later, she'd be grateful, but right now she just wanted to ball up a fist and hit him for being so damned thorough.

Then he pulled the stopper on a bottle of whiskey and poured a river of fire over her leg, and she was too busy holding in the screams to follow through with the threat.

When Wolf fished the needle out of the water, Lizzie gave up trying to be brave. "It's going to hurt, isn't it?" stupid question, since any fool knew it would.

He glanced at her, his gray eyes dark and unreadable. "Probably. I'm not the daintiest of folks. You want to drink some of that whiskey?"

"Maybe later. Let's just get this over with." She gritted her teeth and managed to hold still through two stitches. As he knotted the thread for a third one, Lizzie laid back on the bed, unable to stop shaking. The edges of her vision narrowed. The fourth time he pushed the needle through her flesh, she gave up the fight altogether and fainted.

When Lizzie came to, the fire was down to embers and the lamp had been trimmed to barely burning. Careful of Wolf's handiwork, she shoved the blanket aside and turned up the lamp enough to see. He'd wrapped her leg in strips of clean white cloth that looked suspiciously like the only other shirt she owned. The washbasin was empty and her sewing box was put away. Her rifle was propped up in the corner. By the sheen of oil on the barrel, he'd even taken the time to clean it so no one would know it had been fired.

A half-empty bottle of whiskey sat on the floor beside the bed, within easy reach. Lizzie glanced around the empty room. Nothing hinted that someone else had been there. "Damn," she whispered. Couldn't he have stuck around long enough for her to thank him? She skimmed the edges of the bandage with her fingers. He was an odd man, with the nerves of an outlaw, the manners of a gentleman, and the face of Lucifer himself. She wouldn't mind waking up to see him close by. But it didn't matter now.

Wolf was gone.

CHAPTER TWO

Civil, Texas, April 1890

"Just follow the river and you'll find it," she mimicked her former trail boss's smoke-and-crushed-rock voice. "Well, which damn river?" She glared over her shoulder at the last wide creek she'd forded. "Bet he's never even been to this part of the Texas Panhandle."

Lizzie spit into the dust at her mule's feet. "Damn fool cowpoke. If somebody took the trouble to beat the shit out of him, there'd be nothing left but his boots!"

She hurled a few curses over her shoulder in the general direction of the cattle drive she'd been forced to leave a week earlier. "There ain't no town anywhere around here! I hope you get lost on the way to Dodge City. Durned sidewinder," she groused, her frustrating winding down into exhaustion. She hadn't had a good night's sleep in ten days. If she didn't find shelter, they'd be sleeping in the rain again tonight and she just wasn't sure she could take another damp day in the saddle.

Lizzie urged her tired mule on. "Come on, Yeller. Just a little farther. Let's get to the top of this hill and see what we can see. That town has to be here somewhere. I'd really prefer something more solid than wind at my back tonight." The yellow mule's ears flicked toward her as she spoke, but her mount didn't plod any faster. Lizzie wanted to howl in frustration. "Move it, you stubborn old donkey."

The insult worked. The animal picked up the pace, bouncing Lizzie on its broad back. She wiped the sweat from her face with her sleeve and shifted the heavy pack strapped across her back to a more comfortable position. She carried everything she owned in the pack, including extra ammunition for the pair of Navy revolvers strapped around her waist and the rifle nosed into the saddle scabbard.

If not for a swollen river and the sharp stick hidden in the muddy water, all her gear would be slung across the butt of a horse instead of her. No use crying about the past, though. Better to look forward and see about making some better luck for herself.

Lizzie leaned forward in the saddle as the mule labored up the next rise. Stretching tall, she looked around, eager to call it a day. For as far as she could see, there was nothing but open land, grass and rocks. So much for making her own luck.

Her shoulders slumped and she resigned herself to sleeping in the open again. It wasn't a pleasant prospect. Dampness hung in the air like fog and the wind raced down the long valley with wicked purpose. The clouds were gray and heavy, so low she thought she might be able to climb the next hill and touch one. A storm was definitely coming. A big one. If she couldn't find shelter, she at least needed to find a campsite on higher ground. That meant hauling water up hill.

"Damn that trail boss anyway. Just because I didn't have the personal parts he expected to find..."

She shrieked when the mule stepped into a hole, nearly pitching her into the dirt. "Watch where you're going, Yeller."

She and her cussed mule had been following the Canadian River for the better part of a week. She'd crossed so many streams and creeks she should have grown gills and scales by now. And still, there was nothing but more of the same.

Lizzie expected to find some hint of civilization by now. According to the trail boss, when he'd tossed her off the cattle drive and left her in the dust, there was a town about a hundred miles in the direction she'd been going, but she hadn't found it yet. Hell, the military had been moving people and supplies through the Texas Panhandle toward Palo Duro Canyon for months. She should have at least found some sign of them. But there was nothing out here, not even wagon tracks. Only miles of grass, and an occasional buffalo or two.

Lizzie scanned the sloping land again, starting to feel the tickle of panic. There had to be someplace she could stay the night, anything that might provide cover from the storm. She was so tired of sleeping wet she'd even consider sharing a cave with the native wildlife.

Just as she was ready to admit defeat, a shape caught her eye. *A house!* She stared hard into the distance, trying to see through the wet haze, unwilling to fully believe she hadn't conjured it up in desperation. When the image didn't change, she let out a whoop of delight. Yeller jumped sideways, nearly tossing her from the saddle.

"Whoa, Yeller. Easy, boy. Steady now." Lizzie patted the mule's neck and murmured nonsense until the animal settled down. "Didn't mean to surprise you, but I imagine you'll forgive me if you get to spend the night in a barn. Looks like my luck is returning, after all."

Bumping the mule in the ribs, she trotted the remaining length of the valley toward the chimney she'd spotted peeking over the next rise. The reality was even better than her imagination. The center section of the cabin was made of mud and logs, but the parts on either side sported whitewashed wood planks. "Looks like someone did some expanding, Yeller."

She took her time riding up to the house, careful to stay in the open with both hands showing, but no one challenged her approach. All the shutters were closed, making the place look deserted. The pile of dust and branches in the corner by the door seemed to confirm it. "Nobody's been inclined to sweep lately, that's for sure."

Coaxing the mule to a stop, she studied the shuttered windows. "No lights that I can see, Yeller." Shifting her pack again, she slipped the safety strap from one of the revolvers. No need to be unprepared. "Hello in the house. Anybody home?"

She waited and listened, but all she could hear was the rain coming down the valley. Not looking forward to a drenching, she hopped off the mule.

Still cautious, she dropped the mule's reins into the grass, knowing the animal wouldn't move from that spot. It was just too lazy to bother. Lizzie slid the heavy pack from her back and left it in the dust nearby. Drawing her revolver just in case, she approached the house in silence. Nothing moved. No smell of recent cooking scented the air.

She climbed the single step and examined the porch. Months of dirt and debris covered the boards, marred only by the paw prints of a curious raccoon or two, and a coyote. Or maybe a wolf. She glanced behind her at the approaching dusk. That was one animal she had no interest in meeting up with.

Taking her courage in both hands, she knocked. No answer. She banged on the door, hard. "Anybody home? I sure could use a dry place to sleep tonight."

Still no one answered her summons. Trying the latch, she stepped to one side and pushed the protesting door open. No one stopped her. The room was too dark to see much, with all the shutters closed. She spotted a lantern just inside the door, with a small amount of kerosene in it.

"This stuff looks thick enough to paint with," she muttered aloud, digging in her pocket. "I hope it still burns." Lizzie peeled one precious matchstick from the oilcloth wrapped bundle she carried. Using the backside of her shirt, she scrubbed at the lamp's base to clean off a spot. "Damn. Its glass. Can't strike a match on that." Glancing around, she decided the stone hearth was her best hope for a spark. Dragging the match on the stone, she grinned when it shot to life in a flash of sulfur-born fire.

Lizzie touched the flame to the wick and coaxed it to life. A cloud of smoke filled the chimney when she slid it into place. Coughing and waving away the acrid haze, she trimmed the wick until the light overtook the haze, then lifted the lamp and took a look around the empty main room.

A long table sat askew near the sink. Two benches and two chairs were shoved into the space by the hearth. A rocking chair lay on its side across the room. From the layer of dust on everything, the little house had been deserted for some time. A dark stain on the floor by the hearth spoke of some past trouble, but it was too old to worry over right now.

Grinning to herself, she examined the rest of the house. Empty. Satisfied she would be alone, she hurried back outside. Her mule brayed as she walked by. "Just hold on, Yeller. I promise to get you settled before the rain gets here."

Next, Lizzie went to the barn, delighted to find nothing living other than a mouse or two, judging by the gnawed edges of some of the leather tack left behind. The barn was well organized. Tanning tools lay rusting on the shelves. Rope and leather strapping hung in coils nearby. "Wonder why they left all this stuff?" Talking to herself, she chose a stall for Yeller. "Guess I'll just be thankful they did."

There was only moldy hay for feed, so she led Yeller into the large corral. "Eat fast, mule. I don't know what kind of four-legged critters might come visiting, so I'm putting you in the barn for the night." The mule took her advice and buried his nose in the knee-high grass.

She tried the pump next to the trough, but it was rusted solid. Muttering to herself, she hunted up a bucket in the barn and went to the well. The sun-faded stone structure was waist-high and overgrown with flowering vines. Bees buzzed nearby, drawn by the sweet scent of nectar. The builder had fashioned a flat roof of split logs to connect the four corner beams. A thick rope was tied to the leather handle of a heavy wooden bucket. Its length was tied around a stout crossbar overhead and threaded through a stout pulley with a smooth-handled crank at one end.

Lizzie examined the rope and leather for weak spots before lowering the bucket into the inky darkness of the well. She blew out a breath of relief when it splashed into water. Cranking the handle to lift the bucket before it got too heavy, she hauled it to the top and wrestled it to the edge of the well. Scooping a little water in her hands, she brought it close and sniffed it. Nothing to indicate the water was bad. She let the liquid slip through her fingers before touching the tip of her tongue to her damp palm. Cold and sweet. She scooped a little more and took a sip, quickly spitting it out, just in case there was something wrong with it. Wonderful.

She drank her fill, then untied and hefted the bucket. Struggling with the weight, she splashed her way to the corral and back until the small trough was half-full. "That should hold him for a time. I want to explore the house." She filled the bucket again and carried it inside the cabin.

She wandered through the smaller bedroom first, unnerved to find the beds all made up with blankets. A wooden top lay on the pillow of one. Baby clothes were folded neatly on the shelves of one closet. Whoever lived here hadn't planned on staying away.

The other bedroom was larger, with one window overlooking the valley and barn. The other two had a view of the woods crowding close to the back of the house. Heavy wooden shutters with narrow gun slits cut into the center were shut and barred across every window.

A huge feather mattress covered a rope bed. "My favorite." Memories of life on her grandfather's ships, sleeping in swaying rope hammocks, had her smelling the sea on the wind. Lizzie pounded a fist on the big bed. Dust puffed into her face, making her sneeze. "Yep. They've been gone a while."

There were clothes left behind in this room, too. A small oak bureau was filled with them and dusty bottles were arranged across a fancy dressing table. Lizzie ran her work-roughened fingers along the polished edge. "I wonder if they plan to return anytime soon."

She shrugged her shoulders and surveyed the room. "I'm here and they aren't and I'm staying until this weather blows itself out." Dragging her pack into the room, Lizzie made herself at home.

A flash of lightning made her jump. Before the thunder sounded, Lizzie ran for the corral. Yeller would be out of sorts for a week if he was left out in the rain when there was a barn this close. The big mule was waiting by the gate. More thunder rumbled in the distance, reverberating down the long valley. The mule nipped at her sleeve as she reached for the latch. "I'm hurrying, you ungrateful beast." She opened the gate and Yeller bolted for the barn as the heavens opened, leaving Lizzie to follow.

Scraping at the dried muck, she cleared a stall and led the animal inside, tying a rope across the entrance to keep him there. It took another trip out in the rain to get a bucket of water to keep him for the night. Satisfied he'd be safe, she dragged and shoved the heavy barn door shut and ran for the house.

Soaked through and shivering, she added wood to the fire. The previous occupants had left a healthy pile of carefully split logs right outside the door. She said a short prayer of thanks for their foresight and positioned a third log across the first two.

Lizzie took off her belt guns and laid them close by. She'd dry everything off in a minute. Then she unbuckled the bandolier full of rifle cartridges, lifted it off her shoulder, and laid it out flat on the table. Next came her buckskin jacket. The collar was frayed, and there was fringe missing here and there down the arms, but it still did the job it was made for. A shiver rocked her from head to toe, making her hurry. She peeled off her faded red flannel shirt and the pants made of finely tanned buckskin, and draped both over the benches to dry.

Finally, standing in only a camisole and a pair of old cotton drawers, gray and fuzzy from use, she dragged the rocker closer to the fire and eased her tired bones into the seat. "Aaaah," she moaned. "That feels so good." She took a deep breath and relaxed on a sigh.

Wrinkling her nose, she sat up straight again. Something stunk! "What died in here?" Sniffing, she looked around for the source of the sour odor. Her eyes widened when she realized it was her own filthy clothes stinking up the cabin. "Now, you've gone too far, Elizabeth Ann Sutter. Even Rufus and Cletus smelled better."

Imagining herself as dirty as the two old cowboys who'd visited the Doan's Crossing saloon sent a shudder through her that had nothing to do with the cold. Not giving herself time to consider the wisdom of her action, she grabbed everything and strode outside. No more thunder rumbled through the hills, for which she was grateful, but rain poured from the sky, making washing out her clothes easier.

She was shivering by the time she stripped off her chemise and stood naked in the rain. Gritting her teeth, she stayed in the deluge long enough to clean the dirt and sweat of the last week from her skin and hair. Jumping a muddy puddle up to the porch, she wrung everything out and tossed it back into the cabin an instant before she remembered the filthy floor.

Cursing, she retrieved the garments, rinsed everything again and carried the dripping pile inside, leaving a trail on the sanded wood all the way to the fireplace. Dragging a bench close to the flames, she wiped it down with her wet shirt, then stretched out the buckskin with care. It was all she had to wear and she couldn't have it shrinking to nothing.

Another trip into the rain, and her shirt was mostly clean again. Wringing the water from it as she went back inside, she tossed it over the back of a chair to drip dry. Naked and freezing, Lizzie hurried into the bedroom in search of something to wear. She could wrap a blanket around her, but they were so dusty she'd have to go back out in the rain again.

"Not even under th-threat of death," she muttered through chattering teeth, and went to look through the clothes left by the previous occupants. "I'd rather freeze in my altogether."

In one of the bureau drawers, wrapped in tissue, she found a soft cotton nightdress carefully folded on top of a stack of women's undergarments. The fine white fabric glowed in the dark room. Her fingers traced the lace around the neck and the tiny satin ribbon wound through it to tie at the throat. "This sure feels pretty. I hope she won't mind me borrowing it."

Lizzie dragged it over her head and studied herself in the dressing table mirror. The nightdress hugged Lizzie's body and stopped halfway down her calves. "Must have been one tiny woman."

Wearing a stranger's nightdress, and the matching robe she found hanging on the back of the door, Lizzie hurried back to the fire and propped her cold feet on an overturned bucket.

"Oh," she moaned, scooting closer to the flames. "Oh, oh, oh. That feels *good*." Once her shivering stopped, she went to her pack for her hairbrush and scurried back to the glowing warmth. The firelight glinted off the ornate silver brush. Lizzie turned it over and over, watching the flames reflect in the lines of the finely etched angel on the back.

Her papa had brought it back from England for her the year she was born. The matching mirror had long since been busted. A fancy brush was a foolish thing to keep, but it was useful and she could never find it in her to leave it behind.

Shaking off the long-dead past, she sat forward in the rocker and went to work on her hair. The dark brown strands were growing out, making it more obvious she was female, but she hesitated to cut them short again.

She'd chopped her hair off when she left South Carolina so no one on the wagon train west would know she was a woman. Once in Texas, she let it grow a little longer, but kept it tied in messy braids nobody wanted to touch. When she needed to get out of Doan's Crossing, the disguise had been good enough to get her hired on as a waddie, pushing cattle to Dodge City. Not even that puffed up trail boss had realized he'd hired a woman.

"Don't be a fool, Elizabeth Ann. Just 'cause God gave you a female's goods don't mean you're a woman." Besides, it had been so long since she'd dressed like a lady, she wasn't sure she remembered how to act. Petticoats, hair ribbons, dainty shoes. It was all too much of a bother. "Give me boots and buckskins any day," she declared to the empty cabin.

Putting thoughts of feminine things out of her head, Lizzie tugged the brush through her hair until it dried—but she didn't take her knife to her drying tresses.

CHAPTER THREE

Dawn came, but only a generous man would have called it morning. Wolf knew the sun was up there somewhere, since there was light enough to see the ground, but that was all he would concede. They were a day out of Fort Elliott, too far to turn back. A steady rain had started in the very late hours of last night and it was still falling.

"Pa?" Calvin hunched under a gray rain slicker that was three sizes too big. "When's it going to stop?"

Wolf held on to his temper, barely. "I'm not God, son, and that's a decision only He gets to make. No use complaining about it. You'll be just as wet and you'll irritate your horse." *And me*, he added, but not aloud. He didn't want to upset his son. He was too damned grateful to have him back alive.

Calvin heaved a sigh and patted his horse's neck. "Okay, Pa." They rode in silence for another mile. "Pa?"

Wolf topped a small rise and pulled his horse to a stop to wait for Calvin to catch up. "What now, son?"

"I think Lightning needs to rest. I might be getting too heavy for her."

His irritation evaporated. Wolf turned his face away so Calvin wouldn't see his grin. His boy was not quite eight years old and as small as Wolf was big. "Well, if you think so, we'd better find a spot to stop for a while." He scanned the landscape again. "There's a small stream a couple of miles ahead. Can she make it that far?"

"Sure I ca— I mean, *she* can."

Looking over their back trail for any sign someone was following, Wolf checked the lead rope on the packhorse, then bumped his big chestnut mare in the ribs and set off down the hill with Calvin close behind. The trees that grew near the stream were too small to offer him any protection, but Calvin managed to ride under some of the higher branches, out of the rain. Wolf dismounted and lifted his son from the saddle just for the joy of holding him. Resisting the urge to hug him, Wolf set him on the ground. "Go on. I'll see to Lightning."

Calvin didn't wait for a second invitation, but disappeared into the brush downstream, his slicker flying behind him. When he returned, Wolf was waiting to boost him back into the saddle. "We need to keep riding. There's not enough cover for all of us."

"Okay, Pa." Calvin settled on the back of the chestnut filly that had been a gift from Jake McCain, the Texas Ranger responsible for rescuing his son from the killers who'd kidnapped him. Calvin leaned forward to pat the horse's neck. "Come on, Lightning. We've still got some miles to cover."

One heavy eyebrow rose as Wolf heard his son quote words he'd said many times in the months since they'd ridden away from Lucinda, Texas. Being on the trail was hard, and they didn't cover many miles in a day, but Calvin's company made for more laughter and sunshine, somehow. Wolf stretched tired muscles. He was ready to be home. How much more tired must a young boy be?

"We have enough supplies to keep us for a while yet, so we don't have to go into town first. I expect we'll be sleeping in our own beds in two or three more days." Alone, Wolf could have covered the distance from the fort to Civil in two days.

Calvin glanced at the sky, his face a mirror image of his mother. "Only three more nights on the ground."

"Maybe less, if we get moving."

The boy grinned at him, mischief sparkling in his eyes. "Then what are we doing standing here? You aren't afraid of a little rain, are you Pa?" Without warning, he kicked his little mare into a gallop, splashing through the stream and racing away across open ground. Wolf swung into the saddle, dropped the packhorse's lead rope and shot off in pursuit. The big horse overtook them in seconds, and Calvin squealed when Wolf scooped him from the saddle on the run.

When the reins fell from Calvin's fingers, Lightning slowed and stopped. Wolf turned his horse in a wide circle back to the packhorse, but he didn't stop tickling his son. Their shared laughter rang across the open ground.

"Stop, Pa. Stop. I—can't—breathe." Calvin's plea came out on a giggle.

"Well, maybe I don't want you to," Wolf teased, squeezing his fingers into his son's ribs to coax out one last ripple of laughter. "Being out of air might keep you in line."

Calvin collapsed against his chest, feigning exhaustion. "I won't do it again." He grinned up at Wolf. "Today."

That earned him more tickling. "Today, huh?" Another fit of giggles followed. Wolf hugged him close. "I guess I can live with that."

"Hey, Pa? What's that?"

Wolf stiffened, staring through the steady rain toward the growing shadows on the trail. A sharp whistle brought Lightning along side and he plopped Calvin into the saddle. "Stay real close, son, and be ready to ride if I say so."

The boy grabbed the reins and settled his hat tighter on his head. "I'm ready, Pa." He stared as the shadows solidified into men on horseback. "Who are they?"

Wolf ignored the question, all his concentration on the approaching riders. He recognized the man in the lead. Jefferson 'Black Jack' Hayes was not the kind of man you turned your back on. The man bringing up the rear looked familiar, though Wolf couldn't place him. Probably another from the company Black Jack kept during the war. The other two men with him were unknown, but you could bet they were no better than their leader. Wolf shifted in the saddle, drawing their attention away from Calvin.

"Richards? Is that you?" Hayes pulled his horse to a stop only fifteen feet away. "I didn't expect to see you again."

"Hayes." Wolf nudged his horse forward, staying between the men and Calvin.

"I was terribly sorry to hear about your wife, though I see you found your son. That should bring you comfort."

The man shook his head in what some might have called sympathy. Wolf knew better.

"Did they get your little girl, too?"

Though Calvin didn't make a sound, Wolf felt his son's pain at the man's careless statement. Anger snaked through him. "What are you doing here, Hayes? Last I heard you were swindling folks out of their savings in Saint Louis."

Hayes's lips thinned at the insult. "Saint Louis lost its charm. I've decided to stay in the territory a while, see what opportunities present themselves." The men with Hayes laughed at some shared joke and kicked their horses into motion.

Wolf watched in silence until they disappeared north, in the direction of Civil. Smothering a curse, he tugged Scarlett's reins and turned to ride east.

"Pa, home's the other way."

"I know, son, but we aren't going to ride too close to that bunch. They can't be trusted."

Calvin steered his horse close to Wolf's side. "How could you tell? I mean, that man that you were talking to looked fine. He was dressed all right and all, not like that awful man, Harrison. I mean, I knew he was bad the minute I saw him, before he hurt Amanda. He even smelled rotten. Can you tell me how you knew about Mister Hayes? Someday, I might need to know how to tell that a man can't be trusted. Can you teach me?"

Wolf stared into the distance. His son was too young to know so much about the ugliness of men. "Most of it comes from living, Cal, but I'll try." They rode at an easy pace, sparing the horses, talking about whatever came into the boy's head. The day passed, and sunset brought another night of campfire and hard ground.

Wolf dished up the stew he'd put together. "Good thing we're almost home. I'm getting tired of jerky and hardtack."

Man and boy dug in, wanting to eat while the food was hot. They'd both discovered the taste was a little better that way.

"You can go hunting if you need to, Pa. I'll be all right."

A chill snaked down Wolf's spin, freezing his blood. He hadn't been able to leave his son alone yet. There were times he wondered if he ever would. "We can make do with what we have."

"I could make a snare and catch some rabbits," the boy offered. "But I'm not sure this part of Texas has rabbits. At least, I haven't seen any."

"They're here, but they've gotten pretty good at hiding. Tomorrow, I'll show you how to spot them. We'll set out a couple of snares after we make camp and try our luck."

"I'd sure like to know how to see them. Then I can help keep us fed." Calvin yawned. "Guess it's time for some shuteye." He washed out his tin cup in the stream and put it away in his saddlebag before burrowing into his bedroll. "'Night, Pa."

"Good night, son." Wolf watched his son settle down and drop into sleep with the ease of the young. Pouring the last of the coffee, he leaned against his saddle to watch the stars. Sleep would be a long way off again, tonight.

• ♥ •

Wolf and Calvin topped the last rise, both eager to see their little house come into view at the end of the long valley. It had taken all of the week Wolf had predicted to get here, but tonight they would sleep in their own beds.

"There it is, Pa! We made it!"

He smiled at Cal's enthusiasm. Though Wolf wouldn't admit it to his young son, the ghosts had been riding him hard the past few days, visiting him in the darkness and daylight, reminding him of all his failures. His wife, beautiful, gentle Emily. She deserved so much more than to die because he hadn't been there to protect her. And little Amanda, his baby girl, who shouldn't have known the horror, the violence of men at such a tender age.

"We've still got the better part of an afternoon's travel to get there, Cal. So keep moving."

The sun was setting when they rounded the last bend. The little house looked the same, almost eerily so. The yard was swept of leaves and debris, the porch looked freshly swept, and...

"Pa?" Calvin guided his little horse closer to his father's side, fear and confusion in his voice. "There's smoke comin' from the chimney."

Wolf had seen the wispy white trail more than an hour ago, but had convinced himself it was lack of sleep that had him imagining things. But if Cal could see it, it must be real.

Squatters. Some low life had moved into their home. "Whoever it is, they won't stay long once we get there. Get behind me, son."

He checked the load in both revolvers and his shotgun before bumping his horse in the ribs. As they neared the house, he spotted the lazy freeloader, on the roof of the barn. What the hell was he doing up there? When Wolf saw fresh patches, he realized the squatter was fixing the holes.

That made no sense. All the squatters Wolf had encountered moved into an empty structure and made use of what was there until they were forced out again. He should know. He'd made use of his share of empty houses while he searched for his children.

But the evidence was before him. "This should be interesting," he muttered. Motioning Cal out of sight, he slid a revolver free and rode up to the barn, stopping just out of the shelter of the eaves.

"What the hell are you doing to my barn?"

The intruder spun around, forgetting his precarious perch. Wolf spotted the flash of sun on a barrel, but before he could react, the man lost his footing, let out a squeal, and started sliding off the roof.

Wolf was moving almost before the realization hit. The curve of hip, the narrow waist. He snagged the falling body just short of the ground.

"Damn it. You're a woman."

• ♥ •

Lizzie's breath was knocked from her as she slammed into a hard, male chest. Instantly, she squirmed, trying to break free. A huge arm pinned her in place against thighs as thick as tree trunks while his big chestnut horse danced around, threatening to send them both pitching into the dust. Panic stole her breath all over again. He was as big as a mountain! She'd never get loose. She renewed her struggle against his hold.

"Just take it easy. I'd never willingly hurt a woman." The man muttered a few words even Lizzie had never heard before as he controlled his restless mount. Turning the horse around, he deposited Lizzie in the dust near the house before sliding from the saddle. Thunderclouds darkened his eyes to the color of a stormy sea. For an instant, she swore she'd seen those eyes before.

Lizzie took a step back and came up against the porch. She was a little puzzled that he stopped his advance. It sure wasn't because he was calm. His fists clenched and relaxed, hovering close to his belt guns. Why didn't he come on, then? He had to know she couldn't fend him off. Only when he glanced down and back up did she remember the pistol she held. When had she cocked the hammer? It didn't matter. She had to take the advantage while she held it.

Drawing a deep breath for courage, she raised the barrel a few inches and motioned him back a couple of steps. "Just keep your distance and I won't have to use this." Keeping her eyes on him, she moved to the left, into the open, to give herself some room to run.

"I've got her covered, Pa."

Lizzie swung toward the voice behind her without thinking. The man dove at her so fast she didn't have time to react. He grabbed her wrist and ripped the gun from her fingers as they went down in a tangle of arms and legs. Her breath whooshed from her lungs as his weight settled on her hips.

"I'll leave. I swear it. Just don't hurt me."

The plea seemed to shock him, then made him mad all over again. Other reactions set in too, a growing hardness she recognized. Unwelcome heat curled through her belly. What a time to get attracted to a man. She wiggled around, trying to throw him off, making the heat—and hardness—that much worse.

"How's that knife wound?"

Lizzie's gaze flew back to his. She recognized his eyes a heartbeat later. "Wolf? What the hell are you doing here, you damn outlaw!"

"He ain't no outlaw!"

She'd forgotten the boy. At least, she thought it was a boy. Arching her back, she craned her neck and managed to spot him, but it was kind of hard to be certain when she was seeing upside down. "Who are you?"

"I'm the one that's gonna shoot you if you don't let go of my pa."

Lizzie stared. "I'm not..." Awareness stabbed through the anger and panic. Heat beneath her palms, her fingers. Her hands were fisted in the Wolf's shirt, holding on like she wanted him right where he was. With an unladylike oath, she loosened her fingers and gave him a shove. He didn't budge.

"Get off me," she snapped at him.

Wolf gripped her wrist and pushed to his feet, taking Lizzie with him. It took more courage than she thought she had to meet his gaze. From this angle, he looked more like a mountain than a man. The storm still roiled in the depths of his icy gray eyes.

"What are you doing squatting in my cabin?"

"I'm not a squatter. I took *shelter* from the rain a couple of weeks ago. The house looked abandoned, like no one had been here in a while." She shrugged and looked away, uncomfortable with the intensity in his stare. "I fixed a few things, cleaned up a little. I didn't take anything."

Silence. Thick, uncomfortable, unbroken. The hollow click of the hammer of a shotgun being eased forward shattered it. "I'll get the horses, Pa."

"Thank you, son."

Manners? From a boulder?

"The woman and I will be inside."

So much for a reprieve. Refusing to wait for him, Lizzie climbed the two stairs to the porch, aching from head to heels. He beat her to the door.

"Not so fast." She felt cold steel kiss her neck. "Just in case you aren't alone here."

Her heart hesitated, then pounded out her terror. No witnesses. No one to help her. He reached around her and shoved the door open, motioning her to go first. She couldn't move.

One big hand wrapped around her arm. "Come on. I'm not planning on rape, if that's what's got you so scared." His grip was almost gentle as he urged her from bedroom to bedroom, ensuring no one hid inside. He flinched when he saw her stuff lying at the foot of the big bed, but he didn't comment. When they returned to the main room, he tossed aside a rug in the back corner and opened a tiny hatch built into the floor.

"I missed that." She leaned down to try and see the length of the passage. "Where does it lead?"

"Root cellar," he snapped, then heaved a big breath like he was fighting for control. He holstered his revolver and closed the hatch. "There's a door in the back that lets you out in the trees beyond the outhouse. I put it there so Emily would never be trapped inside the house if..."

He broke off, gritted his teeth and dragged her to the next room. Finally satisfied they were alone, he ushered her to a chair at the table. She sank into the seat because her knees wouldn't hold her up any longer.

"Relax, will you? I said I wasn't going to hurt you."

She lifted her chin and glared at him. "I'm not scared of you, Goliath."

He raised one eyebrow at the blatant lie, but let it go. "You know me, but I didn't ask your name that night in Doan's Crossing."

"Liz—" Now her fear was just making her mad. She cleared

her throat and tried again. "Lizzie Sutter."

"Well, Lizzie Sutter, thank you for cleaning up in here." He rubbed a long finger on the table exactly where she'd sanded away a blood stain. "And for not changing things around. Calvin needs this to be home again." His gaze returned to the dark spot on the floor in front of the fireplace. When he raised his eyes to hers, her breath backed up. Horrible agony, loss, dulled his eyes.

"What happened?" She slapped a hand over her mouth. "Never mind," she rushed on. "It's none of my business."

His gaze hardened again. Without a word, Wolf left the house, taking her grandfather's pearl-handled revolvers and the rifle she kept propped behind the door with him.

As his footsteps faded, she started to breathe again. "How stupid can you be, Lizzie Ann?" she berated herself. She knew better than to question a man. Especially one like Wolf. She knew the code of the west: *don't ask about what don't concern you.* But she was naturally curious, and it got her into trouble more times than not.

Wolf Richards. The man who'd saved her hide and probably her life back in Doan's Crossing. She hardly recognized him without the heavy beard he'd sported that night. Then again, she'd never expected to see him here.

Lizzie rubbed at a sore spot on her backside. That was one big man. Wresting with him could be dangerous to a body, but interesting. Grinning at the thought, she stretched her arms over her head and took stock of her aches and pains. Between falling off the roof and rolling in the dust with a mountain on her chest, she was sure to have a few new bruises. Getting out of bed in the morning wasn't going to be pleasant.

She dropped into a chair with a groan as she realized she no longer had a bed to sleep in. The one she'd been using had to belong to Wolf. Maybe he'd let her sleep in the barn. With the roof patched, at least she'd be dry if it decided to rain again. She pushed to her feet to start packing.

It didn't take her long to have her few belongings stacked by the door. Sniffing the air, she realized the rabbit stew she'd put together for dinner was close to burning. She didn't know if she'd be staying to eat, but it made no sense to waste the food. Stirring the contents of the soup pot, she made a few additions and soon had enough to share between the three of them. A quick pan of biscuits finished the meal. She pulled everything away from the heat just as footsteps sounded on the porch.

The knock surprised her. "Come in?" The door didn't open. It took her a moment for her to realize Wolf wasn't taking a chance that she had another gun hidden away. She moved to the middle of the room and held her empty hands out where he could see them.

The knock came again. "Come on in. I'm unarmed."

The door swung open, but no one was there. Then she saw the glint of light on a barrel. "See? No guns or knives. Not even a sling-shot and rock."

For an instant, she thought she caught a hint of laughter in Wolf's eyes as he peered around the corner, but it was gone before she could be sure. He glanced around the room, making certain she told the truth before motioning his son into the house. He slid his revolver back into the holster at this waist, but he didn't move to take off the gun belt.

"We didn't have time for introductions before. Miss Sutter, this is my son, Calvin."

The boy stepped forward and took off his hat, revealing a wealth of blond hair and summer-sky blue eyes. "How do you do, ma'am?" Calvin flashed a heart-stopping grin at her, then inhaled with an exaggerated sniff. "Something sure smells good."

She grinned back. The boy knew how to get what he wanted. "I made stew." She turned back to the hearth. "It isn't fancy, but there's plenty to share. Would you care to join me?"

"Thank you, ma'am." Calvin headed to the far side of the table and dropped into a chair. When Wolf didn't follow, the boy shifted to face him. "Pa?"

Lizzie glanced over her shoulder. The man stood at the door, looking like he'd seen a ghost. He took a visible breath and shook his head, as if to clear his head. "I'm coming, son." He closed the door and joined them at the table.

Dinner was a strange affair, with the adults eating in silence while Calvin chattered non-stop about all the people he'd met on their journey home from Texas. When the boy finally fell silent, Wolf ended the meal. "Time for bed, son."

"Aw, Pa. I want to stay up and talk some more. And I'm not tir—" A yawn interrupted his plea, and he ended it on a grin. "Guess I am, a little." He carried his plate and cup to the sink. "Thank you for the meal, ma'am." Cal headed for the smaller bedroom at the far end of the room, but the closer he came, the slower he moved. "Pa?" His little voice shook, tearing at Lizzie's heart.

"I'll be there in a minute. Take a candle with you. It'll be all right, son."

Wolf crossed to the shelf over the dry sink to fetch a short stump of white candle. He lit it from the one on the table and handed it to Calvin. When the boy disappeared, Wolf turned his gaze on Lizzie. "What's all that?" He indicated her meager belongings.

"If you don't mind me staying tonight, I'll sleep in the barn. I can be gone at first light," she hurried on as he shook his head. "You mean to turn me out in the middle of the night?" She threw down the ragged-edged cloth she was using to wipe the table. "Then I'll just get out of your way right now."

He snagged her arm as she pushed past. "Slow down, woman. I'm not telling you to leave. There's a storm coming."

Her heart stopped, but she blamed it on the mention of a storm, not on his nearness. "Storm?" On cue, lightning flashed with thunder right on its heels. "I-I don't like storms."

She flinched as lightning flashed again, closer.

"I'll—uh…" She chewed on her bottom lip, mustering her courage. "I'll be all right in the barn with Yeller."

One corner of Wolf's mustache twitched. "Your mule has plenty of company with our horses. There's room for you in here." He motioned toward the bedroom with his free hand.

She blanched, felt all the blood leave her head. "I'm not going in there with you."

He crowded her a little, proving he was aware of her reaction to him. "I can't lie and say I haven't considered it." Wolf played with the end of her braid. "It's been a long time." He released her and stepped back. "But you can have it. I'll bed down in Calvin's room. I'm not so desperate that I need a woman who looks almost as much like a man as I do."

Lizzie felt like he'd punched her. Of all the horrible, nasty… "Fine." Snatching up her pack, she escaped into the bedroom.

• ♥ •

Hurt, anger and confusion radiated from the woman as she stormed off. As Wolf watched her disappear into the bedroom he'd always shared with Emily, his heart gave a funny lurch that he chose to ignore.

Wolf scrubbed his hands over his face. What demon had goaded him into saying something like that? Maybe she wasn't the prettiest thing he'd ever seen—Emily would always hold that place, to his mind. That didn't mean it was fair to treat her poorly. She had what God gave her and he had no right to criticize. But couldn't she at least dress like a woman?

Disgusted with her, himself, and the world in general, Wolf headed outside. The animals were bedded down, and the storm would likely keep everything else tucked up for the night, but he was unsettled. He made a trip around the house, the barn and the corral, but the feeling persisted.

He leaned against the corral rail and studied the house. A soft light glowed in the windows, like it had every time he'd come in after dark. Emily always made sure he could find his way home. And, no matter the time of night, she waited up for him, welcomed him into her arms, into their bed.

Wolf leaned over and tore up a stem of buffalo grass to chew on. Emily had made the house a home. From the day they moved into the tiny one-room cabin he'd built as a wedding present, it felt like a castle, with her its beautiful queen. She'd filled their home to the rafters with laughter and love. Now, it held only ghosts.

He kicked at the split wood fence rail. How the hell was he supposed to make a home for Calvin without her? What did he know about raising a son? A boy needed his mother.

Wolf remembered growing up with only his father. She'd died when he was only a little older than Cal. He knew she was pretty, because his father had told him so many times, but she'd been dead so long he could barely picture what she looked like. Now, every time he tried, he only saw Emily.

Thunder rumbled in the distance. Wolf could smell rain riding the wind. He climbed the steps to the porch and leaned against a post to listen as it raced down the valley toward him.

The door opened behind him. Wolf stiffened, half-expecting Lizzie to shoot him after all.

"Pa? Are you coming soon? I can't make my eyes stay closed, even though I'm real tired. I keep hearing noises and stuff."

Wolf inhaled the cool, damp air. He dreaded going inside. The house was full of ghosts he wasn't sure he could face. He didn't know how he would get through the night, but he had to try. For Calvin. "I'm coming, son."

CHAPTER FOUR

The rain stopped an hour before dawn, leaving behind a warm, dreary morning. Wolf leaned against a post as daylight painted the horizon. Breathing in the morning air, he rubbed the back of his neck, stiff from the few hours he'd spent on a too-small bed. Calvin still slept, unburdened with the memories and worries that kept Wolf awake most of the night.

When he'd gone to bed, the sweet scent of his baby girl surrounded Wolf in the small bedroom. Every time he drifted off, images of her being stolen from him invaded his dreams, and he'd jerk awake to her screams for help. Unable to stand it, he'd come outside to listen to the night.

Now, with morning here, he set the past aside. The future worried him more. How would he support his son? He had to go hunting, capture more horses, begin earning a living again, but he wouldn't—*couldn't*—leave Calvin alone in the house. And taking the boy along wasn't possible. He was still too young to have the skills and stamina needed to keep up.

Wolf stretched his arms over his head, trying to ease sore muscles. He could leave Calvin in Civil, but who could he trust to keep him safe? Millicent Freeman would watch out for him, but Calvin was terrified of the giant, overbearing woman. Wolf trusted Harvard Browning, Civil's saloon keeper and the only man in town Wolf called friend, but Harvard had enough to do. Besides, Emily would never have approved of Cal sleeping above The Fallen Star.

Perhaps Emily's friend, Hannah... He closed his eyes against the grief and worry. And the memories. Everywhere there were reminders of his dead wife.

The door opened behind him and Wolf turned, expecting to see his son. Instead, Lizzie slipped out.

"I looked in on Calvin. He's still sleeping."

Wolf nodded once, a short, sharp movement. That was something Emily would have done. She always checked on the children before starting breakfast.

"It stopped raining." She handed him a cup of coffee, then moved to the far end of the porch.

He murmured his appreciation as he took a sip from the steaming ceramic cup. "About an hour ago. Coffee's good. Thanks."

Lizzie didn't turn around, didn't look at him. Instead, she studied the empty sky as if expecting to see something of great importance written there. Her dark hair was brushed smooth and tied in a single braid that hung halfway down the middle of her back. Wolf studied the thin strip of leather at the end of the braid as it swayed with her steps, drawing his attention to the curve of her waist and her rounded hips. She wore the same buckskin pants and shirt she'd had on the night before, but he no longer thought she looked much like a man.

Letting his gaze roam the length of her from shoulders to knees, Wolf couldn't imagine everyone hadn't seen through the disguise. Unless they didn't care enough to look. "Your hair is longer than before."

"In a place like Doan's Crossing, it wasn't wise to advertise I was a woman. With my hair shorter, and dressed in men's clothes, most folks didn't give me a second look." She set her cup on the narrow railing and tugged the braid over her shoulder to fiddle with the leather tie. "It made me being a saloon keeper a little more acceptable to the high and mighty folks in town. To Orville's family, too."

"Orville?"

"Orville Harris, the previous owner of the saloon. A fight broke out over some re-branded cattle and he got caught in the crossfire." Lizzie threw the braid over her back. "Hell of a useless way to die."

"Is that how you ended up with the saloon?"

She looked him up and down. "I made a death-bed promise to keep it running until Orville's brother could get there and take over. Why do you care?"

"Curiosity." He tossed out the last bit of coffee. "Why'd you leave?"

She finally turned around, leaning against a post as if she hadn't a care in the world. "Folks took exception to a dead man lying in the street, especially his friends. Someone decided to try and pin it on me. I guess I was the convenient target, the new-comer with no one to speak up for me, and ugly as a marsh rat, to boot."

"They arrested you?" Guilt turned like a knife in his gut. "Damn it! I should have stayed."

She waved off his concern. "They had no proof, just a lot of nasty innuendo. Still, they kept harassing me, threatening the few customers I had, diverting my whiskey shipments to the wrong saloon, until I could barely stay in business." She paused long enough to drain her coffee cup. "It was *strongly* suggested I find another town to roost in. One of the marshal's brothers even offered to buy the saloon, then made sure I understood he'd take it by force if I didn't move on. Fortunately, Orville's brother got there before they burned the place down. He sold out and I signed on as a waddie with the first cattle drive that came through town. Figured following a bunch of cows to Dodge City couldn't be too hard."

Wolf didn't respond. What could he say?

Lizzie wrapped her arms across her middle, lifting her curves into better view. "I still don't understand why you helped me that night. I was no concern of yours."

Wolf hesitated.

"Never mind." Lizzie jammed an old, felt hat onto her head. Its brown felt was faded and the brim was drooping over her ears, but it served the purpose. "I'm going to check on my mule."

He grabbed her arm when she charged past. "I'm not sure I

can explain."

She tried to shrug off his hand. "It doesn't matter. You don't owe answers to a half-woman-half-man freak."

Wolf tightened his grip. "Miss Sutter." He paused. What could he say to make up for his careless words? "I apologize for what I said last night."

She went still, her eyes full of suspicion. "Why?"

He stared into her midnight gaze. "Because it was cruel. Because I had no right. Because my mother raised me better." For some reason, that last part made her smile, a tiny curving at the corner of her lips.

"You had a mother? I figured you were hatched under a rock."

His spine stiffened, anger coiling, until he saw the glint of humor in her dark eyes. "I deserved that." He released her arm and removed his hat. "I'm sorry, ma'am. There was no excuse for me acting like such a rattlesnake."

Lizzie shrugged. "Don't go getting all foolish. I don't suppose I can be mad at you for stating the simple truth."

Wolf tried to protest, but she talked over him.

"I can't fault you for seeing me as I see myself." She took a single step back, ending the conversation. "Excuse me. I need to see to my mule. We have a long ride ahead of us."

"Not really." He settled his hat back in place. "Civil is less than half-an-hour west, along the river."

She stared at him. "Half-an-hour? How can that be? I didn't see any sign of a town, not even wagon tracks. That's why I stopped here instead of going on that night."

"You must have come in from the east. If you'd ridden over two more hills, you'd have seen it."

"Two more..." Her lush lips thinned. "That's why you wondered what I was doing here? Figured I liked it better in your house for free than payin' for a room in town, is that it?"

"That's not the reason." Wolf paused, searching for an explanation.

Lizzie didn't give him a chance. She jammed her hat on her

head. "At least I don't have to ride far to get some supplies to repay your *hospitality*." Her sarcasm sliced at his hide.

"Now, just hold on a minute."

She cut off his protest by striding away. Damned stubborn woman. Wolf watched her storm away, hips snapping back and forth with every angry step. His body stirred, just as it had in the saloon in Doan's Crossing. How in the hell had he ever mistaken her for a man?

"Pa?"

Wolf yanked his gaze from Lizzie's backside and turned toward the door. "Good morning, son."

"Where's Miss Lizzie?" Calvin wandered onto the porch, carrying his boots. "I thought maybe she'd make some of her biscuits for breakfast. They sure were good last night."

"She's in the barn. Why don't you go ask her if she'll stay long enough to eat with us?" Maybe over a meal he could find a way to apologize that she would accept.

"Sure. After I visit the privy." Calvin banged his boots upside down against the doorframe to dislodge any unexpected varmints, stomped his feet into them and headed down the steps.

Wolf smothered a laugh. It was like watching a miniature version of himself. A little disconcerting, truth be told. "I'll start the bacon," he called after his son.

"All right, Pa." Calvin waved that he'd heard as he rounded the house.

Wolf was digging through their dwindling supplies when he heard the scream.

"Calvin!"

Shoving through the door, Wolf hit the dirt running. As he cleared the porch, he saw Lizzie race out of the barn, aim her rifle and fire. She never broke stride, continuing in the direction Calvin had gone. Wolf couldn't breathe. The edges of his vision grayed. He wasn't sure he'd survive if anything happened to his son.

He rounded the corner and skidded to a stop. Lizzie had

Calvin in her arms, calming him. One hand was pressed tight against the boy's left calf. Blood stained his pant leg from knee to ankle. And lying a few feet away was a full-grown *javelina*.

Wolf approached the big animal slowly, his rifle ready to fire. The wild pigs were notorious for their bad tempers, sharp tusks and thick hides, but this one wasn't getting up. Lizzie's single shot had gone through its right eye.

"Pa?"

The quiver in Calvin's voice squeezed Wolf's heart. "It's all right, son. It can't hurt you any more. Miss Sutter took care of it." He sat on his heels beside the pair.

"Where did it come from?"

Wolf brushed a hand over Calvin's hair. "Out of the woods. It probably found some nice tender roots under that bush over there and you got a little too close."

"Let's go into the house," Lizzie interrupted. "I want to take a look at that souvenir you've got." Wolf met Lizzie's gaze. "It's not too bad. I got it before it could charge a second time, but the wound will have to be cleaned out good and probably stitched."

Wolf felt the blood drain from his head, leaving his skin cold. He'd stitched on skin many times, but never on a child. On his son. He locked his knees and clenched his teeth, hoping he didn't embarrass himself by fainting.

Once he was sure he wouldn't keel over, Wolf lifted Calvin and carried him to the cabin. Lizzie stayed close, keeping pressure on the wound and talking to keep the boy calm. Wolf was grateful, since it also took his mind off what was coming.

Lizzie went inside ahead of them and grabbed a blanket off the big bed to cover the kitchen table. Together, they settled Calvin on the makeshift pallet, but it was Lizzie who slid a long knife from her boot and sliced the boy's pant leg open along the seam. Wolf's hands weren't steady enough to handle anything sharp.

Instead, he dipped water into a dish pan and soaked a clean cloth to wipe away the blood. When he leaned closer, his head bumped Lizzie's. She moved out of the way until he motioned her forward again. The wound didn't look too serious.

"It's going to need a few stitches," Lizzie confirmed.

Wolf's gut jumped at the thought.

"You're going to sew on me?" Calvin's voice rose to a squeak as he grabbed at Lizzie's hand.

"Now, don't fret, little man." Lizzie smoothed his hair back. "Your pa knows what he's doing."

Calvin looked back and forth between the adults, finally settling on Lizzie. "Wi—will it hurt?"

She grinned at him. "You know, I asked the very same question when he fixed up my leg."

"My pa sewed on you?" The amazement in his voice made Wolf want to laugh. A little of the fear and tension eased and he felt steadier as he turned to the hearth to start heating the bucket of water.

"Yep, sure did." Lizzie brushed Cal's hair out of his eyes. "And he did a fine job of it, too."

"But, you're a girl."

Wolf grinned and Lizzie laughed aloud. "Why would that matter? I've still got legs, same as you."

While Calvin thought over how he felt about his father stitching on a girl, Lizzie crossed to the hearth where Wolf was stoking the fire.

"I have a small bottle of laudanum in my pack. Just a little bit will make this a lot easier on him."

Wolf pushed to his feet. "You carry laudanum? I thought that was for frail, nervous females."

When she started to bristle, he lifted a hand. "Sorry. I'm only trying to rile you—and distract myself. I'd be obliged if you'd give him a little so I don't hurt him too badly." He held out a shaky hand. "I'm not sure I can do this."

She took his hand between hers, warming it. "You'll do fine. You've a fair hand at doctoring. I have the scar on my thigh to prove it." She strode for the barn and returned a minute later with a small blue glass bottle. Pulling out the dainty cork, she poured a tiny amount of laudanum into a glass and added cool water before going back to Calvin. "You need to drink every bit of this. It tastes awful, but it'll help."

The boy eyes the milky liquid. "What is it?"

"It's called laudanum. It's medicine." She held it out again, but he didn't take it.

His mouth turned down at the corners. "I don't think I need any lau-dum."

Lizzie ruffled Cal's hair. "Well, I think you do. Just pretend you're a famous gunfighter and this is whiskey." The ploy worked. Calvin wrinkled up his nose and up-ended the glass.

"Oh, yuck. That tastes worse than cod-liver oil."

"You actually *swallowed* cod-liver oil?" Lizzie shivered. "You're even braver than I thought." She winked at Calvin and grabbed up her rifle. "I'll be back presently."

Wolf looked up from the fire. "Where are you going?"

"I want to be sure nothing comes sniffing around that carcass. And I don't have much stomach for blood." With a wink and a grin, she turned on her heel and left.

Wolf forced a smile for Calvin's sake. The laudanum was making the boy drowsy, but he was still in pain. Wolf could see it in his eyes. "Hang on, son. Everything will be all right." Wolf swallowed. Hard. "I need to take a look at that cut now."

Calvin's nod was uneven, almost drunken. "'Kay, Pa."

It took every ounce of courage Wolf possessed to clean out Calvin's wound. Every sound the boy made sliced into him until he figured he was bleeding worse than his son. By the time Lizzie returned, Wolf was exhausted and he hadn't gotten to the stitching yet.

She washed her hands with lye soap and steaming water before coming over to stand beside Calvin. "How're you doing, cowboy?" Lizzie squeezed Calvin's shoulder, bending over him to make a face, hoping to distract him a little.

The boy's eyes were huge with unshed tears. "I—It don't hurt too bad."

"That's the spirit. I knew you were one brave young man the

minute I saw you. Now, you just close your eyes. Your pa and I will take good care of you."

Calvin nodded, but the motion was jerky. His eyes began to droop. Finally, the laudanum took full effect and Calvin slipped off to sleep.

Wolf panicked. "What's wrong with him?"

"Nothing." Lizzie patted Wolf's back and held the lantern closer. "He's finally asleep, is all. Just do what you have to do."

Concentrating on keeping his hands steady, Wolf made seven neat stitches in Calvin's leg. Even unconscious, Calvin whimpered and shied away from the needle. It didn't take long, but Wolf felt like he'd been at it for days when he tied off the last stitch.

Lizzie bandaged the wound and helped Wolf settle Calvin in his bed. They retreated to the fire, leaving the door open so Calvin would hear them if he woke up. Wolf dropped into a chair at the table and laid his head in his hands.

"Here." She slid a cup in front of him. The bite of whiskey stung his nostrils. "You need this."

Wolf tossed back the contents and didn't argue when she poured him another portion. He swallowed most of it before pushing the cup to one side. "I better check on him."

Lizzie laid a hand on his. "He's fine, Wolf. Don't fret."

He glared at her and grabbed the whiskey bottle.

"Save some for me, would you?" Lizzie dropped into the seat across table and held out a small tin cup.

Wolf filled it to the rim, then added more to his own. "Thank you, Miss Sutter. You saved my son's life. I'll never be able to repay the debt."

"No debt owed." She tossed back half the whiskey.

He disagreed, but let it drop. "Where did you learn to shoot like that?"

She stared into the fire, avoiding his eyes. "One of the old sailors on my grandfather's ship was a marksman in Queen Victoria's Household Cavalry until he was caught with the wrong young lady. He escaped to sea rather than face her irate father.

He taught me to hit a tin cup swinging from a yardarm at forty paces in twenty-foot seas. After that, shooting on dry land is easy."

They settled into silence, each lost in their own thoughts. As Wolf's fear and panic receded, his mind returned to the problem of someone to watch out for Calvin, and he realized he'd found what he needed.

"Miss Sutter?"

"Oh, stop being so formal. We've shared a bottle and you've seen more of me than any other man. Under the circumstances, I think you can call me Lizzie."

"Lizzie, then. What are your plans after you leave here?"

She grabbed the bottle and poured a little more whiskey, but she didn't drink it. She turned the cup this way and that, swirling the liquor close to the rim, then set it aside. "I don't know. I should head for California, but I find I'm not in much of a hurry to get there."

"Have you considered staying in Civil?"

"Civil." She snorted in laughter and slugged back half the whiskey in her cup. "What the hell kind of a name is that for a town, anyway?"

Wolf chuckled. "Millicent Freeman, the wife of our sheriff and blacksmith, came to Watson's trading post about five years ago. She climbed down off her wagon, looked around at the collection of tents and lean-tos and announced she would make the place civil in no time. The name stuck. And Millicent still runs the town, such as it is."

"And what would I do in Civil?" Lizzie slugged down the remainder of her liquor. "I doubt the formidable Mrs. Freeman would welcome a saloon in her community."

"Actually, we have one. Harvard Browning is the proprietor," he supplied. "And before you ask, Millicent wouldn't want another one opening up. But there are other things to do. In fact..." He stopped, waiting until she looked up. "I would like to hire you."

Lizzie pulled her hands off the table slowly, leaning away

from Wolf. "I told you before—"

"That isn't what I meant, although not for the—uh…reason I gave you last night."

"Then just what *do* you mean?"

Wolf turned the whiskey bottle in his hands, watching the firelight play through the amber liquid. Sharing his troubles was something he usually avoided. "I used to make my living by hunting, tracking and trailing."

Lizzie picked up the bottle and poured another round. "What's trailing?"

"Guiding settlers and army families along the trail from Dodge City or Fort Worth to the area around the canyon at Palo Duro. I used to track the buffalo herds and hunted for the army for a while. That's how I met Emily."

"Who's Emily?"

Grief sat heavy on his chest. "Emily was my wife. She was murdered by the Harrison gang, in this very room. They also stole my son and young daughter."

Realization came swiftly. "Your daughter? Merciful God. I'm so sorry, Wolf."

He stared at the dark spot on the floor where Emily's blood stained the wood. Cursing, Wolf downed his whiskey. "We're nearly out of supplies, and since I've spent the last six months finding my son, I don't have the money to lay in much. I'll have to start hunting for the army again, but Cal's too young to go along and I won't leave him behind with someone he doesn't like. He's been through enough."

Lizzie nodded her understanding. "So…do something else."

"Such as?" He poured another finger of liquor and upended his cup.

"Keep that up and you can become Civil's town drunk!" Lizzie corked the bottle and set it on the bench beside her, out of easy reach. "What about trailing? He can go with you."

Wolf shrugged. "That would take us away from the cabin for months at a time. He can't sit a horse that long, especially now, with his leg cut up."

She sipped at her whiskey. "What does all this have to do with you hiring me?"

"I need someone to stay here with Calvin until I get back."

Lizzie made a sound of disbelief. "You don't know anything about me, yet you'd trust me with your son?" She shook her head at the foolishness. "Take him to town."

"Harvard's the only one I know who would put Cal before saving their own skin, but he lives above the saloon. Not exactly an ideal place for a young boy. I'd rather he stayed here with you."

"No." She rose to tuck the whiskey back into her bundle.

Wolf dropped his forehead to his hands. He knew it was her choice, but he wanted to argue, convince her. "Is someone expecting you?"

"As a matter of fact, there is." She rounded on him. "Don't look so surprised. Even somebody like me can have a family."

He shook his head. "Lizzie. Please."

Lizzie took a deep, slow breath and let it out on a sigh. "I have a brother in San Francisco. My mother is there, too, I understand, at least until she finds another husband to support her."

The bitterness in her voice warned Wolf she was finished discussing her family. "Just a few weeks, Lizzie." Wolf shoved to his feet and crossed to stand in front of her, desperate enough to plead. "Stay for three weeks. That should give me time to lay in enough to hold us for a while."

Lizzie studied him for a long, silent moment, then shook her head. "I can't help you. I'm sorry."

Wolf didn't follow when she headed to the barn. The look in her eyes had surprised him. Whatever the reason, Lizzie Sutter was afraid to stay with Calvin.

He heard her ride out an hour later, in the direction of Civil. He could go after her, try to change her mind, but what purpose would it serve? She'd given him her answer.

When he checked on Calvin, Wolf was relieved to see the wound wasn't bleeding and his son slept soundly. The bottle of laudanum sat on the floor near the head of the bed. Lizzie had left it behind for Calvin. In spite of what she said, the woman had a gentle streak in her. She'd make a fine nursemaid.

Wolf snagged his hat from his daughter's bed. It was too soon to leave Cal with a stranger, anyway. Just because Lizzie was a female, and a damn fine shot, didn't mean she could take care of his son.

They had enough supplies to keep them for another day or two, then he'd ride into Civil and talk with Millicent Freeman about keeping Cal. Meanwhile, there was work to be done. The horses needed grooming, stalls needed to be mucked out, and he had to find game close to the cabin or there'd be no supper tonight.

As he closed the door behind him, a shadow caught his eye. He drew his revolver an instant before he recognized the shape.

There, on the far end of the porch, suspended from his skinning rack, hung a gift from Lizzie.

The gutted *javelina.*

CHAPTER FIVE

The sun was high overhead by the time Lizzie rode into Civil. It may have been only half an hour to town on Wolf Richards's long-legged mare, but Yeller had taken more than twice that long, braying and sidestepping most of the way, just to be sure she understood he wasn't pleased with having to hit the trail again. Danged cantankerous critter.

Civil, Texas, huddled into a wide curve in the Canadian River. The main street ran east to west, straight into the river, with buildings spreading out on either side of it like the roots of a tree. The establishments were small and plain, some whitewashed, the rest the gray of unpainted wood left in the sun and wind too long. Beyond the gray hulk of the livery and the peeling front of the church, Lizzie counted a dozen houses, painted yellow and blue and white, looking like fancy lace sewn on the collar of a homespun shirt.

Lizzie glanced around and spotted the general store. Several women and at least one man milled around inside. One of them ought to be able to answer her questions. Tugging on the reins, she turned Yeller that direction and stopped beside a watering trough. She looked around before sliding out of the saddle. She didn't bother tying Yeller to the hitching post, just looped the reins over the saddle horn. He was too lazy to wander off.

Lizzie settled her hat lower and checked that her braids were messy enough to confuse folks. Her buckskins were clean, but they fit a little closer after the recent washing. Hopefully the stains of hard use would be enough to keep folks from looking too close. No reason to give her secret away to anyone here. She wasn't staying long, and folks thinking she was a man had definite advantages on the trail.

At the last second, she dragged her pack off the mule and slung it over one shoulder. Its bulk should hide enough of her from prying eyes to maintain the illusion.

A cheery bell tinkled when she opened the door. All conversation stopped and the folks inside turned to see who was coming in. Lizzie hesitated in the doorway, looking at the faces that were unknown, yet so familiar.

"Welcome to Civil, mist—ma'a—uh, stranger." The man behind a stubby counter littered with haphazard stacks of paper lifted a hand in greeting. "What brings you to our little community?"

Lizzie shifted the weight of her pack and stepped into the store, working hard not to jump when the door closed behind her with another irritating tinkle of the bell. The four women scattered around the room studied her as she strode to the counter. "I need some supplies and a place to stay for a few days. Wolf Richards said you could help me."

"Mr. Richards sent you? Well, then. Welcome to Civil." The man scratched at his temple with one finger. "I said that already, didn't I?" He skirted the counter and stuck out his hand. "No matter. I'm Percy Mercer, proprietor."

She dusted her hand on her buckskins and took his in a firm grip. "Lee Sutter."

"Pleased to meet you, Mister Sutter."

Mercer didn't say anything else, didn't move. "My supplies, Mister Mercer?"

"Oh." He jumped into action. "Of course. What will you be needing?"

"Bacon. Beans. Salt." Lizzie sniffed the air, and smiled. "Coffee, too, please."

"How much of each item, Mister Sutter?"

"A half pound of salt, a pound each of the rest. And I'll need a room for a few days, if you know of an available one in town." Glancing around the store, she was relieved to see three of the women were standing together, talking amongst themselves. At least they weren't staring a hole in her back any longer. The other was picking up and putting down tin cans on the far wall, trying to make a choice and not doing a good job of it.

Lizzie studied the shelves herself, amused by all the little necessities and doodads folks thought important enough to have shipped all the way out here to a frontier store.

"Here you are." Mercer plopped two burlaps sacks on the counter, sending one stack of paper flying. He scrambled to catch the little pieces. "See Mrs. Dorsey, there, about a room."

Lizzie dug out a few coins and paid the man, gathered her supplies and her courage, and faced the women. "Which of you ladies is Mrs. Dorsey?"

The woman who stepped forward was as round as she was tall, with graying hair stretched up into a bun, flushed cheeks and a wide, toothy smile. "I'm Henrietta Dorsey." The giggle she tried to hide behind her gloved hand made her sound like a schoolgirl.

Lizzie lifted her hat a couple of inches. "Pleasure to meet you, ma'am."

Henrietta blushed, the ruddy color sweeping up her cheeks. "Oh, the pleasure is mine, Mr. Sutter." She giggled again, then cleared her throat. "If I may perform the introductions? This dear woman is Millicent Freeman. Her husband, Archibald, is Civil's excellent sheriff."

Lizzie sized up the woman who Wolf said frightened young children. Other than her stature, which was impressive, she didn't look too ferocious. Lizzie nodded slightly in greeting, hoping to stay on her good side.

"This is Mr. Mercer's wife, Audelia." Henrietta pointed over her left shoulder. "And over there is my niece, Hattie Jamison. Come and say hello, Hattie dear." The young woman blushed, just like her aunt had.

"Hattie's husband is a scout for the army, but you probably already know that." Another giggle tickled the air.

Just how a stranger in town was supposed to know anything about anyone, Lizzie wasn't sure. "Ladies."

"Welcome to Civil, Mister Sutter." The others echoed Henrietta Dorsey's greeting.

"Thank you, kindly. Missus Dorsey, I am in need of a room for a few days, until I get rested up for my journey to California. I understand you might be able to help me."

"California?" Henrietta's lips rounded into a perfect 'o'. She covered her mouth with a pudgy hand. "My goodness. That is a terribly long way to travel. Why are you going all the way to California, Mister Sutter? Perhaps you have family there?"

Lizzie wanted to tell the nosy woman to mind her own business, but she really did want to sleep in a bed for a couple more nights while she planned her trip. She refused to acknowledge the part of her that was hoping to see Wolf again before she left. "My brother, ma'am. I'm on my way to join him."

"Wonderful. Family is so very important, don't you agree?" Slipping her arm through the crook of Lizzie's elbow, Mrs. Dorsey powered her way to the door. Lizzie glared at the damned bell as she opened the door, and nearly landed on her backside when Mrs. Dorsey dragged her over the threshold. They careened across the street to a two-story clapboard-front building with a small sign in the window declaring rooms for rent. The whitewashed front was faded to gray, but the inside was as spotless as soap and water and good intentions could make it.

"Room three is open, Mr. Sutter. Top of the stairs and to the left." The woman pointed toward the second floor and held out a huge skeleton key tied to a fancy wooden doodad with the scuffed remains of a number three on both sides in black paint.

"Dinner is at six o'clock sharp, in the kitchen, just through there." She pointed to a small door under the staircase. "Come right on through. We don't stand on ceremony here." She giggled, a high, tinkling waterfall sound. "No need to bother with fancy. Come just as you are. Six o'clock sharp, remember. I don't cotton to latecomers. Oh, and breakfast," she prattled on. "Breakfast is at half-past sun-up. No need to laze away a perfectly good morning, I always say."

Lizzie must have looked as confused as she felt.

"Thirty minutes after the sun comes up," Mrs. Dorsey explained. "Made no sense to say six or seven in the morning, since the sun comes up earlier or later every day. So, half-past sun-up." Satisfied she'd made herself clear, the woman waved Lizzie toward her room and bustled through the door beneath the stairs, her ample girth barely clearing the opening.

"Thank you, ma'am," Lizzie called after her as she started up the squeaking staircase. No one would be able to sneak upstairs, that was for certain. Four rooms opened onto the hallway at the top. Lizzie turned left to room three and inserted the key. The room was small, furnished with only a bed and a chair. One tiny window broke the monotony of the white-washed plaster walls.

Dumping her supplies and pack on the floor, she went to see to Yeller. The animal seemed to glare as she gathered his reins. "Don't be mad at me, mule. Mrs. Dorsey was in a hurry to see me settled, and I don't think there's a way of stopping that locomotive once she gets up a head of steam." She tugged and cajoled Yeller into motion. "Come on. Let's find you a place to be."

By the time she had the mule fed, curried and settled, she was starving. No breakfast, no lunch. "Dinner had better be good," she muttered as she washed up in the trough outside the livery. She glanced at her reflection in the water. "What a sight! I ought to go to my room and at least smooth my hair some, or Mrs. Dorsey's liable to chase me away from the table with a broom."

Lizzie splashed more water on her hands and face before heading back to the boarding house. She made it as far as the bottom stair when Mrs. Dorsey bustled into the front hall. "There you are. Come, come. You're late. Dinner is ready."

"I just want to go up and—"

"No, no, no. No time. I said six o'clock and it is nearly three past. You're keeping the others waiting."

"Others? Now, hold on a minute."

The woman hustled and prodded Lizzie through the door into a small room stuffed with a long table, twelve chairs, and two men. Both rose to their feet, the look of surprise in their eyes at her appearance one Lizzie knew well.

"Gentlemen, meet Lee Sutter. Mister Sutter is staying for a few days before heading on to California to meet up with his brother. Mister Carruthers, will you please make the remaining introductions while I set out your dinner?"

"Why, uh, c-certainly, M-Mrs. Dorsey. It w-would, uh, be m-my p-pleasure."

Though the man had agreed, he didn't say a word, didn't even blink, as Lizzie approached the table. The closer she got, the further back his head tilted, while he kept staring at her face, his mouth opening and closing like a landed trout. His long, pointed nose was even with her chin and his back-East clothes made his arms and legs look like sticks. The mud-brown sack suit he wore was at least one size too small, leaving a good three inches of pale, naked skin and frayed cuff hanging out at his wrists.

All seven buttons on his vest were closed, stretching the fabric over his skinny frame. His pants rode high above his mud-splattered shoes, and the high collar of his starched white shirt was so tight around his long, thin neck, she expected he'd have to unbutton it to swallow. After an awkward ten seconds, the other man laughed.

"That's the first time Carruthers's mouth has shut since I came in here. I'm in your debt." He inclined his head in a greeting more suited to a drawing room than a backwoods boarding house. "Carson Browning, proprietor of The Fallen Star Saloon."

The speaker was long, tall and smooth around the edges. His dark gray suit fit his broad frame well and complimented the burnished blond hair curling over his collar. A neatly trimmed mustache outlined his full upper lip. His nose and high cheekbones gave away his high-class breeding, elegant and perfectly proportioned. A scattering of silver at his temples added to the image of a man who had it all.

His eyes, however, held the pain of living. They were the color of good whiskey, shot through with shards of darker gold that made them look a little sad, somehow. Then he smiled, and became the charming scoundrel once again.

"This speechless gentleman is Willoughby Carruthers." Browning waved a hand in the shorter man's direction. "Civil's schoolmaster and resident poet."

That shook the man from his stupor. "P-poet, yes, well, I d-dabble in the art. Dabble. Indeed." When he finally ran out of breath, he offered a rather small and girlish hand. "A p-pleasure to meet you, Mister S-Sutter."

Lizzie shook the butter-soft hand he held out, scared she would crush bones. "Mister Carruthers."

"A pleasure," he repeated.

"How do, Browning." Lizzie reached around Carruthers to grasp the hand the saloonkeeper offered. As she applied pressure, she glanced down, surprised. The fingers were slightly twisted and arched. The injury was old, though, and didn't hamper his firm, sure grip. As she raised her gaze to Browning's, the saloonkeeper's whiskey-colored eyes narrowed. He swept her from head to boots with an assessing look before a small smile curved his lips. "A pleasure, *Mister* Sutter."

He knew. Just by shaking her hand, Browning had figured out she wasn't a man. His discovery of the truth had a rock of dread settling in her stomach.

She had to divert the conversation. "The Fallen Star, huh? Wolf Richards told me about your place. He called you something else, though. Harvard, I think. Funny name, if you ask me."

His smile broadened, not insulted in the least. "Folks here call me that because I studied at Harvard University."

She thought she detected the polished veneer of society in his speech. "Massachusetts." Lizzie looked him up and down. "Grew up around there, too, I expect. Why Civil?"

As he considered his answer, Mrs. Dorsey brought in platters mounded with food. The three of them filled their plates under her watchful gaze before the woman joined them at the table.

"Everything smells wonderful, Mrs. Dorsey. Absolutely delicious." Carruthers enthused.

Lizzie sniffed the air and decided Carruthers had been drinking. A lot. The scent coming from the platter of meat was heavy, oily. It took three mouthfuls before Lizzie identified the tough, greasy meat drowning in lumpy brown gravy as buffalo, ladled over potatoes that had been boiled to paste.

The bread was altogether different. After one bite of the thick slice, she slathered a generous layer of fresh butter on the rest, took a big bite and chewed slowly in appreciation. When it was gone, she snagged another slice before forcing herself to take another bite of meat and then pushed the rest around on her plate, burying some under the potatoes, hoping Mrs. Dorsey wouldn't notice.

She couldn't imagine why Harvard and Carruthers would willingly eat here more than once, but Lizzie didn't ask. She didn't care to offend her landlady, and she sure didn't want to start a conversation and extend the torture. The sooner they were out of that little room, the happier Lizzie would be.

At the end of the meal, Harvard thanked Mrs. Dorsey and rose to his feet. "Mr. Sutter, why don't you visit my establishment this evening? I'm sure we can find a couple of folks willing to play a hand or two, if you're interested."

Cards. Lizzie almost smiled. If Harvard thought she was an easy mark, he was in for a surprise. "I'll do that, Mr. Browning. I believe I'll do just that."

"Please," he smiled. "Call me Harvard."

• ♥ •

The saloon sat at the river end of the main thoroughfare, where the dirt road curved left to trace the path of the river. From a distance, the two-story yellow structure seemed to block the road entirely. Two windows were cut into the second story like eyes in a wide forehead. Only one boasted a curtain, a swatch of deep blue that made it seem the saloon wore a pirate's patch.

A large square sign hung from two chains above the blood-red double doors, proclaiming the name of the establishment. The painted wood sported a golden star tumbling from its place in the heavens to land in the Texas plains.

Framing the doors, two glass panes, tall as a man and twice as wide, reflected the dazzling sunset. Lizzie blinked against the glare and lifted a hand to try and block the light. Finally, she crossed into the shade of the building to escape it.

Before going in, she studied the room from the doorway. The inside was narrow, smaller than she expected, and smelled of sweat, dirt and beer, under the sharp tang of lye soap. The scents were familiar, beloved, swamping Lizzie under a wave of homesickness as she strode through the door.

Six tables made of wood planks nailed on sawed-off barrels were scattered through the saloon. A dog-legged staircase jutted into the right side of the room, drawing her gaze up to the three doors that opened onto a narrow balcony. Harvard had light-skirts? Lizzie didn't see any evidence of them in the place, but that didn't mean they weren't around.

Two cowboys occupied the table in the back, both leaning against the wall with their boots propped on the tabletop and hats shading their eyes, empty glasses near their ankles. Compared to the outside, the saloon was plain and unassuming.

Except for the bar. The long expanse of teakwood was a thing of beauty. Long as a girl's imagination, the surface gleamed in the light of six oil lamps suspended from the ceiling. She hadn't seen wood that shiny since she stood beside her grandfather on the aft deck as his ship pulled out of port after the winter layover.

Harvard stood behind the bar, his legs spread wide and his arms crossed over his chest, watching her. He'd changed clothes since dinner, and while his longish hair and sad eyes still held the look of a poet, the suit he now wore was pure gambler.

A shiny six-shooter hung on his right hip, suspended from a belt of finely tanned and blacked leather. A vest of dark purple brocade, with seven shiny silver buttons, peeked out from the edges of his tailored black suit coat. A polished silver chain looped from one button to disappear into the vest pocket. No doubt the watch attached to the other end of the chain was impressive, as well. Whether he still had it or not, this man came from money. Generations of it.

Harvard poured a shot of whiskey as she approached the bar. "Welcome to the Fallen Star, Sutter."

Lizzie downed the amber liquid in one gulp and held it out for more. "Nice place."

Harvard smiled as he gave her a refill. "Not really, but it's enough for now." He pointed the bottle toward a table. "There's no wood for table legs, and paint for the walls will take six more months to get here, but, as they say, its home."

"You got girls here?" She poked her thumb in the general direction of the second floor.

"Not yet, but I'm considering it, if only to drive Millicent Freeman out of her mind."

Lizzie threw her head back and laughed. "Should have known you'd be a troublemaker." She sipped at her drink this time. "Impressive bar. Where'd you come by it?"

He caressed the highly polished wood. "If the gentleman in Mobile who sold it to me is to be believed, the wood was part of the starboard deck from the unfortunate paddle steamer *Denbigh*. But he was far more interested in profit than provenance."

She rubbed her hand across the smooth surface, caressed the perfectly curved edge. "If you believed him, you got hornswoggled. The *Denbigh* ran aground near Galveston, not Mobile. The Union Navy shot her to pieces and burned her to the waterline before the tide could float her off the mud." Lizzie flattened her hand on the wood and closed her eyes. She could almost hear the ocean. "Wherever it came from, though, it certainly brings back memories."

"So, you're a sailor. That's a rather unusual occupation for a woman."

"Woman!" Lizzie squared off and clenched her fists, the denial automatic, necessary. "The last man who insulted me like that lost a couple of teeth and—"

"Don't bother." Harvard leaned closer, stopping her words and her breath. "The moment I saw your eyes, I knew there was a female under all that buckskin."

"Shut up, Browning!" She glanced toward the cowboys in the back. "Keep that under your hat, would you?"

"Depends. Who are you hiding from?"

"Nobody," she denied, battling to keep her voice down as her fear rose. "I'm not wanted by anyone," she assured him, surprised at how the double meaning stung.

He stared into her eyes, searching, then nodded. "All right. You have my word. And that's something you can count on." Harvard straightened as three men strolled into the bar. "Unlike these three," he muttered under his breath. "Evening, Hayes. Boys."

Lizzie turned to study the new arrivals. The man called Hayes was duded up like a dandy, all fancy buttons and slicked back sunshine-blond hair. Tall and whip-lean, he strutted with the ease of the powerful. This man was accustomed to being obeyed.

He wore a charcoal suit with narrow black stripes. The black vest was made of a rich fabric that gleamed like fine leather. His white shirt was starched stiff and reflected the lamplight when he moved. The pair of black boots he sported must have cost a small fortune. They were polished to a fine gleam, in spite of the dust he'd just walked through to get inside.

His thick mustache was carefully trimmed to outline a pair of full, perfect lips. The matching pearl-handled revolvers at his waist were clean and shiny. Black Jack Hayes cut an impressive figure. Then he looked at Lizzie and she fought not to take a step back.

His eyes were the color of the sky and flat as death.

The two men following in his wake were plain in comparison. One blond and one dark, both stood half-a-head taller than Hayes, and twice as wide. The only thing clean about them was the guns they wore on each hip. Both followed Hayes to a table and waited until he sat before taking a chair on either side of their boss. The blond sidekick pulled a smooth flat rock from his pocket, tossed it into his left hand, and started caressing it with his thumb, over and over.

"Bring a bottle, Harvard." Hayes kicked a chair out from the table with his shined-up boot. "Take a seat and play a few hands with us."

Lizzie felt the coins in her pocket grow warm in anticipation. "I'll take that chair, if you don't mind."

"Careful," Harvard murmured as he topped up her whiskey. "Don't turn your back on him."

She studied Harvard's eyes over her glass, recognizing genuine concern. She'd have to be extra watchful tonight. With a slight nod acknowledging his warning, Lizzie took her drink and swaggered to the table.

Hayes didn't bother to stand. "I don't believe I've had the pleasure." The sticky sweet drip of pure Southern honey in his voice turned her stomach.

Lizzie kept her voice as deep and gravely as possible. "Lee Sutter." Sliding the chair back with a booted foot, she dropped into the empty chair without shaking the hand he offered. She'd take his money, but she didn't have to pretend to like him.

His eyes narrowed as he withdrew his hand. "Colonel Jefferson Hayes, at your service."

Colonel. That explained a lot.

Harvard thumped a bottle to the scarred table, followed by a deck of cards. Obviously Harvard didn't trust Hayes not to mark his own deck. "Those who've lost to him call him *Black Jack*."

Because she was looking, Lizzie saw Hayes's nostrils flare slightly. Obviously, he didn't much care for the nickname, or the implied slur in Harvard's words.

"Now, now." Black Jack scooped the new deck from the table and began shuffling. "There's no call to disparage my reputation before the game even begins."

"Then deal." Lizzie settled in, tossing her stake in the center of the table. "The night ain't getting any longer." She studied the man's hands as he shuffled and dealt the cards. He was practiced, smooth, and could palm an ace faster than anyone she'd come across. Black Jack Hayes was good, but she was better. She could beat him, fair and square.

They stayed even for the first few hands, then she began to gain the advantage, mostly because she watched too closely for him to deal an extra card off the bottom of the deck. As her pile of coins grew, his mood slipped, until it matched his nickname.

"Two pair." He slapped the cards on the table, beating the hands of his two compatriots.

Lizzie laid down a pair of queens. "And the lady makes three." Lizzie turned over the queen of hearts. For a heartbeat, she thought Black Jack would draw down on her, but he subsided when Harvard laid his revolver on the bar.

Black Jack leaned back in his chair. "Well, Mr. Sutter, you seem to have the luck of Lucifer himself."

She gathered the cards and started shuffling. "Seems like it tonight."

"Where did you come from?"

Lizzie didn't see any harm in answering. "Most recently from Doan's Crossing. I ran a saloon there for a while." The tension in the room grew so thick you could cut it. She glanced up to find Black Jack glaring at her.

"A saloon in Doan's Crossing, you say?" Black Jack leaned across the table. "When?"

"A while ago," she snapped, tired of the interrogation. "You going to play or not?" Lizzie tossed back the whiskey in her glass and twisted in her chair toward the bar. "Bring me another one."

When she faced the table again, Black Jack looked mad enough to murder. What the hell? He subsided when Harvard came over with the whiskey, but his mind was obviously no longer on the cards. He didn't even try to cheat during the next hand.

Deciding she didn't want to be around when the man spit out whatever he was chewing on, Lizzie scooped her winnings from the table. "I truly appreciate your contributions, gentlemen." She pulled a worn leather bag from under her shirt and poured the coins inside. Digging out two bits, she tied the bag closed and tucked it back out of sight.

"You aren't quitting."

Black Jack's question sounded a lot like an order, and his two gunnies shifted to clear their weapons. He dismissed their concern with a sharp flick of one hand. "It's still early."

Fear sizzled through Lizzie, but nothing showed on her face. With a swagger, she moved away from the table, careful to stay out of the line of Harvard's shot. "Not if you judge by the barkeeper's yawning." She tossed the coins to Harvard to pay for her whiskey and tipped her hat. "Goodnight, gentlemen. Thank you for the game."

She ignored the quiet curse Black Jack spat at her back, and the not so quiet ones from his two companions, strode through the doorway, and immediately moved to the left, out of their gun sights, then picked up her pace. It would be purely foolish to underestimate that bunch. And Lizzie Sutter was no fool.

The night was clear and cool. A half moon floated, fat and lazy, in the infinite black of the sky. Once she was out of range, Lizzie slowed down and strolled toward Mrs. Dorsey's, mentally counting her take. She'd won enough money tonight to make the trip to San Francisco in reasonable comfort. Riding the train all the way to California was certainly preferable to the seat of a wagon or—good Lord forbid—the back of a mule. And, she hummed with satisfaction, she could do it without having to wire her brother for some of what she had banked with him.

Lizzie was so occupied with her plans she didn't see the couple waiting near the rooming house until she reached to open the front door. She had her revolver half drawn before she recognized the sheriff and Mrs. Freeman. She dropped the weapon back into the holster and lifted her hands clear, palms forward. "Sorry, Sheriff. Ma'am." Lizzie touched the brim of her hat. "I didn't see you standing there."

"Good evening, Mr. Sutter." Millicent Freeman moved into the pool of light cast by the single lantern burning in the foyer. Her dark blue walking dress stopped just short of skimming the toes of her lace-up boots. "You're out rather late this evening, aren't you?"

Lizzie caught herself as she opened her mouth to tell the woman it was none of her damned business. No need to antagonize her. "Yes, ma'am, I suppose so. I took in a few games over at The Fallen Star." Why on earth did that make Lizzie feel like she ought to apologize?

The sheriff stuck out his right hand. "We haven't been introduced, though I know who you are. Word travels fast, here. Archibald Freeman. Welcome to Civil."

Lizzie shook his hand. "Thank you, Sheriff."

"I thought I saw Black Jack Hayes go in there." Freeman glanced across the street toward the lights of the saloon.

"You did, and his contribution to my future endeavors is very much appreciated." Lizzie patted her pocket.

The sheriff's bushy salt and pepper brows met in the middle as he frowned. "Don't underestimate Jefferson Hayes, Sutter. He's meaner than a cornered grizzly with a sore paw, and twice as dangerous. Not a man to be trifled with."

Lizzie glanced back the way she'd come, considering. Harvard had said almost the same thing. Maybe she should hang around town for a few days after all, and give Black Jack some time to calm down some, get over being beaten. Then again, it might be smarter to get out now, before he had a chance to plan how to get even. "I appreciate the warning, Sheriff. I'll take it to heart."

She moved to go around them, but Millicent blocked her path. When Lizzie glanced up, she had the horrible feeling the woman knew Lizzie wasn't who she pretended to be. Then a dog barked somewhere in the darkness and the moment was lost.

"Good night." Millicent reached for her husband's arm.

"Perhaps we'll see you tomorrow."

Lizzie mumbled a response and escaped inside. Slipping up the stairs and into her room, she turned the key in the lock and slid a chair under the knob. She didn't bother with a candle, just unbuckled her gun and bandolier, toed off her boots, and stretched out fully dressed on the mattress. She kept her revolvers close, not trusting Black Jack Hayes to be a good loser, especially after the sheriff's warning.

Closing her eyes, she began planning her trip. With the money she'd won tonight, she could afford a train ticket all the way to San Francisco from the nearest railway station. There wasn't any good reason to stay on in Civil, except Black Jack's temper, of course. If she left in the morning, and he was mad enough to follow... Lizzie wiggled her hips deeper into the lumpy mattress. Better to stick around town. At least, if it came down to a fight, she'd have the sheriff to help her. She wasn't in a real hurry to get to California, anyway.

Lizzie rolled onto her side to stare out at the stars. She could stand being around the nosy inhabitants of this wide spot on the riverbank for that long. Civil wasn't bad as towns went. The people were a little too interested in her business, but probably nothing much happened way out here in the middle of nowhere, so any stranger was cause for excitement. She supposed a person could even make friends, if they stuck around long enough. Wolf and Calvin were good people, and Harvard seemed to be an honorable sort.

She punched her pillow into a more comfortable shape and let her mind drift. If she stayed for a few days, Wolf Richards might even come to town before she left. Lizzie sat up in bed. "Now why would I care if he did?" she hissed into the dark room.

She dropped back onto the mattress. Maybe it would be better to cut out tomorrow. The sooner she got to San Francisco, the sooner the dreaded reunion with her brother—and her mother—would be over.

Lizzie pulled out the letter she'd been carrying in her pocket for more than a year. Unfolding the creased and stained paper, she angled it toward the moonlight. The faint scent of lilacs enveloped her in a cloud of memories.

Her mother always wore that scent. When Lizzie was a little girl, she'd loved to be held by her, just because she always smelled so pretty. If she closed her eyes, she could still see Mama, her rose satin ball gown shimmering with every step, as she came to tuck her daughter into bed before leaving for another party. Before Papa died, she'd seemed so beautiful, so perfect. Now, Lizzie knew better.

For a moment, Lizzie almost wished she could go back to the time when her mother was just Mama, not Amelia Sutter-Davis-Marlow-Reese, the self-centered man-hunting trollop who destroyed families.

Lizzie flopped to her back, staring at the pen strokes on the fancy ivory paper. She could almost hear the carefully rehearsed tears imbedded in the words. *You'll always be my little girl...miss you every day....so sorry...please come home to me.*

At the end, her brother added his own request that she come to California. *It's time to put it behind us, Lizzie-girl.* That Will took the time to write anything at all was what finally decided Lizzie.

Her brother had been devastated by their father's death. Will, even more than Lizzie, blamed their mother for everything that happened. She and Papa had argued constantly, about how she flirted with any man who would pay her a little attention, and how she was never satisfied. Not with the house or her children, or even with Papa. Mama always wanted more. More dresses, more money, more prestige, a bigger house, more party invitations.

Mama had driven Papa to leave, to book passage on that ill-fated ship bound for the islands. Will believed their father made up the excuse of business just to get away from her. At least, he felt that way the last time they'd spoken, more than ten years ago, on the day he boarded a ship for California, leaving four-teen-year-old Lizzie behind in South Carolina to care for their dying grandfather. Evidently, Will's feelings had changed.

Lizzie folded the letter and laid it beside her on the bed. If her brother could put the past to rest, so could she. But not just yet.

She rolled away from the window and tucked her hands under her head. She'd stay in Civil a week, to rest, eat her fill and pack her supplies. With the money she'd won tonight, she could send a few things out to Wolf and Calvin, to repay him.

Remembering the way she'd accused Wolf of being inhospitable made her face burn with shame. That had been her temper talking, nothing more. The man had every right to be suspicious. He'd stuck his neck out for her out in Doan's Crossing, probably saved her life, and she turned around and bit the very hand that was trying to help.

She owed him an apology, and sending out a few useful items might be the only thing he'd accept. That she might see him again had joy stabbing at her heart, but she slapped it down. Nothing for her there. Not even time enough to make him a friend. She would just be grateful he wasn't an enemy. Once the debt was paid, she would ride west until she ran across the train tracks, buy her ticket and not look back.

In two weeks, maybe three, she would be riding in luxury toward California—to face her past.

CHAPTER SIX

"Dammit!" Lizzie rolled away from the patch of morning sun burning a hole in her eyeball. "Damn it all to hell! I hate mornings," she mumbled under her breath. Scrubbing the sleep from her eyes, she stretched and scratched until she felt awake enough to stand without falling on her face. Yawning, she pushed to her feet and headed for the wash bowl.

With her hair slicked down and her gun belt on, Lizzie felt ready to face the day—and breakfast.

Her stomach rumbled, reminding her she hadn't eaten since the meal Mrs. Dorsey served last evening. Lizzie paused at the bottom of the stairs. If breakfast was more of the same, maybe hungry was better. Deciding to give it a try, she turned toward the dining room and nearly knocked her hostess off her feet. Lizzie jerked back and her hat went flying.

"Excuse me, ma'am," she apologized as she bent to retrieve her hat.

"Mister Sutter!" The woman heaved a dramatic breath, pressing her pudgy palm to her generous breast. "I didn't realize you were still here."

"Why wouldn't I be?"

"When you didn't come to breakfast, I assumed you'd ridden out at first light, instead. I was just on my way up to be certain."

Damn. Lizzie heard the woman's voice in her memory, reciting the timetable for meals. *Breakfast is at half-past sun-up. No need to laze away a perfectly good morning.*

"Does that mean I have to go without this morning, ma'am?" Lizzie tried for her most pitiful look. She really was hungry.

"Well, normally I would have to deny your request, since I've so many chores waiting, but..."

Lizzie widened her eyes a bit, going for hopeful. Her stomach got into the act, rumbling like a thunderstorm.

"Oh, you poor man." Mrs. Dorsey fell for it. "Come along. I'm sure I can find you something."

Something turned out to be thick slices of fresh, hot bread, sweet butter and honey. Lizzie declined the landlady's offer to slice some of the buffalo left from the previous evening and filled up on what was in front of her, along with two cups of strong, hot coffee.

Satisfied, she leaned back and propped one ankle on her other knee. "That certainly hit the spot. I think that's the finest bread I've ever eaten."

"I wish I could take the credit, but Hannah Weaver does all the baking for me. I simply don't have the time."

"Thank you again, ma'am, for taking time to feed me. I truly appreciate it, knowing how busy you are and all."

Mrs. Dorsey ducked her head and blushed. "Why, Mister Sutter, you are too kind."

When she batted her eyelashes, Lizzie knew she'd spread it on a little too thick. "Well, I...uh, I should be going. I've kept you long enough, and I have some business to attend to, myself." Lizzie snagged her hat from the chair beside her. "Good morning, ma'am."

She escaped to the street before Mrs. Dorsey could protest and keep her there. Lizzie slapped her hat on her head and turned toward the livery.

An hour later, satisfied Yeller was well cared for, she left the mule snoozing in the sunny corral and stepped into the rapidly warming morning.

"Good morning, Mister Sutter."

Lizzie spun around and came nose to feather with Millicent Freeman's hat. The fluffy creation was wide enough to shade the county and covered in enough feathers to clothe an entire flock of ostriches. Nearly every color of the rainbow sprouted from the woman's head and dribbled down her neck.

Holding off a sneeze with effort, Lizzie stepped away and met Millicent's gaze. "Morning, Mrs. Freeman." Touching two fingers to the brim of her hat, Lizzie went to pass the woman. To her shock, Millicent slipped her arm in Lizzie's and turned them both toward the street.

"I'm so glad I ran into you. I trust this is a convenient time for our chat, Mr. Sutter."

"Well, actually—"

"Good." Millicent tightened her grip ever so slightly, but Lizzie got the message. They were going to talk. Now.

Walking beside the woman, Lizzie felt ridiculous. The stains on her jacket stood out in sharp relief next to Millicent's immaculate royal blue walking dress, with its upswept layers and bustle. The woman carried herself with elegance and breeding. If not for her flour-dusted russet hair, and the few extra womanly curves, Lizzie might have mistaken Millicent for her own mother.

Lizzie adjusted her stride and tried to walk like a man would when keeping pace with a shorter female, all the while praying she didn't trip over her boots and fall on her face.

They went the length of the main street arm in arm, past the jail and the blacksmith's barn, promenading for the whole town to see. The woman didn't even give the smithy's door a wide berth, though the heat of the blazing fire under the anvil could be felt clear to the sidewalk. They crossed in front of the church and turned north, away from the river, ascending a slight incline to a whitewashed gate. The blue clapboard structure behind it looked like a fancy city townhouse in miniature.

Millicent steered her up two stone stairs onto a curved landing and through a front door boasting a large window, crowded with carved images of peacocks. A tall hat tree and a narrow marble-topped table nearly filled the entry hall. There were two doors on either side and a staircase marched up one wall, its length edged with a polished wood banister.

Lizzie removed her hat and stood in the doorway, fingering

the dusty brown felt brim, her image reflected in the huge, gilt-edged mirror suspended over the table. Fixing her eyes on her boots, she studied the pattern of mud on the toes. Anything to keep from looking at herself—or Mrs. Freeman.

"No need to be nervous."

Lizzie's gaze snapped up as Millicent plucked three wicked looking pins from the froth of feathers on her head. Setting her hat on the hall table, she pointed to her left.

"Hang your hat here and take a seat in the parlor, over there. I'll see to some refreshment."

The sitting room Millicent ushered her into was small, square and lovely. The walls were a lighter blue than the outside of the house. A stone fireplace with a polished wooden mantle took up most of the far wall. Frilly white curtains, tied back with dark blue ribbons, framed the windows set all across the front of the room, facing the street.

Opposite them stood a huge sideboard made from some of the finest mahogany Lizzie had ever seen. It reminded her of the big map box that once sat in the captain's quarters of her grandfather's ship. A cut crystal decanter of sherry and four tiny matching glasses perched on a silver tray atop the sleek and shiny surface.

Millicent returned, carrying a large tray bearing a china tea-pot, two cups and saucers, two small pitchers, and a bowl of sugar. She motioned toward a dark blue damask settee. "Please sit down, Miss Sutter."

Lizzie was halfway down before Millicent's words registered. She bounced back to her feet. "What— What did you call me?"

Millicent insinuated herself into a matching damask chair facing Lizzie. "There is no use in further pretense. I've known since the moment you entered Mister Mercer's store yesterday."

Lizzie dropped back into the seat and closed her eyes. "How?" It seemed the only thing worth knowing at the moment. "How did I give myself away?"

"You didn't, Miss Sutter. Your costume and demeanor are quite convincing. However, one has only to see your eyes, your smile, to realize the truth. Fortunately for you, most people don't bother to look that closely."

They sat in silence, each sizing up the other. Taking pity, Millicent poured two cups of tea, then added a healthy splash of amber liquid from one of the pitchers. "Here. This might help."

Lizzie gulped at the warmth, and choked on the alcohol. Whiskey! *Thank you, God.* She sucked in a deep breath to stop the coughing and attacked the cup again. After three swallows, Lizzie felt reality returning. She set the cup back into the dainty saucer with a click and looked straight into Millicent Freeman's eyes. Her grandfather always told her to come out on the winning end of a losing conversation it was best to attack, gain the upper hand quick as you could.

"Whiskey, Mrs. Freeman?"

Millicent lifted her left eyebrow into a severe arch. "If you tell a soul, I will have you arrested."

Lizzie nearly dropped her teacup. "Arrested! On what charge?"

Millicent smiled. "Why would you think there would need to be a charge?"

"The sheriff—"

"Prefers to sleep with both eyes closed."

Lizzie studied the older woman, the burn of fear starting up in her gut. Until she caught the twinkle in Millicent's eyes. She was teasing. "You have this whole town buffaloed, don't you, Mrs. Freeman?"

Millicent laughed, a full, rolling sound that invited Lizzie to join in. "Don't tell anyone that, either."

While Millicent sipped her tea, Lizzie studied her. Seated in this homey room, without that pile of peacock on her head, she looked much less intimidating, but Lizzie wasn't sure she could trust her.

"What do you want from me, Mrs. Freeman?"

"Please, as long as we are alone, call me Millicent. I only insist on formalities out there," she motioned with her head toward the street. "Most folks think I'm a controlling old biddie."

She took another sip from her steaming cup. "I suppose I am, now that I think about it." She grinned and Lizzie felt her own lips curving in response.

"How do you prefer to be addressed?" Millicent refilled Lizzie's cup, but didn't add any liquor.

"I'm sorry, Mrs. Fre—Millicent. I don't know what you mean."

"I can continue to address you as Miss Sutter, but—"

"Oh, that," she interrupted. "My given name's Elizabeth, but everyone who knows me—the *real* me, that is—calls me Lizzie."

"Very well, Elizabeth. What are your intentions in my town?"

Apparently, Millicent wanted to keep her distance. Lizzie shoved the hurt back into the hole in her heart where kept it buried and sniffed at her cup, hoping a little of the whiskey had stuck around. No such luck. She set it back in the saucer without tasting the tea and forced her mind back to the conversation. "Intentions? I don't understand."

"Really? You ride into town after an extended stay at the Richardses' homestead, of which, by the way, I do not approve. You take a room in town without telling Mrs. Dorsey how long you intend to stay, then head straight to the saloon and defeat the most notorious gambler in this territory."

"Just hold on, there. Black Jack invited me to play. I didn't go in there to challenge him."

"That may be true, but the result is the same." Millicent set her cup aside. "Jefferson Hayes is a very bad enemy to make, Elizabeth."

"So I've been told," she muttered into her cup. "Three times, now."

"Very well. You are a grown woman. I can't force you to heed my warning. Now, about Mister Richards."

"Look," Lizzie interrupted again. "A couple of weeks ago, I was searching for Civil and happened upon a house. I was lost, it was gettin' dark and fixin' to storm. I stopped there for shelter and to rest up. If I'd known Civil was only another short bit away, I'd have ridden into town the very next day. Since I didn't have any idea where I was, I stayed on. The place was deserted, and had been for some time, judging by the dust." Lizzie didn't know why she felt the need to defend herself.

"I understand that, Elizabeth, but you remained in that house after Mister Richards and young Calvin returned."

"Only for two nights! What was I supposed to do, ride out the instant he got home?"

"Yes." Millicent's brow arched again, emphasizing her point. "That is *precisely* what you should have done."

"It was almost nightfall," she protested, "and another storm was coming on. I planned to leave the next morning, but that's when Cal got hurt. I couldn't leave Richards to deal with that alone. He needed me..." She trailed off, appalled. "It just wouldn't have been right."

Millicent didn't say a word, just studied Lizzie like a bug on the window, for a long time. "Very well," she finally broke the silence. "I believe you didn't intend to begin a scandal."

"Scandal? Everyone here thinks I'm a man. What kind of rumors could two men and a little boy sharing a roof start?"

"Lizzie, if I saw through your disguise, it is entirely probable someone else will, as well."

Browning already had. Hoping that thought didn't show on her face, Lizzie pushed to her feet and paced to the fireplace. She thought she'd found a friend, but had a fist full of rattle-snake instead. "Then I'll ride out right now. Wouldn't want to start anyone talking, after all."

"That isn't necessary; at least, not yet." Millicent stacked the cups and saucers on the tray and carried it to the mahogany sideboard. "You may remain in Civil as long as you like, provided no one realizes you aren't who you claim to be. Any hint of trouble or scandal in my town and..."

"I get the picture, *Mrs. Freeman*." Lizzie headed for the door. "Don't worry about me. I won't stay in your precious town any longer than absolutely necessary."

"Elizabeth Sutter, you stop right there. I have not finished!"

Lizzie stopped, shocked at how much like her mother Millicent sounded.

The older woman joined her in the foyer. "If I hear even a hint that you have been found out, I will insist you behave as the young woman you are."

Fear blossomed, an acid in Lizzie's gut. "What do you mean by that?"

Millicent clasped her hands together at her waist, her posture emphasizing her absolute conviction. "From the moment of discovery, you will be expected to dress and act as a woman for the duration of your stay in Civil. Further, you will remain here, under my guardianship, until a proper escort can be found to see you to your brother in California. That is your destination, I believe?"

"But I don't know the first thing about being a female, Mrs. Freeman." Lizzie bowed her head, ashamed of the admission.

Millicent sighed. "Elizabeth, I truly don't mean to cause you any difficulty."

Lizzie faced Millicent. "Pardon me if I find that hard to accept. You threaten to tell folks the one thing I've spent years keeping secret, but you don't mean me any trouble?" Lizzie snorted in disgust. "Guess you're just seeing to my best interests, is that it?"

"Something like that." Millicent handed Lizzie her hat. "Do we have a deal?"

Since Lizzie planned to be out of Civil by sun-up, long before anyone else could figure out who she was, she agreed. Only Wolf and Harvard Browning would ever know the truth.

To Millicent's credit, she didn't hesitate to accept Lizzie's hand to shake on the deal, in spite of the dirt stuck under her nails.

Lizzie felt a shiver of trepidation as they clasped hands, like she'd just done something real stupid, but it was too late to back out. She'd given her word—and Lizzie Sutter never went back on her word.

Lizzie didn't slam the door on the way out, but only because

Millicent held it open for her. Stomping down the two stairs, she slapped her hat on her head and headed for the livery. She made it halfway to the church before a voice called out from the shade of the Smithy.

"Well, well. If it isn't Mister Sutter."

Dammit! Lizzie didn't need to deal with Black Jack Hayes right now. Bad enough that Millicent Freeman had backed her into a corner. If this full-of-himself gambler said the wrong thing, Lizzie was liable to start something she'd regret—and she wouldn't be able to get out of Civil fast enough to stop Millicent Freeman.

"What's your hurry, Sutter? It isn't time for dinner, and I'm certain you wouldn't be rushing to a bath."

His two shadows laughed, the sound low and nasty.

Lizzie swallowed the lump of fear choking her. "Why do you care, Hayes?"

"I'm hoping you will give me a chance to win back some of my money."

"It's *my* money now, and no, I don't want to gamble today."

"Tomorrow, then." Hayes oiled his way into the dusty street to stand in front of Lizzie. His two gunnies followed. The ugly one took up a position to Hayes's left, leaving enough space in case he had to draw fast. The big one stopped behind Hayes, but stepped in close enough to offer his boss some shade.

Lizzie glanced at the two thugs, then back at Black Jack. "Ain't gonna happen, Hayes. Witnesses."

The gambler's eye narrowed to coal-black bottomless slits. "You know, Sutter, I don't like to lose. I like losing a business venture even less."

She squared off with Black Jack, ready to give him a tongue-lashing he would never forget, and spotted Millicent Freeman standing in her doorway. Damn it! If Lizzie gave in and started a fight, she'd be wearing bloomers by morning. Trapped, Lizzie fisted both hands, digging her nails into her palms and focused on the pain rather than how badly she wanted to plant a fist in Black Jack Hayes's face. "Get used to it."

Lizzie shoved past the bigger of Hayes's two henchmen and stomped down the street before her temper got the better of her and she ended up wearing a damned dress.

She thought she'd gotten away clean when a voice called out from the doorway of The Fallen Star.

"Hayes, word has it you got beat! Glory be. I never thought I'd see the day." The cowboy cackled. "Guess you should press on for Alaska, after all. Might have better luck there."

She definitely had to leave town in the morning. No way was Black Jack going to leave her alone until he cornered her into another poker game. And what was that about a business venture? Lizzie glanced back to see how Black Jack was taking the cowboy's ribbing, and wished she'd kept walking.

Hayes's temper flashed and his right hand twitched toward his belt gun. Lizzie braced herself for a three-on-one fight, but, before she could blink, his anger vanished, as if it had never been. His face was blank as he turned his gaze on her. A shiver ran up her spine and set her scalp to prickling. Black Jack would find a way to get even. No doubt about it.

The promise was in his eyes.

• ♥ •

"Calvin, for the last time, I can't make biscuits or bread or pie or cake."

"But, Pa—"

"Not another word!" The instant he shouted, he regretted the burst of temper, but he couldn't take the words back. "Look, son. I'm sorry. I didn't mean to yell."

"I just wanted something to go with my stew, Pa." Cal's lower lip trembled as he scooped a spoonful of the thick mess Wolf had cooked and let it plop back into the bowl.

"I know, son. It would probably taste better with bread, but we don't have any and I don't know how to make it."

Calvin grabbed hold of his pant leg and repositioned his injured limb. The grimace of pain that twisted his little face made Wolf feel even worse.

"Do we have to have *javelina* again?"

The whiny edge to the question made Wolf long to break something. Anything. Instead, he gritted his teeth and tried to stay calm. "Not if I managed to snare a rabbit or two."

Calvin brightened at the mention of a change in their diet. "When did you put out traps?"

"Snares," Wolf corrected. "You remember. Traps are iron and take a long time to set. I put out a couple of snares last night after you went to bed. I didn't go far, son," he hurried to reassure Calvin, whose face lost all color as he realized he'd been left alone while he slept. "I wasn't gone long. I could see the light in the cabin the whole time."

Calvin finally looked away to take a tiny bite of the stew, wrinkling his nose at the smell. "It's all right, Pa." He put down his spoon. "I'll clear the table so you can go check your snares."

The boy showed no sign of pain when he dragged his leg off the bench. Not even a twinge when he took a step. Wolf had the feeling he was being played.

Deciding to be thankful for what he had, he picked up his rifle and stuffed some extra cartridges into his pocket. "I'm leaving the loaded shotgun for you, son. Be careful when you move it around."

"I know, Pa."

Cal limped to the table and checked the load in the shotgun. He handled the big gun well. Wolf didn't know whether to be proud of him or sorry the boy had to learn to be prepared so early in life.

"I'll let you know it's me before I come in."

"That'd be a good idea. Wouldn't want to put a hole in you by mistake." He grinned at his father, then turned back to the washtub and the pile of dirty breakfast dishes.

The snares were a bit farther from the cabin than Wolf had owned up to. Heading to the north and over the hill at a jog, it took him ten minutes to reach the shaded valley where he'd set the snares. As he stepped across a small stream and ducked under the low branches of a willow tree, he found blood. Not a lot, but enough to tell him his catch was probably gone.

The first had been destroyed when a four-legged hunter had discovered an easy meal. The second wasn't in much better shape, but could probably be repaired. Wolf inspected the ground around the snares.

"Coyote." Tracks circled the area twice, then a single set of almost dainty prints dug into the soft ground near the stake Wolf had used to secure the snare. "Damned prairie wolf!"

He settled into the grass to try and make a usable snare from what he had left. With a curse for his rotten luck and a prayer that the thing held, he reset the snare and turned for home, hoping to find something along the way with which to make a meal. Cal wasn't the only one sick to death of wild pig stew.

His luck didn't improve. No rabbits, no ducks, nothing. Even taking a longer route back, he was still empty handed when the house came into view. Dropping into the grass under the huge old cottonwood tree at the top of the hill overlooking his homestead, Wolf leaned his rifle against the rough bark and dropped his hat into the dust beside him. Leaning his head against the trunk, he closed his eyes, just for a minute.

He was tired. It had been weeks since he'd slept through the night, either because his son had nightmares—or he did. Last night Cal jolted him out of a sound sleep screaming for his baby sister, Amanda. By the time Wolf got there, he was in such a state it had taken an hour to calm him down and get him back to sleep. Wolf sat up the rest of the night, watching over his son while the ghosts of his wife and daughter slipped through his mind and lacerated his already bleeding heart.

Closing his eyes, Wolf imagined Emily was there beside him, her favorite blue dress spread into a perfect circle around her as she plucked petals from a daisy. The bright yellow petals fell from her fingers and she chanted a silly rhyme in her sweet, sweet voice. Heaving a sigh, Wolf slid deeper into the day-dream. He could almost smell the rose-water Emily dabbed behind her ears every morning.

He loves me. He loves me not. He loves me. He loves...

One by one, the petals fell, drops of sunlight scattering on her dress. Then one hit with a splash of red. Then another. And another.

Wolf jolted awake, tearing himself from another nightmare of blood and death, another reminder of how he'd failed his family. Shoving to his feet, he trudged down the hill. Cal saw him coming.

"Didn't you catch any rabbits, Pa?"

Another failure. "I did, but a prairie wolf got to them first." He took the shotgun Cal held and broke it open. "I'm sorry son."

"That's all right, Pa." He scuffed the toe of his boot across the dusty porch. "We'll get by."

He followed his son inside, trying to think of some way to make it up to him. What might make his son happy again?

"Cal, how about I try to make us some biscuits for supper?"

The boy spun back to his father, hope lighting his blue eyes. "But you said you didn't know how."

"Then it's about time I learned, don't you think?"

"I'll help, Pa. Together, we can do it, I'll bet."

An hour later, Wolf nearly conceded defeat. The last of his flour dusted the floor and covered them both. He'd mixed and mixed, adding flour, then water, then more flour, in a cycle that ended with two dozen piles of soggy dough side by side in a pan. He'd bake the things, but he doubted they'd be edible.

The only highlight of the whole wasted afternoon had been the fit of giggles that beset Calvin when Wolf had given the uncooperative dough a frustrated stir and sent flour flying everywhere. At least, something good came of the mess he'd made.

Wolf plunked the baking pan close to the fire. He refused to try and figure out how to regulate the cast iron stove Emily had loved so much. It had taken him six months to earn the money and four months of waiting to get the damned thing, but she'd crooned over the hunk of metal like a mama over her newborn. He'd been glad to leave her to it. Now, he wished he'd paid more attention.

He only knew how to cook over an open fire. Meat, beans,

bacon and coffee. That was the extent of his knowledge. Grumbling about another of his failings, Wolf cleaned up the room, spared one last glance at the blobs by the fire, and headed for the barn. He had a few minutes before they'd need to be turned around so the other side could bake. In the meantime, he had work to do.

Wolf was brushing out Scarlett's tail when he smelled it. Smoke! Dropping the brush in the dirt, he shoved past the big horse and ran for the house. Wispy tendrils of gray curled out every open window.

"Cal! Where are you, son?" Dear God, don't let him be trapped inside. "Calvin!"

"What's wrong, Pa? Fire!" Cal spotted the smoke as he rounded the house from the direction of the outhouse, and started to run as fast as his limp allowed. "Pa, the house is on fire!"

Wolf skidded to a stop in the doorway and stared into the house. There, on the hearth, smoldered a pan of smoking black rocks that were about the size of what used to be his biscuits. "Well, hell!" He took a deep breath of clean air and strode to the fireplace. Using a hunk of towel and a piece of kindling, he scooped the smoking pan from the coals, dropped it to the floor and scooted it out the door with the toe of his boot.

Cal joined him to stare down at the dismal lumps. "Guess we won't be having biscuits tonight, after all."

Wolf hugged his son to his side. "Afraid not. I'm sorry."

"That's okay. We'll get by." Cal fished out one that didn't look too bad and kicked the rest of the smoldering remains into the dust by the stairs where they wouldn't do any harm. "I'll go stir the stew."

To his credit, Cal ate his dinner without complaint, mostly. He even tried to eat the not-too-badly charred biscuit he'd salvaged. He turned it on the side and gnawed at an edge, but nothing came lose. He had a go at the other side.

"Ouch!"

"What now?" Wolf dropped his spoon and it splashed stew

across his sleeve.

"I tink I boke my toof," Calvin managed around the fingers he'd stuffed into his mouth.

Wolf closed his eyes and hauled in a breath, praying for strength. "Come here and let me see." Cal shuffled around the table to stand between his father's knees. "You have to take your hand out of there, son."

"Hur's."

"I know it hurts, but I have to be able to see it." Once he could actually see the front tooth, he relaxed. "No blood, and the tooth is still in there." He touched it gently. "It's a little loose, though."

Cal's eyes filled with tears. "I don't have to let Mister Evans do nothin', do I?"

"No, son. I won't make you see Mister Evans." Thadeus Evans was a peddler who came through Civil twice a year, on his way to and from Santa Fe. Somehow, he'd managed to convince most of the folks in town he was a dentist. Wolf considered him a snake-oil salesman, an opinion seconded by Harvard. "We'll just wait and see. Might be it was about ready to come out anyway."

"Yeah, I am growin' up, after all." Cal swaggered back to his seat and scooped up the biscuit.

"No more, Cal." Wolf took the brick of dough away from his son. "We'll try again another time."

Cal spooned up another bite of stew, then shoved the bowl away. "It's my fault we don't have anything else to eat, ain't it?"

"What? Calvin, no. Why would you think that?"

"'Cause you ain't gone hunting and you'd be able to go if it wasn't for havin' to watch out for me."

The sadness in the boy's eyes nearly broke Wolf's heart. He held out his arms and Calvin rushed into them, burying his face against Wolf's chest. "Now, you listen to me, Calvin Richards." He smoothed the boy's hair away from his tear-streaked face. "None of this is your fault. None of it." He slid two fingers under Cal's chin and urged him to look up. "We'll get by just fine. As soon as you can ride, we'll try to do some hunting close by, lay in some meat to tide us over."

"Why don't you go into town? Mister Mercer might have something we can buy to eat."

Wolf ruffled his son's blond hair. "Tired of my cooking?"

Cal ducked his head. "Yeah. A little."

"Me, too. I'm so sick of *javelina* stew I can't stand it." Wolf grinned at his son's expression. "A few more days and you'll be well enough to ride. Then you can come with me."

"You can go to town without me, Pa. It ain't far."

Wolf swallowed hard to keep the stew down. The thought of leaving Cal alone, even for a few hours...

"Pa, I'll be all right. Really. I can still shoot. My aim ain't injured, just my leg."

Wolf turned to Calvin and was surprised to see the stubborn set to his jaw, along with a healthy dose of insult lurking in his shining eyes.

"There're all kinds of things I can do 'til you get back, Pa, like carry in wood and sweep the floor. I can start slicing up the rest of the *javelina* for jerky, too. I know how. Honest. Mama teached me. No reason to waste it." Cal straightened but didn't quite release his hold on Wolf's shirt. "I don't need someone to watch over me all the time, Pa. Besides, you'll be back before I have time to miss you."

Wolf tried to smile when Cal quoted what he always said to his children before leaving to go hunting, but his face felt hard, brittle. "Cal— "

"Don't you trust me, Pa?"

Wolf closed his eyes, shutting out the hurt he saw on his son's face. "Of course I do, Cal." It was himself he didn't trust. Too many things could go wrong.

But he was backed into a corner. If he didn't make the trip into Civil, he would feel better, but Cal would be hurt and would probably end up even more scared than he already was. "All right, son. I'll leave in the morning. That way I can get to town and be back in time to eat the noon meal with you."

"What will we be having, Pa?"

Wolf tickled Cal and hugged him close.

"Pig stew!" They shouted it at the same instant, and collapsed into shared laughter.

CHAPTER SEVEN

Wolf angled Scarlett toward Civil, his packhorse trailing behind on a lead rope. He was only twenty minutes from the cabin and he'd nearly turned back twice already, terrified of leaving Calvin alone, even for the few hours it took to get to town and back. But there was no help for it. They'd lived on the meat of the *javelina* Lizzie shot for the last few days, but it wouldn't last much longer.

"Thank the Lord for small favors." A man could only tolerate gamy wild pig for so many meals in a row. Wolf puffed out his breath to encourage a fly to be on its way and glanced around. Maybe he would flush a few doves on the way to town. They didn't offer much in the way of meat, but the change would be welcome.

He leaned back in the saddle as Scarlett descended a hill. In the distance, Wolf spotted a small mud house that hadn't been there eight months before. Civil had grown while he was gone.

That would have made Emily happy. She'd always taken pride in the little town they called home, even though she lived nearly an hour from it. She said she didn't mind being so far from town, but he knew she missed the company of other women. If only he'd given in and moved them closer.

He shook off a little of the sorrow weighing on his heart. Wishing wouldn't bring her back, and there were other things to concentrate on, like who he could ask to stay with Calvin while he went trapping.

During the long months after Emily's murder, while he searched for his children, he swore, once he found them, he'd never leave them alone again. The reality of what could happen when he wasn't there to protect them haunted him, day and night. Try as he might, he couldn't think of another way. Trapping was the fastest way he knew to make enough money to see them through the winter.

Wolf crested another rise and aimed Scarlett for the river that ran beside town. At least the rain had stopped. The land wore the shimmering sweetness of damp earth and new growth. He inhaled the scent, relishing the quiet, the peace.

He probably would have ignored the small tan lump lying near a chunk of exposed rock if it hadn't moved. Wolf palmed his revolver and pulled his horse to a stop. The lump straightened into a man, then slumped to the ground again. Wolf rode forward, eyes restless, watching for an ambush. Nothing moved but the long prairie grass in the fitful wind. He got within ten yards before he called out.

"You there. Mister. Need some help?"

The man rolled to his feet and tried to run. He managed half a dozen steps before collapsing with a groan. Recognition flashed through Wolf.

"Lizzie!" He leapt from the saddle and ran to her side. "Lizzie? Can you hear me?"

She turned her head toward his voice, but she couldn't have seen him through the blood running into her eyes. Curling into herself, Lizzie looked like she expected to get hit some more.

"Take it easy, Lizzie. It's Wolf Richards." He dropped to his knees beside her. When he touched her arm, she screamed, biting the sound off almost immediately. Wolf snatched his hands back. "Sorry."

He smoothed her hair away from her bruised cheek, checking a gash on her forehead that still bled a little. "That cut's not too bad. You're going to be fine. I'm going to take you back to the cabin now." He scooped her into his arms, and her head lolled back, coming to rest against his shoulder. He could see the bruises darkening the skin of her jaw and another blooming beneath the laces of her buckskin shirt. Someone had kicked her there. The outline of a boot toe was visible on her skin. "God, who the hell did this to you?"

She swallowed, hard, and dragged in some air. "Not sure," she whispered. "Maybe Hayes," she panted. "From behind. A rock. Knocked me off Yeller." She licked at her dry lips.

"Let me get you some water." He whistled to bring Scarlett closer, then eased Lizzie to the ground, a little relieved that she didn't seem to have any busted ribs to go with the broken right arm. Supporting Lizzie with one arm, he helped her sip a little from his canteen, then poured some on his handkerchief and wiped some of the blood off her face.

She slumped back and closed her eyes. "Where's my gear?"

"I'll come back and look for it later."

"Yeller?" She coughed, and grabbed at her ribs, gasping in pain when the movement jostled her busted arm. "Damn!" She worked at getting her breath back for a minute. "Heard—a shot."

That would be just like Black Jack, to shoot a defenseless animal. He loved to watch things bleed. Wolf hissed a string of curses into the wind, trying to get rid of some of the helpless fury burning in his gut. "Enough talking. Let's get you to the house."

It was a testament to her pain that Lizzie didn't argue. In fact, she didn't make a sound as Wolf lifted her into the saddle and climbed on behind, though she had to hurt like hell. He held Scarlett to a walk, trying not to jar her too much, but the ride seemed to go on forever. He didn't think he'd ever been so glad to see the cabin.

"Calvin!" Wolf's call brought the boy limping to the porch, a shotgun cradled in his arms.

"What happened, Pa?" Cal hurried down the steps and grabbed the reins Wolf dropped. "That's Miss Lizzie!"

Wolf dismounted as easy as he could, but Lizzie whimpered in pain when his boots hit the ground. "Put Scarlett in the corral, then bring in a couple of buckets of water. Carry it in a little at a time so you don't make your leg worse," he cautioned. "I can't take care of two of you."

"Sure thing, Pa."

Climbing the stairs to the porch wrung a moan from Lizzie. "Hang on, honey." He crossed the main room and laid her on his bed. "Lizzie? Come on, now. Let me see those pretty eyes."

One eye opened a slit, enough for Wolf to see a hint of her usual fire flashing within. "Liar."

He grinned. "Nice to have you back. Where do you hurt?"

"Everywhere but my little finger," she groaned and closed her eye again.

Wolf unlaced her deerskin shirt, but couldn't find a way to get it off her without hurting her worse. Her right arm seemed bent the wrong way somehow, and he was pretty sure the bone was broken. As he pulled at the stiff material, she gasped and sweat broke out across her forehead. With a curse, he yanked the knife out of his boot and sliced through the seams. Maybe she'd be able to fix the damn shirt somehow.

The pants went the same way, and he didn't even hesitate before cutting off her undergarments. He thought she'd fainted, until embarrassment stained the very pale skin he'd uncovered. "I'm sorry for this, but I don't want to move you any more than necessary."

"Just do what needs doing."

As he exposed more skin, he pulled a blanket over her, trying to preserve a little of her pride. Finally, she lay naked beneath the wool. The remains of her buckskins lay spread beneath her like a deer skin on a stretcher.

"How bad is it?"

Wolf moved into her line of vision, so she didn't have to move. "You've got some bruises on your right side, but I don't think they busted any ribs."

"My arm got in the way," she muttered.

"Looks that way. They were none too kind to your face, but

they left your sass intact." Her reply made him grin. "Just rest now. I'm going into Civil for the doctor."

"Calvin?"

"He'll be in the other room."

"Will he be all right with you gone?"

It touched him that she would think of his son when she was hurt so badly. "He'll be fine. I won't be long."

That seemed to satisfy her, because her breath slid out on a sigh and she dropped off to sleep.

• ♥ •

"How is she, Pa?" Calvin had three buckets of water sitting inside the door, and another heating by the fire. "Is Miss Lizzie gonna be all right?"

Wolf ruffled his son's tangled blond hair. "I think so, but I'm going to go get Doc Browning, just in case. Can you keep an eye on her 'til I get back?" Leaving Cal alone again was the last thing he wanted to do, but it couldn't be helped.

"Sure, I can. And I'll make sure she stays put, too. Just let me know it's you before you come in. I'll shoot anything else." The boy stared up at his father, a pint-sized version of the man he would grow to be.

"You do that, son. I'll be back as soon as I can."

Calvin watched his father mount up and ride for Civil. Taking his job seriously, he closed and barred the door, then made sure every window in the house was secure. He considered making coffee, but he didn't really know how, and he didn't think Miss Lizzie would want any, anyhow. He shoved and dragged a chair close to her door, then went back for the shotgun and leaned it against the wall within reach.

Finally, he couldn't resist. "Need to make sure she's breathing, don't I?" He reasoned his way into the bedroom and right to her side. It seemed kind of odd to see her brown hair spread all over the pillow instead of his ma's long blond braid, covered in a night cap. Ma had real pretty hair, he remembered.

"Who's there?" Her hand moved in a jerky pattern, like she

was trying to find something.

"It's me, Miss Lizzie. Calvin Richards." She calmed down as soon as he said his name. Calvin leaned closer so she could see him. "You just stay real still, now. Pa went to fetch the Doc. I'm going to keep you safe until they get back."

She smiled just a little. "Lucky for me there are two men in this house."

Cal plopped onto the bed and jumped off just as fast when she groaned. "I'm sorry! I didn't mean to hurt you."

"I know." She breathed in and out real fast a few times, then licked her lips. "It's my arm." She breathed in. "I could use…" Another breath. "Water."

"Sure thing." He limped to the buckets and scooped a cup full, sloshing and dripping all the way back to the bed. There he stopped, looking between the cup and her. "How're you gonna drink this?"

She opened her good eye. "You need to drink about half that first." He took two big gulps and wiped his mouth with the back of his hand.

"Good. Now come over by my right arm. Climb on the bed. Easy," she panted when he sat down too hard.

"Sorry," he whispered. Seeing her hurt this bad made his leg hurt all over again.

"It's all right. Now, help me hold up my head a little."

Together they managed, though most of the water spilled on the bed. "That's enough."

Cal stayed by her side, plucking at the wet spot on the bedclothes. "You ain't gonna die, are you?"

"Not a chance," Lizzie whispered. "I just hurt a whole lot. But don't you worry. I'll be right as rain in a few days."

"You want some more water?"

"Not just now, Sir Calvin. I need to rest a while."

"Then I should go sit by the door and protect you. I promised Pa I would."

"Why don't you settle down right here beside me? That will

make your job a little easier, don't you think?"

"I think you might be right. Let me just get my shotgun." He scooted off the bed, favoring his left leg.

"How's your *javelina* souvenir doing? I'll bet you're going to have quite a scar to show off to your friends."

"Oh, you bet." Cal laid the gun on the bed between them and climbed back in real easy. "Pa said it's gonna be a fine one. I got to keep the two big front teeth." He stuck fingers in the air in front of his mouth, pointed up.

"Tusks," she corrected.

"Yeah, that's what Pa called 'em, too. Since you skinned the javelina for the meat, I got to keep them tusks to remember by. I just wish…"

Lizzie cracked one eye open. "Wish what?"

"I just wish the darn thing hadn't been so big. I'm real tired of pig stew."

Her lips curved up on one side. "When I'm feeling better, maybe I can come up with another way to fix it."

"Could you, really? Pa tried to make biscuits and they were mostly burned and too hard to eat, but I tried anyway and dang near broke my tooth." He leaned close so she could see it. "Pa said I don't have to see Mister Evans about it, though." He wiggled down until his head was on the pillow beside Lizzie. "Why did you call me Sir Calvin?"

She smiled again, just a little, and Cal thought it must hurt, 'cause she didn't do it for long.

"You're protecting me, like a knight in shining armor would have many years ago. People always called the knights Sir something-or-other, depending on their name. So that makes you Sir Calvin."

"Oh. I like that."

"Good. Now I'm going to rest my eyes for a minute. You should do the same. A knight has to save his energy for the upcoming battle."

Calvin stretched out beside her, slipped his hand into hers, and slid into sleep.

• ♥ •

Wolf tore into Civil like the hounds of hell were snapping at his heels. "Harvard!" His shout as he shoved into the saloon startled the lone cowboy sprawled against the bar. His boots landed on the floor with a thump, but he staggered backward when he tried to stand.

Wolf caught him before he hit the floor. "Where the hell is Browning?"

"Right here, Richards." He stuck his head out of the back room, wiping down a bottle of whiskey.

Wolf met him halfway across the saloon. "Mister Sutter was ambushed a few miles from here." If she played poker with Black Jack Hayes, she'd probably kept up her pretense of being a man. Wolf wasn't going to be the one to ruin her disguise.

"Damn." Harvard checked his gun belt. "Was it Black Jack?"

"She—he thinks so. I found him between my place and here." Wolf waited until Harvard looked up. "He needs a doctor."

Harvard paled. He opened and closed his right hand, then started rubbing at the joints, as if it pained him. "Ask someone else."

"There is no one else. You're a doctor." Wolf pulled his hat off and ran his fingers through his hair. "I understand how you feel, but there's no one else I trust."

"No one can understand." Harvard stared at Wolf with haunted eyes, pulling the cloth through his fingers again and again, as he battled the past. "Fine." He tossed the cloth on the bar. "Simmons, drink up. The saloon is closed."

The cowboy gulped the last of his beer so fast half of it poured down his neck. Jamming his hat on his head, he rolled off the bar stool and stumbled toward the door.

Wolf followed the cowboy out. "I'll go saddle your horse."

"Let me get my bag and go with you," Harvard turned toward the back of the saloon. "Otherwise, I might talk myself out of coming."

It only took fifteen minutes to get underway, with Wolf barking at the boy who worked in the livery the whole time.

"Damn it, Richards. Calm down." Harvard tied his black medical bag behind the saddle of a leggy buckskin gelding.

"I have to get back. Sh—he's alone with Calvin." He lifted the reins and set his heels to Scarlett, leaving Harvard to follow. As they neared the valley where Wolf found Lizzie, he veered to the left and signaled a stop.

Wolf slipped the leather tie from his belt gun so he could draw easily.

Harvard followed suit. "Why are we going this way?"

"This is where I found Sutter. I want to take a quick look around, see if they left anything of hers—his behind."

Harvard turned his mount onto a parallel track, scanning the horizon for other riders. "You don't have to bother."

"With what?" Wolf skirted a small outcropping of rocks.

"I figured out Sutter was a woman the moment I met her."

Wolf studied the doctor in silence.

"The eyes," Harvard explained. "And her skin, of course." He reined in. "Much too soft for a man."

A stab of something ugly dug under Wolf's tough hide. He sat back in the saddle. It couldn't be jealousy. Not possible. He was just concerned that Doc knew Lizzie's secret. "What do you plan to do with the knowledge?"

"Absolutely nothing, which, as my friend, you should know by now, you hard-headed son of a bitch." Harvard lifted the reins to continue down the hill. "There's something shiny over there."

The men reined in beside the smashed remains of the mirror. "Damn him," Wolf cursed as he stared down at the pieces. Only the carved wood that'd surrounded the silvered glass was worth the trouble of salvaging. He swung out of the saddle and squatted by the debris. It had to be hers. The frame was only busted in a couple of places. Maybe he could fix it for her.

Wolf glanced around and spotted a small mound of leather a dozen or so feet away. It was her pack—or what was left of it. The leather had been slashed, the contents smashed or stolen. Everything was gone, including her guns. "Son of a... They busted everything they didn't steal." He examined and tossed aside a thick hunk of curved glass.

"I tried to warn her Black Jack made a bad enemy, but she seemed to believe she could stay out of his way."

Wolf secured the frame to his saddle. "She wasn't sure it was him, but this looks like his work. Let's get to the house."

"Hold on." Harvard pointed at two long-legged coyotes in the distance. "What do you suppose could be of interest to them, out in the open like this?"

Wolf watched the animals stalk along the rim of the next hill. "What's left of Lizzie's mule, I'm guessing." To be sure, they rode that way, scaring off the coyotes. What they found confirmed Wolf's guess. "They probably shot it just to see it bleed." He yanked his hat lower on his brow. "I'm going to kill the son of a bitch for this."

"You didn't see him do it," Harvard cautioned. "And she isn't sure. You can't prove he attacked Lizzie, and you know how Sheriff Freeman is about proof."

The truth was bitter. "Still..."

"Stay out of it, Wolf. This isn't your concern. The woman will heal in a week or two, and go on her way. She'll likely never see Black Jack Hayes again, but you live here. *If* Black Jack did this, he's an enemy you don't need."

"Too late," he muttered as he unbuckled Lizzie's saddle, yanked it free and climbed back onto Scarlett. For a long minute, he stared up at the buzzards circling high above the mule's carcass. "Let's get to the house."

Harvard reined his horse around to follow. "You should have back-shot that bloodthirsty bastard when the opportunity presented itself."

Wolf didn't disagree. Just another regret to add to the long list of his life.

They approached the cabin from the north. Wolf stayed in the open so Calvin could see him. They rode right up to the porch and still Calvin didn't open the door.

"Calvin? You in there?" Silence. Nothing moved. No one answered.

Terror froze Wolf in place, seized his lungs and made it hard to breathe. He dismounted and ran up the porch steps, but the door was barred. Motioning Harvard to go the opposite direction, Wolf slipped around the house, checking doors and windows for a sign someone had gotten to his son. Everything was locked up tight. When he reached the bedroom window, he straightened enough to peer in through the rifle slit, and came nose to barrel with a loaded shotgun.

"Who?" The voice was so soft Wolf barely heard.

"It's me. Wolf. Are you two all right?"

The barrel disappeared. He heard the scrape of the bar being lifted and the shutter opened. "Can't get to—door," she panted, slumping against the wall.

"Where's Calvin?" Before she could answer, Wolf caught sight of his son, sound asleep on the bed. He holstered his revolver. "Doc?" He glanced toward the other man, standing ready at the far corner of the house. "Everything's all right. I'll open the door." He boosted himself onto the sill and rolled over it and into the room.

Lizzie watched through her one good eye. "Show-off."

Wolf tossed a grin over his shoulder as he checked on Calvin, then unbarred the door for Harvard.

"What are you doing here?" Lizzie snapped at Harvard as the men approached. She managed a half-hearted protest that faded into a moan of pain when Wolf lifted her off the floor and carried her to the bed.

Harvard washed up in the basin on the dressing table. "I was told you needed a doctor."

"Saloon-keeper *and* sawbones? Do you have to poison your

clientele to get any patients?"

"Now, that's not fair." Harvard dried his hands and opened his bag. "I should at least have a chance to prove myself before you label me a charlatan," he joked.

Only Wolf knew how forced Harvard's humor really was.

"That's an awful lot like what Black Jack Hayes said about his card playing." Lizzie eyed the stethoscope like it was a snake.

"Just relax," Harvard reassured her. "I was a very good doctor. Once." He bent over Lizzie. "Tell me where you hurt."

As Harvard got down to business, Wolf moved Calvin to his own bed. He stoked the fire and turned the bucket of water around so it would heat through. He groomed both horses and released them into the corral with plenty of water. He made coffee. And Harvard was still with Lizzie.

Twice, Wolf started for the door, determined to barge in and make sure she was all right. Twice, he paced the length of the room, vague panic clawing at his gut. The last time he'd done this was the night his son was born. "She isn't Emily," he reminded himself, his whisper harsh in the silent room. Disgusted with his worry over what amounted to a stranger, he dug through their meager supplies for the makings of soup. Stranger or friend, Lizzie would need to eat.

He nicked his finger with the knife when Harvard called his name. "Damn." Shaking the stinging wound, he strode into the bedroom.

"Do you need a doctor for that?" Harvard indicated Wolf's bleeding finger.

Wolf bit back what he wanted to say. No need to take out his rotten mood on Harvard. "How is she?" He nodded in Lizzie's direction.

"*She's* just fine," Lizzie snarled. "Not that you asked *me*."

"That's right. I didn't." Wolf turned back to Harvard.

"I don't think her right wrist is broken, though the swelling keeps me from being certain." Harvard pointed at the rough splint he'd fashioned from flat pieces of wood and strips of white fabric. More fabric looped from her neck and around the splint in a serviceable sling. "That should keep it stable enough until I can be sure, as long as she leaves it on." He raised an eyebrow in Lizzie's direction to make his point.

"My word I'll behave." She lifted her left hand and held it palm out in a pledge. "I won't risk my shooting hand."

Harvard shook his head. "I should have known." He turned his attention back to Wolf. "Nothing else looks too serious. A couple of banged up ribs, a nasty bruise on her left thigh, and she won't be seeing out of her right eye for the next few days. All in all, I'd say she was fortunate."

Lizzie snorted. "Fortunate? If this is what you consider fortunate, I'd hate to see—"

"Shut up, Lizzie." Wolf cut her off, then turned back to Harvard. "What do I need to do for her?" He knew she wasn't leaving for a while and he needed to know how to help her. Knowing she was in pain made his gut hurt.

"I suspect she wouldn't take laudanum if I prescribed it." Harvard dug a bottle of whiskey out of his bag. "I know you don't have any here, because you haven't been into the saloon to buy a bottle." He poured Lizzie a generous amount. "Drink this and try to sleep. It'll work as well as laudanum and it tastes better."

Lizzie gulped it down and held out the glass for more. "Not a hell of a lot better, but it'll do."

"Don't malign my whiskey, Miss Sutter, or I'll take it with me." A grin gave away his bluff as he poured another shot, then set the bottle on the dressing table.

"Doesn't matter. I have my own." She turned her gaze on Wolf. "Where's my pack?"

Wolf hated to tell her, knew it was going to cause pain of a different kind. "It's gone."

She stared at him. "What do you mean, gone?"

"Whoever did this was thorough. There was nothing left but slashed up leather and the busted frame of your mirror."

Tears shimmered in her eyes. "My grandfather's revolvers? My money? Will's mirror?" The last was barely a whisper.

Wolf shook his head, feeling like a knife was digging into his gut. "There was nothing left."

She sniffed. "Yeller?"

He didn't have to answer. She covered her eyes with her good arm. "Leave me alone. Please."

When the first tear leaked down her cheek, Wolf wanted to break something. Instead, he set the whiskey on the floor by the bed and followed Harvard out of the room.

Harvard accepted the coffee Wolf poured. "She'll argue, but she needs to stay put for a while. A month would be best, but we can move her into town after a week or so. I don't want to risk injuring her further by trying to take her there sooner."

"She can stay here as long as she needs to."

Harvard lifted his cup. "You realize Millicent will be incensed when she finds out Lizzie's here."

"This is none of Millicent Freeman's business." Wolf sat on his heels to poke at the fire. "I'd hate for the women in town to think poorly of Lizzie, though, just because she's here."

"You want me to send someone out to stay with Lizzie?"

Having a woman here to cook and clean would be helpful, but Wolf didn't want another woman in Emily's house. Still, Lizzie might not care to be alone here. "I'll ask her before you go."

"Ask me what?"

Both men spun toward the voice. "You don't follow instructions well," Harvard admonished. "I told you to rest. What are you doing out of bed?"

Lizzie ignored Harvard. "Ask me what, Richards?"

When Wolf didn't answer, Harvard explained. "I think you should stay here and recuperate for a few weeks, but the ladies in Civil will likely take offense at the idea of you being here alone with Wolf. They could make your life difficult."

"Like it isn't already?" She snagged Wolf's coffee cup on the way to the rocking chair near the fire. He barely registered its absence. At her first moan of pain, Harvard was at her side, helping her to sit.

"Thank you," she breathed.

Wolf could only stare. She was dressed in Emily's favorite nightgown and wrapper. Sitting in what had been his wife's favorite chair, Lizzie opened the door wide for all the ghosts. He couldn't think of anything but his wife and daughter. Gone. Forever.

"Wolf? Wolf!" Harvard's voice yanked him back to the present. "You all right, old friend?"

"I need to check on Calvin." Wolf knew he wouldn't be able to concentrate on anything until he knew his son was safe. Lizzie eyed him strangely when he left the room, and no one spoke until he returned and dropped into his seat at the table.

Lizzie tried to set her cup on the floor, but couldn't bend over that far. Harvard took it from her and set it on the table, touching her shoulder in sympathy. Wolf watched his old friend pamper Lizzie, his thick blond hair falling into his eyes as he leaned close to speak with her. Whatever Harvard said made Lizzie laugh. The sound sizzled through Wolf's blood.

Wolf shifted on the bench, drawing Lizzie's attention.

"So, is your offer still good?"

He stared at Lizzie, confused. "What offer?"

"To stay with Calvin while you go do whatever it is you need to do." She flexed the fingers of her left hand then fisted them on the arm of the rocker.

Wolf stared at the contrast of pale skin against the dark wood. But where Emily's hands were small and soft, Lizzie's showed strength, experience. It disturbed him to realize he liked that in a woman.

"Damn it, Richards. Pay attention. I'm asking you for a job, here!" Lizzie banged her fist against the chair arm, then flinched in pain. She grabbed at her ribs with her good hand.

Wolf refilled her cup and returned it to her. "Here, hold onto this. Might keep you from hurting yourself further." He stepped out of reach before she could fling the contents at him. "Just keep your temper, woman."

Harvard laughed. "I'm not sure her staying here is a good idea, after all. You two are liable to slice each other to ribbons and I don't have the time to keep patching you up." He leaned toward Lizzie. "You're pretty good at poker. Why don't I stake you? You could earn your traveling money that way."

"And who would I play? By now, word has gotten around I beat Black Jack more times than skill or plain luck should account for."

"Did you cheat?" Wolf knew, if she had, Black Jack would never give up. This attack would only be the beginning.

"Hell, no, I didn't cheat! Didn't have to. He's not that good." She rubbed at her arm above the sling. "Not that it matters. No one who hears about it is going to sit at a table with me. I didn't worry about it at the time, since I wasn't planning to stick around, but now?" Lizzie shrugged and rubbed at a sore spot on her leg with the tip of her little finger.

"How about tending bar?" Wolf knew she could do that.

She waved a hand in the general direction of her bruised up face. "Would you buy whiskey from someone who looks like this?"

"You'll heal," Harvard soothed. "Just be patient."

"Not something I'm good at, Doc. In the meantime, I'll have to owe you for patching me up."

Harvard waved off the offer. "It's on the house. I feel responsible for what happened."

"Black Jack Hayes is responsible. The bastard," she hissed, then glanced around as if to be sure Calvin hadn't heard her language. Since her good hand was full of coffee cup, Lizzie tried to blow a strand of hair from her face, growling when it flopped back into her eye.

Harvard laughed at her frustration.

"It isn't funny," she snapped.

Lizzie glared at him, which only made Harvard laugh more. "Let me get the whiskey. Maybe that will calm you down."

"I don't need whiskey. I need a job." She huffed in annoyance, then balanced the cup on the chair arm long enough to rake the hair out of the way. "If my pack is gone, then Black Jack, or whoever the hell did this, took everything, including the money I won from Black Jack, fifteen day's pay from a God-forsaken cattle drive and what was left from minding Orville's saloon." Lizzie glanced up at the sound of surprise from Harvard. "Didn't know you were patching up a competitor, did you?"

"He got *all* your money?" Now Harvard looked ready to hunt Black Jack down and beat the money out of him with his bare hands. Wolf understood the feeling completely.

"Not all of it. I'm not totally without sense." At Harvard's bark of laughter, Lizzie glanced at her coffee, seeming to give serious consideration to flinging the cup at his head. "I wired most of my money to my brother in California before I headed west. What was in my pack was to see me to San Francisco."

She turned her blue eyes on Wolf. "You need someone to keep Calvin safe and fed while you go off and earn your living. I have to make enough money for supplies and a train ticket. We can help each other. You offered the job to me before. I just want to know if the offer is still open."

"What about the ladies of Civil?" Harvard argued.

She laughed, then caught at her ribs. "Damn, that hurts." She took a couple of careful breaths before answering. "I don't give a hoot what they think of me, and my being here isn't going to harm Calvin's reputation. Or his," she stabbed her chin in Wolf's direction.

"He battered his reputation beyond recognition years ago." Harvard capitulated. "Fine, but I doubt Millicent will agree, if she finds out you're a woman."

"She already knows," Lizzie countered. "Not that her opinion matters to me."

"Millicent Freeman can mind her own business." Wolf stood. "The job is yours. I'll leave as soon as you're on your feet."

"Done." Lizzie handed Wolf her cup and stuck out her left hand to seal the deal. Wolf enveloped it in his much larger one. Her hand felt small, feminine, but with rough edges, just like Lizzie herself. She was one strong woman.

Wolf held her hand long enough to see a blush color her cheeks. Interesting, she looked almost female with that bit of pink heating her face. Lizzie yanked her fingers free, muttering under her breath.

"What's done, Pa?"

The adults welcomed Calvin into their circle. Wolf wrapped an arm around the boy's shoulder. "Miss Sutter is going to stay with us for a while, son, until she heals up."

Cal rubbed at his eyes and covered a yawn. "Is she going to be here while you go hunting?"

Wolf crouched down in front of his son. "Would that be all right with you?"

"I guess so." The worry lines between his eyebrows smoothed. "Maybe Miss Lizzie can teach me how to shoot them *javelinas*." The boy turned his blue eyes on Lizzie. "Could you, ma'am? Please?"

"We'll see, Cal. It'll be a while before I can hold a rifle, let alone do any target practice on cantankerous wild pigs. For now, you need to get back to bed. Your leg needs rest as much as my arm does." Lizzie watched Calvin go into his bedroom, rubbing her right arm just above the splint. It had to be hurting or, Wolf suspected, she wouldn't show even that much weakness. A moment later, she caught him watching. The rising color in her cheeks told him she didn't like being caught showing any pain.

Harvard took pity on her and asserted the rights of his profession. "For now, you need to get some rest, as well. Doctor's orders," he cut off her protest. Wolf started forward, but Harvard got to her first and helped her out of the rocker. "The more you rest, the faster you'll heal."

"That's a good idea." Lizzie leaned on him and Harvard accepted her weight without comment. "The sooner I can shoot, the sooner Black Jack Hayes gets to meet his maker."

"The devil will have to wait a while longer." Harvard steered her into the bedroom, Wolf following in their wake. "Of course, if Hayes shows his face in Civil, I'll be happy to dispatch him to hell for you."

"I appreciate the offer, but it isn't your fight, Doc." Lizzie sucked in a breath as he eased her into bed. A tiny groan was the only indication the movement hurt.

"It is now." Harvard talked over her protest. "One, you played cards in my saloon and you beat him, fair and square. Two," he continued. "You're my patient."

"I wasn't when he waylaid me," she grumbled.

"A technicality I choose to ignore. Three, whether or not he knows it, he struck a woman. No man has that right. Period."

When she took a breath to argue, he brushed her hair off her forehead. The tender gesture shut her up.

"Nothing you say will change my mind, Miss Sutter, so save your breath."

"Fine," she huffed. "But you'd better not kill him before I get back on my feet. That pleasure is all mine."

When Harvard offered Lizzie a splash of whiskey to help her sleep, she yanked the bottle from his hand and slugged back a healthy swallow.

"That's enough." He took it away and held it out of reach. "Now rest. I'll be back to check on you in the morning."

"No need. I'll mend just fine without any more doctoring."

"In the morning," he insisted, leaving the room before she could argue any more.

Wolf stepped back and followed Harvard to the hearth, where Harvard stood staring at the flames. He handed Wolf the bottle of whiskey. "Put this away where she can't find it. She's mad enough right now to down the whole thing."

Shaking his head, Wolf set it on the table. "I don't think she'd ever give up that much control."

"I'm not so sure about that." Harvard settled his hat in place and picked up his bag. "What supplies do you need? I'll bring them when I come to check on her in the morning."

"I'd be obliged. There's not much here. Only what we had with us." Wolf paused, rubbing at the back of his neck. "Tell Mercer to put everything on my summer credit."

Harvard paused, staring out over the land, avoiding Wolf's gaze. "I'll cover the supplies for you."

"No." Wolf studied his friend a moment. "Mercer and I have an agreement."

"Not anymore." Harvard tied his bag to the saddle and faced Wolf. "After what happened to Emily, folks stopped being quite so trusting. Audelia convinced him it was foolish to give credit to someone who might never come back to town."

"Meaning me." Wolf clenched his fists and fought the urge to kick in a fence rail.

"Meaning all of us. Mercer refused to single you out, so no one gets credit at the General Store. I'm sure Audelia will soften up again, but, for the time being, that's the way things are."

"For the time being," Wolf echoed. "What the hell am I supposed to do in the meantime?"

"Let me take care of it."

"No! I don't want to be beholden to anyone, least of all a friend."

"You stubborn backend of a mule." Harvard closed the distance between them, getting in closer than was wise. "If a friend can't help out at a time like this, who the hell can? Shut up," he bit out when Wolf opened his mouth. "I'm paying! Got that? Settle up with me when you sell some furs or horses."

He ended the argument by swinging into the saddle. Heels to the ribs sent the horse into a gallop, but Harvard didn't go far. Reining in his mount, he circled back. "I don't have to remind you to keep an eye out for Black Jack. It would be like him to come back and see how much havoc he managed to wreak."

"He won't take me by surprise." Wolf stroked the horse's nose. "I know him too well."

Wolf stepped back and watched until Harvard disappeared over a hill, then went in search of Calvin. His son had followed them out of the house, but wandered off. He found the boy in the barn. "What are you doing in here?"

"I wanted to take care of Yeller. Didn't you bring Miss Lizzie's mule with you?"

Wolf blew out a breath. More death for his son to cope with. "Her mule is gone, son."

The boy stood stock still, staring at his father. "Stole gone? Or dead gone?"

"The men who attacked Miss Lizzie shot Yeller."

Calvin's eyes rounded in shock. "But why? Yeller wasn't very fast, but they didn't have no reason to shoot him."

"You're right, son. But these men don't care if anything lives or dies. Killing is a sport to them."

The boy kicked at the dirt. "I don't understand why God makes men who'd do somethin' like that, Pa. I really don't."

"Neither do I. Just remember, God also makes men who won't let them get away with it."

Calvin wrapped an arm around Wolf's waist. "That's what we're here for, right, Pa?"

Wolf hugged his son close. "That's right, son. Now, come on. You have to help me finish making the javelina stew I started this morning."

Together they put together a passable meal, using some leathery old vegetables Calvin found in the root cellar and a few of the young greens growing wild in the kitchen garden. Wolf gave it a final stir and dished some up.

Calvin wrinkled his nose at the gamey taste, but dug in for a second bite. "I sure wish we had some of Miss Lizzie's biscuits to go with this. That might make it taste better."

"You should have roasted the meat first," she quipped from the bedroom door.

"What are you doing up?" Wolf stood as Lizzie limped to the table. "Why don't you sit in the rocker?" He tried to head her away from Emily's chair at the table. "You'll be more comfortable trying to eat."

"I'll be fine right here." She eased into the chair opposite Wolf, eyeing him as he dished up a bowl of stew and sat down again. "If making biscuits isn't too unmanly, Calvin, I can teach you how. Then you'll never have to go without."

"Would that be all right, Pa? If I learn how, I can make them for you." He turned back to Lizzie. "Pa loves biscuits."

"He does? Then maybe he'd like to learn to make them, too." Her smile lit up her eyes and Wolf's heart missed a beat.

It was only because she sat in Emily's chair, he reasoned. His heart was banging in his chest because another woman sat in the place his wife should be.

Certainly not because he'd just discovered a simple smile made Lizzie Sutter one very pretty woman.

CHAPTER EIGHT

By the time Harvard got back to Civil, more than half the day was gone. If he was going to make any money in the saloon today, he needed to get the doors open. Not that there was much of a living to be made in a town like Civil these days.

Years before, when he first came out west, before Millicent Freeman arrived, the banks of the Canadian River played host to hunters, trappers, soldiers and mountain men. Every man, trying to make his way out on the Texas high plains, eventually came to the trading post and accompanying settlement that squatted along the water's edge. With some canvas for a roof and a sign to point the way to a bar made by tying together a dozen small tree trunks dumped on the riverbank by the spring rains, Harvard opened the only watering hole to be found north of Fort Elliott.

Then one enterprising man brought his wife, along with his blacksmith tools, to the trading post, and everything went to hell. Under Millicent Freeman's iron thumb, canvas tents became wood and stone buildings, horse trading became commerce, and rowdy, uncivilized mayhem gave way to marriages, Sunday morning church meetings and schooling for the children. Wild looking buffalo hunters were replaced by a few thirsty cowboys and an occasional army patrol with a few hours of leave.

Civil now boasted a boarding house, a sheriff and a schoolmaster. The town was growing.

And all the fun was gone.

Harvard took the wooden walk fronting the general store in two strides and shoved the door open. "Mercer! Where are you?"

"He's in the back, Mister Browning, filling an order for me."

Harvard managed to hold back the curse that crowded his lips and tipped his hat. "Good afternoon, Mrs. Freeman. I didn't see you there." Although, how he could possibly miss seeing a woman of her stature challenged the imagination.

"I shouldn't wonder. Your mouth was working before your intelligence made it through the front door." She arched one graying eyebrow and glared down her slightly pointed noise at him. Even wearing that ridiculous green hat with a pile of pink feathers and half-dead flowers perched on top of her towering hair, she managed to make him feel like a little boy caught with dirt under his fingernails at the supper table. At times like this, Harvard wondered why he stayed on in Civil.

"My apologies, ma'am." He tipped his hat again and escaped across the room to search through a small pile of ready-made clothes. Something here might fit Lizzie. When she saw what Wolf had done to her buckskins, there'd be a mighty ruckus. Everyone in Civil would probably hear the explosion.

Lizzie Sutter was certainly a surprise. He could see the necessity of disguising her gender while traveling alone on the frontier. A female alone was considered fair game by a lot of men, and unfit company by their wives. By posing as just one more in a sea of drifters, she would be left to herself, even by those who weren't certain she really was a man.

How anyone could be fooled by the ruse was what amazed him. Lizzie moved through the ranks of the males as if she'd been raised as one, but she couldn't hide her true self, not if you took the time to look. She had a fire inside that shone in her eyes. With her natural compassion, a backbone of iron and a temper honed to a fine edge, she was all woman.

Harvard dug deeper in to the pile of clothing. He'd briefly considered letting his friend face Lizzie's fury on his own, but he couldn't do it. Wolf had been through enough this past year. Having a woman slide into the place your beloved wife had occupied, even innocently, as Lizzie had done this morning, had to be hard on a man.

When Lizzie walked out of the bedroom wearing what had to be Emily's dressing gown, the blood had drained from Wolf's face so fast, Harvard expected to have to catch him. One shock like that was enough. And what it would do to Calvin didn't bear thinking about. Lizzie needed clothes of her own.

He chose two pairs of pants and two white shirts, then threw in a set of braided leather suspenders to hold up the trousers in case nothing fit. As soon as Millicent left, he'd try to find a chemise or two, and maybe some drawers. The undergarments wouldn't be fancy, but a woman needed something against her skin besides cotton and wool, no matter who she was pretending to be.

When Percy Mercer emerged from the back room, he greeted Harvard with a hint of distraction. "Be right with you, Mister, uh, Mister Browning, just as soon as I deliver..." The tiny man squinted at the package he carried. "Well, Mrs. Freeman, I believe this is what you requested." He turned the bundle toward the light and lifted a corner of the paper wrapping. "Can't see it real well. Must have left my glasses in the back."

"Six yards of burgundy wool?" Millicent unwrapped and shook out the fabric, holding it in the sunlight to scrutinize every inch. "This will do quite well, Mister Mercer." Satisfied there were no flaws in the weaving, she folded it again. "Mind you, I'm still waiting to receive the lace I requested. I will never understand why your suppliers won't send everything you order at the same time. Honestly, you'd think we were living in the middle of nowhere instead of in a thriving community." She gathered up a parasol that matched the green of her dress. "Mister Freeman will be by to settle up with you at the end of the day."

Mercer escorted her to the door. "That'll be fine, Mrs. Freeman. Any time that's convenient for Sheriff Freeman. You have a wonderful day, now."

Harvard laughed under his breath when Mercer, his bad eyesight warping his sense of distance, nearly closed the trailing end of Millicent's voluminous skirt in the door.

Mercer pulled out a starched white handkerchief and mopped his brow. "Thought that woman would never leave," he muttered. "Who in their right mind wants wool at this time of year?" He swiped at the back of his neck, before refolding the damp white square and tucking it in his pocket. "Now then, Mister Browning." He squinted in Harvard's general direction. "Where are you, and what can I do for you today?"

Harvard stuffed two chemises into the middle of the pile of clothes he'd chosen and rolled them into a bundle. Without his glasses, Mercer wouldn't know for sure what he had. "Wolf needs supplies to see him through to winter. And Calvin needs new clothes. I told him I'd make the choices for him and deliver them tomorrow. I'm helping make repairs to his place," Harvard offered as explanation. "There are a lot of things that need fixing after eight months."

"I'm sure that must be true," Mercer agreed. "Very true, indeed."

Harvard pointed at the coffee, beans and salt. "Start with those, same amount as he bought the last time."

Mercer started scooping and weighing. "Won't this be a bit much, what with the most unfortunate events of last autumn?"

Oh, hell. How could he explain this and not tie Wolf up in a knot of lies? "That boy of his is growing like a dandelion in sunshine. To be truthful, there's not a lot of boy left in him."

Mercer smiled. "Of course. Calvin. I should have considered him. Please tell Wolf how happy we are that he recovered his son. And our condolences on his losses."

"I'll be happy to," Harvard agreed. "To that order, add four pounds of bacon. Is that too much?" he asked when Mercer straightened in surprise.

"Well, if he's going off hunting, who will be eating it?"

Harvard improvised. "Calvin. And Wolf will need supplies on the trail."

"True enough. Flour and sugar, too, I expect. And a few sticks of candy for Calvin. I wonder who will keep the boy while Wolf is gone. Or perhaps he'll go along with his father.

But is he old enough? I wonder."

Mercer headed for the storage room, muttering to himself about supplies and weights. Just before he disappeared through the canvas curtain covering the doorway, he glanced back over his shoulder to Harvard. "You go on and write down whatever you've chosen for the boy. I'll gather up the rest of the supplies."

Harvard stepped behind the counter to record the clothing in Mercer's ledger. The chemises he marked as undergarments. Not a lie, just not real specific. Let Mercer think everything was for Calvin. No one would be hurt by the assumption.

"Mercer," Harvard called out. Percy poked his balding head through the canvas curtain over the stockroom doorway. "I'm going to go open up before someone starts a rumor I've left town and Millicent tries to convert my saloon into the new church she wants to see built. Would you mind delivering everything to me there? I'll have the money for you then."

"Not at all, my friend." Mercer waved him away. "I'll bring it myself this evening, after closing. Happy to do it."

"Good. I'll take the clothes with me and see you at the saloon in a few hours."

Harvard escaped into the street before Mercer asked any more questions he didn't want to answer. Nodding to the cowboys lounging in front of The Fallen Star, he reached for the key in his vest pocket. "Come on in, gentlemen. The bar is open."

"About time. I'm so thirsty I nearly gave in and had me some tea, like that woman said we ought to be drinking 'stead of your—uh—wha'd she call it, Jamie?" He scratched at the straw-colored hair poking from under his hat. "I remember," he crowed. "Divil's brew. That's right, ain't it, Ricky." He slapped the shoulder of his nearest companion. "The unholy drink of the divil," he intoned, one finger pointing at the sky and the other hand fisted over his heart in a pretty fair imitation of Audelia Mercer. The temperance-minded woman considered it her sacred responsibility to drive Harvard out of business.

Damned interfering female.

The cowboys dogged Harvard's heels as he unlocked the doors. As soon as they cleared the threshold, the talker dumped his saddle in a corner and tossed his dusty hat in the general direction of the hat tree. A second, who looked like a narrower version of the first, mirrored the movement. Both hats twirled once around a hook and settled down like well-trained hounds.

The shortest of the three dumped his saddle, kept his hat and made a beeline for the bar. "Not even you could be desperate enough to drink that sissy stuff, Willie," he ground out in a voice that had been calling after cattle for a lot of years. "Tea'll rot yer insides for sure." He shook a small pile of coins from a leather pouch onto the bar, counted out four, and put the rest away. "Keep giving me whiskey until that's all spent."

His partners did the same and, for the next couple of hours, the three of them drank and argued about everything that came to mind. Each time they'd circle around to an agreement about something, they'd nod like three identical saplings in a burst of breeze, drain their glasses, and bang them onto the bar, waiting for a refill.

While Harvard poured, one would dig around for an old memory, a second would disagree with his remembering of it, they'd square off and launch into another argument. The routine was such an old one that, if one man forgot what he was going to say, another would speak the line for him.

Since they weren't interested in anything more than flapping their gums and soothing parched throats, Harvard tuned them out. The bang of a boot on the walk outside had him reaching for his shotgun. When Millicent Freeman swept past the door, he returned the weapon to its place.

The wind picked up and something hit the window. Again, his fingers closed around cold steel, only to release it a moment later. The third time it happened, he was across the room, wiping down a table. As he spun for the bar, it dawned on him. He was expecting—*hoping*—Black Jack would walk through the door so he could get into a *discussion* about what that animal masquerading as a man had done to Lizzie.

And wouldn't that be a foolish thing to do? That kind of discussion could get him killed.

Just to have something to do with his hands besides reach for the shotgun every time the building creaked, Harvard started polishing glasses. He had no business confronting Black Jack without some proof the bastard had attacked Lizzie. She wouldn't appreciate him exposing her secret to the whole town. Or that he might fight a battle she considered her own.

He remembered the look of utter despair that had washed into her eyes when Wolf told her everything she owned was gone. For an instant, Harvard saw the woman she was, not the man she pretended to be. She didn't stay down long, though. Inside of an hour, she had a splinted right wrist and her chin stuck out in defiance and determination.

Lizzie Sutter was quite an enigma. Nothing at all like Julianna.

With no warning, memories rose up and rolled over him in a flood. Julianna. Her hair, her eyes, the scent of her perfume. The sound of her laughter. The glistening of tears in her eyes when she'd told him...

The smashing of glass on the floor shattered the memory.

"What the hell?" One of the cowboys leaned over the bar to study the remains. "What happened?"

Harvard stared at the shards. Just like him. Broken in too many pieces to ever be whole again.

"Just clumsy, I guess. You boys ready for another?"

With a splash of amber liquid, the arguments started again. Harvard got the broom from the back and swept up the broken glass and dumped it out, just like Julianna had tossed him aside to grasp ambition with both hands.

The cowboys rambled and ranted at each other for most of the afternoon. When their money finally ran out, so did the conversation. Nodding their thanks and weaving in perfect unison, the cowboys disappeared in the direction of the livery stable, presumably to retrieve the horses that went under the gear they carried slung over their shoulders.

He'd barely had time to wipe off the bar when Percy Mercer pushed through the door.

"Good evening, my friend," the little man called out. "Is this a good time?"

Harvard shook his head. Mercer, like most of the folks in town, acted as if The Fallen Star was Harvard's living room instead of a place of business, just because he lived on the second floor. Maybe it was time to build that set of stairs on the outside of the building so his neighbors had a different door to knock on when they came visiting. Of course, they'd have to come in here first, to tell him they were calling, so he could go upstairs and answer. Waste of good lumber, in his opinion.

"It's always a good time in a saloon, Mercer. What can I get you?"

"Oh, well," Mercer glanced toward the door, no doubt checking that his wife hadn't spotted him coming in here. "I don't know that I should."

"How about a shot of whiskey on the house? Consider it payment for personally delivering my order."

The man scrubbed a hand over his balding head and under his too-tight collar. "Well. When offered in such a manner, it would be inexcusably rude to refuse."

Harvard poured a generous shot of his better whiskey. "Enjoy." As he capped the bottle, he glanced out the door. "Speaking of my order..."

"Oh, of course." Percy coughed a little as he half inhaled his liquor. "I took the liberty of sending it all to the livery. Couldn't see a need to bring it here when you'd only have to haul it there in the morning."

"Good thinking, Mercer. Have another drink."

With the careful application of whiskey, Percy Mercer turned into one of the best gossips in Civil. In no time, Harvard was able to coax out of the man any rumors and facts he knew about Lizzie, and whether Black Jack had come back into town to gloat. He also learned a few things about Sheriff Freeman that might come in handy later.

Once he was sure Mercer was pumped dry, Harvard put the whiskey under the bar and poured a cup of coffee for the storekeeper.

He always kept a pot on the stove. Some folks thought it was an extravagance, but Harvard considered it a public service. Many a man had been saved from a lecture on the evils of drink when he came home with coffee on his breath instead of smelling like whiskey. And a happy man meant a repeat customer.

While Mercer sobered up again, Harvard let him prattle on about whatever came to mind. The mention of Wolf Richards caught his attention.

"What did you say?"

"I know. I was as shocked as you." Mercer pulled the kerchief from his pocket to pat at a dribble of coffee on his shirt. "Mrs. Freeman told Mrs. Mercer that she believes it is high time for Wolf Richards to marry again. She said—Millicent, that is, not my Audelia—she said that his boy needs a woman's guidance and that Mister Richards must see to getting a new wife soon. Of course—" He leaned toward Harvard to whisper and nearly lost his balance. Harvard eased him back onto the stool and refilled his coffee cup.

"Thank you," Mercer mumbled and slurped a little from the cup. "Of course, she has a candidate in mind. Though my wife didn't share the name, I feel sure it's one of the single women in town."

Harvard snorted. It sure as hell wasn't one of the married ones. Unless Mercer thought Millicent Freeman was considering instituting polygamy in Civil?

"Thanks for the warning. I'll pass it on to Richards when I see him."

"Don't tell him you heard it from me. If it were to get back to Mrs. Mercer..." His gaze darted to the door and back.

"Your secret is safe. We men have to stick together."

"Quite so, my friend," Mercer smiled. "Quite so." He slid from the bar stool and made his way to the door. Harvard watched for any sign of drunkenness that the man's wife might notice, but Mercer walked a straight path toward the setting sun shining through the opening. "You be sure to let Baker's boy load those supplies for you," he called back over his shoulder. "I already paid him to complete the task."

Harvard laughed. "Thank you, Mercer. I'm in your debt again."

"Not at all, my friend. Not at all. Sticking together, isn't that what you said?"

"Quite so," Harvard mimicked, as Mercer disappeared down the street.

So that busybody, Millicent Freeman, thought she'd just inform Wolf it was time to replace Emily and he'd fall in line? Harvard shook his head. The town of Civil was in for quite a showdown.

CHAPTER NINE

"What do you mean, I have to stay here?"

Wolf stepped back and let Lizzie stomp past. "Doc said—"

"I don't give a pirate's treasure what that saloon-keeper said. He isn't in charge of me."

"No," Wolf reasoned. "*I* am. I'm responsible for all this."

She whirled to face him "And just how do you figure that? You didn't bushwhack me."

"May as well have. If I hadn't upset you, you might have stayed put instead of going into town—"

"That wouldn't have changed anything. I'd have played poker whatever day I went into Civil. Black Jack Hayes is just a damn poor loser."

She rubbed at the edges of the splint on her wrist. It obviously pained her, but she hadn't complained when she got up this morning, and it certainly didn't slow her down as she circled the room like a caged animal.

"He's more than that." How well Wolf knew. "Sit down, Lizzie. You're getting upset for no reason."

He knew the instant the words were out it was the wrong thing to say. The storm exploded in her eyes first, flashes of lightning reflecting on a deep blue sea.

"No reason?" She clenched her good fist and took a single step forward. "No reason?"

The quiet repetition definitely boded ill. He focused on Lizzie as she stalked him across the room. "Stop it, Lizzie. You aren't thinking straight."

The woman snarled. Wolf stared in amazement. Her lip curled and she actually snarled at him. Now what? He had no experience in calming down an irate woman. Emily had never raised her voice, let alone lost her temper.

"Sorry." He held up his hands, palms out, in a gesture of surrender. "Bad choice of words. What I meant was, you aren't going to change my mind by ranting at me. So you may as well plant yourself in that chair and rest like Harvard told you to. You can yell at me from there, if it makes you feel better."

When she hauled in a breath to start arguing again, he scooped her off the floor, stalked to the rocking chair, and deposited her in it. "Now stay put."

He ducked the first shoe she threw. The second one clipped his shoulder. "Cut it out, Lizzie." Wolf swept the flying footwear from the floor. "It's for your own good."

"I don't need to rest. And give me back those slippers," she hollered as he closed the door.

"Not a chance," he called through the thick wood.

He thought he heard something break, but didn't go back inside to check. She wouldn't bust anything that wasn't hers—he hoped. When he entered the barn, Calvin looked up from his chores.

"Pa, what are you doing with those?"

Wolf glanced at the slippers he carried. They were so small in his big hands. Funny, he'd never thought of Lizzie as having small feet. "I'm hoping Miss Lizzie will stay inside if I have her shoes with me. She is the most pig-headed, stubborn cuss of a female I have ever met."

"But aren't those Ma's?"

The shoes suddenly seemed to burn his hands. For an instant, he considered throwing them across the barn. "Yes, son, they are." Cautiously, he stroked the soft leather with one callused thumb. "Since Miss Lizzie doesn't have any of her own now, I thought she could borrow these."

"Is that why she's wearing Ma's clothes, too?"

Wolf swallowed against the pain. "That's right. The bad men who hurt her stole all her stuff." He hunkered down in front of his son. "Is it all right with you if she uses some of your mama's things?"

Calvin bit down on his lower lip when it started to tremble. "I guess so." He reached out with one small finger and stroked the leather shoe, just as Wolf had.

Wolf gathered his son close when the first tear fell. "Go on and cry son. I miss her, too."

Calvin leaned in and whimpered. "Why, Pa? What did those men have to hurt Ma and Amanda?"

Wolf's heart cracked a little more. "I don't know, son. Some men are just bad inside and they do bad things."

Cal wrenched free. His little face showed such pain, such hatred. "Then why doesn't God kill them!" He threw down the pitchfork he'd been using and ran from the barn.

"Calvin! Wait." Wolf tucked the slippers into a pocket and chased after his son. The boy ran toward the creek, not slowing until he reached the speckled shade of an old, gnarled cottonwood.

When Wolf caught up, the boy was on the ground, sobbing into his folded arms.

"It's not fair, Pa." Calvin pounded the ground. "Not fair. Not fair."

He dropped into the grass and pulled the boy into his lap. "I know, Cal. It isn't fair, but it's how it is."

"I didn't even get to s-say g-goodbye," Cal wailed. "I screamed and screamed for her to help me, but she didn't get up." He cried even harder, deep, tearing sounds. "I want her back, Pa. I want Mama and Amanda to come back!"

Wolf tucked his son's head under his chin and rocked him back and forth, staring toward the spot on the hill where Emily was buried. "Me, too, Cal. God help me. Me, too."

He stroked his thumb back and forth across the back of Calvin's hand where it was fisted in his shirt. With each stroke, he could feel the scars on his son's wrist, still tender, where an animal who walked on two legs had tied up a small boy, leaving him to starve...

The rage that was his constant companion nearly ripped

through his control. His muscles tightened, breathing quickened, and for a moment he couldn't see past the red killing haze filling his mind.

Harrison! He'd died too easily. He deserved to suffer, had earned a slow, lingering, torturous death. He should have felt everything he'd done to his victims, blow for blow, cut for cut, agony for agony, but he'd been spared. One bullet had sent him swiftly to hell, while those left behind suffered on. Cal was right. It just wasn't fair.

Wolf pounded his clenched fist in the dust, over and over, while rocking Calvin until the boy's sobs tapered off. Still Wolf continued, rocking and pounding, trying to drain off the useless fury. It was done. His wife and daughter were dead. The past couldn't be relived. But what he wouldn't give...

"God *damn* it!"

Calvin stirred at Wolf's outburst. "Pa?"

Hugging his son close, Wolf tried to be thankful for what he had, but why did it have to hurt so much?

"I always knew you'd come for me."

The soft statement drew Wolf's full attention.

"What?"

"When those bad men took us, I knew you would come and kill them and get us back." Cal sniffed. "Get me back."

The knife in Wolf's heart turned a little, slicing him, bleeding him. "I'm sorry I didn't find you sooner, son."

Cal slid his arms around his father's neck and held on. Wolf returned the hug, sitting in the dusty shade of the ancient tree, listening to the sound of the wind and the steady beating of his boy's heart.

They stayed that way long enough for Cal to doze off. Wolf patted his son's back gently. "Time we got back to work, son." When Calvin straightened, Wolf set him on his feet, then stood. "You ready?"

Calvin didn't answer. He stared behind Wolf, squinting into the sunshine. "What's that?"

Wolf twisted around and found what Cal had spotted. He

studied the dust cloud boiling up from the meadow grass for a less than a heartbeat. "Inside, Cal. Now."

Together they ran for the house. When Wolf's long legs overtook his son, he scooped him off his feet. As they reached the porch, the door opened.

"Both rifles and the shotgun are loaded. I only found two belt guns. You got more?" Lizzie slammed the door on Wolf's heels and dropped the heavy bar into place. She had an arsenal laid out on the table. Guns and ammunition waited in easy reach. All the windows had been barred, the furniture was shoved out of the way, and the fire was blazing. "Just in case somebody gets a hankering to dust out the chimney on their way inside," Lizzie answered his unspoken question.

Wolf grinned. He wouldn't have believed it possible, but he felt the corners of his mouth lift. "You are something, Lizzie Sutter."

"Flatterer." She flashed him a smile that made her one un-damaged eye dance with laughter. Tossing him a saucy wink that looked more like a squint, she hefted one of his Colt re-volvers and pointed toward the meadow with her chin. "Any idea who might be in such a hurry to pay us an unannounced visit?"

He handed the smaller Winchester rifle to Lizzie, along with extra ammunition, and strode for the bedroom. "I have a good idea," he called back over his shoulder as he flipped open the heavy lid of the chest at the foot of the bed. When he straight-ened, he had two more pistols in his hands. Moving quickly, he carried them to the table and gave Lizzie one to load while he stuffed cartridges into the other. "Cal?"

"Yes, Pa?" The boy stood in the center of the room, looking lost and just a little confused.

"You all right, son?"

Cal's little shoulders heaved up, then down on a deep breath. "I think so."

"Good. Take this." He held out the long shotgun. "Keep watch out the south window, but be sure you stay down out of sight."

"Yes, sir." Calvin cradled the shotgun in both arms, filled both fists with extra shells, and moved to the window that faced the wide-open meadow to the side of the house. The empty expanse made it easier for Cal to see anyone approaching the house, and gave Wolf extra time to react if he did. No way would his son have to shoot a man. Not if Wolf could help it. He was too young to have that kind of blot on his soul.

"Wolf?" Lizzie's voice snapped him back. "You gonna enlighten me about who it is?"

"I'm betting on Hayes. It would be like him to drop in just to see how much trouble he'd caused."

She lost a little of her color. "He can't know I'm here," she argued.

"Why do you think you made it to that particular valley before he attacked you? Once you crested Morgan Hill, you were closer to this cabin than town. Anyone finding you would know that and would bring you here for help. It was his way of controlling the situation. Something he's too damned good at."

He checked the load on the big Sharps rifle he held and dropped a handful of shells into his pocket. "Hayes probably found out you'd been here before you went into Civil. Even if you didn't tell him," he talked over her denial. "Someone else could have. I imagine the minute you bested him at cards, he started planning to get even. It's how the man thinks."

"You sure know a lot about that snake." Lizzie put her good eye to a gun slit to look around.

Wolf hesitated, but only for an instant. "More than I want to." He silenced her question with a sharp look. "I scouted for him in the army in seventy-eight, up in Montana."

"What happened?"

Wolf shook his head, trying to dislodge the memories of just how wrong everything had gone. "Same thing that always happens when Jefferson Hayes is around."

The pounding of hooves on hard-packed dirt got louder, then three riders crested the hill where he and Calvin had been only a minute before. A fourth horse, saddle empty, followed behind on a lead rope.

"Hayes," he confirmed.

"And his two sidekicks," Lizzie growled. "Damn, but they're ugly. Where's the one that belongs in that empty saddle?"

When Wolf glanced her way, she was leaning against a window frame, balancing the Winchester in her left hand. She had the men in her sights and her finger was stroking the trigger.

"Sheriff Freeman frowns on killing without cause."

"I've got a helluva lot of bruises that say I've earned a shot." She shifted, gripping the rifle tighter.

"I can't argue that point, but let's see what they want, first." Wolf may have said the right words, but his posture mirrored hers. He didn't feel much like talking, either.

"If it comes to shooting, Hayes is mine." Lizzie left no doubt she wouldn't miss.

"Richards! You in there?" Black Jack hauled his mount to a stop a full two hundred yards from the house.

"He's such a chicken-shit!" Lizzie hissed. "Won't even ride close enough to give me a decent shot. Give me your rifle."

"Why?" Wolf studied the area around the house, looking for more riders.

"'Cause that big buffalo gun will cut him down even from this distance. Give it here."

"What do you want, Hayes?" Wolf yelled through the gunslit. "No," he answered Lizzie a split second later.

Hayes stiffened in the saddle. "Is that any way to greet your commanding officer?"

"Afraid I'll spill some blood on the lawn?" Lizzie reached for the big-barreled rifle Wolf held.

"Stop it, Lizzie," he hissed, swallowing down the vile taste of memories. "*Former* commander…and *former* officer," Wolf yelled at Hayes. "I'm not asking again. Talk, or ride out."

Hayes pushed his hat to the back of his head and leaned forward to cross his arms on the saddlehorn. "We've had a long morning in the saddle. I'd like to come inside, rest a while."

"No," Wolf snapped out.

Black Jack managed to look hurt at Wolf's obvious distrust. "Well, I thought you believed in hospitality to strangers. Your dead wife certainly did." He paused, as if letting the stab sink in deep. "Do you mind if we at least water our horses? Surely, that can't hurt."

"Pa?" Cal called out in a trembling whisper. "There's something moving over here."

Wolf glanced at Lizzie. He knew she wanted to argue, but she eased away from her spot at the window, taking care not to let anyone see her move.

"Go ahead, Hayes, but keep your men where I can see them." A shot rang out from behind him, followed almost instantly by a yelp of pain. "All of them."

Hayes's black-eyed glare pinned Wolf in place like a dagger, just as it always had. It was like looking into the eyes of Lucifer himself. Hayes held him there for a long moment, then relented. "Wilkins!"

Wolf nearly laughed when Hayes's sometimes-sidekick limped around the house in a hurry. His bare, balding head gleamed in the sunshine. Lizzie squeezed off another shot, striking the dirt behind his heels. The man stumbled, righted himself, and picked up his pace.

"Lizzie," Wolf warned in a whisper.

"He shouldn't have gotten so close," she argued, her tone reasonable, as if they were discussing the weather. This time, Wolf let loose the laugh tickling the back of his throat.

"What the hell is so funny about shooting at a man, Richards? Why don't you share the joke with the rest of us?"

"I'm only doing what you taught me," Wolf goaded. God, but the words tasted foul.

Hayes watched the man clamber onto his horse. "Your son has gotten to be quite a shot, evidently. Did he learn that from the men who stole him from you?"

"That's enough water, Hayes." Wolf was done being nice. "The next one who speaks gets a bullet between the eyes. Now, get the hell off my property."

Hayes hesitated for one long moment and Wolf found himself praying the man would say something. Anything. Just make one little sound and he could rid the world of the pestilence called Jefferson Hayes. Instead, Hayes yanked his horse into a tight turn and rode toward Civil.

No one in the cabin moved until Wolf was sure all four were gone. When Wolf relaxed, Calvin whooped behind him.

"Wow, Pa. Did you see that? She clipped that man's hat right off his head. And he was way over behind the barn still."

"Really." It wasn't a question. He met Lizzie's gaze. "I knew you could shoot, woman, but that was—"

"Nothing," she cut him off. "Now, if he'd been riding in hell-bent, with bullets flying, that would have been something, but standing still in the shade, a hundred paces away..." She shrugged, sloughing off the compliment.

"But your shootin' arm is hurt," Calvin argued, still dancing around her, hero-worship clear in his gaze. "You did that with your left hand."

"Just takes practice, Sir Calvin. Lots and lots of practice." She took the shotgun Cal had used and cracked it open, removing shells and checking to be sure it was empty. Next, she peered down the barrel. "Needs to be cleaned."

"I can do it," Cal yelled, and grabbed for the shotgun.

"Hold off," Lizzie scolded, her voice hard and cutting. Cal froze in place and stared at her. "Don't you ever treat a gun like a game, you hear me?"

The boy heaved a sigh and scuffed at the floor with his toe. Wolf took a breath, ready to tear her apart for yelling at his son, but Lizzie crouched down in front of Cal with a grimace of pain, cutting off his rebuke.

"I don't say that for meanness, Calvin. Even if you're positive it's unloaded, always treat this hunk of iron and wood like it's dangerous, 'cause it is. Never forget that. Not even for a second. Understand?"

"Yes, ma'am."

"Oh," she cuffed him gently on the shoulder. "Don't call me ma'am. Makes me feel like an old woman."

Cal blinked, all innocence and youth, and Wolf knew what was coming. "Well, you are, aren't ya?"

Lizzie's jaw dropped and she stared at the boy, flummoxed. Then Cal grinned, his eyes sparkling with humor.

"Aw, I'm just funning you, Miss Lizzie." He punched her arm, just as she'd done his. Wolf saw her flinch when he hit a sore spot, but she hid the pain from Cal.

"I see. You're a funny-man. Hey, Richards." She glanced over at him. "Maybe you could sell him to one of them traveling shows. He'd earn his keep, and wouldn't be around to trouble me."

She made a face at Cal that had him giggling. When she tried to push to her feet and couldn't, the boy slipped a shoulder under her arm to help. Then he held out his hands for the shotgun. "I really can clean it, Miss Lizzie. Pa taught me how."

Lizzie surrendered the big weapon, leaning on the Winchester rifle for a moment. Wolf could see the perspiration beading over her full upper lip, and he doubted it was because of the temperature of the room. He crossed to her, took the rifle and tucked her to his side, helping her to the rocking chair. "Stay put for a while."

"I think," she blew out a breath and hauled in another one, making her breasts fall and rise under the cotton nightdress she still wore. "I'll do that," she finished. Leaning her head back against the carved wood, she closed her eyes.

Wolf looked down at her for a long moment, studying her face. She was pretty, truth be told. High bones in her cheeks, smooth forehead, straight nose, generous lips. And from the view he had while she talked with Calvin, she filled out her clothes, too. An attractive package.

And why was he noticing now?

Pondering the question, he joined Cal at the table and helped clean all the weapons and return them to their places, ready for the next time they were needed.

"She's asleep, Pa." Cal's whisper was loud enough to wake her, but Lizzie didn't move. She might be playing possum, but Wolf doubted it. She was exhausted.

"I think you may be right, Cal." Wolf kept his voice low, teaching by example. "She's got a lot of healing to do."

He put away the last of the rags they'd used, and strapped on his belt guns. "Let's go to the barn and let her rest." Together they eased from the room, closing the door behind them.

The instant the door bumped in the frame, Lizzie lifted one eyelid. "About time you left me alone," she muttered. Rocking forward, then back, and forward again, she let her momentum lift her from the rocker. Catching herself against the table, Lizzie waited to get her land legs back, then shuffled to the bedroom.

"Clothes. I've got to have some clothes." She pushed aside the cloth covering the closet opening. "Something has to fit." She searched through everything on the shelves, then heaved open the lid and dug through the chest. "Nothin' but dresses and skirts and shirtwaists." Lizzie bit back the urge to spit. Dresses and all that frippery was for real ladies, and she couldn't be further from that kind of fanciful creature.

When the cabin door opened without warning, Lizzie dove to the floor and stabbed her hand to the bottom of the chest, feeling for the pistols Wolf had tucked back inside.

"Lizzie?"

The doctor. Lizzie sat back on her heels and puffed through the pain in her knees from slamming them into the plank floor.

Harvard stuck his head into the room. Spotting her on the floor, he hurried to her side. "What happened? Did you fall?"

"I didn't fall. I was getting a pistol."

"What?" He ducked a little, glancing over his shoulder. "Does Wolf know you're here?"

He slipped a hand under each arm and levered Lizzie to her feet with surprising ease. Steadying her with an arm around her shoulders, Harvard helped her sit on the bed.

"We spoke before I came inside. I understand you had some

visitors this afternoon."

"Hence the reason I was looking for something to shoot when you waltzed in without knocking." Lizzie tried glaring at him, but all Harvard did was laugh.

"No waltzing. I was never very good at it, and you're in no shape. I spotted Black Jack and company riding hard for Civil as I came over the hill."

"And you still marched through that door without declaring yourself?" She gave him a shove. "Are you plumb crazy?"

"Not at all. Wolf told me the weapons were cleaned and put away. Here." He dodged the next punch and held out a paper wrapped bundle, tied with rough twine. Obliging her unspoken request, he slid a long bowie knife from his boot and sliced through the twine.

"Clothes!" Lizzie went from wanting kill the man to nearly hugging the stuffing out of him. "How did you know?"

"That you'd rather not be wearing a dead woman's things?"

That snapped her attention back to him.

"Actually, I bought them for Wolf, so he and Calvin wouldn't have to see you wearing Emily's clothes." He aimed a pointed look at the lace-edged shirtwaist still bunched in her fist. "Their loss is still too new."

Lizzie smoothed the creases she'd made in the cotton and laid the garment aside. "What happened?" She glanced at Harvard, half expecting him to refuse to answer.

"You should ask Wolf that question."

"Are you kidding?" She pulled the first bit of cloth she put her hand on out of the bundle, blushing when she realized she held a chemise. "He gets this look on his face that says he wants to break something and I'm half afraid it will be me."

"I added two of those to protect your skin." Harvard nodded toward the undergarments. "New cotton always chafes. The other one is rather fancy, but those were all I could find."

Next, she shook out the pants he'd brought her and held them up for size.

"Wolf would never hurt you," Harvard insisted, returning to

their conversation.

"I know that," she assured him. "I just mean whatever happened hurt him a lot. I'd rather not ask, but I don't want to put my foot into it accidentally, either."

"She was raped and murdered. In this room."

Lizzie leaned over to see around Harvard. Wolf stood in the door, hands fisted, jaw clenched. Without saying another word, he stalked to the closet to grab his hat. He closed the front door very quietly as he left.

It sounded like a cannon shot in the silent cabin. Harvard glanced at her.

"I'll talk to him," she muttered. "Why don't you stay to supper? It'll be better than what Mrs. Dorsey will serve, and I have a feeling we'll need an intermediary."

Harvard's laughter rang through the room. "I'd be delighted."

With his help, Lizzie started a pot of soup, using small bits of javelina she fried in a skillet and several shriveled potatoes Harvard found in a basket in the root cellar.

It took longer to get herself dressed. The pants fit fine, though they were a little short at the ankles. The homespun shirt was too big, but that made it easier to drag on over the splint. Satisfied she was sufficiently covered, Lizzie stuffed her feet into her old dusty boots and straightened everything she'd upended in the trunk before heading out to search for Wolf. She owed him an apology.

She found him on the hill overlooking the house, digging in the dirt under a huge oak tree. "I'm sorry you walked in on that."

Wolf stabbed his knife deep into the earth and turned up a large clump. "But not for talking *about* me instead of *to* me."

Lizzie aimed the toe of her boot at the pile of grass he'd tossed aside. "You seem a little testy on the subject. I just didn't want to hurt you further."

She took a step back when he buried his knife all the way to the hilt. "*Testy* doesn't begin to describe how I feel. *Damn* it!"

Wolf surged to his feet and stalked away.

Lizzie stayed where she was and watched him go. "I knew I should have asked Harvard." A wilted flower caught her attention. She hunkered down to stroke a petal, and realized there were a lot of them scattered about. Wolf had been planting flowers. A half dozen were stuck in the ground in a row, and more waited to join them. She glanced around.

"Damnation," she breathed. This must be her grave. A crude wooden cross marked the head of what had to be a resting place. The flowers had to be for his dead wife. "How you must have loved her, Wolf." Lizzie tugged his knife out of the ground and finished the planting. When she returned from the cabin with a bucket of water, Wolf was waiting.

"Thank you." He stood with his back to her, a few steps from the gravesite, staring out over the rolling landscape. "Emily loved primroses. I thought there should be some here."

"You did a good thing, Wolf." She dipped water over each plant with a tin cup. "I'll keep them watered while you're gone. Just until they catch their breath from being moved. By summer's end, you'll have a real nice patch of pretty."

Wolf knelt beside her and brushed a bit of dirt off one petal, but he didn't answer. Lizzie started to her feet. "I'll leave you be, then."

"I was off hunting."

She stopped, but didn't turn back around.

"Making money so I could have more horses, instead of protecting my own. I was late getting back. I told her I would be back in time for services on Sunday, but I didn't make it. Two hours. Just two hours," he repeated, almost to himself. "I got home at sundown. They'd attacked that afternoon. My children were gone. My wife died in my arms."

He heaved a deep, noisy breath, and his whole body shook as he released it. "I can't think about what they did to her before leaving her to bleed to death. In our bed."

The last was said so softly, Lizzie missed it. "What?"

"They caught up with her in the kitchen," he resumed his

tale. "That's her blood staining the floor. Then they dragged her to our bed to finish what they'd started. By the time I found her, there was nothing I could do but hold her for the few minutes she had left." He looked back at the gravesite, and the tears coursing down his cheeks broke Lizzie's heart.

"I buried her here, went into town to tell the sheriff, and spent the next six months searching for my children."

And he'd come back with only Calvin. "Dear lord, Wolf. I'm sorry."

"Amanda was so pretty," he choked out. "Bright as a penny, the kind of little girl that made you smile just by being in the world. I don't know what happened to her. Calvin still can't talk about it."

"You mean he saw..." Lizzie thought she understood Wolf's need to break things.

"All I know is my son was rescued from a cave, where he'd been tied up and left alone, half-starved. If Ranger McCain hadn't come across him—"

"Don't," she interrupted. "Don't play that game of what might have been. He's alive. That's enough."

"*It isn't!*" he raged. "My wife is dead! My baby girl... My sweet little Amanda..."

"No, Wolf." Lizzie laid a hand on his arm. "Don't dwell on it. You can't change it." She swallowed the tears she wanted to cry for him. "It wasn't your fault."

"Wasn't it?" He clenched his hands into fists until his knuckles were white and the skin stretched tight.

She took one of his hands in hers and smoothed her thumb over his fingers, trying to give him some ease. "Some Satan's spawn are at fault, not you."

Lizzie expected him to argue, to bellow out his fury at fate, but he didn't. Instead he wrapped an arm around her, dropped his head to her shoulder, and sobbed like a child.

CHAPTER TEN

Lizzie sucked back a curse as he squeezed the breath right out of her. She patted his shoulder, hugged him gently, then touched his face. Wolf knew he should let go, but he needed… His grief overwhelmed him again and, when he tightened his hold, she hugged him back, her tears falling right along with his.

"Let it out, Wolf," she whispered, stroking his back and hair in long, gentle motions, a comfort he hadn't expected. "Let go of it. Otherwise, the pain will just eat away at you until there's nothing left."

Minutes passed, washed away with their mutual tears. As the storm of grief eased, Wolf stiffened, realizing where he was. Who he was holding. And how good she felt in his arms. Lizzie loosened her hold to let him go.

Before he could consider the wisdom, Wolf shifted back slightly, tugging her off balance, until she was using him as support. When she looked up, probably to remind him she could stand on her own, he closed the distance between them, covered her lips with his, and kissed her.

Just a short, easy meeting of man and woman. He pulled back a bit, giving her time to tear a strip off him, but she only stared, her dark eyes luminous. Taking her silence for permission, he went back for more, letting grief become something darker, exploring the sensitive edges of her lips, teasing the corners with the tip of his tongue. The brush of his mustache along her upper lip had her sagging in his arms like she couldn't stand on her own.

Lizzie turned her head a little, breaking the contact and hauling in a breath. "Wolf?" She slid her good hand down his arm, probably to push him away. "What are you doing?"

"Kissing you. Do you want me to stop, Lizzie?"

Please say *yes*, a part of his mind begged, because he wasn't at all certain he'd be able to stop if he kissed her again.

"No."

Wolf jolted at the single syllable. Desire stormed through him, blanking that part of his mind that knew ending this was a better idea. He ran his hand from waist to shoulder then all along her good arm, leaving goose flesh in his wake. Gently wrapping her wrist with his fingers, he tucked her hand around his neck, right back where it had been.

When he changed the angle of his head, Lizzie went right with him. His chuckle vibrated between them. "Hold still, woman," he whispered against her lips, and changed his angle again. The easy twist he put on her mouth urged it open and he took possession.

The sparks they'd made burst into flame, burning down his good intentions. Pressing against him, breast to chest, Lizzie dove into the kiss like she was starving for it. Wolf snugged her even closer, then took her to the grass and stretched out beside her, his long body half-pinning her to the ground. Lizzie seemed to pour everything she had into the kiss. Wolf was nearly overwhelmed. It was a long time before he came up for air.

"God in heaven, you taste good." Wolf dipped in for another sample and Lizzie met him halfway.

"Probably the soup." She panted for air and licked her lips, tossing more tinder on the fire in his blood. "I snuck a taste while Harvard wasn't looking."

The mention of the doctor broke the spell. He suddenly realized where he was—and who he was with—and guilt doused desire. Emily. Wolf stared down at Lizzie for three heartbeats, then rolled off her to lie on his back in the grass.

"Wolf?" He felt her hand brush his shoulder. "What's wrong?"

He couldn't think how to answer. He was embarrassed, both by his tears and his behavior after. Lizzie didn't deserve to be used just because she was handy. He could have asked first. Covering his eyes with an arm, he lay still, waiting for his body to ease up on the demands it was making, before he tried to talk. To apologize.

"Lizzie, I'm sorry." Silence. No surprise there. "I had no right to take advantage of you like that."

He at least expected a smart-mouth remark, but she didn't make a sound. Wolf rolled over to face her wrath.

She was gone. Bolting to his feet, he spotted her on the other side of the barn, limping away as fast as her legs would carry her. She had both arms wrapped around her middle, no doubt favoring her busted wrist after he'd grabbed at her like a barely grown man with his first willing woman. "Damn it."

The first clang of the bell on the porch caused his stomach to bunch. The second had him spinning for the house. The third doused the fear. Dinner. That's all those three metallic clangs meant. He saw Calvin jump off the porch rail, where he'd been kneeling so he could reach the big iron triangle. Three strikes had always been Emily's signal that food was going on the table and you'd best not let it get cold.

Emily.

Wolf looked back at the freshly planted flowers lined up before the wooden cross he'd fashioned last fall, right next to the spot where he'd lost himself in the flavor of another woman. Ashamed of himself, of his loss of control, Wolf scooped his hat off the ground and headed for supper.

Lizzie joined them a few minutes later, evidently having walked off her mad. Not that Wolf blamed her. He'd acted like a fool, giving no thought to whether she wanted to kiss him, let alone the paining her ribs must have been giving her.

Harvard took her arm and helped ease her into the chair nearest the fire. Emily's chair. But he knew now how different Lizzie was from his wife. A single beam of sunlight struck fire in her hair, drawing Wolf's attention. The display of autumn among the strands was amazing. He'd thought her hair was just brown, but there was copper and cinnamon, too. Not sure what to say to her, Wolf dropped into his chair at the opposite end of the table.

Calvin and Harvard kept the conversation going, talking about everything from the weather to Lizzie's secret of using soured cream in the biscuits. Wolf couldn't keep track. He kept reliving the kisses he'd shared with Lizzie.

Lizzie didn't say much either, and the moment the meal ended, she bolted from the room, mumbling something about needing to rest. Wolf knew she was avoiding him, but it wouldn't help. He'd apologize, eventually.

"I have to get back to town." Harvard stacked dishes beside the sink and reached for his hat. "I can't afford to lose any more business."

Wolf walked him to the corral. "I appreciate you bringing the supplies, and the clothes for Lizzie. I owe you."

"No, you don't." Harvard didn't even look back.

While his friend gathered up the saddle and tack, Wolf checked his gelding's legs and hooves for cuts, and pried a couple of small rocks from around the horse's new shoes. "I can't let you pay for those supplies. It wouldn't be right."

Harvard tightened the cinch around his mount. "You've done far more for me over the years."

"But—"

"No more." Harvard cut of the conversation by climbing into the saddle. "When will I see you in town?"

Wolf dropped the subject of paying him back. He'd even the score later, when he got paid for the hides and furs he'd bring in before winter. "I'm not certain." Wolf stroked the gelding's cheek. "Thanks to you, we have enough supplies to get by for a while. Once Lizzie is strong enough to protect Calvin, I'll head into the foothills to do some hunting, maybe lay some traps."

"You won't miss the fourth of July festivities, surely."

Wolf arched one eyebrow. "That's Cal's birthday. He'd never forgive me. We'll be there."

Harvard gathered the reins and turned his mount toward Civil. "I'll see you then, if not before." He lifted his hat in a wave. "See that Lizzie gets some rest," he called back, then put his heels to the horse, and cantered away.

Wolf went back inside, intending to just let Calvin know he was going hunting, but he found Lizzie in the rocker, staring at the fire.

"Cal went to his room to find a book for me and fell asleep looking, so I let him be." She shifted a little in the chair, as if trying to find a more comfortable position.

"I came in to let you know I'm going hunting. Maybe we can have something besides wild pig tonight." She nodded, but didn't say anything. "I'll be back well before dark." Another nod.

Damn it, he was no good at this, but there were things that needed saying. "Lizzie," Wolf approached slowly, gathering what he hoped were the right words as he went.

"Don't." She glared at him then looked back at the fire. That brief glance said she knew where he was heading with the speech and didn't want to hear it. "No need."

"There is need." When she didn't argue, he forged on. "I owe you an apology for—"

Lizzie bolted for the bedroom, leaving Wolf with his mouth full of *I'm sorry* and no one to tell it to.

Deciding to leave her alone for a while longer, Wolf loaded the small rifle and leaned it against the wall just outside the bedroom Lizzie had claimed as her own. He resisted the urge to look in on her. He figured he didn't have the right. "Rifle's right here." He spoke through the curtain over the doorway, just loud enough for her to hear. "I won't be gone long." He left before she could find something to throw at him for daring to speak to her.

• ♥ •

The sun warmed his shoulders as he worked his way along the tree line behind the cabin. His heart pounded harder as he lost sight of the house, but he forced his feet to keep moving. Cal was safe. Lizzie wouldn't let anything happen to him. That didn't rid him of the fear tying a knot in his gut, but it helped.

Constantly scanning the surrounding area for movement that didn't belong, he strode south, away from Civil. When he crested a short hill an hour later, he stopped to rest.

A light breeze ruffled his damp hair and dried his sweat-soaked shirt. Wolf studied the horizon, where clouds massed and stacked on top of each other. Though more rain would be welcome, he doubted they'd get anything but a lightning show from those clouds. Resigned to another hot day, he crammed his hat back in place and turned west, looking for game.

Three shots brought down three rabbits. "That'll get us through tonight," he decided when he'd dressed the last one. Reloading as he walked, he headed for the stream to quench his thirst and wash up. He spotted a couple of fat mule deer grazing nearby and reached for his rifle, then changed his mind. He was too far from the cabin to play pack mule with a hundred pounds of venison.

Turning for home, Wolf stopped long enough to dig up a few wild onions with the blade of his skinning knife, and gathered some fresh greens to add to the meal. He couldn't stop the sudden pounding of his heart as he climbed the last hill, but he didn't rush down the other side, either.

Lizzie and Calvin were both bent double in the garden, pulling weeds and loosening the soil around the few volunteer plants that were struggling to survive. As Wolf got closer, he heard Calvin instructing Lizzie on how to weed the garden.

"I think these are turnips. We can leave them be." Cal brushed at the heat-withered leaves then scooped some water from the bucket in front of him. "This little devil," he wrinkled his nose at the next plant as he yanked it out of the dirt. "This is pigweed. Pa called it a rogue plant, whatever that means. We have to keep it away from the horses 'cause it'll make 'em sick, but Mama really liked the pretty flowers."

"At least it's easy to pull." Lizzie yanked another specimen from the ground and glanced up at Wolf, arching one brow. "Most rogues are a lot harder to get rid of."

"Pa!" Calvin jumped to his feet and wrapped dirty fingers

around Wolf's free hand. "Miss Lizzie and me are gonna see what we can save in the garden."

"Good for you." He let Cal lead him through the plants, stepping around the muddy water trailing through half the rows. "Have you found anything worth eating for dinner?"

Cal pointed to a small mound of green on the porch. "That's all the beans we could find. If we ain't—*aren't* too late with the water, we should have more in a few weeks."

"That should be enough for dinner if we add these." He pulled the rabbits from the pack slung over his shoulder. "There are wild onions and some greens we might be able to use, too."

"Yippee!" Calvin spun in a circle. "No pig tonight." He ran around the garden, chanting *no pig, no pig.*

Wolf closed the distance to Lizzie. "Doc told you to rest."

Lizzie glared at him, then rolled from her knees to plop into the dirt. "There! I'm resting. Happy?"

He fought a grin. "Where's your splint?"

"Don't need it. Nothing's broken and my wrist will only get stiff if I don't use it. Now, move." She smacked his boot with the back of her hand. "You're blocking the weeds."

He stood his ground until she looked up again. "I owe you an apolo—"

"Sun sure was hot today." She cut through his words.

"Lizzie, I—"

"Might be in for some rain, though, judging by those clouds. That's why we didn't haul a lot of water to the garden."

"Just listen to—"

"I wonder how many more chickens we can find? How many did you have in the first place?"

"Damn it, woman, hush! We have to talk."

"No! We don't." She wiggled herself past him and a little further down the row. "Enough, Sir Calvin." She interrupted Cal's frenzied celebration. "Come back here and help me. These weeds won't jump out of the ground by themselves, you know."

Wolf counted to ten—forwards and backwards—trying to cool his sudden temper. The woman would drive a saint to abandon heaven. "Fine. I'll drop it. For now. Let me go skin these rabbits, and I'll come back to help. Another pair of hands will make it go faster."

Lizzie shook her head and yanked another wilted plant from the ground. "There's a hole in the barn roof on the east-facing side that I didn't get to before you came home. And you could see what can be done to patch up the chicken coop. Cal coaxed a couple of your hens into a cage with bits of leftover biscuit, but they won't start laying if they don't have some privacy."

Calvin stopped spinning. "Really? They need their own rooms before they'll make eggs? Why?"

Wolf left Lizzie to explain. She put the idea in Cal's head; she could get it out again.

Lizzie tried hard not to watch Wolf walk away—and failed. Why did the man have to be so... *Overbearing*, came to mind. Handsome was hard on its heels.

Lizzie glanced at what she was doing then back to where Wolf was working. Handsome didn't hardly cover it. And overbearing wasn't all that bad, as it turned out.

"Miss Lizzie, are you listening to me?" Cal stuck his nose right up to hers, scaring her half out of what was left of her wits. Daydreaming about Wolf Richards. Had she lost her mind?

"Sure, I am, Sir Calvin. Which ones should I pull now?"

Calvin clucked his tongue. Lizzie felt heat climb into her cheeks. "I knew you didn't hear me. I just said we need to get the grass out from under the pepper plants."

"Sorry about that. Which ones are peppers?"

"These over here." Cal lead the way to half a dozen tall, scraggly plants, sporting three tiny white blossoms each. "They don't look very good, do they?"

"Well, not at the moment," she agreed. "Let's give them a little extra help and see what comes of it. Nothing lost but a little time." Lizzie knelt beside the bedraggled vegetables and started loosening the soil. "What do you do with these, anyway?"

"Cook with 'em. They burn your mouth something fierce. Mama only grew them 'cause Pa likes them so much."

Calvin picked at a leaf that had fallen from the plant. After tearing it to shreds, he swiped at a spot on his cheek.

Lizzie captured his hand before he could do any damage. "Careful, there. If these are as hot as you say, they'll make your eyes hurt worse than your mouth." She grinned and went back to weeding, expecting him to argue, but when Cal stayed quiet, she glanced back, shocked to see tears making tracks in the dust on his face.

"Hey, what's the matter? I didn't hurt you, did I?"

Cal shook his head and scrubbed his eyes with his shirt-sleeve. "I was just thinking about Mama and Amanda," he whispered. "I couldn't stop those men from hurting them."

Just like his father, Lizzie thought as she opened her arms and gathered him close. "I'm so sorry that happened." She rocked back and forth, patting his back, soothing him. "You know there's nothing you could have done to stop them, Cal, don't you? Not a thing."

Cal's thin shoulders heaved on a sigh. "That's what Pa said, but I still wish I could've."

She let him ramble about that day in hell, about the months of horrors that came after, hoping that by talking about it, the boy could begin to accept what happened.

The longer Cal went on, the more heartsick Lizzie became. She had to grit her teeth to keep from saying things she knew she just shouldn't say in front of a little boy. Even if they'd been drawn, quartered, and hacked into little pieces, those sons-of-bitches died too easy. Damnation! She wanted to go dig every last one of them out of the graves they rested in and kill them all over again. Beatings, starvation, and who knew what else. Where the hell was God when those poor babies were being hurt like that?

"Ranger McCain cut me loose with my own knife." Cal reached into his boot and pulled it out to show her. "Be careful. He helped me make it real sharp and I don't want you to get cut."

Lizzie made a show of studying the blade before handing it back, hilt first. "That's a fine knife, Cal. Real fine."

"I know." He slid it back into the boot scabbard. "I keep it here 'cause that's where Pa and the Ranger keep theirs." He tugged his pant leg over the boot. "Ranger McCain took me to this town called Lucinda. They named it for this really mean old woman and they hunt for gold, even though Mister Gerard says there isn't much to find anymore."

She made an encouraging sound and went back to piling up the weeds they'd pulled.

"Pa was almost right behind us, all the way to the town, only we didn't know it. I never saw him. Then I met Nathan and his sister, but I didn't think I should stay there because the bad men were looking for Miss Rachel. That's why they kept hurting Amanda, 'cause she looked a lot like..."

Cal stopped mid-sentence. His face grew pale and his lower lip trembled. Tears welled again in his sad blue eyes. Lizzie dropped the handful of weeds she was carrying and stepped over two rows of plants to get to him.

"Calvin, baby, it wasn't your fault." She ruffled his hair and smoothed it out of his eyes. "You have to believe me. Bad men did this, not you."

Cal fisted his hands around the weeds he held. "I tried to stop him from hurting her. I tried so hard and I kept trying until they tied me up so I couldn't anymore."

Lizzie's heart broke for him. He was too young to have to cope with the evil of the world. "Honey, I know you did, and Amanda knew, too. What happened wasn't your fault." Repeating her words, she hugged him close and rocked gently, side to side, fighting back the urge to cry right along with him.

The sun slipped toward the horizon, taking the heat of the day with it, and still Calvin cried. For a while, Lizzie thought she was going to have to call Wolf over to calm the boy. Finally, Cal pulled free and used the tail of his shirt to wipe off his face. "I'm all right now, Miss Lizzie."

She smiled at him and thumbed off the last bit of wetness from his chin. "I can see that, Sir Calvin. How about we finish up here and then we can get started on that chicken coop?"

"I can do that myself, I'll bet."

Lizzie smiled at the return of his enthusiasm. "I don't doubt it a bit."

• ♥ •

The first roll of thunder belled across the plains while Wolf was still on the barn roof, nailing down another patch. The hole Lizzie had spotted wasn't large, but it was one of three that needed fixing before the rain he'd thought wouldn't come arrived. A few minutes later, a flash of lightning split the sky. Wolf pounded faster. Fat drops of rain heralded the beginning of a downpour as he drove in the last nail. He was soaked to the skin before he could climb down the ladder.

Cursing the summer storm with every step, he strode to the house. His rifle would have to be broken down and dried, along with his belt guns. Every tool in the box he'd had with him on the roof needed toweling down and greasing, as well, so nothing would rust.

Wolf set everything on the porch, out of the rain, then stripped off his shirt to wring the water out of it. "At least it won't need washing." He spotted Cal inside the barn, still hammering at the chicken coop door. Wolf could have made the repairs in a quarter of the time, but Cal wanted to do it himself. So he'd shown the boy what to do and left him to it. From the look of it, he'd be at it for a while, yet.

"Cal? I'm going inside to get the rain off the rifle."

"Okay, Pa." Cal waved with the hammer he held, then swung it at the piece of wood in front of him.

Wolf wanted to laugh. What the boy lacked in skill, he made up for in enthusiasm. Leaving Cal to it, Wolf gathered up the weapons and tools, and hitched the door open with his hip.

• ♥ •

Lizzie stared. She couldn't help it. Wolf crowded into the room, his arms full, and his bare shoulders glistening with rain drops. She swore she could smell the heat coming off his skin, even from across the room. When he turned to close the door, her breath backed up. The naked expanse of his back made her fingers itch to touch.

Wolf turned and caught her staring. She waited for his remark, almost prayed he'd say something cutting and break the spell that held her in place. Instead, he stared back. The rain on the roof drowned out all sounds in the room but their breathing, his deep and steady, hers shallow, rapid. The room heated—or maybe it was her.

He didn't look away as he set everything on the table and crossed to stand in front of her. Close up, he was overwhelming. Lizzie licked her lips, fighting the urge to taste one of the raindrops. As if he read her mind, Wolf eased closer, bringing all that skin within reach.

"Lizzie."

Wolf's gruff whisper broke the spell. She jerked away and shook her head, trying to get rid of the haze coating her good sense. She stepped back. Wolf came forward. She moved right. He tracked with her. She lifted her chin to give him a piece of her mind—and he kissed her.

Just like that, they were back on the hill, her back pressed into the grass, his big body covering hers. Some sense of self-preservation was banging at walls of her mind, yelling at her to get away. Her body ignored the warning, and crowded his, soaking up his heat like a flower in the early spring sun.

Wolf stroked a work-roughened thumb along the curve of her jaw, from ear to chin, leaving chill-bumps in its wake. She leaned into his touch, mesmerized. When he began a feather light exploration of her throat, she turned her face away, offering her neck to his roving fingers. When the brush of heat made her breath catch, he hesitated, then continued on his way, down her throat, across her collar bone, to the delicate skin of her shoulder.

"So strong and so beautiful," he whispered, the words as soft as his touch. His lips replaced his fingers, warm, smooth. Never still, he retraced the path he'd taken, teasing, tasting, until she swayed in place, her knees weak. What was he doing to her? The next breath lifted her breasts to his magical fingers.

At the first touch on her sensitive curves, Lizzie gasped, opening further for him. She knew she ought to end the kiss, wanted to tell him to stop, but the words came out as a whimper that was like setting a match to dry tinder. A deep, rumbling groan came out of Wolf. He cupped her breast, brushed his thumb across her hard, beaded nipple, and wrapped his other arm around her waist to drag her tight against the skin she was desperate to taste.

Her hands roamed his long back, his wide shoulders, while he explored her mouth. When he broke the kiss, she leaned forward and sipped a drop of rain from his chest. His whole body shook. She tried it again. With a soft curse, Wolf framed her face in his big hands and reclaimed her lips.

What was left of her common sense went up in flames. Lizzie pressed closer, wanting to touch him everywhere. Never had she felt so edgy, restless. She wasn't innocent, but what burned under her skin was new, unexpected. There was something she needed, but she hadn't a clue what it was. She had the feeling Wolf did.

He nipped his way down her neck and back again. "So soft."

Her hands had a mind of their own, and they wanted to touch more of this man. Burrowing still closer, she reveled in the heat radiating from his skin.

"Wolf. What's happening to me? I feel so... I can't stand it. Do something."

"Lizzie," he groaned, his big body shuddering as her palms skimmed to his waist. When she slipped her fingers beneath the fabric of his trousers, he sagged, his weight pressing down on her, bending her backward. Thrilled she could affect him, Lizzie stretched onto her toes and explored all the skin she could reach.

Wolf tasted his way along her jaw and down her neck to her shoulder. The brush of his mustache raised gooseflesh clear to her toes. Exploring, he skimmed his hands from her shoulders to her hips, learning her angular form. Digging her nails into his neck, she urged him toward the bedroom. Staggering a little, they made it as far as the doorway before he stopped to kiss her again. Without releasing her lips, Wolf lifted her from the floor. Lizzie shaped the muscles of his arms, then buried her fingers in his hair and pulled him closer. Just a couple more steps and—

"Hey, Pa!" Calvin hollered from the yard.

"Damn!" Wolf dropped her feet to the floor and leaned against the doorframe, panting for air. Lizzie let her hands slide out of his hair, down his neck and chest. She felt the rise and fall of every breath against her palms. She glanced up and her gaze was snagged by his. Eyes the color of a stormy sky glittered beneath the heavy arch of his brows. She lifted her face, pushed to her toes, wanting—*needing* him to kiss her again. When she heard Cal step onto the porch, Lizzie jumped and lost her balance. Wolf's arm tightened around her, holding her close, steadying her.

"I'm all right," she hissed. "You can let go." When he didn't, she gave him a little shove. "Now. Before he makes it to the door."

Wolf straightened a little and she ducked under his arm. Still he skimmed his fingers all the way down her arm to capture her hand as she stepped away. Lizzie whipped around, intending to tell him to cut it out, but the words wouldn't come. The raw desire sparkling in his storm-silver eyes held her enthralled—and speechless.

"Pa, it's time I took my bath." The latch on the door rattled. "We're going to church tomorrow, aren't we?"

Lizzie barely managed to scoop up her sewing basket before Cal opened the door and stuck his head inside.

CHAPTER ELEVEN

"Pa? Did you hear me?"

Wolf stayed where he was, leaning against the bedroom doorframe. He wasn't sure his legs would hold him if he tried to walk. "I heard you, son."

"Well, are we going? I want to see Raymond and Orville." Cal looked from his father to Lizzie. She stayed quiet. The decision was Wolf's to make, though he would welcome her input. Maybe she'd tell him what he wanted to hear. *Stay home. No need to run into all those people who will remind you of Emily.*

But staying home would be for him. Calvin needed to see his friends, needed something to return to normal. And the clawing of panic in his belly shamed him. "You're right, son," he gave in. "I guess I lost track of the days. Want to help me bring in the water for our baths?"

"No need." Lizzie tapped a full bucket with her toe. "There's probably enough here to get started, unless you want to fill a whole tub." Lizzie pushed to her feet. "I'll go check on the horses while you..."

Calvin took off his shirt and tossed it aside. Wolf caught her eye and reached for the buttons of his pants. A becoming peach flush climbed Lizzie's neck. "Would you mind checking Scarlett's shoes? She was favoring her right front hoof a bit this morning."

"Happy to do it." The look on her face clearly said *anything to get me out of here before the bath-taking starts.* She grabbed up her rifle and slid through the door as Wolf loosened his belt and let his trousers hit the floor.

Wolf went looking for her after the last bucket of murky water had been emptied. He found her sitting behind the barn, measuring the darkness and smoking a small ivory-stemmed pipe. The smoke-stained bowl was carved and decorated, the partial silhouette of a ship in full sail showing around her fingers.

"Where'd you find that?" He leaned against the rough wood, inhaling the night blended with the acrid scent of tobacco.

"Only thing besides my boots that Black Jack didn't take and you didn't cut to ribbons." A soft, red glow lit her features, flaring with each hiss of air. "It was in the pocket of my buckskin jacket. Just lucky they didn't smash it when they left their boot prints on my ribcage. I didn't remember it until tonight."

"How could you forget? Most folks I know keep better track of their tobacco than they do their money."

She shrugged. "I'm not most folks."

"True enough." He declined her offer to share the pipe. "I didn't know you smoked."

"Don't much. Only when I'm circling something in my mind."

He couldn't help wondering what she was gnawing away in that head of hers. None of his concern, he decided. "You plan on going into Civil with us in the morning?"

"Nope."

He gave her time to elaborate, but she kept puffing in silence.

"Do you want me to pass any greetings along?"

"Nobody but Harvard knows I'm here. And probably Black Jack." She took one long drag and held the smoke inside for a ten count. "Can't see a need to enlighten the rest of them."

He ignored the relief he felt that she didn't care about seeing Harvard again. "Folks in town are good people, for the most part." Wolf wasn't sure whom he was trying to convince.

"Never said they weren't." She tapped the pipe against the sole of her boot to empty it, then crushed the smoldering tobacco into the dirt until no trace of fire remained. "You'll want to ride the gray gelding."

"Smoke," Wolf interjected. "That's Smoke."

"Well, Smoke is getting lazy and Scarlett could use the rest. Calvin's little mare—" She raised a hand before he could interrupt again. "*Lightning* is ready to go, too."

Wolf helped Lizzie to her feet, steadying her with a hand on each shoulder. "I appreciate you looking after the horses." The moonlight glinted in her eyes, the light just bright enough to see she wasn't looking at him. The fine wrinkles of a frown deepened between her brows.

He gained her attention by brushing a thumb along her jaw. He kissed the surprise off her lips. The earthy sting of tobacco smoke was odd and intriguing on the lips of a woman. Wolf went back for another taste. Before he could deepen the kiss, Lizzie pushed out of his hold and limped off, digging in her pocket for the tiny pouch of tobacco and a match.

• ♥ •

Civil had grown. In only eight months, more people had moved into the little town. Ragged half-tent structures had been replaced with wood and stucco buildings. Before long Millicent Freeman would realize her dream: Civil would be civilized.

Cal pointed at one of the new houses as they rode into town. "Wonder who lives there?"

"I have no idea. Someone new in town, I suppose." He clucked his tongue at his horse, picking up the pace. "We've been gone a while."

"Maybe there's someone new in school." To Wolf's surprise, Cal sounded eager to find out.

"We'll ask Mrs. Freeman. She'll know."

Cal's mouth turned down. "I'd rather ask Raymond. He doesn't look to see if I cleaned my fingernails."

Wolf frowned. He remembered that Sunday afternoon clearly. No matter how much Emily had scrubbed, Calvin managed to get dirty as soon as she turned her back. Millicent's obvious disapproval had only heightened Emily's embarrassment. It was no wonder Cal was afraid of the woman.

"Fine. You ask Raymond and we'll try to avoid Mrs. Freeman today, all right?"

Cal's little face brightened as they rode into town. Folks called and waved as they passed, and a couple of Cal's friends ran over to meet them as they dismounted in front of the little frame church.

"You're back. Pa said that Mister Mercer had told him that Mister Browning had been out to see you."

"Did they hurt you?"

"Where'd you get the horse?"

The questions came from all sides. Cal took a couple of steps closer to Wolf, leaning into him for protection. Maybe this was a bad idea. The boy wasn't ready for all the memories. Wolf laid a hand on his son's shoulder. If he wanted to leave, they would mount up and ride out. Raymond Fisher pushed to the front of the crowd of boys.

"I sure am glad you're back, Cal. Mister Carruthers ain't let me get by with nothing since you left. I even had to partner with Sara Haney in the spelling test."

Cal tried to laugh with the others, but to Wolf he sounded scared. "Come on, Raymond." Cal play punched his friend in the arm. "I'll bet it wasn't that bad."

The other boy shrugged. "You don't think so? *You* be her partner next time. Then we'll see if it ain't so bad."

The others laughed and jostled Raymond, teasing him about liking Sara Haney more than he let on. Gradually, Cal relaxed and joined in the fun. Wolf stayed close until the tension left Cal's shoulders. Once he was satisfied his son would be all right, he stepped out of the way, gathered the reins of both horses and walked to the livery.

Ever since Millicent Freeman decided having horses and wagons scattered about outside the church wasn't proper, everyone took them to the livery. Macon Douglas and his brother, Malcolm, didn't work on Sundays. Instead, they left the big doors open, and water and grain available to any who needed them, trusting that they'd pay for what they used.

After stripping the tack from Lightning, he turned the horse loose into the large corral with the dozen or so others. He knew Sheriff Freeman was waiting nearby, but Wolf couldn't find it in him to hurry. Rejoining his life here was turning out to be even harder than he'd expected.

Taking his time, he checked his mount's hooves and legs. The gelding was used to carrying gear, not a rider, but didn't seem any worse for wear. When there was no more reason to linger, he gave Smoke's haunches a gentle slap and left the corral. The sheriff opened the gate for him.

"Glad to see you back, Richards." Freeman's handshake was firm, his words sincere. "Damn sorry to hear about your daughter. I hope the sons of bitches responsible enjoy hell."

There was no question, no doubt that his wife and daughter had been avenged. Wolf was known to be the kind of man who had no give in him for what needed doing.

"I wasn't the one who sent them there, but, yeah, it's done."

They turned together toward the church. "The missus and I wondered if you'd come back here or start again somewhere else. God knows this can't be easy on you." The sheriff glanced toward the boys crowding around Calvin. "Either of you."

Wolf touched the brim of his hat in greeting as they approached a knot of people near the entrance. "Cal needed home. Guess I did too, more than I realized. Lot of changes around here, though."

"We've grown a mite." Freeman looked around. "A few new houses, another couple dozen citizens. And it's good growth, for the most part."

Wolf glanced at the sheriff. "What part isn't good?"

"A couple of speculators showed up about a month ago, interested in buying land cheap." Freeman ran his fingers through his hair, roughing up the graying strands. "What they're doing isn't illegal, just annoying. I told them I'd arrest them the second that changed."

"Thanks for the warning. You see them, tell 'em to stay clear. I'm not selling, and speculators try my patience."

Freeman chuckled and clapped Wolf on the shoulder.

"Good to have you back." The men joined the other parishion-
ers chatting outside the church. The handshakes and kind words
were subdued but sincere as Wolf was welcomed back into the
family of the town. A few of the women refused to meet his
gaze, and one or two of the men avoided him all together, but
most expressed their condolences on his loss, then continued
their conversation. Though it was hard to accept, life in Civil
had moved on.

A bell rang overhead, startling Wolf. Rodney Fisher, Raymond's father, laughed and clapped him on the back. "Millicent's latest addition. Claimed no self-respecting church could
be without one. Convinced the town council right quick."

"When did they decide to spend our money on that?"

"Oh, last spring, I th—no, it was February last. You was off
hunting for the army, I imagine. Emily probably…" Fisher
cleared his throat and slid a finger under his too-tight collar.
"That is… Uh. Well, anyway, it took more than a year to get the
durn thing from some bell-makin' foundry up to Maryland.
Came as far as Liberal on the train, then four of us drove Wil-
son Matthews's wagon up there to bring it the rest of the way.
Gittin' it across the river was no easy thing, I can tell you. That
thing weighs close to five hundred pounds! A man can't reach
across it, it's so big. Well, you could, but not me. No, sir. Took
six of us to hoist it up there and hold it in place while they got it
installed. You can probably hear the ringin' clear to Dodge City.
No excuse to be late for church, now." He slapped Wolf's
shoulder again and headed for the door.

Wolf rubbed at the sudden tightness in his chest. Of course,
Emily would have known about the bell. From the day she arrived in the brand new buggy her parents had given them as a
wedding present, Emily had made it a point to stay up with all
the happenings in Civil, who was new, what was planned. Another thing he was going to have to take on. How was he supposed to earn a living and keep up on what was important, too?

As the crowd of waiting worshippers thinned, Wolf spotted
Cal standing off to one side with a tiny, brown-haired woman.

Hannah Weaver. His gut rolled once before he ruthlessly twist-ed the life out of the reaction. She had been Emily's dearest friend. Seeing him and Calvin again had to be scraping her grief raw, too. He could at least be man enough to say good morning. She beat him to it.

"Welcome home, Cain."

He nearly turned tail and ran for the horses. Only Emily had ever called him by his given name. Hearing it from Hannah's lips was almost too much.

"Good morning, Mrs. Weaver." She stiffened at the formal greeting, but he couldn't go back to what was before. When Emily was alive, he'd always leaned down and let tiny little Hannah kiss his cheek, but not now. He turned his hat round and round in his fingers, disgusted that he was too much of a coward to even shake her hand. As though she read his thoughts, Hannah closed the distance between them and placed dainty gloved fingers on his thick wrist.

"Don't expect so much of yourself, Cain."

Wolf glanced at her face, still unlined, though she was only a few months younger than he. "You're too kind to me, Han-nah."

She only smiled and held out a hand to Calvin. "Would you escort me inside this morning?" She glanced back at Wolf, her summer green eyes flashing in the sunlight. "I do believe Calvin has grown three inches since last summer. He'll be as tall as you before long."

Calvin preened under her attention and offered his arm like a gentleman. Wolf could only be grateful she'd managed to focus the boy's attention on a happier time.

As he followed the pair into the sanctuary, he could feel eve-ry eye turn their way. It wouldn't be long before the rumors began, before the women folk would have Hannah taking Emi-ly's place. Anger and disgust warred in his mind as the service droned on.

Women unfolded fans to stir the air as the temperature in the crowded room rose. All the different colors looking like a horde of butterflies hovering within the congregation. Men mopped at their faces and necks with starched white cloths. Wolf glanced at Hannah when he saw her reach for her bag, but instead of a fan, she removed a pale lavender embroidered handkerchief. Only then did he notice Cal's tears. He'd been so caught up in his own demons he hadn't spared a thought for how being back here, among all the memories, might upset his son.

Protectiveness roared through him, drowning out Reverend Stephens as he preached of kings and prophets. He leaned toward Cal, intending to carry him outside, away from all the sympathetic looks, but Hannah shook her head. *Leave him be*, she mouthed. She dabbed away the streaks of moisture on Cal's face, then smiled at Wolf. "He'll be fine," she whispered.

Wolf wasn't. The pitying glances from some, the speculation from others, brought out a need for violence. He gritted his teeth and faced forward, silently begging the minister to finish so he could escape. Finally, the last hymn was sung, the organ wheezed into silence and the congregation stood to leave, filing past the preacher on their way out the door.

"Your sermon was a little under two hours, Reverend. Decided to go easy on us, eh?" The man in front of Wolf harangued the minister good-naturedly, prompting laughter from everyone within earshot, including the preacher.

"It was getting a bit warm in the sanctuary. The wind from all the fans threatened to blow my notes away, so I cut it short this morning, Mister Plotts." Reverend Stephens greeted Mrs. Plotts and the six Plott children as they skipped past, before turning to Wolf.

"It's good to have you back among us, Mister Richards. I've missed seeing you in the congregation." He shook Wolf's hand, his grip strong and steady. Honest. "And I'm glad you're here, too, Calvin." He patted Cal's shoulder before going on to the next in line. "Good morning, Mrs. Peterson. How is your cold this morning?"

Wolf settled his hat in place as he stepped into the hot sunshine. Hannah had slipped away in the crowd leaving the pews, before Wolf could thank her. She'd cared for Calvin as Emily might have, with a gentle, loving touch. He owed her more than she realized.

"Pa, can I go say goodbye to Raymond?" Cal squinted against the bright light, searching for his friend.

"Sure, just don't be long. We need to be getting back."

He spotted Hannah with two women he didn't recognize. When all three heads turned his way, he realized she must be answering their questions about the stranger in church. Not long ago, everyone would have known him, because everyone knew Emily.

Not wanting to make anyone's acquaintance today, he turned for the livery. Before he went three steps, a slick-dressed man wearing a fancy suit and shiny bowler hat stepped into his path.

"You must be Cain Richards, Wolf to your friends." The exuberant greeting was bad enough, but the man stuck out his right hand. "Johnson's the name. Jeremiah Johnson. You've probably heard of me."

"No." Wolf moved to go around the man, but he kept pace.

"Well, you will. Yes, sir, you certainly will. I'm a land broker, perusing possible home sites for new settlers. I understand you own a nice parcel outside of town."

Wolf stopped, forcing the man to back up. "My land isn't for sale."

"Perhaps not yet, but you haven't heard my offer." He squared his shoulders, ready to launch into a prepared sales pitch in his pinched-off whiny voice.

"Don't bother. I'm not selling." Wolf stalked away, leaving the man sputtering in the sun.

"Irritating son of a bitch, isn't he?"

Wolf spun toward the voice. "Browning. I was just coming to look for you. I didn't see you in church."

Harvard laughed as he gripped his friend's hand in greeting. "Me? In there? If I put a toe through the door, I fear, just like Jericho, the walls would come tumbling down."

"Unlikely, Mister Browning. God's house is built especially for sinners like you." Reverend Stephens joined them, an unfamiliar couple in tow. The man was broad and stocky, with gray hair and leathery skin that shouted *farmer*. The woman at his side was nearly as tall as her husband, with a wealth of graying brown hair piled on her head. She smiled when Wolf removed his hat, making her pale blue eyes twinkle. Funny how the simple curving of lips could make even a plain woman lovely.

Lizzie was like that, turning from plain to pretty with just a smile.

"There is no sinner quite like me, Reverend." Harvard tipped his hat, a smile on his face and in his voice. Obviously, the argument was an old one. "Afternoon, folks."

"Sven and Alice Peterson, allow me to introduce Mister Harvard Browning. He owns the rather successful establishment in the center of Main Street."

Harvard cackled. "Can't even say *saloon*, Reverend?"

"Not on a Sunday," the minister teased. "You know I won't give up on bringing you into the fold, Mister Browning."

"I'd be disappointed if you did, Reverend."

The preacher indicated Wolf. "And this is Mister Richards. Sven and Alice moved to Civil in the fall. He's been hoping to speak with you for some time."

"How do you do?" Peterson had a thick accent and he spoke carefully, as if his English was newly learned. "I belief I have your horses."

Wolf halted in the process of shaking the man's hand. "What did you say?" He must have misunderstood.

"I belief I have your horses," the man repeated more slowly. "Soon after the unfortunate happening." He bowed his head, a gesture of respect that touched Wolf more than any other condolences he'd received. "Two weeks after, maybe three, I went hunting. As I sat concealed near the river, five mustangs, all with halters on dem, came to drink. They didn't run from me, even when I walked up to them. When I returned home, they followed like five big hounds." He laughed, a wheezing, cracked sound. "The Reverend thought they might be yours. You notched their left hind hoof, yes? A mark dat looks like a long-footed E with a J swooped up at da end of it?"

Wolf didn't know what to say. That was definitely his mark. Emily hated spoiling the horses' beautiful coats with a traditional brand, so he'd devised one he could carve into the inside of their hooves using Emily's initials: E and J. Everyone who knew Wolf could tell which horses belonged to him. The rest learned fast.

Peterson waited for Wolf to confirm his assumption with the patience of a man who made a living watching things grow. "They probably are my stock."

The man nodded. "I thinked so," he crowed, his glee stealing his new language skills. "Dey are only five, but such shining coats, such long manes. I told my Alice, 'deez horses are no more meant to be vild.'"

"Well, I'll be damned." Harvard pumped the man's hand like the horses were his own. "You come by the Fallen Star, Mister Peterson. The first drink is on me."

Peterson looked tempted, but one glance at his silent missus and he declined. "I don't need dat, but I tank you for da offer."

Wolf couldn't believe it. When he road up to the house that horrible afternoon, the horses were nowhere to be seen. He'd assumed the thieves took them, too. "I owe you a great debt, Mister Peterson."

"Nah," he scoffed. "No debt. Tanks is enough. You come now and get dem." He plopped his battered brown felt hat on his head and turned toward an old, beat up buckboard, pulled by a pair of well-aged mules. "Erik! Orville! We go now." Two lanky boys broke off from the cluster near the front steps of the church and loped over to climb into the wagon.

Wolf shoved his fingers through his hair. "I need to get my boy home first. He can't ride that far."

Harvard clapped him on the shoulder. "Don't worry about Cal. I'll take care of getting him home."

With that problem resolved, Wolf agreed to follow the Petersons and collect his horses. Sven whistled at the mules, tipped his hat to Reverend Stephens, and headed west out of town. Wolf thanked the preacher for his assistance.

"I'm glad I was able to help in some small way. Good day, Mister Richards. Mister Browning." Reverend Stephens shook their hands and returned to the church.

Wolf faced Harvard. "I appreciate you seeing Cal home."

"Happy to help. I'll get him some food before we ride out to the house." Harvard lowered his voice, not wanting anyone to know about Wolf's houseguest. "I need to check on..." He let it go at that.

"It would be helpful. It'll take me two or three hours to bring the horses in, if they're mine. I'd rather not have him in the saddle that long. The souvenir he got from that *javelina* is still tender. Lightning is over at the livery."

"Lightning?" Harvard tried not to laugh.

Wolf grinned. "*I* didn't name him." He stepped into the sun, searching. "Calvin?"

The boy ran up. "Hi, Mister Browning. Whatcha want, Pa?"

"Mister Browning is going to ride home with you, while I go to the Petersons. They've been taking care of some of our horses."

"Really? Which ones?" Cal had considered the big animals pets, just like his mother.

"I won't know until I see them. They may not even be ours." Wolf ruffled his hair. "I want you go with Mister Browning, and mind what he tells you."

"Yes, sir. Is he coming to make sure Miss Lizzie is doing all right?"

Wolf took a swift look around, grateful no one was close. "We don't mention our guest where anyone can hear, remember? We talked about that on the way to town." Cal's brows wrinkled and looked as if a question was coming. "We'll discuss it at home, son. Go on, now."

Cal heaved a confused sigh. "All right, Pa." He scuffed his boots a couple of times then ran after Harvard. "Wait for me,

Mister Browning."

The questions started before they were out of earshot, but Cal was only interested in the horses. Breathing a sigh of relief, Wolf saddled his horse and rode to catch up with the slow-moving wagon.

CHAPTER TWELVE

"Hey, Miss Lizzieeee!"

Lizzie looked up from the revolver she was cleaning and squinted into the bright sunlight. Calvin was at the top of the hill on the far side of the creek, standing in the back of a wagon full of hay and straw and waving for all he was worth. Lightning was tied on a lead rope, following in their dust boiling up behind. Lizzie returned the greeting, studying the man holding the reins. Too narrow in the shoulders to be Wolf. Fancy white shirt, string tie, six-shooter at his hip. Had to be Browning.

"Damned whiskey-peddlin' sawbones," she groused. "And where the hell did he leave Wolf?" She waited for him to appear, expecting him to be riding far enough behind the wagon to stay out of the dust, but he wasn't there. Steadying the revolver against her knee with her bad hand, she went back to polishing the barrel, trying hard to ignore the unwanted sting of disappointment.

"Whatcha doin'?" Cal jumped from the wagon as it stopped under a tree and bounded up the steps. "That's one of Pa's extra pistols, ain't it? Can I help?"

Lizzie didn't stop rubbing. "Horse."

"Huh?"

"Where's your horse?"

Cal looked from Lizzie to Lightning. "Right there."

"Is that where he's supposed to be after following behind a wagon and breathin' dust for more than an hour?" She glanced sideways at the boy.

"No, ma'am." Cal toed a clod of dirt.

"Go care for your noble steed, Sir Calvin. I'll still be here. Be sure there's enough water in the trough," she reminded him. "And bring a bucket full for Mister Browning's horse, too."

"I can take care of my own horse." Harvard turned to follow the boy.

"No, sir." Calvin lowered his head, looking rather put upon. "I can pump water for them both." Cal snagged Lightning's reins and kicked at clumps of grass all the way to the corral, making Lizzie grin.

"He shouldn't be required to care for those horses. The saddles are too heavy for a boy his age to lift."

"I know that," Lizzie snapped. "I'll handle the tack, but he has to remember to always consider his horse first. Someday, the lesson may save his life."

"You're a wise woman, Miss Sutter." He moved into the shade of the porch and started pointedly at her right hand, wrapped around the cylinder of the revolver. "That doesn't look much like resting your arm to me."

Lizzie almost snarled. Some days a man was more trouble than he was worth. "I'm resting my *leg* at the moment. My *arm* will be next."

Harvard laughed. The damned irritating man actually threw back his head and laughed like a hyena. "You don't like to be laid up, do you, Lizzie?"

She puffed a strand of hair from her eyes. "Makes me madder'n a cornered badger. That's something you'd do well to think on the next time you go dishing out unwanted advice."

"Ah, but, as your physician, I'm honor-bound to remind you. For your own good," he talked right over her objection.

"Where's Wolf?" She figured changing the subject would be a good idea. Maybe then she wouldn't be tempted to shoot Harvard where he stood. Her surly mood wasn't any of his doin', but that didn't make him any safer.

"Sven Peterson, a farmer with a spread north of town, thinks he found several of Wolf's horses. He rode out to the farm to be sure. He'll need the feed if he brings them home."

Lizzie stopped polishing. "Do you think they're his?"

Harvard leaned against a support post and crossed his long legs at the ankles. "I hope so. Wolf had plans to raise horses for the army. Those mustangs were to be the breeding stock, his starting herd."

"Mustangs? Nice horse for this part of the country." She closed one eye and studied the inside of the barrel she was cleaning, then hunted up a clean corner of the rag she was using. "Did he buy them?"

"He caught them when they were just weaned. Before Emily was killed, he had more than a dozen. The man has a gift with animals." Harvard glanced over his shoulder and watched Calvin for a moment. "You didn't answer Cal's question. Is that Wolf's revolver?"

"Yeah. He loaned me the pair until I can earn enough money to buy my own. I did some shooting with it this morning, but it pulls to the right beyond fifty feet. I thought cleaning it might help. There's a nick in the end of the barrel." She held out the gun for him to inspect. "That might be the cause of the pulling, but I can't be certain until I clean it up good and shoot it some more. First, though." She set everything on the porch beside her chair. "I have to help Cal with the horses and move that feed into the barn."

"I'll take care of it." Harvard pressed a hand to Lizzie's shoulder to urge her to sit down again. "You keep on resting that leg."

The man winked before he swaggered off toward the corral. If she didn't know better, she'd swear he was flirting. God only knew why. She might be a female, but she was just about the furthest thing from a woman in these parts.

Lizzie studied Harvard as he led his horse, with the wagon rolling behind, toward the barn. Positioning the contraption in front of the door, he called Calvin over and helped strip tack off Lightning. Without the dandy coat he wore in town, she could see muscles moving beneath his snowy white shirt.

He might be put together in a nice package, and have sad eyes that had seen their share of troubles, but he was still a gambler at heart. Not at all the kind of man she would be at-tracted to. If she were interested in a man…

An image of Wolf came to mind, bare chest gleaming with raindrops in the firelight. For a moment, she could feel his smooth skin under her fingers instead of the cold metal barrel she was cleaning.

Lizzie's face heated and she nearly threw the revolver into the dust. What the hell was wrong with her? First, she couldn't resist the man's kisses, now she couldn't stop thinking about him.

Disgusted, she loaded the revolver and stuffed it into her waistband, then heaved herself out of the chair and hobbled off to the barn. Maybe mucking stalls and moving straw would get her mind back to its own business.

• ♥ •

By the time Wolf returned, five tamed mustangs on lead ropes strung out behind him, the day was nearly over. Lizzie and Harvard came out of the barn at Calvin's shout.

"Pa's back with the horses. Look at 'em, Miss Lizzie. Ain't they a sight?" He grabbed her hand when she came close enough and pointed out each animal. "That's Paint in the lead, then Angel and Big Red. The black one with the white sock is Midnight, and the yellow horse is Dandelion. Amanda named that one."

Cal got quiet, and the sadness on his face broke her heart. "Every time you see that horse, Cal, you remember your sister when she was happy. I imagine she would like that."

He wiped his nose on his sleeve and nodded, then took off running. "Pa!"

"Not too close, Cal," Lizzie called after him. "You'll spook the horses."

"I know," he hollered back, slowing his headlong pace.

At a signal from Wolf, Cal swung open the corral gate, care-ful to stay out of the way as the horses were herded inside. Wolf guided his dove gray gelding to the water trough and swung down from the saddle. Even from a distance, Lizzie could see his pride and relief at getting some of his stock back.

The pump handle squealed with each long stroke as he filled the trough in the corral, then a couple of buckets for his mount. Harvard clapped him on the back in congratulations. Lizzie caught up on the conversation as she joined the men.

"Peterson took decent care of them. He kept them in a pretty small enclosure, so they were a bit of a handful at first. Kept wanting to stretch their legs out and run." Wolf studied each in turn. "Their hooves could use trimming, and Angel is favoring one leg, but for the most part, they're in good shape."

Harvard crossed his arms on the top rail of the corral. "Did he say where he found them?"

"Over near Adobe Bend, about a mile from his homestead, still on our side of the river. I'm surprised they let him get that close. A wild-born horse usually reverts pretty fast." Wolf leaned over the trough and ducked his head and neck into the stream of water coming from the pump.

Lizzie stepped out of the way of the splashing. "Maybe the others are still around."

"Can we go looking for them, Pa?" Calvin climbed through the corral fence. "I can ride fine now." He tried hard not to limp, but none of the adults were fooled.

"I appreciate the offer, Cal, but I'll search the area while I'm out hunting." He swung his son into the gray's saddle. "Take Smoke to the barn. I'll be there shortly to brush him down."

"We've got grain, Pa. Should I give him some?"

Wolf turned immediately to Harvard.

"In celebration, old friend." Harvard grinned, not in the least put off by the glare in Wolf's eyes. "I brought a wagon load of hay and straw, as well. Not a lot, but enough to keep you for a while."

"I can't accept another gift." Wolf's jaw jutted forward, signaling the start of an argument.

"Then you can pay me when you go hunting. A wild turkey and a nice venison haunch should cover it."

"Deal." Wolf shook Harvard's hand then glanced toward

Lizzie. "Any trouble today?"

"Not a bit, unless you count not catching the fish I'd planned to cook for supper. I never could get the hang of it, no matter how many times Ol' Timothy showed me."

"We'll make do. Come on, Cal. Let's get these horses settled." Wolf turned on his well-worn boot heel and strode for the barn.

Harvard moved to help her back to her seat on the porch. "I'll make a try for the fish if you tell me about Old Timothy."

"He was a sailor on Grandfather's ship." Lizzie shrugged off his help. "He'd hopped over the deck rail and hid out on some island until the Marines stopped looking. When Grandfather sailed by, he signed on. Old Timothy swore he'd been in the King's navy since Victoria's grandfather was a baby. He certainly looked old enough for it to be the truth. Mostly, he was a kind old man who never tired of answering my questions." Lizzie smiled at a memory. "And I asked a *lot* of questions."

Harvard sat on a step close to Lizzie and crossed his fancy boots at the ankle, getting comfortable. "I imagine you did."

• ♥ •

Wolf watched from the shade of the barn. When Lizzie smiled at whatever they were discussing, Harvard leaned a little closer, probably drawn by the same surprising light that made Wolf want to stay nearby. He beat back the streak of jealousy that sizzled through his middle and went to gather up the curry comb and brush.

"We done good, didn't we, Pa? Me and Mister Browning and Miss Lizzie." He tossed a forkful of straw in the general direction of a stall. "It took us a long time, but we cleaned out all the old mess and made it back into a proper barn."

"The place looks good, Cal." He led the first mustang into the open space in the middle of the barn. "Thank you for helping out around here."

"We wanted it to be ready when you got here with the horses and it was."

Cal jabbered on about straw and grain and pounding on fallen boards with Wolf's big hammer while Wolf kept brushing horse hide, gradually settling the horses back into their old stalls.

"Good thing we got a big barn, Pa." Cal counted animals, then stalls. "Or there wouldn't be enough rooms for all them horses."

"I have to get you back in school, Calvin. Your language is getting worse by the day."

"I know," he chirped, hanging up the pitch fork. "I can do better, I just have to think on it."

"Then think on it, son."

Cal giggled. "Where you wanna put Paint, Pa? There ain't—*isn't* another clean stall," he corrected, at a look from Wolf.

The boy's laughter lightened Wolf's heart. Maybe everything would be all right, after all. "How about the one over there?" He pointed with the brush. "Paint likes to be close to Angel."

Cal grabbed the pitchfork and started tossing moldy straw into the pile near the back wall. "Do you think the other horses are somewhere close, Pa? I sure would like to find Blackhorse."

Blackhorse, named for his obsidian coat, had been Emily's horse. The gentle mare was stout and strong, perfect for pulling their small wagon to town and back. Wolf used his sleeve to wipe the sweat from his face.

"I doubt it, son. I can't imagine she's still around."

"Will you look for her, Pa? Please?"

"I promise. Now, let me see those ropes you—"

The sound of gunfire cut him off. Dropping everything, Wolf snatched up his rifle. "Stay here!"

He eased to the barn door and looked around. There was no one on the porch. The front door was shut tight. Another shot came from his right, in the direction of the stream. Wolf angled that way, taking care to stay low.

He slipped into the protection of a large tree and listened. No voices. No sounds of a struggle. Another shot rang out, followed instantly by the whine of a ricochet.

"Fine shot, Lizzie. That pile of dirt had to be a hundred

yards away." Harvard's voice sounded normal.

"No pull this time, either." Lizzie's reply was muffled, as if she was facing away.

Trying to calm down, Wolf topped the hill as Lizzie fired off another three rounds. Each shot pulverized one of the pecan-sized rocks lined up on a fallen willow tree twenty yards downstream. "What the hell is going on?"

Lizzie spun in his direction, the revolver aimed dead center at his chest. The instant she recognized him, she raised it toward the sky. "Damnation! Don't sneak up on me like that. I could-a put a hole in you. Not to mention you scared a year off my life!"

"That's only fair, since I thought we were under attack again." Wolf tightened his grip on his rifle, fighting the urge to punch them both. He was overreacting, but he couldn't hold it back. The grief. The helpless fury. The reminder of all he'd lost.

Harvard wedged his makeshift fishing pole into a rock cairn on the bank. "Sorry, old friend. We came down to do some fishing. I wasn't thinking when I insisted Lizzie show off her shooting abilities."

Wolf walked away, trying to regain control. He examined the tree limb Lizzie had used as a target. All that was left of the three rocks was powder. "You can shoot with your left hand."

Lizzie holstered the revolver awkwardly. "I'm not much on the draw yet, but I can defend myself."

"And Cal."

She hesitated briefly before nodding. "Him, too, should there be a need."

Something relaxed deep inside. His son would be safe here with her. "I'll go tell Cal everything's under control."

As he walked away, Lizzie colored the air blue, cursing her own stupidity. Good. Maybe next time she'd think to tell him she was going to practice shooting something.

Wolf stayed in the middle of the yard as he approached the barn, letting Cal see him coming.

"Come on in, Pa." The voice came from above Wolf's head.

As his eyes adjusted to the gloom in the barn, he spotted his son standing on the seat of Harvard's wagon. "What are you doing up there?"

"I couldn't see out all the windows from the floor." Cal handed his shotgun to Wolf. "From here, I can watch the front and the back at the same time."

Wolf lifted the boy off the wagon and hugged him close. "Good thinking, Cal. I'm proud of you." He lowered Cal to the floor and ruffled his hair. "Everything's fine. Lizzie's just testing the aim on a revolver. Let's finish getting Paint settled in."

Cal went back to sweeping out the stall, his eagerness sending clouds of dust and straw into the air. Wolf stared back over the land, toward the creek where Lizzie and Harvard remained. He didn't realize he had a death grip on his rifle until his hand started to ache.

• ♥ •

Thunder rumbled from slate-colored clouds on the horizon. "Another storm? I hate storms." Cussing all the way to the house, Lizzie stayed one step ahead of the rain, Harvard hard on her heels. At least it'd held off long enough for them to catch plenty of fish. While she settled on the porch to clean their catch and chop the water roots she'd dug up, Harvard ran for the barn to lend Wolf a hand.

It took longer than it should have to clean the roots, since her right wrist was still tender and weak, but, thanks to the knife Wolf had sharpened for her, she was getting the job done. Lizzie stopped to rest her hand, inhaling the scent of rain and clean land. Now that the thunder had stopped, she found she kind of liked the rain.

Cal clomped up the steps, knocking mud off his boots before he crossed the porch. "What're those?" He crowded close to watch Lizzie clean the mess of roots and cut them into small chunks.

"This is Pickerelweed, that long, fat root there is Cow Lily, and the other is Three-Square. I found them in a little backwater a couple of hundred yards downstream. We'll stew and mash 'em up to go with the fish. They're kinda like potatoes, only they taste a bit different."

Cal wrinkled his nose at the pile of roots. "How different?"

Lizzie mock-threatened Cal with her knife. "Guess you'll have to taste them to find out, swabbie."

"What's a swabbie?"

"The sailor whose job it is to clean the decks." She pointed to the muddy footprints on the porch. "Get to it, or ye'll walk the plank, me bucko."

Cal giggled when she tickled him with an elbow to the ribs, then grabbed the broom and threw water everywhere.

"Hey, you little rascal. Watch where you're slinging that stuff. I don't want to have to rewash all these roots."

"I'm not a rascal, I'm a swabbie." Still, he eased up on the enthusiastic sweeping and managed to get most of the puddles and mud off the wood. "What's next, Miss Lizzie?"

"Make sure there's enough wood for the fire." Lightning flashed and thunder boomed a split second later. Lizzie flinched. "On second thought, help me get these inside."

"What's the matter, Miss Lizzie? Don't you like storms?" Cal dragged out his shirttail and turned it into a basket.

Lizzie shoved the cut roots into his makeshift pouch and snagged the bucket of cleaned fish. "No, I hate them. And don't ask me why, 'cause I truly don't know."

She jumped at the next roll of thunder. "Damnation," she muttered, looking for something to put the roots in to cook. "Cal, fill that big pot with water, please."

"I don't think there's enough in the bucket." He poured in what water there was, then tipped the pot so she could see. "I'll go get some more."

Before she could protest, he skipped out of the house into the rain. "Calvin Richards, you're going to be a challenge while your Pa is gone. I can see that." She shook her head and went to find something to dry him off with.

"Calvin Joseph Richards!" Even Lizzie flinched when Wolf hollered at his son. "What are you doing?"

"Miss Lizzie needs water," came the reply. Thirty seconds later, another boom of thunder heralded a deluge. Harvard ducked through the door, followed closely by Calvin and Wolf. All three were soaked to the skin.

Harvard grabbed a towel from the pile on the table and tossed one to Wolf. "I told you to stay on the porch, but would you listen to me? No."

Wolf fired the cloth at Harvard's chest. "You're just too smart for your own good, you know that?" He laughed when Harvard returned the volley

Lizzie tried to keep her head down, but she couldn't stop herself from looking. Wolf's shirt molded to his body, reminding her of the day before, when he'd come inside without one, water glistening on his...

"Miss Sutter, you're staring." Harvard's teasing whisper came from right beside her ear.

She jumped. "Back off, Saw-bones," she mock threatened, brandishing the knife. "Or you'll need your own services to plug up a hole or two."

Harvard held both hands up in surrender. "Never mind. Sorry I mentioned it."

Wolf watched the byplay from the doorway. When Lizzie glanced his way, he was fighting laughter. She could see his mustache twitch. Embarrassment made her face so hot she should have scorched the roots in her hands.

"I got the water for you." Cal struggled to the fire with a bucket filled to the brim.

"Looks like you got more than just a bucketful, swabbie." She took the heavy bucket from him before he dumped it on his boots. "Go put on some dry clothes, and bring your boots back to dry by the fire," she called after him as he ran for his room.

"I know," he hollered, pushing through the doorway.

"It would be a good idea for you two, as well." Lizzie stared at the fire to keep from looking at Wolf again.

"Yes, ma'am," Harvard teased. "Richards, you got something

dry I could wear?"

Wolf pointed him toward the bedroom. "In the chest at the foot of the bed."

Lizzie dipped water from the bucket into the cooking pot, trying desperately to ignore Wolf, but the closer he came, the harder it was to concentrate.

"It would go faster if you poured it."

"Then I wouldn't have anything to do but look at you."

He stopped close enough for her to feel the heat coming off his big body. "And you don't want to do that?"

"Oh, I do," she fessed up. "But it would only get me in trouble."

"You're probably right, but we could sure have some fun getting there."

Wolf stroked her cheek with the back of his fingers, brushing down her neck toward the open buttons of her shirt. She closed her eyes, relishing the tingle that followed his touch. When he stopped, her lids fluttered up to find him studying her closely, his eyes darkened to the color of a stormy sky. Then he turned to go without saying a word.

Lizzie watched him walk away toward the bedroom, hips rolling beneath cotton. Of all the nerve! How dare he stoke the fire then just waltz away? She glared at his back. *Two can play that game*, she vowed.

The rain kept up the rest of the day, locking them all inside together. Lizzie took advantage of the opportunity and tried to tease Wolf as often as possible without being too obvious. She didn't want Browning to notice

As she served the meal, she made sure she brushed against Wolf's arm as she set down his plate. With the wind blowing hard, the windows had to stay shut. As the still air in the cabin grew warm, Lizzie stood where he could see her lift her shirt to fan a bit of coolness under the fabric. He watched, but gave no indication he was affected.

She even did the most feminine thing she could think of— brushed her hair off her damp neck and tied it back with a piece of rawhide. Nothing. The man was infuriating.

By dusk, Lizzie was ready to scream. Between Wolf ignoring her best efforts and Calvin's constant chatter, she had to get out of the little house, into the air, even if she risked being caught by the next storm.

"A fine meal, Lizzie. I don't believe I've ever had fish better prepared." Harvard gathered plates and carried them to the sink. "Where did you learn to cook like that?"

"Mr. Cornelius Barnstable. He was the cook on The Anna-Carolina."

"What's that?" Cal dropped next to her on the bench and crowded close.

Lizzie shifted away. She didn't want to hurt his feelings, but it was just too hot to touch.

"*She* was my grandfather's ship. I sailed on her for more than eight years. Barnstable finally got tired of all my questions and taught me a few of his secrets." She snagged the last scrap of fish before Harvard cleared away the platter. "This recipe was one of his best." She popped the small bite into her mouth and smacked her lips in appreciation.

Cal laughed and moved closer. "What else could he cook? I'll bet he's the one who taught you to make biscuits, and that's why yours are so good."

"No, he couldn't make decent biscuits to save his skin. His were hard as a clam shell." Lizzie moved away until she was in danger of falling off the bench.

"Like Pa's!" The boy opened his mouth wide and leaned closer to show her. "'At's the toof I a'most bwoke on his."

Wolf saw her squirming and took pity. "Calvin, move over. You don't need to sit on the same foot of wood as Lizzie."

"She don't mind," Cal grumbled as he scooted over an inch. Heaving a sigh, he crossed his arms on the table. "So what are we gonna do, Pa? It's too hot to play games."

Harvard finished washing the last plate and went to toss the wash water out the door. "It's still raining, but the wind has lessened." He propped the door open with a bucket and lifted a couple of windows. "That should cool it off in here without getting us too wet. If you don't mind, I'll stay here a little longer. Perhaps the rain will stop altogether. In the meantime, how about you and I read something, Calvin?"

Cal eyed Harvard with mistrust. "You mean study?"

"No." He ruffled the boy's hair. "I mean *read*. For fun. Where do you keep your books, Richards?"

"They're in my room." Cal led the way. "What do you want to read?"

"Let's see what we have to choose from."

Lizzie tuned Harvard out as he read through all the titles on the shelf. She pretty much knew which ones were there, since she'd perused them herself, just after she arrived. She'd even read one to get through a couple of particularly long nights. But the thought of being stuck inside while Calvin read aloud was more than she could bear.

"I'm going to check on the horses," she announced to no one in particular, and fled.

CHAPTER THIRTEEN

Wolf followed Lizzie to the door and watched her hurry across the open yard, dodging puddles, to disappear inside the barn. He still found it hard to believe that Lizzie had been teasing him all afternoon. On purpose. Of course, he was finding she could do that just by being in the same room.

What was it about her? He'd always thought he knew the type of woman he preferred. Dainty, feminine, totally his opposite, totally female. Emily. But something about Lizzie drew him in ways Emily never did.

From the clothes she wore to her deadly aim with a knife, she did everything possible to make a body think she was a man. She even cussed like one. God knew there was nothing feminine about her, but neither was there a doubt she was female. It was in the way she walked, her laughter when Calvin said something that tickled her, or how she swept her hair away from her heated skin. She was definitely a woman.

And even though she was nothing like his wife, she attracted him like a buck to water on a hot summer day. When she propped her booted feet on the table after a meal, he wanted to pull them into his lap instead. It took all his control not to follow her across the room. Even her rough language and strong will drew him.

And his body's reaction was primal. It was nothing like his desire for Emily, which had always been gentle, shadowed with his need to take care of her. Emily had been fragile, breakable. Lizzie was strong, balancing him in every way. And he realized he liked that about her the most.

"Where did Lizzie run off to? I wanted to thank her again

for the excellent meal."

Wolf moved aside to let Harvard through the door. "She's in the barn. I imagine she needed a little breathing room."

Harvard bit off the end of his cheroot, then struck a match on the clasp of his watch chain. "Not used to company, is she?"

"So it would seem." Wolf looked into the cabin. "Where's Calvin?"

"I sent him to bed." Harvard puffed the cigar to life before putting the match out in a convenient puddle. "He fell asleep against my shoulder halfway through the third chapter." A slow inhale interrupted his words. "Took some convincing, since it's not quite dark out, so I promised you'd finish it for him tomorrow night."

Smoke drifted into the twilight as the men fell into an easy silence. An owl hooted from the woods behind the cabin. For a moment, a cougar was silhouetted against the night sky as it loped over the small rise to the north.

Wolf inhaled the familiar scents. It was good to be home.

Harvard studied the glowing end of his cigar. "Are you certain leaving her alone here with Cal is a good idea?"

He knew his friend meant well, but this wasn't a conversation he wanted to have. Wolf lowered himself to a dry spot on the top step and leaned back against a post. "She can shoot, cook and read. Cal is comfortable with her."

"Several people in town can say the same. Way out here, they will have no one to help if…" Harvard let the words slide, but they still felt like salt in a raw wound.

Wolf rubbed at his neck, stiff and sore from battling five ornery mustangs. "What choice do I have? Should I continue living off charity like I've been doing?"

"It isn't charity for a friend to offer a helping hand." Harvard blew a stream of smoke into the air. "You've done it often enough for me."

"I know, but it doesn't feel right to me. I need to make my own way."

"You always have. No one doubts you will again. That

doesn't mean you need to run off and do it right now."

"I have debts to repay," Wolf ground out through gritted teeth. "After I finally got on my feet here, I swore I'd never again run up a tab at Mercer's store. And the Petersons deserve something for five months of caring for my horses."

"Did Peterson ask you for recompense?" Harvard pushed at Wolf. Hard.

Wolf shook his head. "No, he refused me when I offered. Told me to forget it. But I can't do that." Wolf turned to meet Harvard's gaze. "I can't just pretend I don't owe the man for saving some of my herd, some of the way life was before this hell began."

Wolf leaned his head against the post and closed his eyes. Why was everything so damned hard? "For my own sanity, I have to go. I've got to put what happened behind me, prove to myself I can keep on living. I have to let Emily and Amanda go, and this is the only way I know to get started."

Harvard puffed in silence for a while. "Be sure Lizzie knows I'll take them in without a single question, if she wants someone guarding her back."

"I'll tell her." Wolf studied the horizon before continuing. "I owe you."

Harvard's oath cut through the quiet night. "Damn, but you are one hard-headed son-of-a-bitch." He pulled hard on his cigar, the end glowing brightly with each puff. Wolf knew his friend was angry, but that was too bad. Some things a man just had to do for himself.

When Harvard finally reached the end of his cigar, he crushed it beneath his boot and bent to pick up the butt. "I think I'll take you up on that offer of a bed. I don't want to change a busted wagon wheel in the mud between here and town." Taking out another cheroot, he struck a match and puffed the tobacco to life. "I brought a small bottle of brandy with me. An excellent French vintage." He pulled the liquor from his pocket, then drew out another cigar, offering it to Wolf. "Care to join me?"

• ♥ •

An hour later, the rain finally stopped and Lizzie felt a little more relaxed. It was amazing how far brushing horsehide went toward calming the soul. With the horses settled for the night, she had no reason to remain in the barn, but she couldn't bring herself to go back to the house. She'd never been around a youngster before, and the constant noise and chatter was wearing on her nerves.

She patted Angel's velvet nose and slipped out of the stall. "Now that you look all sleek and beautiful, I think I'll spend some time on me." She sniffed at her clothes. "I need a bath." Before she talked herself out of it, Lizzie grabbed a piece of soap and a large, clean cloth from the pile in the barn and headed for the creek.

She glanced at the house as she passed. The men were lounging on the porch, each holding a glass. A half-empty bottle sat on the porch rail between them. She could smell Harvard's cigar from here. For the first time, Wolf actually looked relaxed, at ease. Unwilling to disturb them, she waved and strolled off into the gathering darkness.

All evidence of the rain was fast disappearing into the sun-dried ground, but she still had to watch her step to keep from slipping in the terra cotta colored mud. The grass growing near the water's edge offered better footing, and felt wonderful beneath her bare feet when she tugged off her boots and socks.

"Ah!" Lizzie wiggled her toes deeper into the damp grass. "One of the simple pleasures of life." Stripping down to the new chemise, she looked back toward the house. "Hope nobody comes looking, 'cause they'll get an eyeful." The finely woven cotton undergarment was just about the fanciest thing she'd ever put next to her skin. Even in the failing light, she could see the dusky color of her nipples. "Sure doesn't leave much to the imagination."

She spread out the rest of her clothes nearby. The trousers and shirt needed washing, after cleaning fish and grooming horses, but that would have to wait. As water-heavy as the air was, it would take too long for them to dry. Laying her revolver on top of the pile, where she could get to it, she waded into the water.

Lizzie angled a few steps upstream toward a small rock outcropping. It wasn't much of a change in height from the rest of the bank, but the jutting stones would block her from view if anyone wandered over from the house. The rushing water had cut away the creek bed here, making a pool deep enough to get all of her wet at the same time.

"Damnation, that's cold." She splashed water over her arms and shoulders to get used to the temperature before lowering herself gingerly beneath the surface. The difference between the water and the steamy air was shocking. Chill-bumps roughed her skin and her nipples hardened to aching points.

Crossing her arms over her breasts to spare them the brunt of the icy water, Lizzie sat on the rocky stream-bed, took a deep breath, then ducked beneath the surface to wet her whole body. Shivering, she rubbed the soap over her skin and hair, dunking again to rinse.

Feeling cleaner than she had in days, she rolled to her back to watch the clouds scudding across the dusky pink and peach colored sky.

Though the sun had dropped below the horizon, she had another hour or so of light. Lizzie closed her eyes and lay still, soaking up the silence. Her hair drifted around her, meandering in lazy circles in the slow current.

Lost in the warm evening air and the chilly water of the stream, she didn't realize she wasn't alone until Wolf scooped her from the water. She opened her mouth to give him a tongue-lashing for scaring the liver out of her, and Wolf crushed his lips over hers. The heady taste of brandy warmed her as his tongue stabbed into her mouth, filling her, demanding a response. And she gave him one, matching him kiss for kiss.

Striding from the stream, Wolf took Lizzie to the ground, his hands rough, desperate. He pinned her in the grass, grinding his erect shaft at the juncture of her thighs without releasing her lips. Lizzie's hands roamed, frenzied. Little mewls of encouragement were coming from her mouth, her very soul. She'd never felt anything like this. She wanted—no, *needed* to go where he was taking her. Had to go. Would die if they didn't get there.

He loosened the buttons of his pants with quick jerks and freed himself from the fabric. Pushing a knee between hers, he slid into place and supported his weight on his arms, towering over her, ready to drive home. She should probably stop him— or at least slow him down—but the only thought she could form was *finally*.

Reaching for his wide shoulders, she fisted her fingers in his shirt and held on tight. Without warning, he stopped, as if her grip had brought reality crashing in on them. Wolf seemed to realize where they were and what he was doing. Shame dulled his feverish eyes. With a curse, he rolled off her and lay on his back.

"What's wrong?" Lizzie shook with unfulfilled desire.

"I'm sorry, Lizzie. I can't... We shouldn't..." Heaving an uneven, disgusted sigh, he covered his eyes with his forearm. "I had no right to attack you like that. You deserve some gentleness. Your first time shouldn't be like this."

Lizzie colored the air blue with her response. Still cursing, she straddled his hips and brought her heated core in contact with his still-exposed shaft, desperate to recapture the feelings that lashed through her when he touched her. "It isn't my first time." His length hardened even more beneath her, caressing her aching flesh until she worried they might strike sparks. Fumbling, nearly frantic, she rose to her knees and tried to impale herself.

Wolf smoothed his hands up her thighs to frame her body at her hips and hold her still. "Easy, girl. Take it easy."

Lizzie didn't want to take it easy. She wanted the aching to stop. Her mind was wrapped in cotton batting, unable to think, to reason beyond the feverish need.

Though his hold was gentle, Wolf refused to cooperate. When she tried again to join their bodies, he rolled, putting her beneath him, and captured her hands.

"Lizzie, stop." He kissed her once, an easy brush of lips, then laid his forehead on hers. "Please, Lizzie-girl. Listen to me."

"No! If I'm not female enough for you, you should have left me in the damn creek!" She wanted to hurl a few more curses at his head, but he eased his full weight onto her and she could barely breathe, let alone talk.

"You gonna hear me out, now?"

She inhaled slowly, planning exactly what she would say before she ran out of breath. He must have guessed, because he leaned in for another kiss. By the time he raised his head, she was seeing stars, and not only from lack of air.

"Still think you aren't female enough to interest me?"

Lizzie shook her head. That small motion had him easing off to lie beside her. The air was cold without him warming her from shoulders to toes. Reaching over her head, he snagged her shirt.

She grabbed at the cloth and covered herself as best she could. Mortified, that's what she was. Utterly and completely mortified. One good look at her less than impressive curves, and Wolf didn't want her anymore. Lizzie closed her eyes against a wave of shame and tried to swallow the lump of failure in her throat.

"Why?" The single word was all she could manage.

Wolf brushed the side of his hand over one distended nipple. "Because you were shivering with cold."

"Not that, you bull-headed stallion." Lizzie smiled a little in spite of her embarrassment. "Why did you stop me? Before, I mean."

"Because you deserve better."

She glared up at him. "I told you it wasn't my first time."

"That has nothing to do with it." He cuddled her closer, sharing his body heat.

Lizzie didn't need warming. The steam coming out her ears could power a locomotive. "Don't make me force you to talk."

Wolf chuckled—and blew the lid right off her temper.

Before he could move, she snatched his belt gun from the holster on his right hip. He went perfectly still when cold steel kissed his temple.

"You really don't want to laugh at me right now."

He blew out a breath, half frustration and half pure outrage. "Put it down, Lizzie."

"Not until—"

He dodged forward and knocked her arm aside at the same instant. Without giving her a chance to recover, he rolled on top of her, pinned her left wrist to the ground, and grabbed her gun hand.

Lizzie came face to face with one purely pissed off male.

"Put it down." Wolf's eyes were flat and cold. She'd pushed too far. She lowered her arm slowly, until she felt grass against her wrist, and eased her fingers off the revolver.

Sweeping up the gun, Wolf rolled to his feet and stuffed it back into his holster. "Get dressed."

He turned his back, allowing her a little privacy, and she didn't waste time. In minutes, she was dressed and standing before him.

"I'm sorry. My temper... Sometimes I don't think, I just act and to hell with the consequences."

He reached out with his left hand and combed his fingers through her hair, easing out a couple of snarls. His right hand stayed where it was, thumb hooked in his gun belt, in front of the revolver. "My stopping had nothing to do with how you look."

She fiddled with a button on his shirt. Wolf lifted her face with gentle fingers under her chin, until she had no choice but to look at him.

"Lizzie, I don't consider you less a woman because of the clothes you wear. Even in trousers, you've had me tied in a knot for hours. Days."

Lizzie fought a feminine surge of triumph. "I meant to."

"I know." He tugged on a lock of hair. "Little hell-cat."

"So why'd you stop? You weren't leading me anywhere I didn't want to go."

Wolf stayed silent, smoothing tangles from her hair.

She started to get mad all over again and turned away rather than start another fight. "Fine. You don't want to say what put you off me, I won't ask again."

Wolf spun her back and kissed her senseless. When he released her, she couldn't remember what she'd asked.

"I stopped, Lizzie-girl, because I don't want a fast coming together with you. When I take you," he paused to kiss her again. "Our first time won't be out in the open with an interruption just over the hill."

"If you hadn't stopped, we'd be done and they'd be none the wiser." Frustration simmered just under the surface, made worse by the rugged man standing so close she could almost taste him with every breath.

Wolf framed her face with his big hands. "Lizzie, why do you want to hurry through it?"

She blushed. Lizzie thought she was beyond embarrassment, but she felt the heat rise in her face. What the hell was she doing, standing here discussing *this* with him? "I don't..." She blew a strand of hair out of her eyes, but it flopped back again. "Just 'cause it isn't my first time doesn't mean I'm what you'd call experienced. I guess I don't know any other way to...uh, to do it than fast."

He smoothed the troublesome lock of hair off her face. "Who was he?"

"None of your damn business." She pulled free and flopped into the grass to stare at the creek. She rubbed at her sore right wrist, still not healed from Black Jack's attentions. Wolf sat behind her and pulled her into the notch between his thighs. She felt the stiff rod of his desire against her buttocks, and she wiggled a little closer, grinning when he moaned under his breath.

"Witch," he whispered close to her ear, nipping at the lobe in retaliation. "Now tell me."

She gave brief consideration to trying for his belt gun again, just to see if she could get it a second time. Wolf captured both wrists and wrapped his arms around her, pinning her hands beneath his. "Don't even think about it."

"I wasn't." She shrugged off his snort of disbelief. "Not seriously, anyway."

Held close in his arms, Lizzie fell silent, hoping he'd let the matter drop. His hold tightened, telling Lizzie he wouldn't.

"You're worse than a starving dog with a ham bone." She tugged at her hands until he released them, and pulled a long blade of onion grass from the ground to chew on. "Why does it matter?"

He lifted her, laying her across his legs and hugging her close. "Because it still pains you."

Lizzie smoothed his mustache and traced his lips with her fingertips. Her breath caught when he nipped her thumb, then eased out on a sigh as he soothed the little sting with his tongue. "How could you tell?"

"You don't want to talk about it and you haven't changed the subject yet."

She feigned a punch to his shoulder. "It hurt once. Not anymore. Not really. Tommy was a sailor. Nineteen, and real handsome. I was thirteen and just figuring out why men and women are made different. Easy prey."

She shrugged away the remembered heartache. "We spent a few frantic minutes together in back of a boat builder's barn down at the wharf." She wrinkled her nose. "I still can't abide the smell of sawdust and pine pitch." Shaking off the thought, she continued.

"Tom fastened his trousers over what was left of my innocence and walked away, leaving me to find my own way home. His ship hauled anchor with the next tide. He's lucky he made it out of the harbor before my brother caught up with him. Will planned to thrash the tar out of him, then stand us up in front of a preacher."

Wolf tucked a strand of hair out of the way behind her ear. "Did you want to marry him?"

"Hell, no. Not after he turned tail and ran away as fast as he could. Damned coward."

He stroked her skin with his thumb, light, teasing touches along her jaw, down her neck. "You never found someone else who captured your heart?"

"I never looked. I was too busy caring for my grandfather. He refused to give up the sea, though being on the water for months was becoming too much for him. That same spring, we were caught a hundred miles off the coast in a major blow. I'd never seen waves that high. It came up so fast. One minute, the sky was blue; the next, we were fighting to keep the ship from getting knocked onto her side."

Lizzie closed her eyes, remembering. "My grandfather was on deck, helping the crew strike sail, when the mizzen snapped. He slipped on the wet deck and couldn't get out of the way. Damn near took his leg at the knee." She toyed with the buttons of Wolf's shirt as the memories flooded in.

"We lost most of the goods we were transporting in the storm. Then Gramps took sick with lung fever before we could make port. Will and I used every bit of money we had saved up just to pay the crew so they wouldn't leave."

She leaned into Wolf's touch as he tugged her closer to his side. "We promoted the first mate to skipper, but after a couple of seasons of too many storms and cargo losses, we had to sell the ship to cover our debts." Lizzie played with the dark hair dusting Wolf's chest so she didn't have to meet his gaze.

"My brother signed on with another ship in order to earn a wage, but no one would take me on as crew. Women aboard ship are bad luck, you know. Whispers started that I was to blame for what happened to my grandfather. Even a few of the sailors I'd known my whole life started to believe it." She tried to laugh, but the pain of that final betrayal hurt too much.

"I stayed ashore with Gramps, tried to make a home for us. We took what money remained from the sale of The Anna-Carolina and bought a run-down tavern on the wharf. Between caring for Gramps and cooking and pulling drinks for the customers, there wasn't time to consider taking on a husband." She shrugged away the could-have-beens. "Hell, the only men I saw were sailors, and I wasn't going to fall for another one who could hoist canvas and disappear over the horizon. Besides, what do I know about being a female?"

Wolf captured her lips and set about showing her just how much she did know. When she finally pushed him away so she could catch her breath, Wolf lifted her right hand and kissed her fingers, one by one, teasing the sensitive skin between them with the tip of his tongue. "You are an incredible woman."

Lizzie slapped at his shoulder. "Now, don't go and spoil everything with fancy talk."

"Not fancy. Truth." He nuzzled her ear. "Was he the only one, then?"

Lizzie frowned. "Only one, what?"

"Your only man."

"No." Why was she sitting here, telling him all about a past she'd rather forget? She tried to get up, but Wolf held her close, ignoring her struggles. With a huff, she subsided, but turned away. "I got needs, just like any other woman."

Wolf cupped and shaped her left breast, teasing the sensitive nipple. "I can see that," he teased.

Lizzie batted at his hand. "Stop it." When he moved to her other breast, she moaned, helpless to resist the feelings he sent through her.

He planted a row of kisses the length of her neck. "Go on."

"I tried again a couple of times, but there was nothing special about a quick tumble with a man in the back room." she finally admitted, a little ashamed. "I figured it must be me."

That brought his head up. "What do you mean?"

"I'm not..." She gathered her pride and lifted her chin to meet his gaze. "I'm just not enough woman to enjoy sex."

Wolf stared at her for two heartbeats, then captured her lips in a searing kiss. He slipped his tongue passed her lips and teased hers into a sensual dance. Releasing her hands to roam where they would, he laid her in the grass and followed her down, stretching her out full-length beneath his weight.

The contrast of the cool earth at her back with the heat of his body sent sparks shooting to her core. She could feel him, from nose to toes, and a shiver shook her, tingling her scalp, tightening her skin.

Wolf must have felt it, too. He deepened the kiss, stroking his tongue over hers and stoking the fire higher. He buried one hand in her hair, combing it out to spread around them in a dark arc. His other hand smoothed up her side, under her shirt, teasing her sensitized skin all the way to her breast.

He cupped the slight weight in his palm, strumming his thumb across her nipple like the string of a fiddle, over and over, until her whole body vibrated in rhythm with the tune he was playing.

Releasing her breast with one last caress, Wolf eased to one side and started on the buttons of her shirt. It was slow-going, since he insisted on touching her, kissing the skin he exposed, tangling the fingers of his other hand in her hair, tugging her lips to meet his again and again.

Lizzie smiled at him and licked her lips, tasting him there. His gray-blue eyes turned molten pewter as his desire flared, making her feel truly beautiful. She went to work on his clothes, anxious to feel him—all of him—against her skin.

"Pa?"

Wolf stilled when Cal called out from the front porch, then dropped his forehead to hers. The exasperated curse he muttered made Lizzie chuckle.

"You tried to warn me," she teased.

Kissing her once more, hard, he rolled to put himself between Lizzie and discovery. Behind his broad shoulders, she buttoned her shirt again, not an easy task when her hands were trembling. Lizzie giggled like a schoolgirl as she struggled to tuck her shirttail into her pants without standing up.

Wolf glanced over his shoulder at her, his eyes the color of pewter, glittering with humor. Just like that, her world, everything went away. There was only him, her—

"Where are you, Pa?"

And Calvin, coming on fast.

• ♥ •

"Over here, Cal, by the creek." Wolf looked at Lizzie once more, sorry to see she was fully clothed. Still, better that than the inevitable questions his son would ask if she wasn't.

Cal dropped into the grass beside Wolf, and flopped onto his back. "What are you doing out here? Counting the stars?"

"Something like that." Behind him, Lizzie snorted with laughter. "You're supposed to be in bed."

"Aw, Pa, it ain't really even dark."

"It's late, son, and tomorrow comes early regardless of how long the evening stretches."

"But I'm not ti—" Cal's declaration was interrupted by a yawn. "—ired, Pa. Honest. I don't want to go to sleep yet."

"Where's Mr. Browning?"

"Snoring in Amanda's bed." Cal wiggled around until he could lay his head on his father's thigh. Wolf lifted him onto his lap and Cal snuggled closer. "Where are you gonna sleep?"

Wolf turned to Lizzie, delighted to see the deep blush color her cheekbones. "Probably in front of the fire. Don't worry, I won't be far."

"Okay." His son yawned once more, and within two breaths was asleep. Lizzie eased closer, until he felt her warmth against his arm. Together, they enjoyed the quiet evening as the cicadas and tree frogs began to sing up the night.

Wolf would have been content to sit there until dawn, but he felt Lizzie shiver. "Ready to go back inside?" He wrapped her hand in his. "You're getting cold."

"I need to take a brush to my hair or I'll have to skin my head come morning."

"I'd be happy to help brush it out." The thought of having his hands in her silky hair had a predictable effect on his body. Wolf shifted a little, trying to get comfortable again without waking Calvin.

"I'd be happy to let you," Lizzie whispered, leaning close

enough to brush a kiss on his jaw. "Need any help getting up?"

Wolf shook his head, tightened his grip on his son, and pushed to his feet. Once she'd gathered all her belongings, he nodded for Lizzie to lead and followed her back to the cabin, enjoying the view every step of the way. The sway of her hips was a siren call. By the time they made it to the porch, Wolf wasn't sure he'd be able to climb the stairs.

Lizzie opened the door and stood aside, staring pointedly below his belt. The little minx knew exactly what she did to him. Wolf elbowed aside the curtain over the doorway and eased Cal back into bed. After pulling the blanket over his shoulders and watching a moment to be sure he still slept, Wolf leaned down to kiss his forehead.

"Are you planning to tuck me in, too?"

"Go to hell, Browning."

Harvard chuckled, a low, friendly sound. "Wish Lizzie pleasant dreams for me."

Wolf slipped behind Lizzie as she sat in the rocker, staring into the fire and working to comb the tangles from her hair. He crowded her into the rocker and captured her lips for a long kiss. "God, woman," he moaned softly. "It's been too long since I did that."

She tweaked his nose and kissed him again. Snagging the brush, Wolf lifted her from the rocker and sat down. Then he settled her on his knees and went to work.

"Mmm." Lizzie leaned into his touch. "That feels so good."

Wolf stroked the length of her hair, then slipped his hand under the heavy mass. His cool fingers against the warm skin of her neck made her shiver. He took advantage and traced the neckline of her shirt, around and down until he found the tight pebble he sought.

Her sigh turned to a soft, breathy moan. Filling his palm with her warm weight, he teased her until she dropped back against him, then slipped a button free and delved beneath the fabric.

"Damnation, your fingers are cold," she hissed, wiggling

away, trying to evade his touch.

"Not for long," he whispered. Refusing to release her soft flesh, Wolf pinned her against his chest and explored until her moans threatened to wake Harvard and Calvin. Easing his hand from her shirt, he retrieved the brush.

"Give me a minute and I can probably sit up."

Wolf pressed her back against his chest. "No need." Dividing her hair, he pulled half forward to drape over her shoulders. With each stroke of the brush, he caressed her breast. By the time her hair was smooth and dry, he was as hard as a fence post between his legs.

Lizzie rolled her hips in a slow circle, stroking his shaft through their clothes. She reached behind her and massaged his hard flesh once, twice, then rose from her seat. A hand on his shoulder told him to wait. She disappeared into the bedroom and came back wearing her nightdress and carrying a quilt. Folding the colorful fabric into a bedroll, she spread it on the floor in front of the fire and held out her hand to him.

Words weren't necessary. He doubted he could say anything coherent anyway. How had she known that he couldn't yet bring himself to take her to the bed he'd shared with Emily?

He eased out of the chair and knelt beside Lizzie. The chance of discovery here was great, but the memories in the bedroom were still too powerful for him to face.

Lizzie wrapped her arms around his neck and kissed him, her tongue sliding past his lips to tangle with his, bringing his attention back to her. He let her lead the way for the moment, enjoying her first foray into the beauty of what could happen between a woman and a man.

When her hands got busy with the buttons of his trousers, Wolf stopped her, holding her away from her goal. He kissed her fingers, one at a time. "Not this time, honey." He teased her palm with the tip of his tongue until she forgot all about protesting. "Tonight is for you."

She threaded her fingers into his hair, fingernails scraping his scalp, awakening feelings he'd forgotten existed. "You don't hear me complaining."

He kissed her quiet. "But I want to show you another way."

She relaxed, letting him take the lead. Wolf skimmed her soft angles with his palm, fingers to jaw, shoulders to knees, and back again. Each time, he came closer to her most feminine curves and the sensitive flesh at the juncture of her thighs.

When he stopped to shape her ribcage, her whole body undulated, trying to get closer, to bring his hand to her breast. He sealed his lips to hers, then gave her what she wanted.

Though he'd touched her there before, teased the rosy center to a hard peak, the softness was a shock. She was so strong, so sure of herself, it was easy to forget she was all woman beneath the clothes she wore.

Lizzie tore her mouth away, gasping for air. "How much more?" she panted, rubbing against him with every breath.

"We're just getting started, baby." He teased his way to the neckline of her nightdress and slipped one tiny button free, then another. Each bit of flesh revealed had to be tasted, savored. Lizzie lost patience and shoved her hands beneath his to finish the task.

Instead of a lover's reprimand, he lifted one breast free of the fabric and relished the gift. When her moans of pleasure threatened to wake Harvard, he covered her mouth with his hand.

Lizzie licked at the skin he offered, nipping until he replaced his hand with his lips and tongue. He explored the soft skin of her neck and throat, returning to lavish attention on her other breast. When he latched onto her nipple, Lizzie's body bowed from the floor. Both hands ran the length of her, testing the strength in her taught muscles.

As much as he wanted to feel all of her against his own naked body, Wolf had to be content with stroking her soft skin, shaping her thighs as he slipped a hand under her nightdress to find her slick heat.

At the first light touch, she arched her hips off the floor, trying to get closer. "Wolf?"

"Shh, baby. I'm right here."

"What are you..." She inhaled sharply. "*Damnation.*"

"Come with me, Lizzie-girl. Come along with me."

He slipped one long finger into the heat that beckoned. With each breath she took, Wolf eased in a bit further, teasing, exploring her riches. He covered her mouth with his and breathed her deep moan into his lungs, stroking sensitive flesh until she pushed against him, seeking more.

She was perfect, searing him with heat, striking a spark to his control. Lizzie kissed him deeply as he set an easy rhythm, stoking the fire until it seared them both, confined, raging to be set free. And still he held to the pace, easing her toward the edge, letting the conflagration consume them both.

He watched the first flutters of her pleasure spark in her beautiful dark eyes. Moving faster, he pushed deeper, driving her to the peak and over, tumbling with her, muffling her cries of completion with his lips.

Breathing hard, it took long minutes before he could force himself to release her. Settling her between him and the fire, he covered her tempting skin and held her close to his chest. He caressed her body, from shoulder to knee, exploring her strong legs and the feminine pitch of her hips, not willing to let her go yet. When his big hand settled over her belly to share the tiny quivers still coursing through her, she threaded her fingers through his.

Neither said a word, comfortable in the silence. The wonder in her eyes told him enough. When she drifted to sleep, Wolf carried Lizzie to the bed and wrapped her in the quilt that still held the scent of their lovemaking.

Leaving her to her dreams, he returned the rocker and waited for the ghosts in his memories to join him.

CHAPTER FOURTEEN

"I'm going hunting."

Wolf made the announcement suddenly, while the three of them cleaned up after breakfast. Harvard had hitched his rented wagon and set off for town at first light.

Cal stopped wiping the table. "When, Pa?"

"I'll head out this morning, once chores are done. You'll need meat to get you through when I go trapping."

"When are you coming back?"

"Tonight, if the hunting's good. Tomorrow, at the latest."

"Oh. Okay." Cal rubbed at a spot on the table. "Can I go with you?"

Wolf ruffled his son's hair. "Not this time. Miss Lizzie needs your help around here."

"Oh." He looked so downcast it was as if he'd been told Christmas wasn't coming this year.

"You want to help me with the horses this morning?"

Cal shrugged without enthusiasm. "I guess so."

"Then get moving, boy. Daylight's wasting." Wolf followed Cal to the barn and set him to work feeding the horses. He put a halter on Midnight and led him out of his stall.

Wolf turned to find Cal staring at him. "Why are you riding that one instead of Scarlett?" He brought a bucket of feed and set it in front of the horse.

Wolf patted Midnight's neck and ran his hand along the smooth hide, checking for scrapes or sores. "He's due to spend some time under a saddle. We don't want him to forget everything I taught him last summer." He kept talking while he brushed the black hide to a gleam. Cal would need to know all this one day. "I also need to know how he'll take to a little shooting. This is a good trip to start him on."

Cal followed Wolf around the horse, patting and stroking as he went, so the big animal would know where he was. "Makes sense to me. And if he doesn't like it, you won't be gone too long." The boy leveled a sidelong glance at Wolf. "Unless he dumps you in the dust, of course."

Cal's giggle turned to a howl of laughter when Wolf swung him off the floor and tickled him.

"What have you been telling Midnight? Huh? Have you been teaching him bad manners?"

"No, Pa." Another peal of laughter made the horse shy. Wolf took two steps away from the big hooves. "I'll tell him to take real good care of you. I promise."

Wolf hugged Cal one last time before setting him on his feet and handing him the reins. "Hold him steady while I check his hooves."

Cal stroked the long, smooth neck. "He sure is a handsome cuss."

"Calvin." Wolf bit back a chuckle. "Where did you hear that?"

"I don't know." Narrow shoulders rose and fell in a shrug. "Maybe one of my friends."

He tried for innocent, but Wolf wasn't buying it. It sounded more like Lizzie, to him. "Well, next time think it through before you just repeat what your *friend* said."

Cal grinned, making Wolf remember seeing himself in a mirror when he was that age. Other than his mother's hair, Cal was just like him. And didn't that promise a few proper dust-ups ahead between them, as it had with Wolf and his father.

Wolf gestured with his chin. "Walk him over to the trough and give him some water. I'll lead out the rest once they're done eating."

"All by myself?" Wearing a smile the size of Texas, Cal chuckled at the horse. "Come on, Midnight. Let's go get you a drink."

Two at a time, Wolf led all the horses out of the barn and set them loose in the corral. When he came back with everything he needed to groom the horses, Lizzie was waiting for him, holding a bundle tied up in red-and-white checked cotton.

"You know, it would have been easier to put the corral next to the barn."

He pulled his hat off and wet his bandana in the trough to wipe the sweat from his face and neck. "Before too much longer, I'm hoping it will be."

Lizzie squinted against the sun to study his face. "The corners of your eyes aren't crinkled up, so you must be serious. Do barns around here get up and move in the night? That's something I'd like to know before you leave."

Wolf laughed as he settled his hat back in place. "No, ma'am, not in my experience." He accepted the bundle and peeked inside. Biscuits, still hot from the oven, steamed around a healthy pile of fried ham. She'd tucked a good-sized portion of jerky in there, as well. "Thank you, Lizzie. You didn't have to go to all this trouble."

"No trouble. Cal asked for biscuits to go with the chili I'm fixing for dinner, so I made some extras. The jerky will hold you over if you can't get back before nightfall. Now tell me about the barn."

"I plan to build a bigger one, over there, on that flat spot beyond the corral." He tucked the food into his saddle bag while she studied the land. "It'll have stalls enough for twenty or thirty horses. Someday."

"Makes sense. Expand the corral to meet it and you'll have a nice set up. Good thinking, Richards."

"Why, thank you, ma'am." He grinned at her teasing tone.

"You look ready to ride."

That sobered him. "I should have been on the trail by now, but I need to groom the horses and muck the stalls and—"

"Cal and I can handle the chores. It might be better if you get going."

Wolf started to argue, to list all the reasons he needed to

stick around a little longer. Cal wasn't ready to let him ride out. He looked for his son and found him walking among the horses, talking softly as he cut out one to begin grooming.

"He'll be fine, Wolf. And you'll be back by tomorrow, at the latest."

Lizzie was right. He knew it. That didn't make it easier to put his foot in the stirrup. Turning away from the temptation to stay, Wolf climbed into the saddle. "I'll be back as soon as I can be." He gathered the lead line of the packhorse, Paint.

"We'll be here." Lizzie stepped away from the big horse.

Wolf guided Midnight to where Cal waited, straddling the top rail of the corral. Wolf caught him in a close hug. "You do what Miss Lizzie asks, you hear me?" Cal nodded, refusing to loosen his grip.

"I'll be back no later than tomorrow, son."

He set Cal back on the corral fence, working hard to ignore the tears shimmering in his blue eyes. "Nothing's going to happen. I swear it."

Wolf tugged on the reins and aimed the horses toward the south, following the creek toward where he'd spotted the deer a few days ago. At the crest of the hill, he glanced back. Cal had his arms around Lizzie's neck. Guilt punched him in the gut. He should stay. He could let the folks in Civil help a while longer.

Even the thought of taking charity, no matter how well intentioned, made him feel like a failure. But what did that matter, compared to his son's happiness?

Wolf looked back once more. Lizzie and Cal were climbing into the corral to start grooming the horses. Something she said made Cal laugh.

He'll be fine, Wolf. Lizzie had made a promise, too, one he knew she planned to keep.

Wolf lifted the reins and bumped Midnight in the ribs. "Git up, horse." Midnight obeyed and Paint came right along, too. With every step the horses took, Wolf prayed he'd be able to keep his promise to his son.

• ♥ •

"Calvin Richards, sit down and eat." Lizzie leaned back in her chair, exasperated. "I won't ask again. You get up again before your plate is empty and I'm feeding your dinner to the crows."

"But Pa might be coming." Cal dragged his feet all the way back to the table. He shoveled in another bite, proving he was hungry, but his head popped up at every sound from outside.

"That was the wind. Eat."

Another bite, another sound. This time, his behind lifted off the bench.

"A hawk. Eat!"

The midday meal had been the same, with Cal leaping to the window every couple of minutes. And all afternoon, through every chore Lizzie could come up with to pass the time and wear the boy out. It was enough to drive a person plumb loco.

Another sound. "That was a horse." Lizzie hid a smile when Cal stayed put this time, intent on finishing his biscuit with honey. She waited until he swallowed the last bite. "Now, go out and help your pa."

Cal's mouth dropped open. "He's here? But I didn't hear nothing."

"Cal? Lizzie?"

"Pa!" The boy's boots barely touched wood as he scampered out the door. "You're home!"

Lizzie followed, a whole lot slower.

"I told you I would be," Wolf agreed, catching him in a hug and spinning in a circle that made them both laugh.

Lizzie approached the loaded packhorse. "Looks like the hunting was good."

"I didn't have to go far, after all. There's enough venison to keep you and Cal fed for a month and to pay back Browning for the straw and feed."

She stroked the weary mustang's cheek and nose, then set to work untying the knots holding the load in place. "I don't see a turkey, though."

"He'll have to settle for a couple of rabbits instead." Wolf grinned. "As long as he can eat it, he won't mind much."

"One less meal at Mrs. Dorsey's?" Lizzie shuddered at the remembered hunk of leathery buffalo swimming in greasy gravy. "No, I'm sure he won't mind." She glanced at Wolf. "You had anything to eat today?"

"Nothing hot," he admitted. "I've made do with the jerky you sent along."

"Go on in and eat. There's plenty of chili. It's in the cast iron pot on the stove."

"It's good, too, Pa. Got enough of them peppers you like to burn a hole clean through your tongue."

Wolf laughed. "Sounds perfect. Let's see to Midnight and get this load off Paint, then I'll take you up on that offer."

Wolf led the horse to the far edge of the porch, under the large nails driven into the ceiling, where Lizzie had suspended the javelina. Wolf had put them there for just that purpose: to string up large game for skinning. Lizzie followed him with the brace of rabbits and two plump Prairie Chickens she found tucked in a saddlebag.

"These will make a nice meal." She set them apart from the rest. "I'll get some water boiling and pluck these before I work on the rabbits."

While Wolf and Calvin took care of the horses, Lizzie gathered everything they would need to skin and dress the game. Nothing would be wasted, not if Lizzie could help it.

"Let me clean up and I'll give you a hand with that."

"Go on and eat. Cal and I can get started here. Calvin," she called across the yard. "Bring yourself over here and let's put that knife you've got to work."

Wolf brought the pot of chili and a spoon to the porch.

"There are clean bowls, Richards." Lizzie scowled at him. The last thing Cal needed was another bad habit to break.

Wolf just shrugged. "Can't see a reason to mess up another dish when I'm going to eat everything in here." He dug into the pot with relish. If his exaggerated moan of pleasure over the first bite was any indication, he approved.

"Thank you, Lizzie." He carefully wiped his mouth and hands with a clean cloth after finishing off the chili. "That was delicious. I sincerely hope you put the last of the javelina in there."

"Tired of wild pig?" She grinned at him without looking up from the bird she was plucking. The pile of feathers at her feet grew quickly.

"Damned right I am," he teased. "Although, I must say you put it to good use. If I hadn't known that was the only meat in the house, I'd have sworn you used fresh beef."

Lizzie smiled. "It's all in the spices. Peppers, salt, some wild onion. I learned a few tricks from Cookie on that trail drive out of Doan's Crossing. I wasn't with the outfit long, but at least I didn't waste what time I had."

"I don't think you ever do." By the puzzled look, Wolf doubted she even recognized her constant need to learn, no matter where she found herself. He rinsed the cook pot with hot water from the bucket heating by the small fire Lizzie had going a dozen or so feet from the house and set it aside. "What do you need me to do first?"

"String up one of the deer. It's too heavy for us. We tried, didn't we, Cal?"

"Yes, ma'am. Durn near slung us both off the porch when it fell back down."

Wolf bent to check the rope tied around the animal's legs. "So that's the thump I heard."

Calvin giggled. "Miss Lizzie said *discreshun* is part of...part of..." He scrunched up his face, thinking hard. "I can't remember what you said."

"Discretion is the better part of valor." She repeated her earlier words.

"Yeah. Whatever that means," he whispered to his father.

"I heard that," Lizzie barked, pitching a handful of feathers at him. "It means a body's gotta know when to quit." She tried to look fierce, but she was laughing too hard at his silliness.

They worked side by side for the rest of the evening. An

hour after the last light of dusk had faded, Wolf sent Cal to wash up. "Time for you to take a bath and get to bed, son."

"But, Pa—"

"No arguments. It'll take you an hour to get clean."

Lizzie stood and stretched her back. "I'll go set a pot of beans to soaking for tomorrow."

She rinsed her hands in the bucket of water Wolf put on the porch for that use, and slipped into the house to give Cal some privacy. Lizzie tossed a palm-full of salt into the pot of beans and water, then cut a small slit in one of the dried hot peppers and threw that in, as well. Through the open window, she could hear splashing water and the quiet conversation between father and son. Good sounds. Normal sounds. They didn't need anyone else to help them get along with living.

So why did knowing that make her heart hurt?

By the time Wolf got the boy bathed and into his nightshirt, Cal was practically asleep standing up. He tucked the boy into bed while Lizzie went back to work on the venison.

Three of the haunches, including the one destined for Harvard were already cleaned and cut into usable hunks, so she hung them in the root cellar to age. Picking up one of the knives Wolf had just sharpened, Lizzie sliced paper-thin strips of meat off the remaining haunch and dropped them into the pot of seasoned brine beside her. An hour in the mix of water, vinegar, molasses, onion and salt, and the jerky would be ready to spread flat on the drying rack Wolf had made of lengths of twine strung on a wooden frame. Two identical racks were already covered in meat from the ribs and shoulders of the animals. Three more waited to be filled.

Wolf closed the cabin door behind him and went to stoke the fire. Logs of damp mesquite made a nice smoky heat that would add its own flavor as the jerky dried. He placed the wood on the side of the fire, not wanting to kick up the flames or scatter ash on the meat.

"This is looking good enough to eat." He rearranged a few of the strips to catch more of the smoke. "I'd try a piece if I had the energy to chew."

Lizzie wiped the sweat from her forehead and upper lip with her sleeve. "We're making good progress."

He studied her face, recognizing fatigue in the slope of her shoulders. "You've done enough for one day, Lizzie. Let me take over."

"I'm not that tired yet," she managed through a yawn. "The more we do now, the less there is to do tomorrow."

Wolf shook his head at her stubbornness, but didn't argue. They still had a ways to go, and doing it now was as good as in the morning. "Is that the last of them?"

"Yes, thank heavens. The rest are hanging in the root cellar."

"I'll take Harvard's portion into town on Sunday. Cal wants to see his friends and I need to let Hannah know I'll be gone." It took him a minute to realize she'd stopped working.

"Who's Hannah?"

"Hannah Weaver. She's a widow, been in Civil for..." He had to stop and think. "Going on eight years, I believe. Hannah and Emily practically grew up together. She moved here to be closer to us."

"I guess she's a good friend of yours."

He nodded, concentrating more on the hide he was stretching than the conversation. "Cal's pretty fond of her, too."

Lizzie got to her feet so fast she knocked over the chair she'd been sitting in. "I need to turn the jerky."

Wolf stared at her ramrod-straight back. If he didn't know better, he'd say she was mad about something. But nothing they'd been discussing should have...

He bent his head over the stretching rack so she wouldn't catch him grinning. *So, Miss Lizzie was the jealous type. Interesting.*

When Lizzie came back on the porch, he kept working like nothing was out of the ordinary. Around midnight he called a halt. "That's enough. The rest will hold."

Lizzie laid out the last of the meat from the brine bucket. At least she didn't seem upset anymore. "Agreed. Do you want to put out the fire, and move the jerky inside for the night?"

"No, I'll sleep out here with the fire." He rubbed at the back of his neck, trying to give sore muscles some ease. "With the bigger fire, the jerky will be done by midday."

"I'll relieve you in a few hours." Lizzie dunked her knife in the bucket of wash water and dried it on a cloth that had started the day clean. "We need fresh wash water."

"I'll get it." Wolf took two buckets to the pump. When he came back, Lizzie had gone into the cabin. She came out a minute later, carrying soap and clean clothes, with a revolver stuffed into the waistband of her pants. "I'm going to wash up in the creek." She glanced up at him from beneath her lashes. "Care to come along and soap some of the parts I can't reach?"

Wolf grabbed her and tugged her close. "Nothing I'd like better, but—"

"You can't leave the fire," she finished for him. She leaned into his strength for just a moment. "I doubt I've got strength to spare for any shenanigans, anyway." Straightening, she lifted her face for a kiss. "If I'm not back in fifteen minutes, come save me from drowning." With a saucy wink, she strode into the darkness.

CHAPTER FIFTEEN

If he didn't go trapping soon, she was going to kill him. Lizzie yanked the pump handle harder than necessary, sending water spurting over the rim of the bucket and onto her boots.

"Damnation!" She jumped out of the way, knocking the bucket over on the way.

"Something bothering you?"

She didn't turn around. If she did, she'd either chew the man up and spit him out, or fall at his feet and beg him to make this horrible, itching *want* go away.

Never in her life had she felt, day in and day out, that she was missing something. Not until that night in front of the fire, when Wolf showed her some of how it could be. That had been days ago and he hadn't touched her since.

No, that wasn't true. He'd touched, smoothing her hair out of her eyes, squeezing her shoulder as he walked past, helping her into the house with a hand at her waist.

A minute ago, he took away the full bucket she carried and his fingers brushed against her wrist and palm. The touch was light, accidental. And just enough to make her want to scream.

"I'm fine," she forced through gritted teeth. Righting the bucket, she filled it again and stomped off toward the garden. Though it had rained like Noah's flood three days earlier, the relentless sun had dried the earth to cracking. If she didn't keep the plants watered, there'd be nothing usable by the end of the week, let alone for canning at the end of the summer.

The few seeds she'd discovered in the root cellar were planted in short rows on the north corner of the house, where the structure would offer the tiny plants a little respite from the afternoon sun. She emptied the bucket at the base of the pepper plants, and stepped out of the way of the run off.

"That ought to do it for today." Wolf approached with two full buckets. "I'm going to check on the primroses."

Lizzie watched him go. She knew his dead wife was the reason he didn't get closer, wouldn't follow through on all the promises made by every touch, but that didn't calm her temper.

"Get back to work, girl," she snarled to herself. "Nothing like sweat and sore muscles to take the starch out of your mad."

A saying to live by, according to her grandfather.

Lizzie glanced to where Calvin worked on the chicken coop—or pretended to work. "Cal, be careful where you're swinging that hammer," she called to him. "You're gonna get hurt."

"I am *not*." He underscored his opinion with a loud bang, followed by several wild swings. The need to yell at him was strong. The boy's mood was darker than a summer thundercloud and he quibbled about every little thing.

Monday, he'd whined about doing his chores. Yesterday, he didn't like her biscuits anymore. This morning, the bacon was too burned. She'd heard *my ma never* a dozen times in the last three days. The longer the week went on, the more fractious he became. She knew he didn't want to stay behind with her. The boy couldn't make it clearer if he walked up to her and shouted in her face.

The fact was enough to fray her already-strained nerves. How the hell were they going to get through six or seven weeks together?

"Where's Pa?"

Cal still carried the big hammer he'd taken from Wolf's tool box.

"He went up the hill to tend your ma's grave."

It was the wrong thing to say. She knew the instant it left her mouth. Cal clenched his fists and his lips flattened until they nearly disappeared. Lizzie faced him, ready to move if he decided to take a swing at her.

"Calvin Richards, don't even consider it."

Lizzie held Cal's gaze with her own. "Stay out of this, Wolf. This is between me and Calvin."

"I won't allow him—"

"I said stay out of it."

"Don't you talk to my pa that way!" Cal lifted the hammer over his shoulder, holding it with both hands, and took a step forward. Threat vibrated in every line of his young body.

"You're mad, Cal, but not at me. You're mad at your pa for leaving you behind, mad at your ma for dying, mad at the whole dang world right now." Lizzie closed the distance, leaning down until they stood nose to nose. "You better learn to control that mad, or it'll get you into real trouble."

She straightened. "Now take a swing if you think you have to. But remember, there are consequences. Make your choice."

For a split second, she thought she'd played it wrong. She braced herself, but Cal dropped the hammer in the dirt and ran for the creek. Wolf made to go after him, but this was something Lizzie had to take care of on her own.

"Stand your ground, Richards."

Wolf stared after his son. "I won't allow him to act that way. He knows better."

"And I'll remind him." She laid a placating hand on Wolf's arm. "But Cal and I have to settle this, or we won't be able to stay here when you head out."

She checked the load in her revolver, in case she ran into critter trouble of the four-legged kind, another thing Cal had to learn to consider. Ramming it back into the modified holster at her waist, she went after the boy, tracking him through the creek and into the woods on the far side of the valley.

Once into the tree line, she could hear him, the sobs loud in the shadowed quiet. "Cal, I'm coming in."

Lizzie spotted him about ten feet away, sitting on the exposed root of an ancient tree. Letting the silence build between them, she found a dry spot on the other side of the massive trunk and settled down to wait him out.

"I'm sorry, Miss Lizzie."

When he started to wipe his nose on his sleeve, she tugged a hankie from her pocket and tossed it to him. "Use this."

Satisfied the weeping was drying up, Lizzie turned to face him, planting her elbows on her knees and leaning close. "You want to explain now or later?"

Cal shrugged, his narrow shoulders still quaking.

"Not good enough, Cal. I know you're sorry, but you gotta tell me for what." She heaved a loud, exaggerated sigh. "I know it isn't an easy thing, admitting when you're wrong, but sometimes, we just have to."

"I didn't mean to yell at you, or start to take a swing at you." His head popped up. "I never would've hit you, Miss Lizzie. Honest."

"I believe you. Any idea why you're so mad at everything?"

"I don't want Pa to go," he whispered, the last breaking on another sob. "What if he don't come back this time?"

Lizzie moved to sit beside him. "Do you really think anything could keep him from coming back for you? He followed you halfway across Texas to bring you home once. Don't you believe he'd do it again?"

"I know, but I don't want to—"

"And there isn't a chance in hell of it happening, Cal. I gave my word to protect you. I never break my word."

"But you still can't shoot good with your gun hand."

She flexed her still-healing right wrist. "My arm is only a little sore, now. True, it still doesn't work as good as it used to." With her left hand, she whipped the revolver out of the holster and cocked it in the blink of an eye. "But this hand works fine." By the stunned admiration in the boy's eyes, he hadn't expected that.

"Wow. Will you teach me to do that?"

Lizzie eased the hammer forward and dropped it back in the holster. "I can do that, as long as your pa doesn't mind." She stood and held out her hand. "You ready to go back?"

"He's gonna be mad at me."

She nodded, squeezing his fingers and winking to reassure

him. "Probably. You'll just have to explain it to him like you did to me. Okay?"

"Yes, ma'am."

Wolf was waiting just out of the trees. Cal gave Lizzie a long, pleading look.

"Uh-uh. Time to own up to what you did and take your medicine."

Heaving a put-upon sigh, Cal trudged the ten or so steps to face his father. He started pleading his case before he got there. "I know, Pa. I shouldn't have lost my temper and I shouldn't have even thought about hitting Miss Lizzie with the hammer even though I never would have done it."

"I'm disappointed, son." Wolf didn't relent, his anger obviously still simmering.

"I'm sorry, Pa." Cal started to kick at the dirt, then stopped and looked straight at Wolf. "I apologized, and I'll learn to control my temper. I promised Miss Lizzie."

Wolf glanced at Lizzie and she nodded, a small movement, just to confirm Cal was being truthful. "That's good, but I don't know yet that it's enough for me. You go on back to the house and finish what you were doing. I have to think on this a while longer."

"Yes, sir." Cal trudged down the hill, hopped across a narrow spot of the creek, and headed for the barn and his remaining chores.

"Do you think I need to punish him?" Wolf tucked a stray strand of hair behind her ear. It took a second for Lizzie to focus on what he said.

"I can't blame him for acting on what we're all feeling. If I had that hammer here, you might be dodging a swing or two right now."

Wolf's grin was slow, sexy, shining in his eyes before his lips curved. "What's the matter, Lizzie-girl?"

"As if you didn't know, you devil." She scraped her fingernails along the front of his trouser buttons. Discovering he wasn't as unaffected as he pretended did her heart good. Pressing a little harder, she massaged the growing ridge again. Then, with a grin and a wink, she ran for the house.

He caught her under a big willow tree and swung her behind the trunk before capturing her mouth in a hard kiss.

Lizzie put up a show of struggling for a heartbeat before melting into his hold, not even caring that she couldn't breathe. She was seeing stars when he finally let her up for air.

"Lord, woman, I've wanted to do that for the longest time."

She punched his shoulder. "Then why the hell didn't you?" Lizzie hit him again. "You've been teasing the wits out of me all week, but you wouldn't come close enough to touch."

"Couldn't," he groaned against her ear. "Cal's been too close. And I didn't think I'd be able to stop. I'm not sure I can now."

Lizzie fisted her hands in his silky black hair. "Damnation, Richards. I don't *want* you to stop." She took the lead, dragging him down for a scorching kiss and wiggling her fingers beneath his waistband.

"Stop. Lizzie, hold up." Wolf was breathing hard. "We have to stop now."

"Hellfire and dam-*nation*!" She dropped her forehead to his chest and concentrated on slowing her heartbeat. She didn't pull her fingers out of his pants until Wolf tugged them free. "I can't go on like this," she admitted in a low voice, more than a little embarrassed.

"Neither can I." He lifted her face and kissed the tip of her nose. "I misjudged how much I want to feel you beneath me."

"Good. I'll go wear Cal out so nothing short of a military tattoo will wake him up tonight." Wolf grinned at her teasing, sending heat clear to her toes.

"We'll be quiet." Wolf tugged her back into his arms. "Lizzie? Are you sure?"

She raked her nails down the stiff evidence of his desire. "Definitely." Swinging her hips, she sashayed off, thinking of all the things she planned to do to the man the second she got the opportunity.

• ♥ •

By the time supper was over, Lizzie felt like a long-tailed coon up a really short tree. Every noise had her jumping. Her skin was so prickly she could barely stand the feel of her clothes. Wolf wasn't helping matters. All through the meal, he took every opportunity to touch her hand, bump her feet with his beneath the table, brush against her when he helped clear the table. He'd driven her nearly crazy.

She tugged a clean chemise over her damp skin. While Wolf and Cal went to the creek to wash up, she'd commandeered the remaining hot water and bathed in the bedroom. Hurrying now, so she didn't get caught half dressed, she slipped on a fresh shirt and trousers. For just an instant she wished for a pretty dress to wear, then snorted at her own foolishness. Wearing a skirt wouldn't change who she was, and Wolf seemed to want her anyway.

Tossing the contents of the bucket out the bedroom window, she returned to the main room and took up the sock she was trying to darn. Even in the dim light of the fire, she knew it was a hideous job. Just this once, she wished she could do some of the things a woman was expected to do. Sure, she could hunt, and clean and cook what she shot, but surely, she was smart enough to learn to sew or embroidery or darn a damned sock!

She cussed an unladylike streak when she stabbed herself with the darning needle for the third time. "Keep it up and maybe the blood will hide the pitiful sewing," she groused.

"Talking to yourself?"

Lizzie jumped a foot. "How the heck do you do that?"

Cal shouldered his way past Wolf. "Pa's the quietest there is. He snuck up on me and Nathan and Miss Rachel, and we were expecting him to be there."

"I'm inclined to believe it." *Who is Rachel?* she mouthed at Wolf. He just shook his head, a sure sign he didn't want to discuss the woman in front of Calvin.

"You gonna finish that book for me tonight, Pa? Mister

Browning promised you would." Cal wandered across the room to look over Lizzie's shoulder. "You're bleeding, Miss Lizzie."

Wolf spun around and crossed the floor in three strides. "Bleeding? What happened?"

Lizzie pulled her hand free. "It's nothing. Me and this needle keep meeting in the middle is all. Ouch!" She bit back another curse when she stuck herself again.

"Ma was real good at stuff like that. She said Grandma showed her how when she was a little girl. Didn't you have anybody to show you?"

She rubbed her smarting finger on her trousers. "Not my mother, that's for sure. One or two sailors taught me to sew on canvas, but those needles are lots bigger. Ouch! *Damnation!*"

Wolf laughed. "I can only imagine what you said when you stabbed yourself with one of those."

"Nothing I can repeat in polite company." She took one more careful stitch before realizing both males watched her closely. "Don't you two have something to do?" She glared at Wolf. "Like maybe a book to read?"

He chuckled, obviously enjoying her embarrassment. He'd pay for that later.

"Why don't you fetch the book, Cal? I'll light a lamp."

They settled close together at the table. "Moby Dick."

Wolf was watching her when Lizzie glanced up, smiling. "One of my favorite stories."

"'Cause it's about sailors, I'll bet." Cal was studying the illustration at the beginning of the chapter.

"That's right. And a really big, boy-eating whale."

Cal giggled. "He's trying to eat the *man*, Miss Lizzie. Not a *boy*."

"Oh, sure he is. I just forgot."

Wolf leafed through the pages briefly. "Where did Mister Browning stop, son?"

"I don't know. The last thing I remember is something about some picture and not being able to tell what it was."

Together they found the spot. Wolf backed up a few pages

and started to read. Lizzie closed her eyes and enjoyed the sound of his voice, rising and falling with the rhythm of the words. She was being truthful when she said the story was a favorite. She'd read it enough times to know it by heart. But she'd never enjoyed it as much as she did now.

"Did I put you to sleep, too?" She jolted when Wolf spoke close to her ear.

She yawned and rolled her neck to ease the stiffness. "I suppose you did. Where's Calvin?"

"Dreaming of whales, no doubt." Wolf nipped at her earlobe, then soothed the spot with the tip of his tongue.

She moaned softly and tilted her head a little more to the side. "Nightmares, more likely. What on earth was Harvard thinking? A whale impaling himself on the mast-heads. Knots of human hair." Lizzie shuddered. "That stuff is guaranteed to disrupt the sleep of the stoutest of constitutions."

"His twisted idea of a joke, probably. Keep Cal awake, keep us apart."

"He wouldn't dare."

"He'd find it amusing to think he might have succeeded, if only for a moment."

"The man is loco." She glanced toward Cal's room. "You're sure he's asleep?"

"Absolutely. Shall I carry you to bed now?"

She tossed the half-darned sock in the direction of her basket and wrapped both arms around his neck to pull him closer. "Only if you're coming with me."

Wolf swept her from the rocker, making her giggle. Then he kissed her, long and deep, and she forgot to breathe. "Put me down and I'll get a blanket."

"Not this time," he whispered, his warm breath raising chill bumps on her skin. "I want you in my bed."

Deciding now was not the time to point out it had been his wife's bed, too, she tugged him down for another kiss.

Six steps had them in the bedroom, where he dumped her on the mattress and followed her down. The ropes creaked with their weight as they rolled and tussled across the wide mattress. Lizzie tried to match him, kiss for kiss, touch for touch, but she could barely think with the things he was doing to her body.

Wolf leaned in for another kiss, half covering her with his body and the ropes groaned like the rigging of a ship in a gale. He pulled her closer and the bed marked the motion, making her giggle. Wolf might be ready to be in this bed, but with Calvin sleeping only a few feet away, Lizzie was afraid of making this much noise.

She gave Wolf a push and turned away from his kiss. "The bed," she managed when he set to work exploring her neck and throat. "The noise."

Wolf stopped mid-nip. His exasperated sigh made her smile. The man didn't like to be interrupted. While he was busy considering, she slipped out from under him and held out a hand to pull him to his feet. Tugging the quilt off the bed, she folded it and tossed it on the floor on the far side of the room. That would keep the bed between them and the door, just in case. Then she launched herself at Wolf and let him take it from there.

Stumbling around the edge of the quilt, he set Lizzie on her feet. She started to lie down, but Wolf stopped her. His big hands skimmed her arms, her shoulders, coming to rest at the neck of her shirt. One by one, he opened buttons, his eyebrows climbing as he uncovered the fancy chemise. "Lizzie-girl, you are always a surprise."

A heated flush warmed her cheeks. This man could embarrass her so easily. "I wore it for you, so you'd best appreciate it."

"I do." He leaned forward and ran the tip of his tongue along the lace edging the bodice. "I definitely do."

Lizzie smiled at him and licked her lips, tasting him there. His blue-gray eyes warmed to pewter as his desire flared, making her feel truly beautiful.

His hands were shaking as he finished with the buttons and eased the shirt off her shoulders. When she reached to return the favor, he captured her hands.

"Slow down, Lizzie-girl. We got all night."

Her breath caught as his fingers traced the same path his tongue had taken, roughing the lace just enough for her to feel it. His tongue returned, teasing her with darting forays under the edge of the fabric, while his hands made short work of her pants. When she stood in nothing but the lacy chemise, he bit down on the end of the ribbon that laced it closed and tugged it free, using only his teeth and that magical tongue.

Never had she felt what she was feeling now. Shivers rippled up and down her skin. Her legs felt weak, her head was spinning. Wolf unlaced the ribbon all the way to her navel, stopping along the way to tease her heated flesh.

When the ribbon finally floated to the floor, she hauled in air to keep from fainting and her breasts lifted clear of the fabric.

Wolf stared. "You are so beautiful."

Lizzie folded in on herself, trying to hide from his heated gaze. By the light of the candle, his eyes looked like melted pewter, running hot and liquid, burning her deep beneath her skin.

Wolf stroked her shoulders, her back, relaxing her. His hands were warm as they slid across her ribs, sliding the chemise out of his way as he went. The fabric tickled her thighs and calves as it fell to a heap on the floor.

This time, when she reached for his buttons, Wolf helped. "I need to feel you, Lizzie," he whispered, adding fuel to the smoldering blaze in her belly. "All of your soft, warm skin." He shrugged out of his shirt and tossed it aside. His trousers quickly followed.

They stepped toward each other at the same moment, Lizzie just as desperate as Wolf. She wrapped her arms around his neck as he gathered her close, one hand in her hair, one shaping her spine until he pressed her against his hardest flesh.

She wasn't sure whether he urged her down or her knees gave out from the onslaught of feeling, but Lizzie found herself stretched out full-length on the quilt with Wolf on top, touching her. His tongue tangled with hers in a kiss hot enough to burn down the house.

Lizzie whimpered, knowing where this was going and wanting to get there faster. Wolf didn't argue. He pushed one knee between hers, urging her to make room for him. When he tested her slick channel, he moaned into her mouth, the sound matching Lizzie's own muffled cry.

"So hot, so ready for me," he whispered, his warm breath adding fuel to the fire of sensation sweeping through Lizzie.

Settling between her thighs, Wolf moved his hips, stroking her with his stiff shaft, then pushed into her burning core.

Lord, the man was big everywhere. Lizzie gasped for air. It was too much. She wasn't ready. But her body took over, weeping, relaxing, and easing his way.

Wolf stopped moving, giving her time to adjust, but she no longer wanted to wait. Wrapping her legs around him, she managed to bring him closer, urging him deeper. He pulled almost all the way out, ripping another moan from her.

"Lizzie?" Concern was etched in every line on his handsome face. "Are you all right?"

"I will be, as soon as you get back where you belong."

His chuckle teased all the way through her. He gently rocked forward, again and again, each time going deeper, until she took all of him, to the hilt. Lizzie breathed his deep moan into her lungs.

He stopped again, pressing his forehead to hers, peppering her face with gentle kisses. "Lizzie." She forced her eyes open at the wonder in his voice. "We fit."

She wiggled a little. "Lord, yes, we certainly do."

"Never before." He lifted his weight to his arms and stroked long and deep, grinding their centers together. "No woman has ever taken all of me."

"Show me," was all her addled brain could come up with. "Now, Wolf."

A sexy grin spread across his face, his lips curving, his eyes sparking fire. "Yes, ma'am." And he started to move.

Every stroke drove her higher, until she thought she'd die of the pleasure. With a little experimenting, Lizzie figured out how to squeeze his shaft, driving the sensations higher for both of them, if his gasp was any indication.

"You like that?" She moved once more, dragging a low moan from Wolf.

"Again," he whispered, the sound hard, forced. He caressed her thighs and behind her knees, curving her legs toward her chest, letting him get deeper. "Do it again." This time it was a demand.

She gasped at the invasion, but not in pain. Lizzie's hips arched on their own as her insides coiled tighter. "Wolf?" A ragged whisper was all she could manage.

"I'm right here, baby. Let go. I won't let you fall."

Taking him at his word, she leaped into the blaze, unable to hold back the cry of pleasure that was torn from her very soul. Wolf's cry came on the heels of hers. His big body quaked, arched into hers as completion ripped through him, dragging her along on the wild, wonderful ride.

He collapsed over her, his weight driving what little air she had left from her lungs. Lizzie didn't care about breathing. She never wanted these feelings to stop. His panting breaths puffed near her ear, warming her. She smoothed one hand the length of his back to the softer skin of his buttocks while the other tangled in his silky hair. She would never get enough of touching it. Touching him. Too soon, he eased out of her and rolled to his side.

Tucking her close to his chest, Wolf laid his head over hers. There were no words to describe... Lizzie found his hand and brought it to her lips, kissing each finger and the center of his palm.

"'Thank you' seems inadequate." She spoke softly, not wanting to shatter the peace in the room.

She felt his smile against her hair. "I was going to say the same thing." He kissed her forehead. "You ready to get off this floor?"

She twisted until she could see his eyes. The silver depths

were warm, brushed with contentment. "You sure you want to be with me in that bed?"

His grip tightened on hers. "How did you know?"

"It stands to reason. She was your wife. You made children in that bed." She swallowed against a knot of envy. "You loved her."

Wolf was silent for a long time. "Emily was—perfect, is the only word that comes to mind."

A stab of hurt pricked her heart. The slice stung all the more because he probably didn't mean the words the way she took them.

"When she agreed to marry me, I thought I finally had it all. Everything I ever wanted."

"You can have that again, Wolf. Another woman will come along who can help build that life for you." Lizzie knew it wouldn't be her. In spite of his tenderness toward her, she wasn't the kind of woman a man thought of marrying.

Wolf got to his feet and lifted her, quilt and all, from the floor. Placing her gently on the bed, he covered her up, kissed her forehead, grabbed his trousers and walked out without saying another word.

"Damnation," she whispered into the empty room.

And the half-formed dream she didn't realize she was building around him burned to ash.

CHAPTER SIXTEEN

Lizzie watched from the shade of the barn as Wolf and Calvin worked side by side in the little garden. Calvin's posture mirrored his father's, hat tipped back, down on one knee, pulling weeds with both hands. They moved alike, the boy a smaller version of his father.

Cal laughed at something Wolf said, then tossed a weed—large clump of dirt and all—at Wolf, hitting him square in the hat. The dusty black felt went flying and Cal took off running, Wolf on his heels.

The man didn't try too hard to catch him as he chased him around the perimeter of the corral. Muscles shifted beneath Wolf's shirt, making her insides clench with need. Lizzie stepped out of sight and leaned against the rough barn wall, breathing like she was the one running.

For three days now, ever since—fool that she was—she'd mentioned the sainted Emily, Wolf had avoided getting near her. Lizzie was close to losing what was left of her mind. The man wound her into a ball of want without even trying, and now, he wouldn't even touch her.

Hearing a shout of laughter, Lizzie stepped into the sun, not wanting to miss the come-uppance. Wolf had Cal dangling over his shoulder like a sack of flour and was heading for the water trough. He didn't stop until water splashed over his boots when Cal's hands batted the surface.

"Stop. Pa. Stop." Cal's laughter broke his words into short chunks. Wolf joined in, the deep rumble rippling up Lizzie's spine like a lover's fingers. She turned away, disgusted with herself. She was getting too attached. If Wolf didn't go soon, she would shoot him and put herself out of her misery.

"Lizzie?"

She blinked her way back to awareness and walked out of the barn, her hand resting on the revolver at her waist. "Right here."

Cal was still head down over Wolf's shoulder. A line of damp was visible halfway up the boy's sleeves and his hair was still dripping. "We're going to church in the morning so Cal can see his friends once more before I leave. Care to join us?"

Lizzie flexed her fingers, trying to work out tension that had nothing to do with her gun hand. "I don't think that would be wise. Best I just stay out of sight until you get back."

"You can come—" Cal started to argue, but subsided with a giggle when Wolf gave him a little shake.

"If you think that's best, we'll abide by your decision." Wolf grabbed one of Cal's wrists and flipped his boots to the ground. "We need to finish up here and get cleaned up. Tomorrow is going to start early."

• ♥ •

Long after the sun set, Lizzie sat on the top rail of the corral, watching the darkness and puffing on her pipe, the stale tobacco smoldering in the carved whalebone bowl. She'd told Wolf she only smoked when she was worrying about something. Tonight, it was him.

"Something wrong?"

Lizzie knew Wolf was there before he spoke, but she wasn't inclined to talk.

"Lizzie?"

"No." She inhaled and blew a stream of smoke into the still evening.

He walked over to lean against the fence, so close his sleeve brushed her hip when he crossed his arms over the rail. "Weather should hold for a few more days."

"Probably."

"Cal's sleeping."

Which meant they were alone. And still, he didn't touch her.

Lizzie wanted to throw back her head and howl at the nearly full moon rising over the horizon.

"Do you need me to pick up anything while I'm in town to-morrow?"

"No."

Wolf huffed out a breath, and the impatience in the sound gave her hope the wanting wasn't all one-sided. "Are you going to talk to me about what's bothering you?"

Lizzie tapped out the tobacco ash from her pipe, watching until the last glow winked out in the dirt. Then she slipped the pipe in her pocket—and launched herself at Wolf.

Their arms and lips met at the same instant. Wolf spun a full circle and pinned her between his big body and the corral rails. Tongues tangled while desperate hands tugged at buttons. He yanked her pants down while she freed his straining erection from his. Lizzie wrapped her legs around his waist and they came together hard, all fire and wild need.

The explosion came fast, first him, then her, leaving them both spent and panting. Wolf loosened his grip so she could breathe and she let out a yelp as tender flesh scraped down rough wooden slats.

He kissed her before she could holler again, then propped one boot on the bottom rail and plopped her on his leg. The feel of well-worn denim against her abraded behind was both pleasure and pain.

"Do I need to kiss it and make it better?" One heavy eyebrow arched and he made as if to look at her backside.

"If you laugh, I swear I'll belt you into next week." Lizzie threatened him with a fist and tried to find mad somewhere in her mind, but there was nothing but satisfaction. "You about drove me crazy! Why'd you wait so damned long?"

Wolf helped her dress, then lifted her to sit on the top fence rail again, this time facing him. He moved between her knees, holding her close enough to pet while he answered her question. "After I left so abruptly the other night... I guess I wasn't sure you'd want me back in your bed."

Try as she might, she couldn't stop the warmth that flooded her face at his plain talk. The mad she'd been searching for earlier, flared. "So instead of asking me, you decided the best thing was to avoid touching me all together." She combed her fingers into his hair, grabbed a silky handful, and yanked.

"Ow! That hurts, woman."

"Good." She dragged his mouth to hers for a kiss. "Don't ever try to think for me again. Ask, dammit."

His mustache tickled her lip when he grinned. "Yes, ma'am."

They passed a pleasant hour, talking softly, touching whatever part of each other they could reach, and kissing often.

"I suppose I should check on Calvin and call it a night. You coming?"

In answer, Lizzie wrapped one arm around his neck and let him carry her back to the house and straight into the bedroom. By the time he checked on Cal and got back, she was lying naked beneath the quilt. Without a word, Wolf undressed and joined her.

CHAPTER SEVENTEEN

"Cal, what's gotten into you?"

"I hate her!"

The shout bounced off the walls and set a match to Wolf's temper. "Mind your manners, boy."

"She ain't my ma, and I'm not staying with her!"

Cal threw the door open with a bang and ran for the barn.

Wolf started after him. "Calvin Richards! Come back here and apologize."

"Let him go." Lizzie turned back to the sink and poured hot water into the dishpan.

"He can't talk to you like that."

She calmly shaved soap into the steaming water, acting like nothing out of the ordinary had happened. "Just this once won't hurt."

"No, I won't allow it." Wolf reached behind the door for his holster. "What the hell got into him? I thought we'd gotten past all that the other night."

Lizzie glanced out the window, like she was watching Cal. The first rays of the rising sun warmed her skin, making him wish for another hour alone with her.

"I've been expecting it."

Wolf glanced up from tightening his gun belt, surprised. "Why? I thought he liked you."

"He likes me fine." She grabbed a cloth and plunged it into the dishpan. "But he'd rather be with his father."

This feeling of frustration and failure was becoming familiar. He checked the load in both belt guns, the motions automatic. "I'll talk to him. He can't come with me."

"He knows that, Wolf, but knowing doesn't stop the wanting. Give him a few minutes to cry it out in private. No man likes to cry where others can see. Not even a half grown one."

Remembering how he'd leaned on Lizzie when his own grief became too much did nothing to improve his mood. She was wrong, though: most times, a man would rather not cry at all.

Settling his hat in place, he went in search of Cal. He found him in the barn, throwing hay around with angry abandon.

"Son?"

"I don't want to stay here with her." He stabbed the pitchfork into the pile of straw and heaved it toward a horse.

"Enough!" Wolf crossed the barn in four strides and snatched the pitchfork out of his hands. "You're going to hurt one of the horses."

"No, I won't!" He turned on his father, fisting his small hands on narrow hips. "I'm not a baby. I know how to muck out a damned stall."

Wolf didn't say a word, just raised one eyebrow and waited. There were tears on Cal's cheeks and his shoulders heaved with righteous anger. His manhood had been called into question and his pride pricked. It took longer than Wolf liked, but finally the boy calmed enough to realize what he was doing: facing down a grown man—his father—with fighting on his mind.

"You ready to talk, now?" Wolf put the hay fork back in its place on the far wall. No need to embarrass the boy further by watching while he took the measure of the slice of humble pie he had to eat.

When Wolf turned around, Cal was waiting.

"I'm sorry I lost my temper, Pa."

"I appreciate you saying so, son, but the apology has to be made to Miss Lizzie."

Cal kicked at a pile of dirty straw. "I know."

Wolf hunkered down so he was on eye level with Cal. "You know I can't take you with me, son. Not this time."

"But I can ride all day now, Pa. I won't slow you down, I swear."

"That won't be enough, Cal. I'll be in the saddle from dawn to dusk for nearly a week just to get where I'm going. You're growing up fast, son, and your leg is healing fine, but you aren't ready to make this trip."

"I hate being a little kid."

"I didn't say you were a kid, Cal. Someone has to be here to help Miss Lizzie. She's still hurting, and she can't do everything around here that needs doing. I'm counting on you to take care of her while I'm gone."

The boy's blue eyes met his while he considered Wolf's words. "She does need me, don't she, Pa?"

"She'd never admit to it, but, yeah, she does."

Cal's chin went up. "I can take care of her. You won't have to worry at all."

Wolf squeezed his son's shoulder. "I'm much obliged." Straightening, he pulled Cal into a quick hug. "I love you, son. More than you can ever know. Now go make it up to Miss Lizzie. Waiting won't make it easier. I'll be right here."

"Yes, sir."

Wolf watched him go, footsteps dragging all the way. The boy was becoming a man faster than he realized. "I wish Emily was here to see it." Accepting the stab of pain, he led Scarlett from her stall. "Come on, girl. Let's get you saddled. We've got a long way to go."

In truth, he should have been gone before first light, but he'd had a hard time making himself leave Lizzie. He turned to look toward the house. Had Cal heard them? Was that what set him off again?

He picked up the brush and started grooming Scarlett. Lizzie was something special. He'd never laughed while making love to a woman before. Hell, he hardly ever laughed, period. But she had a way about her. Tough as nails on the outside, soft as moonlight on the inside. Nothing at all like Emily.

Wolf shook out the saddle blanket and tossed it onto Scarlett's back. He still loved Emily—probably always would—but being with Lizzie had eased the hurt. Knowing his son would be safe with her while he worked to get them back on their feet helped, too.

"Pa?"

Wolf glanced at his son. "Did you talk with Miss Lizzie?"

"Yes, sir. She accepted my apology and said we'd start fresh from here." He walked over to Scarlett. "You're almost ready to go."

"I need to get on the trail, Cal. The sooner I get started, the sooner I'll be home again." He lifted the saddle into place and tightened the cinch straps. "You want to take her up to the porch for me?"

Cal shrugged. "I guess so."

Wolf swung him into the saddle and handed him the reins. Cal stared in shock. "You mean I get to ride her over there? By myself?"

"You're old enough to handle her. Just go easy, since you don't have stirrups. It's a long way to the ground from up there."

"I'll be careful." Cal took hold of the saddle horn and lifted the reins. "Get up, Scarlett."

"Give her a little water on the way," he called after Cal before leading Smoke from his stall.

In just a few minutes, he had the tall gray gelding groomed and the pack saddle secured. Wolf took a last look around the barn, just to be sure nothing needed doing before he left, then led Smoke to the house where Scarlett stood. Cal was still on her back, but the reins were looped twice around the porch rail. Lizzie had carried his saddlebags to the porch and stood beside Scarlett, praising Cal on his horsemanship.

"I think he'll be riding Midnight before long. Don't you agree, Wolf?"

Wolf plucked Cal from the saddle and carried him to the porch. "Probably." Swapping boy for saddlebags, he tied his gear on then took his rifle from Lizzie and secured it in the scabbard. He had plenty of extra ammunition in the satchel on Smoke's saddle, along with his traps, leather thongs and anything else he thought he might need. At the last minute, he added two extra blankets. This late in the season, he might have to go higher in the mountains to find game. Though it was still hot in the foothills during the day, nights could get cold enough to snow.

"This should keep you." Lizzie handed him a bulging leather bag. When he opened the heavy pouch to check the contents, the rich scent of roasted venison made his mouth water. Beneath the oilcloth-wrapped meat he found beans, bacon, ground coffee and salt. "Thank you." The fewer nights he had to stop early to hunt and cook, the more ground he could cover.

"The venison should hold you for three or four days, anyway." She watched him stow the provisions. "Which way are you heading?"

"I'll follow the Canadian River west, toward the Turkey Mountains, over in New Mexico Territory. There's good grazing land there. If the trapping isn't good, I can at least bring down a couple of buffalo and elk, though I hate the thought of wasting meat just to get hides."

"That's a long way to ride for furs."

He nodded. "If I see sign of game closer, I'll follow it, but I don't expect to be that lucky, with summer almost here."

Cal played with Scarlett's reins, bending and twisting the leather. "When will you be home, Pa?"

Wolf checked the knots holding everything to the saddles one last time. "It'll take the better part of two weeks just to get there and back. Don't look for me much before the first of July."

"You'll be back for my birthday, won't you?" Cal stared up at him with eyes so like Emily's Wolf almost couldn't bear it.

Wolf ruffled his hair. "I haven't missed one yet." Giving Cal a hug, he swung into the saddle. "You take care of each other, now. And if you need anything, remember Harvard offered."

Lizzie scoffed at his concern. "Would you quit fussing? We'll be right here when you get back. Now get going."

Lizzie climbed the steps and held out a hand for Cal to join her. Turning Scarlett in a tight circle, Wolf headed toward the river. When he crested the first hill and glanced back, a shiver wormed its way down his spine, making him queasy.

Lizzie and Cal stood side by side on the porch, waving, exactly as Emily and the kids had last fall, when he rode away and lost nearly everything he loved.

CHAPTER EIGHTEEN

Harvard leaned against the frame of his office window, staring out at the river sparkling in the late morning sun. This view would be better from the second floor, but it made no sense to heat the upper floor through the winter when only two of the rooms would be used. Unless he decided to bring in girls to use the other rooms, which would also bring in money. The account book lay open on his desk behind him. He'd been working since before dawn. All the income and expenses had been entered, but he needed a break before trying to add the columns of figures, hoping they came out in his favor.

He reached for the teapot on the nearby table and refilled his cup. The bone and gold-gilded china was delicate for a man, as Wolf reminded him every time the man had to use the stuff, but Harvard still enjoyed the finer things in life. And using the china, crystal and silver never let him forget where he came from. And whom he'd left behind.

Returning to the view, Harvard sipped the tea and watched the glow on the eastern horizon expand. Steam curled up from the cup, obscuring the view. Or maybe it was just his tired eyes. He hadn't been able to sleep with Black Jack's threat replaying in his mind.

I can get another bottle where I found the first.

Lizzie and Calvin were not safe, no matter how good a shot she was. Black Jack would charm her into hesitating, just for a moment, but it would be enough.

"Mr. Browning."

The knock on the locked saloon door came simultaneously with the voice, startling Harvard. Tea sloshed out of his cup, burned his hand and dripped onto his boot. What the hell was *she* doing here this early?

Setting his cup out of sight on the desk, Harvard tugged a handkerchief from his pocket and wiped his hand on the way to the door. If that woman insisted on disturbing him, she could damn well wait.

For a split second, he considered answering the door without his suit coat, but the moment of enjoyment he would gain from the slight wasn't worth the antagonism. He refused to greet her with a smile, however.

Swinging open the door, he crossed his arms and planted himself in the doorway. "What do you want, Mrs. Freeman?" He hesitated when he realized she wasn't alone. "Mrs. Weaver. What a surprise."

"We must speak with you." Millicent stepped forward, forcing Harvard to give way.

Behaving like the gentleman he'd been raised to be, Harvard motioned for them to enter. "I was just having some tea in my office. May I offer you ladies a cup?"

"Thank you, Mr. Browning," Hannah Weaver spoke before Millicent had a chance to decline. "Tea would be very welcome. Mrs. Freeman got me out of the house before I could brew my own."

While they seated themselves, Harvard dusted out two more cups and saucers, and carried the pot to Hannah. Her movements were graceful as she spooned a bit of sugar into her cup, filled it with the steaming liquid, and then topped his cup after Millicent declined.

"Thank you, Mrs. Weaver." Harvard settled back in his chair. "What brings you ladies here so early this morning?"

"I understand Elizabeth Sutter is staying at the Richards place."

Harvard stared at Millicent. How the hell had she found that out so fast?

Millicent's hands fisted in her lap. "You don't deny it."

He sipped at his tea, deciding how much to say. "You never

cease to amaze me, Millicent. I doubt Wolf has been gone more than an hour, but you already know he left Calvin behind. How?"

"My source doesn't matter."

"It does if you want my help." He smiled. "I assume that's why you're here."

"It's unacceptable for the Richards boy to live out there with Miss Sutter."

"Why? She isn't going to do anything to put him in danger."

"Just staying in that home is unsafe. I would have thought the unfortunate loss of his wife and daughter would have convinced Mister Richards of that."

In that moment, Harvard hated Millicent Freeman.

"Calvin doesn't want to come to town. He's afraid he'll be forced to stay with..." He hesitated to voice the reason.

"With me," Millicent finished for him. "You needn't try to spare my feelings, Mr. Browning. I'm well aware I frighten the boy. Never having been a mother, I seem to lack some of the instincts required to make children comfortable."

Harvard felt hips lips twitch with a grin. "I imagine it has more to do with your insistence that he bathe daily than your motherly instincts, Millicent. He is a boy, after all."

The older woman nodded. "I'll have to remember that."

"Mr. Browning. Harvard." Hannah leaned forward in her chair. "Why didn't Wolf ask me to take Calvin in?"

He set his tea on the table at his elbow, then reached for her hand. "I think he's afraid people will get the idea there's a future for you and him. Perhaps, that you'll get that idea."

"I see." Hannah closed her green eyes, trying to hide her feelings, but the tightening of her fingers in his told him how right Wolf was. Hannah was in love with him.

"I'm sorry, Hannah."

"No, that's all right. I should have realized Wolf will never get over Emily."

Harvard wasn't certain that was entirely true, after seeing him with Lizzie, but he wasn't about to say anything to the women. He gave Hannah's fingers a gentle squeeze and released her hand. "You still haven't told me what you plan to do?"

The frown on Millicent's face made it obvious she'd had plans that included Wolf and Hannah, as well. But, to her credit, she didn't pursue the topic. "I've spoken with the members of the Ladies League and we are all in agreement. Elizabeth and young Calvin need to be brought into Civil. Mrs. Weaver has offered to take them in."

"She won't come." Harvard was certain of that.

"She will have no choice. According to the sheriff, they are not safe where they are."

"On that, we agree." Harvard rose to pace the room. "I had a run-in with Black Jack last evening. I took one of his comments to be a veiled threat against Lizzie."

"Do you believe he knows where she is?" Millicent stood when Harvard nodded. "There is no time to waste."

"How are you going to convince her you're right?"

Millicent smiled—and it wasn't a pleasant sight. Harvard waited, but Millicent refused to elaborate. "Perhaps it would be best if I ride out and talk with Miss—"

"I will accompany you." Millicent stood. "Between us, I'm certain she can be made to understand the wisest course of action is to move into town."

"At least until Wolf returns and—"

"At which time," Millicent interrupted, "the boy will, of course, be allowed to go home. It is entirely out of the question for a young woman to live with an unmarried man and his son, no matter *how* innocent you believe it to be."

He rose to face her. "No one knows Lizzie is a female but the three of us, Wolf and Calvin."

"That state of affairs will be remedied the instant she moves into town."

Harvard glared at Millicent. "I'm certain Miss Sutter has a good reason to keep her identity secret. We have no right—"

"She gave her word. That gives *me* the right." She held up one gloved hand to stop his protest. "There is no purpose in continuing this discussion. Miss Sutter will agree. I am on my way to the livery to hire a buggy. If you wish to accompany me, Mr. Browning, you may do so, but I'm leaving now."

Hannah's eyes offered an eloquent apology. "I'll go home and get ready for company." She held out her right hand to Harvard. "Please tell Lizzie I'm looking forward to meeting her, and having her and Calvin as my guests."

"I'll do that, Mrs. Weaver." Harvard escorted the women to the door. "I'm sure it will relieve her greatly to know she will be made welcome."

• ♥ •

"Remember, the ace can be a high card or a low card. Depends on where you need it."

Calvin laid his two cards down, counted on his fingers, and picked them back up to be sure he saw them right. "If I have it as my high one, that counts eleven, right?" His lips moved as he recounted his hand. "That's too many. I think."

"Then count it as one point and ask for another card. You want to get close to twenty-one, but not go over. Remember, though." She hesitated before dealing. "If you have more than fifteen points, another card will probably be too many."

Calvin huffed in frustration. "I don't understand."

"Didn't I tell you studying your figures in school was important?" Lizzie folded her own cards and set them aside. "Let's have a look at what you have. We won't count this hand."

Calvin turned over a black jack, followed by an ace of hearts.

A shiver ran her spine at the reminder of her attacker. "That's twenty-one. You would have won, boy." Lizzie learned across the table and slapped his shoulder.

"Durn it!" Cal shoved his chin forward in a pout. "We didn't count that one."

"That's all right. We'll just deal again." She gathered the cards and started to shuffle. "We're just practicing, anyway."

"But if I win, you're gathering the eggs tomorrow, right?"

Lizzie laughed at the hope in his eyes. "And if you lose, you wash *and* dry the dishes all day."

Cal straightened in his seat. "I'm gonna win this time."

"Don't count on it, swabbie. I'm pretty good at this *poque* stuff, too."

"What's *poque*?" Cal picked up his cards, one at a time, and started adding, his lips forming the numbers so clearly Lizzie didn't even have to see her hand to bet.

"It's a fancy French term for poker. At least, that's what the sailor told me when he taught me to play." She laid the home-made deck of cards aside and glanced at the two she'd dealt herself.

"Those sailors sure taught you lots of stuff."

"There wasn't much else to do once my chores were done. Or when the wind quit blowing. What you gonna do?"

"I'll take…uh…one more. I think."

She bit back a chuckle and dealt Cal another card. "I'll hold on these. Show your hand."

Cal turned over a king, a ten, and seven.

"Twenty-seven is six too many." She flipped over her hand. "Nineteen for the dealer. I win, and you have to wash the supper dishes."

The sound of an approaching buggy drowned out his automatic complaint. Lizzie was on her feet and across the room in a heartbeat, revolver drawn and ready. "Somebody in a one-horse buggy. I think that's the doc driving. Who's riding with him?"

Cal peeked around the frame of a window across the room. "Mrs. Freeman." He shrank back a step and sidled closer to Lizzie. "What's *she* doing here?"

"Let's go out and ask her. Then we'll both know."

Lizzie holstered her revolver as she opened the door. "Afternoon, Mrs. Freeman. Browning. A little hot for a social call, isn't it?"

"We would have been here sooner if Mr. Browning wasn't so particular about the conveyance we procured."

"Now, Millicent, I would have been remiss if I'd brought you out here in something that might not make the return trip."

"There was nothing wrong with that wagon and you know it, Mr. Browning. You were intentionally delaying us, hoping I would change my mind about coming."

After sorting through the fancy talk, Lizzie figured out Harvard had kept Millicent away as long as he could.

Millicent waited while Harvard tied the horse to a porch post and came around to help her climb down. She brushed some of the dust from her dress before pinning Lizzie with a glare.

Damnation. "Who told you I was here?"

"That doesn't matter."

"It does to me."

"May we come in?" Without waiting for an invitation, Millicent mounted the steps and swept through the door, coming to a halt just over the threshold. "What is going on here?"

"Poker," Lizzie snapped back. "What does it look like?"

"You're teaching this child to gamble?"

Lizzie squeezed past her and gathered up the cards. "What's the harm? It isn't easy to be good at poker. It's an important skill for a man to know. Passes the time and puts you in places to pick up valuable information. The kind that can save your life." She slid the cards into a leather pouch and laid it on the mantel. "Besides, it keeps his mind working. Consider it schooling in adding and subtracting."

Millicent looked like she'd gotten a whiff of something dead. "It will take him into saloons and houses of ill-repute!"

"Beats the hell out of playing solitaire and drinking alone," Lizzie retorted, thinking of the night she met Wolf.

Millicent's mouth opened and closed like a freshly landed trout. "I will thank you to mind your language. There is a child present."

The barb stung. Lizzie had forgotten Calvin was sticking to her heels like weeds to a fence line, soaking up every word she said. "You're right, Mrs. Freeman. I apologize for my outburst. Calvin," she shot him a glare. "Don't repeat what I said until you're nineteen. Now what can I do for you two? I don't think you came all the way out here to remind me how to talk in front of a boy."

Millicent reached up and removed two pins the length of Lizzie's arm from her hat. "I understand Mr. Richards is gone."

Lizzie nodded, not sure where Millicent was heading. "He rode out this morning for the Turkey Mountains. Plans to be back by July fourth."

Next Millicent lifted the feathered creation off her fancy hair. "And he left you in charge."

That was too obvious to need a response.

"I'm sorry, Elizabeth, but it simply isn't proper for you to be out here alone with this boy."

"His name is Calvin, and Wolf hired me to be here."

Millicent laid the hat on the table and faced Lizzie. "Nevertheless, you cannot remain. I forbid it. It isn't safe. The only appropriate action available is to move into town until Mr. Richards returns."

"Can't do that, Mrs. Freeman." Lizzie flopped into a chair. "I promised Wolf we'd stay right here." She pointed at the floor to emphasize her words.

"Miss Sutter," Millicent started in.

"No."

"You must listen—"

"Hell, no."

"Elizab—"

Lizzie jumped to her feet. "God. Damn. Hell. No!"

"Elizabeth Ann Sutter, be quiet."

Lizzie's voice finally failed her. "How did you..." She had to swallow a couple of times before she could continue. "How did you know my full name?"

"A lucky guess," Millicent admitted with a shrug. "Now be quiet, and listen to me."

Lizzie could feel her temper heating up for another blow. Evidently, so could Millicent.

"If you interrupt again, I will simply take Calvin into town and wire his grandparents to come for him."

"No! Don't let her do that, Miss Lizzie."

The very real fear in the boy's voice tossed Lizzie's anger into an icy stream. She gathered Cal under one arm and tucked him close to her side. Her other hand was curled into a fist at her side. "I won't, Cal. I promise." Lizzie turned a glare on Millicent. "I'm listening."

"Thank you." Millicent seated herself in the rocker before continuing. "Your presence here is known. If no one was aware of your gender, the issue would not raise a single eyebrow." Millicent glanced at Calvin. "But several people in town are aware."

"More than this time yesterday," Harvard muttered.

Millicent glared at him a moment before shifting her attention back to Calvin. "Are they not, Master Richards?"

The boy squirmed under her scrutiny. Suspicion bloomed when Lizzie tried to catch his eye, but he refused to look at her.

"Cal?" Lizzie knelt in front of him and waited until he met her gaze. "Do you know what she means?"

"I didn't tell anyone," he denied, then dropped his chin to his chest. "'Cept Raymond." The admission was barely a whisper.

Lizzie dropped to one knee and turned him to face her, her hands gentle despite their slight shaking. "Tell me."

He met her eyes for an instant before returning his gaze to the floor. "Me and Raymond were just talking about Pa leaving and me coming back to school, and it sorta slipped out. I didn't mean to tell." He picked at a button on his shirt. "I'm sorry."

She swallowed the curse that crowded the back of her teeth. "What's done is done. I know you didn't intend to cause any trouble." She hugged him close and chucked him under the chin just to see him smile, before standing to face Millicent. "Spit it out, Mrs. Freeman."

"Beyond the probability of the scandal that is bound to follow when news of you living in Wolf Richards's home reaches the community, there is the problem of Black Jack Hayes."

Lizzie dropped into a chair, rubbing at the tense muscles of her neck. Cal stuck to her side like a burr.

"What does that bad man have to do with them knowing you're here, Miss Lizzie?"

"He and I had a bit of a disagreement, that's all."

"After he hurt you so bad?"

"Before." Lizzie tried to smile a little reassurance. "Nothing for you to worry about."

Harvard shifted, just enough to draw her attention. "He threatened you last night."

Lizzie rose slowly to her feet and planted her fists on the table. "What did you say?" She leaned forward and pinned Harvard with an icy stare. "Nobody gets away with threatening me, I don't care who—"

"Quiet, Elizabeth."

Lizzie shut up, but stayed on her feet, glaring at Millicent. The woman didn't even glance her way. "Continue, Mr. Browning."

"Hayes and his two enforcers were waiting in front of the Star when I passed on my way to dinner, supposedly hoping to buy a bottle of whiskey. The excuse didn't wash, since he bought one four days ago and he never drinks that much. He hates being out of control."

Millicent's brows furrowed. "Could the two ruffians who work for him have finished it?"

"They'd be dead if they did. He doesn't share anything he considers his." Harvard tapped his index finger on the tabletop, considering. "Maybe I'm reading too much into it, but Hayes made a comment about Carter and Spears finishing a bottle they'd *acquired* recently." He met Lizzie's gaze. "I think he meant the one they stole from your pack. Hayes said he would just get another from the same source. He knows you're here."

"He can't be sure—"

"Can you take the chance?" Harvard fell silent, waiting.

"You cannot possibly remain here, now. It's too dangerous." Millicent rose to pace the room. "I warned you that your decision to play cards with Black Jack Hayes was unwise. It only made matters worse when you defeated him. It doesn't matter that the game was fair. He is a very bad enemy, Elizabeth, totally unscrupulous. Don't think the fact that you are a woman will stop him. You'll only put young Calvin in danger."

"I can keep him safe."

"Not from Hayes." Harvard threw his support behind Millicent. "He never travels alone, and he never plays fair. You're good, Lizzie, but not that good."

"Damnation," Lizzie muttered under her breath. She knew Millicent was right. If she knew Lizzie was here alone with Calvin, so did Black Jack.

She tossed out the only reasonable argument she had left. "What about Wolf? He expects us to be here when he gets back. I gave him my promise. He shouldn't come home and find the house empty again."

Cal whimpered and Lizzie pulled him into her lap, rocking him gently. "I'm sorry, baby." She rubbed his back as he burrowed closer. "I know how much hearing that makes you hurt." She hugged him close before looking up at Millicent. "And what am I going to do about Wolf's horses? We can't leave them to fend for themselves." Lizzie gazed out the window at the small herd relaxing in the sunshine of the corral.

"Zeke Williams might be willing to look after them," Harvard offered after a moment's consideration. "He isn't much for human company, but he's good with animals and can be trusted. He could keep an eye on the place until Wolf gets back."

Lizzie felt Cal squirm and loosened her hold. "Would he be willing to leave his own work?"

"Zeke doesn't have steady work," Harvard hedged.

"Mr. Williams is a vagabond," Millicent broke in, "a shiftless drifter, a drunken—"

"That's not fair, Mrs. Freeman." Harvard faced her straight on. "Zeke may be unable to ride a horse and herd cattle any longer, but he's a decent man and doesn't deserve your condemnation."

"He's an old cattleman?" Lizzie watched the exchange with interest. Harvard was the first person she'd seen stand up to

242 ♥ Tracy Garrett

Millicent Freeman.

Harvard nodded. "He rode for the Rocking Falls Ranch, south of here, for more than twenty years, and was responsible for all their saddle mounts for another ten. And he's handy with a gun…should it come to that."

"Why isn't he with the Rocking Falls any longer?"

Millicent arched one eyebrow as if daring Harvard to be honest.

"He developed a taste for whiskey," Harvard confessed.

"Does he drink when he's working for somebody?"

He shook his head, the movement sure, decisive. "No."

"Sounds more than qualified. I'll pay him out of my wages from Richards. If he can wait until then to get paid, he's got the job."

Millicent's mouth pursed like she'd eaten something sour. "*You* pay him? That would hardly be appropriate."

"Too bad," Lizzie snapped. "This mess is none of Richards's doing and I won't have him paying the price for my mistakes."

"You have a valid argument," Millicent agreed. "But, perhaps you would allow Mr. Browning to handle the transaction for you?"

Lizzie rolled her eyes. "If that's what it takes to keep scandal from the door, Millicent, we can play it your way."

"Your sarcasm is unwarranted and unladylike, Elizabeth. You have a reputation to rebuild. I suggest you begin immediately." Millicent glanced around the room, considering. "Come along, Master Calvin. Let's gather what you'll need." She held out her hand, clearly expecting Cal to take it.

"Go on," Lizzie whispered. "If she bites, I'll bite her back for you."

Cal giggled when she audibly snapped her teeth. "All my stuff is in here, Mrs. Freeman." He led the way into his bedroom—but he didn't take Millicent's hand.

"Don't forget your schoolbooks," Millicent reminded him. "I know Mr. Carruthers will be glad to have you back in class."

Lizzie waited until they were out of the room to confront

Harvard. "Are you sure?"

He didn't pretend not to understand. "I don't see another way, Lizzie. Black Jack would have no compunction about Calvin if it meant eliminating a witness."

She clenched and released her fists, trying to work off the frustration boiling under her skin. "Dam-*na*-tion." She huffed out a breath. "Guess I'd best get packed."

"I'll feed and water the horses. They should be all right until Zeke can get out here."

"Saddle Lightning and Midnight." At his blank look, she laughed. "The chestnut with the white star and the stallion."

"Millicent will have a fit if you ride into town on that."

"Too bad." Lizzie stuffed the deck of cards into the bottom of a burlap sack. "The horse is just getting used to the saddle again. I don't want him to backslide on me."

"Then let me ride him."

"And leave me next to Millicent all the way into town?"

"An excellent idea, Mr. Browning." Millicent swept into the room carrying a bundle of Cal's clothes. The small smile on her face told Lizzie she'd heard that last comment. "It will give us an opportunity to make plans. I'm certain Master Richards is able to ride his own horse into town."

"Yes, ma'am." Cal bounced along in Millicent's wake, carrying his books and another bundle of clothes. "Can I, Miss Lizzie?"

"May I," Millicent corrected, her tone of voice so gentle even Harvard stared. "*Can I* calls your ability into question. We know you can ride. To ask permission, you use *may I*."

Cal rolled her words around for a minute before his expression cleared. "Oh, I never knew that before." He spun to Lizzie. "May I ride Lightning into town?"

Lizzie didn't know whether to laugh or swear. "Go help Mr. Browning saddle Lightning and settle the rest of the horses." She grinned and shook her head when he whooped in delight and tore out of the house.

"You're doing the right thing, Elizabeth." Millicent rolled up her sleeves and plunged her hands into the waiting dish water. "You go and gather your things. I'll clear up in here."

An hour later, Lizzie climbed into the buggy and picked up the reins. The cabin was put to rights and the horses were settled. She'd written a note explaining where to find them and laid it on the kitchen table where Wolf would see it.

She clucked her tongue and shook the reins to get the swaybacked old gelding moving. The buggy jerked forward a couple of times before settling in, rocking back and forth as they climbed the hill away from the house. At the top, Lizzie glanced over her shoulder. Nothing moved. The horses were in the barn, out of sight. No smoke rose from the chimney. Her heart twisted.

We'll be right here when you get back. Those were her parting words, her promise, to Wolf. Now, he was going to come home and find the house empty, his son gone. Just like before.

Harvard reined in beside the buggy, riding out Midnight's fractious mood. "Something wrong?"

"This doesn't feel right. If Wolf comes home to find the place empty again..."

"I'll make sure Zeke understands he has to stay until Wolf gets back. It'll be fine."

"I hope so, Harvard. If Wolf doesn't find that note..." She trailed off. She couldn't let herself think about what he'd do if he missed seeing it.

The sound of hooves pounding the dirt interrupted them. Harvard eased his mount away from the buggy, motioning for Calvin to move closer. A few seconds later, three riders came into view. "Hayes." Harvard said it like a curse. "His timing is uncanny."

"A little too perfect to call coincidence." Lizzie checked the load in her rifle. "What the—" She managed to stop the curse that almost spilled out when Millicent plucked it from her grasp.

"You're better with a revolver than I." Millicent hefted the rifle and sighted down its length. "This weapon, I can shoot with some accuracy."

Lizzie grinned. "You never cease to surprise me, Millicent."

"No one lives long out here without knowing how to defend themselves, Elizabeth."

She couldn't argue, since she wholeheartedly agreed with the sentiment. Studying the approaching riders, she made sure her belt guns were loaded. At the last second, she stuffed her braid out of sight under her hat. "You think someone tipped him off about you and Harvard coming out here?"

"Do you have a better explanation for his presence?" Millicent settled the long gun across her lap.

There was nothing more to say. "Do we push on for town or wait for them to get here? The odds are pretty good, three against three."

"Four," Calvin corrected. Lizzie glanced at him, only a little shocked to see the heavy shotgun cradled in his arms. If Lightning wasn't trained to stand still when the reins went slack, he'd get dumped in the dirt at the first shot fired, but Cal was obviously willing to try. "All right, four. But you don't pull that trigger unless the Doc or I tell you to, you hear me?"

"Yes, ma'am." With the stock tucked under his arm and the barrel leaning against his knee, Cal held the shotgun with the muzzle pointed at the ground. His jaw was set, his eyes hard, giving her a hint of the man he would become. A man just like his father.

Black Jack never slowed his approach, pointing his horse straight at them. When he was fifty yards away, Harvard raised his pistol. The three men immediately reined in.

"What kind of a greeting is this, Browning?" Black Jack called out. "You'd think we were strangers to you."

Harvard didn't respond, waiting for Black Jack to fill the silence.

"I see." The braggart tipped his hat back with a lazy motion and leaned one arm on his saddle horn. "I was on my way to see Richards. He still at home?"

"What do you want with him?" Lizzie hollered, her finger stroking the trigger, itching to take a shot at the sonofabitch.

"My business doesn't concern you, *Mister* Sutter." He straightened in the saddle. "I take it he's unavailable. No matter, I'll speak with him another time." He tipped his hat to Millicent and gathered the reins to ride on. "By the way, Sutter, how's your wrist? Healing, I hope."

Without giving Lizzie a chance to respond, he kicked his horse into a gallop, angling away from the house toward the west. Lizzie yanked the rifle out of Millicent's hands and sighted down the barrel. She'd never shot a man in the back, but a snake like that needed its head chopped off. Before she could pull the trigger, Millicent nudged the rifle until it pointed at the ground. Nobody said a word until the sound of hooves had faded away to nothing.

"He did it, didn't he?" Calvin's lips were pulled thin, his small body quivering with fury.

"We don't know for certain," Harvard cautioned.

"Like hell we don't," Lizzie growled.

"We'll take this up with Sheriff Freeman," Millicent soothed, "the instant we get to town."

Harvard took the lead, with Calvin right behind him. Lizzie kept the buggy rolling as fast as she could without it rattling apart under them. Still, it took more than an hour to reach Civil. Millicent pointed her toward the jail.

"Stop here, Elizabeth. Archibald needs to know what happened."

Harvard swung down from the saddle as Lizzie brought the ancient horse to a halt. The dust kicked up by the wheels overwhelmed the wagon, sending her into a fit of coughing. Millicent simply closed her eyes and covered her nose and mouth with a handkerchief until the air cleared. Once it was safe to breathe again, she tucked the square of dyed cotton inside her sleeve, accepted the hand Harvard offered, and climbed to the ground. "Master Richards, can you manage both horses as far as the livery?"

Calvin preened under the trust implied in Millicent's question. "Yes, ma'am."

"Excellent. Come back for the buggy once you've turned your mounts over to Mr. Douglas. Please inform him I will be in to settle up before nightfall. When you're satisfied the horses are taken care of, meet us at Mrs. Weaver's home."

"Yes, ma'am." Cal tipped his hat like a gentleman, reached to take Midnight's reins from Harvard, and bumped Lightning in the ribs. "Come on, boy. Let's ride."

CHAPTER NINETEEN

"There you are. Come in." Hannah Weaver opened the door wide and stepped back to let them inside, waving them toward a sitting room. Lizzie studied the woman as she entered the house. They'd never met, but Millicent had told her a little about Hannah during the trip into town.

She already knew Hannah had been close friends with Wolf's dead wife. Hannah Weaver was an army widow. According to Millicent, the only reason Hannah moved to Civil was because Emily was living here. With Emily gone, everyone in town expected Hannah and Wolf to marry, for Cal's sake if nothing else. Knowing that certainly didn't make Lizzie feel more at home here. Just thinking about Wolf with another woman brought on an aching in the center of her chest.

Trying hard to set aside the hurt, Lizzie watched as she pointed Harvard toward a door down the hall. "Put Miss Sutter's things in there. Calvin will have to make do with a pallet in the kitchen. I've hung a blanket across the corner to give him some privacy," she explained to Lizzie like it was her right to approve of the accommodations.

"He'll appreciate you going to the trouble, Mrs. Weaver."

"Please call me Hannah. This house is entirely too small to be formal. I can't imagine stepping over each other every morning at breakfast and not becoming very *close* friends."

The way she emphasized *close* made Lizzie smile, relieving a little of the tension. "Hannah, it is—as long as you call me Lizzie."

When Harvard rejoined them, Millicent rose. "You are in the best of hands, Elizabeth, and I must get on home. Mr. Freeman will be expecting his supper soon. I will see you both in the morning."

"So soon?" Lizzie was stunned. "Don't you have better things to do for a while?"

"The ladies are anxious to get started, and I see no reason to delay. Sooner started, sooner done, I always say. Expect us by eight o'clock. Come along, Mr. Browning." Millicent took Harvard's arm and turned him toward the door. He had no choice but to accompany her back into the sunshine.

The buggy was missing from in front of the house. Evidently Cal had already collected it—or, more likely, the horse had taken itself back to the livery. Lizzie had figured out ten minutes into the trip that the animal knew where it was going and didn't require the assistance of a human to get there. All she had to do was hold onto the reins.

Harvard paused in the doorway. "If you or Cal need anything, Lizzie, anything at all—"

"We'll be fine," Lizzie assured him. "If that changes, you'll be the first to know."

"Why don't you join us for dinner this evening, Mr. Browning?" Hannah invited. "You'll be able to reassure yourself they're settling in."

"That is most kind of you, Mrs. Weaver. I accept."

"We eat at six," she clarified. "Don't be late, or you may not get any pie."

Harvard rolled his eyes in exaggerated rapture. "For a piece of your pie, Mrs. Weaver, I'll arrive an hour early."

Hannah laughed at his antics, the sound gentle and full of joy. Harvard assisted Millicent down the two steps before waving to the women. "Until this evening, ladies."

"Good lord, that man could charm the hide off a badger." Hannah laughed as she led Lizzie down the narrow hallway. "Come on back to the kitchen. Even with a fire in the stove, it's a little cooler back there with all the windows open."

The house was a simple design, with doors at either end of a narrow hallway and opening off it both left and right. The design drew the air through the house, keeping it reasonably cool, even in the heat of summer. Lizzie glimpsed what looked like a library on the right, directly across from the small sitting room. A heavy mahogany desk dominated the space, and was flanked by shelves covered in books and papers.

Two bedrooms faced each other. The one on the right was painted white, with delicate, feminine furniture and snowy white curtains at the window that reminded Lizzie of the ones in Millicent's sitting room.

Hannah pointed across the hall. "This is your bedroom." She urged Lizzie to take a look. "It isn't very large, but I think you'll be comfortable."

Lizzie walked slowly to the center of the room. "It's so pretty." The walls were lavender, the delicate color glowing in the light coming through the open window. The curtains were the same shade, as was the cloth draped across the small dresser. The quilt on the four-poster bed had embroidered posies in shades of purple scattered across the fabric. Lizzie looked around with a sense of awe. "I haven't slept in a room this pretty since I was a little girl."

"I'm glad you like it." Hannah smiled in pleasure and led the way to the kitchen. "Make yourself at home, Lizzie. There will be enough going on to keep you off-balance in the next few days. I want you to be comfortable here."

"I'm sure I will be." Lizzie accepted the cup of tea Hannah offered. "What did Millicent mean, the ladies were anxious to get started? On what?"

Hannah set the teapot down with a thud. "She didn't tell you?"

Dread rippled through her at Hannah's suddenly wary tone. "Millicent didn't say a word beyond who you are, where we'd be staying, how I'd be safe here from Black Jack Hayes, and how wise I was to come around to her way of thinking."

Hannah shook her head and joined Lizzie at the small square table. Wide planks had been trimmed and smoothed, then the grain matched as they were nailed together, forming an attractive surface. The patina that only came from regular use and loving care helped make the kitchen an inviting place to linger.

"Out with it. I hate surprises." Especially when she knew she wasn't going to like it.

"She means well, Lizzie. Try to remember that." Hannah sipped at her tea, wrinkled her tiny little nose at the taste and added another spoonful of sugar. Lizzie didn't bother to sample it before reaching for the sugar.

"Millicent has rallied the Ladies League to assist her in turning you into..."

Lizzie set her cup down. She had an idea where this was heading and she didn't want to have anything in her hands to throw. "Into?"

"She plans to remake you into a proper woman."

"A woman?" Lizzie yelled as she bolted to her feet. "I'll kill that meddling female."

"Lizzie, wait." Hannah grabbed her wrist and tugged her back to the table. "Let me finish. If you still want to take a bite out of her hide after that, I won't stop you. I might even help."

The soft admission left Lizzie gaping at Hannah.

"Well, she has no right to meddle, but then Millicent pays no attention to rights. At least, not anyone's but hers."

Lizzie dropped back into her chair and buried her face in her hands. "Why me?"

"Because you present a challenge Millicent can't resist, I'm afraid."

"Damnation," Lizzie muttered, drawing a soft chuckle from Hannah. She glanced up to find the woman smiling at her.

"You probably are going to hate it, Lizzie, but try to cooperate with her on this. It will make the next few weeks so much easier, and you might be surprised what you find at the end. Besides, you don't have to keep it up. The moment Wolf comes home and you leave Civil, you can go back to being whomever you wish, and there will be nothing Millicent can do about it."

Something in Hannah's voice when she mentioned Wolf caught Lizzie's attention, but she was too riled at Millicent to give it much thought. "And if I refuse?"

The woman glanced at Lizzie and looked away again. "She mentioned you'd made some kind of deal that insured your cooperation."

Lizzie knew when she'd been dealt a losing hand. She sat back with a huff. "I'll try."

"Good. It won't be so bad. You'll only have to suffer through the ladies' company for a few hours each day, then you can forget all about it for a while."

"Hours," Lizzie repeated in dismay. "Wait. *Every day?*" She slugged back her cooling tea and held out the cup to be refilled. "You'd better tell me everything."

"Forewarned is forearmed?" Hannah teased as she poured.

"Something like that."

• ♥ •

"Hurry up, Calvin. You're going to be late for school." Hannah bustled around the kitchen, clearing away breakfast. Lizzie shuddered at her show of energy so early in the morning.

"You, too, Lizzie. The ladies will be here soon, and you haven't even brushed your hair."

Lizzie grabbed her cup of coffee before Hannah wiped it off the table and into the floor. "What difference does it make? They aren't going to like what I do with myself anyway," she groused. "Calvin!" she called, without turning her head.

"I'm going." Cal barreled into the kitchen, snatched the bandana-wrapped bundle Hannah held out and bolted for the back door.

"Calvin Richards," Lizzie yelled at his back. "What do you say to Mrs. Weaver?"

"Thanks for making..." He paused to jump from the wide porch to the ground, his boots barely missing Hannah's tomato plants as he spun toward the street. "My lunch, Mrs. Weaver." His words faded away as he raced for the schoolhouse.

Hannah waved back from the doorway. "What's his hurry?"

"The Fisher boys saw what happened yesterday at the livery. Cal's determined to get to school before them and tell the story his way." Lizzie chuckled as she drained the last of her coffee. "It'll be a long time before I forget how he looked when he came in, dripping wet and spitting mad."

Hannah joined her at the table. "Poor boy. I can't imagine being shoved into a water trough by an old sway-backed mare dragging a buggy behind."

"I knew that horse was of a mind to get back to its oats. I made sure to set the brake before I climbed out of the rig, but it didn't stop that ornery beast. I never dreamed it would drag the buggy all the way back to the livery like that.

"Unfortunately for Calvin, he was between the horse and its destination.

"I'm not sure what was worse for him, the dunking or having his friends witness the humiliation."

"Knowing Cal, he's still trying to decide."

Hannah giggled, but the sound turned to a gasp when someone knocked at the front door. She glanced at the watch she had pinned to her bodice. "Oh, lordy, that's probably Millicent."

"It isn't eight o'clock yet." Lizzie bolted to her feet.

"Millicent believes arriving on time means you're late." Hannah shoved her toward the hallway. "Go!"

The thought of Millicent seeing her while her hair was still a mess from tossing and turning in the bed all night had her running for her bedroom.

"Can't even enjoy my last hour as myself in peace." Lizzie strained to hear their conversation through the closed door, but couldn't understand a word of it. Cursing Millicent, Civil, and women in general, she pulled her hair from its braid and dragged the brush through it a few times, then tied it back with a bright yellow ribbon Hannah had loaned her. She pulled on her drawers and a clean chemise, but glared at the wrapper hanging on the back of the door, also courtesy of Hannah. In a last moment of rebellion, she dressed in her own pants and shirt, and stuffed her feet into her boots. "Take that, Millicent Freeman."

Three hours later, wearing only her undergarments, the rebel in her cowered before seven members of the Ladies League of Civil, Texas.

"Forty and seven-eighths inches, as I measured before." Audelia Mercer kneeled beside Lizzie, stretching a tape from her waist to the floor. The two women seated close behind her nodded in agreement.

"You were correct, Mrs. Mercer. I just didn't realize Miss Sutter was so tall."

"I stood a head above most of the sailors on—"

"Quiet, Elizabeth."

"Yes, ma'am." Lizzie had given up trying to maintain any semblance of control about two minutes after Millicent arrived. Then the woman was joined by Audelia Mercer, Henrietta Dorsey, young Hattie Jamison, Virginia Stephens, the preacher's wife, and a couple of others Lizzie couldn't keep straight. From the moment they settled in, she'd been ordered to turn this way and that, was poked, prodded, pinched, stabbed with pins, and measured to within an inch of her patience.

"I believe that will do for this morning."

Lizzie sagged in relief. It was finally over.

"We will reconvene in two hours with our needlework."

"What?"

Millicent did no more than arch one eyebrow and Lizzie subsided again. Hannah caught her attention and winked.

"Don't encourage her, Mrs. Weaver."

"I'm merely bolstering her courage, Mrs. Freeman."

The look in Millicent's eyes said she didn't believe it for a moment. Gathering her basket of pin cushions, fabric pieces, and drawing pads, she led the procession of chattering women out the door. The instant it thumped closed, Lizzie flopped onto the settee.

"Ouch!" She sat up perfectly straight, fighting the urge to cry.

Hannah hurried into the sitting room. "Pin?"

"Pin," she sniffed. Arching her back, Lizzie held still while

Hannah marked the position of the instrument of torture before slipping it free of the fabric. "Do I dare ask what they intend to do to me with their needlework? Cover me like a footstool, I suppose."

Laughing, Hannah tossed the lavender wrapper to Lizzie. "No, silly. Only two can work on your dress at one time. The rest will spend the time doing embroidery. Or maybe today it's needlepoint. I don't remember which one Millicent decided you should learn first."

"Whichever one involves filling my hide with the most holes will be the one she picks."

"Come on, it isn't as bad as that." She held out a hand and pulled Lizzie to her feet. "You get dressed while I make us something to eat."

"I don't suppose I can put on—"

"Don't say it. Don't even *think* it." She scooped up a pile of mud-brown muslin. "Mrs. Dorsey finished hemming the skirt before she left so it's long enough to hide your boots. The bodice hasn't been altered, but you can still wear it. Mind the pins, though," she added, a false look of wide-eyed innocence plastered on her face.

"Tell me you didn't say *pins*," Lizzie growled.

Hannah was still laughing as she shoved Lizzie into her bedroom and closed the door.

True to Millicent's orders, the ladies trooped through the door at precisely one o'clock, armed with small hoops, multiple colors of thread, and needles. Long ones, short ones, and even a couple of wicked looking curved ones, were plied in and out of squares of fabric, completing a design only they could see. All the while, the women chattered like a barn full of wrens. The noise was enough to drive anyone batty.

Lizzie bit down on her bottom lip and squinted at the cotton handkerchief she was practicing on. Hattie Jamieson had loaned her an embroidery hoop and helped seat the fabric so Lizzie could see the pattern that had been lightly sketched on it. Unfortunately, Lizzie's results didn't resemble the pattern at all.

"Well, you knew it would take practice."

Lizzie glanced over her shoulder at Hattie. "I'm not sure there are enough days left in my life to get this right."

"Don't fret. If I can learn how, you certainly can. In no time, we'll have you doing needlepoint. Then Aunt Henri can teach you to tat lace."

"Lace," Lizzie repeated with dread. "How marvelous." Intent on her work, she nearly jumped out of her skin when Millicent announced the time.

"Three quarters of the hour, ladies."

Immediately, the women threaded their needles into a corner of their project, dumped everything into their basket or bag, and scurried for the door, leaving Lizzie sitting in her half-completed shirtwaist.

"Tomorrow morning, we gather at Mrs. Mercer's," Millicent reminded them. "Same time."

In seconds, the women were gone and the parlor was quiet. "Would you like some tea, Mrs. Freeman?"

"That would be most welcome, Mrs. Weaver." Millicent lowered herself into a chair with a grateful sigh. "A very productive day, all told. You did well, Elizabeth. I know this is difficult for you."

Lizzie rubbed her tired eyes with a hand marked by dozens of needle pricks. "You have no idea."

"On the contrary, I believe I do. That blend of tea smells delicious." As Hannah poured, Millicent rummaged in her sewing basket and drew out a small, flat bottle of amber liquid.

"Is that what I think it is?" Lizzie inhaled deeply when Millicent pulled out the cork. "Whiskey," she whispered reverently.

"We've earned it." Millicent added a splash of liquor to her own tea, then offered the bottle to Hannah, who declined.

Lizzie accepted and poured it into her cup until the tea nearly sloshed over the rim.

Millicent watched, her disapproval obvious. "In truth, those women nearly drive me to distraction with their constant chatter." She sipped her tea and sighed with pleasure. "Still, they do their part."

"What part is that?" Lizzie gulped half the contents of her cup to make room for more whiskey.

Millicent arched one eyebrow as Lizzie refilled her cup, but didn't comment. Instead, she waited for Lizzie to set the bottle down, then corked it and slipped it back into the basket at her feet. "Those ladies are vital in our efforts to tame this town. Too many settlements shrivel and die because there is no stability.

"The women provide a necessary foundation. In turn, their husbands have become fine, productive citizens, and that productivity attracts more of the same. It's the only way to stay on the map, as it were."

Lizzie topped her cup, this time with plain tea and added a little sugar. "I certainly can't argue with you. I've watched towns like Civil spring up overnight and die away almost as fast."

"That won't happen—not if I can prevent it." Millicent set her cup and saucer on the table and checked the time on the watch pinned to her bodice. "I should be going. The school bell will be ringing any—" The peal of the church bell interrupted her. "Excellent. Right on time."

Hannah and Lizzie followed Millicent into the hall and watched while she pinned her hat in place. "You look rather pretty, Elizabeth, in spite of the pins." She studied Lizzie's reflection in the mirror. "Quite a surprise, actually." Gathering her basket, she led the way to the front door. "Now then, tomorrow morning at eight, we will meet at Audelia's for our sewing circle."

"Sewing circle?" Lizzie was confused. "I thought I was done."

"Nonsense. We're just getting started." Millicent arched one graying eyebrow. "We have to finish altering the dress you're wearing, and you'll need two or three more serviceable garments, and one suitable for the July celebration." She ticked them off on her fingers, then eyed Lizzie. "You *are* able to sew, aren't you?"

Lizzie wasn't sure stitching up canvas, or darning the odd sock, qualified as sewing. "Better than I can embroider," she hedged.

"Wonderful. Bring what you have on, if you don't finish altering it this evening. Mister Mercer should have the fabric you need for another one. A nice calico, don't you think, Mrs. Weaver?"

"Fabric?"

Hannah squeezed her arm, silencing her questions. "I'll help her choose something easy to work with."

"And notions, of course," Millicent listed. "I'll stop by the general store and tell him to expect you tomorrow morning around seven-thirty."

"Notions?" Lizzie looked back and forth between the women, settling on Hannah. "What is she talking about?"

"I'll explain later." Hannah opened the door for Millicent. "We'll join you in the morning."

Harvard stood at the bottom of the stairs, looking every inch a gambler in a shiny black suit and dove gray vest, with a gold watch chain looped from the second buttonhole. He removed his matching black hat in greeting and tucked it under his arm to offer a hand to Millicent. "Allow me to assist you, Mrs. Freeman."

"Thank you, Mr. Browning." She frowned at the cloth-covered basket he held in his other hand. "Gifts?"

"Gifts." He inclined his head slightly. "Good day, Mrs. Freeman."

Millicent walked on a few steps, then turned back. Harvard just smiled. Shaking her head, Millicent headed for home.

Harvard climbed the two stairs to join Lizzie and Hannah. "Good afternoon, ladies."

"Don't you look like a man interested in trouble," Lizzie snapped, turning away with a flick of her recently lowered skirt hem.

Hannah had the nerve to laugh, out loud. "Come in, Mister Browning. We were just enjoying a cup of tea. Won't you join us?"

"You're most generous, Mrs. Weaver."

"*You* were enjoying tea, Hannah. I would rather have whiskey." Lizzie flopped into the nearest chair. Harvard came to stand before her.

He sketched a credible bow and presented the basket with a flourish. "Your wish is my command, my lady."

Lizzie lifted one corner of the blue cloth and peeked inside. "Browning, you're forgiven." She lifted a bottle of amber liquid free of the basket.

Harvard looked to Hannah for an explanation. "Forgiven for what?"

"For that disgusting display of civility back there," Lizzie explained. "*Allow me to assist you, Mrs. Freeman*," she mimicked with an exaggerated air, then grimaced. "Disgusting." Lizzie slugged the last of her cold tea and filled the cup with amber liquor. "But this makes you my favorite person again."

"You're cheaply bought, Miss Sutter." When Lizzie glared in his direction, he laughed. "Begging your pardon. Lizzie."

She laughed at him and toasted his health before taking a healthy swallow of whiskey. "Ah, now that's what I call heaven. Where the hell does Millicent get her whiskey?"

"Millicent Freeman?" Harvard looked shocked. "She buys whiskey?"

"Oops." Lizzie looked to Hannah to bail her out.

The other woman allowed Harvard to seat her and poured herself another cup of tea. "You'd best learn to keep your mouth shut, Lizzie. Millicent never forgives that kind of slip."

"I won't tell a soul," Harvard swore, hand over his heart. "No one would believe it anyway." Then he chuckled. "So…the old battleax nips a little."

"Harvard," Lizzie started, warning clear in her tone.

"Don't worry, Lizzie. No one will hear it from me, I swear." He accepted a cup of tea from Hannah with a nod of thanks. "But I *would* like to know where she buys her supply."

"It comes in with her shipments from New York," Hannah

confided in a low voice, glancing toward the open window to be sure no one else was near. "An old friend out east includes a bottle or two with her order each time. The first time it was a surprise, I believe. Now, she counts on it arriving. Oh, not that she's become a lush, you understand, but she does enjoy a splash now and then. Please understand," Hannah hurried to reassure him. "She can't purchase it from you. Someone might see."

"I understand completely. On the contrary, I find this little chink in her otherwise impervious armor of unrelenting goodness to be rather reassuring."

Lizzie drank the last of her whiskey and eyed the bottle for a moment.

"No, I've had enough," she decided. "Not even spending the day with the Ladies League is a good enough reason to become the town drunk. But joining their sewing circle tomorrow just might do it." Lizzie groaned and dropped back in her chair. "What was I thinking, telling Millicent I can sew? I've stitched sails, not doilies."

Hannah laughed, a soft, gentle sound. "Don't worry, Lizzie. I'll help you learn. We can practice on what you're wearing."

"Ah, I see." Harvard settled back to drink his tea.

"What the hell do you see?"

"Lizzie!" Hannah scolded. "Your language."

"Now I understand why there are a dozen pins sticking out from your sides and shoulders."

"We haven't had time to finish her dress. She's been busy all afternoon, learning to embroider."

Harvard choked on his tea. "I beg your pardon?"

"And tomorrow she will join the sewing circle," Hannah chirruped.

Lizzie could see Harvard fighting a grin, even as the corners of his lips quivered and curved. Finally, he gave up, threw his head back, and guffawed.

"I just can't see it. Sewing? Embroidery? What's next?"

"Needlepoint and lace," she grumbled, sending him into another fit of laughter. The deep, warm sound washed over her, reminding her of Wolf. For a better part of the day, she'd been too busy to think of him. Now, she missed him all over again.

Harvard whipped a handkerchief from his pocket and wiped away tears of mirth. "I can't wait to see that."

Lizzie slumped lower in her chair. "Oh, shut up and finish your tea, Browning."

CHAPTER TWENTY

After five weeks of hunting, Wolf was finally on his way home. Two more days, three at the most, and he'd be eating at his own table. The trip had been profitable. With what he'd made off the pelts and meat at the last trading post, plus those he was bringing home to Civil, he'd have the funds to repair and even expand some at the ranch.

Looking east, toward home, he studied the land. There were a couple of hills jutting up from a flat plain, with a broad, lazy river running away to the south. The bumps in the landscape were mostly grass-covered, with few trees to shield someone intent on surprising him. The second one ahead had a flat spot halfway up the side with enough bare dirt to build a fire.

He'd used the campsite before. Perched high on the side of the hill, it gave him a broad view to the front and sides, and solid rock at his back. There was grass and water, too, so his horses would be fine. The incline was gentle enough he could ride right to the well-blackened fire ring.

The sun was setting fire to the western hills when he stripped the gear off Scarlett and Smoke and led them to a patch of grass. Dinner would be the rabbit he'd snared over-night and a pot of strong coffee. He considered frying up few slices of bacon, too, but he was just too tired to bother. He could wait until tomorrow and whatever concoction Lizzie would have cooking.

Filling his coffee pot in the stream that splashed down the rocky hillside a dozen paces away, he added a pinch of salt, then tucked it in close to the flames to boil. He skewered the rabbit on a sharpened willow branch and balanced it on a couple of forked limbs to roast.

While the food cooked, he groomed Scarlett and made a circuit of the camp, just to be sure he was alone. By the time he returned, he was glad of the warmth from the small fire. Though the day had been hot, the air was cooling quickly now with the sun gone.

Sliding the coffee pot out of the fire, he dumped in some ground beans and set it aside to steep. Wolf ate fast, before the air could steal the heat from the food, and sat back with a second cup of coffee to study the land. Movement caught his eye. Easing to his feet, rifle in hand, he spotted a single rider starting up the hill toward him. Since it was an odd place to aim for in the dark, Wolf figured whoever it was had to be familiar with this campsite, as well. Half an hour later, the stranger rode up to the edge of the clearing, both hands in sight.

"Evening. Mind if I share your fire?"

The dancing light glinted off the revolvers at the man's hips. Wolf shifted slightly, just in case. "Depends."

The stranger tipped his battered hat back with one finger. Firelight bathed a face that had seen its share of years.

"Name's Kincaid. Texas Ranger Christopher Kincaid, according to my commission. My friends call me Kit."

"Help yourself to some coffee." Wolf settled back against a large boulder, his rifle within easy reach. "There's plenty."

"I'm obliged." The ranger dragged his right leg over the horse's wide haunches and slid to the ground, landing hard on both boots. If Wolf hadn't been watching, he would have missed the flash of pain cross the man's face. Kincaid hesitated a few seconds before leaning over to loosen the cinch and lift the saddle from a handsome black gelding.

He dropped the saddle to the ground on the opposite side of the fire from Wolf, and spread the saddle blanket over it to dry. Then he pointed toward the grass and gave the horse a gentle pat on its long, elegant neck. "Go on and eat your fill. I'll brush you down later." The horse's nose was buried in a clump of grass before he finished speaking.

Striding back to the fire, Kit rummaged in his saddlebags for a cup, then reached for the coffee pot. "Don't you want to see some proof of who I am?"

"No need. You walk the same as another Texas Ranger I know."

"They teach us that in the first week of training," Kit drawled, his East Texas heritage obvious in his voice.

Wolf grinned into his cup. This was a man he could come to like. Just like Jake McCain.

Kincaid eased himself to the ground and stretched his legs in front of him. When he took off his hat, his red hair blended into the sunset over his left shoulder. "Thanks for the coffee." He took another mouthful, studying Wolf over the rim of a battered tin cup. "You look familiar."

Wolf didn't look up, but he shifted slightly closer to his rifle. "You ever in the army?"

"Once upon a time, but not for years."

"I used to scout for them, up in Montana and down around Fort Elliott. Maybe you saw me there."

"No. More recent." The ranger poured them both another cup of coffee, then settled back against his saddle again, totally at ease. "You rode with the Harrison gang."

Wolf froze, the coffee halfway to his mouth. The only sound was the crackle of the fire. Slowly, he lowered the cup to the ground and nodded. "For a time, though not because I wanted to."

Kincaid didn't move, but Wolf sensed he was ready to draw if it became necessary. "Then why?"

"They had my children. Ranger Jake McCain will vouch for me, if necessary."

Wolf watched the lawman relax and some of his own tension eased. He picked up his cup again and drained half the contents.

"Richards, right? I heard about your wife and daughter. I'm sorry for your losses. Glad you found your boy, though I wish..."

"Me, too," Wolf ended the conversation. Kincaid dug

around in his saddlebags and came up with a small bottle of amber liquid. Wolf tossed out the last of his coffee and accepted a splash of whiskey.

"To those we've lost." Kincaid lifted his cup, tossed back the contents, and poured himself another shot. Wolf declined a refill.

Wolf didn't have to ask whom the man had lost. He recognized the look in his eyes. He saw that same look in the mirror every time he shaved. Though that wasn't true anymore, he realized. The grief had eased some, thanks to Lizzie.

Wolf settled back to sip his whiskey. She'd made a big difference in his life in such a short time. What was he going to do when she left?

As the fire burned down, the men spread out their bedrolls and tethered their horses nearby, Scarlett on Wolf's side, Kincaid's gelding on his.

"Do you mind me asking what you're doing here?" Kincaid dropped to his knees and stretched out on his blanket.

"I've been trapping in the Turkey Mountains. Heading home. You?"

"I'm hunting someone."

Wolf heard the bite in his voice. Whoever the ranger hunted had eluded him, probably for quite some time. "Care to tell me who?"

"Jefferson Hayes."

Wolf looked up, the ease of the evening gone. "Black Jack Hayes?"

"You know him." It wasn't a question.

"Yes." Wolf nodded. "You could say that."

Kincaid's voice held steel and frustration, laced with a little hope. "Know where I could find him?"

"Could be." Why the hell had he said that? Helping take Black Jack down would give Wolf no end of satisfaction. So why did he hesitate to tell the ranger what he knew? That was easy: Lizzie.

"A couple of gun shipments were diverted from their destination and somehow ended up in the hands of the cattle rustlers who've been raiding ranches south of here." Kincaid tossed his cold coffee into the flames. "I've a mind to ask him how that happened."

So Black Jack had finally shown his hand and someone intended to see that he answered for his many crimes. "I had a run-in with him several weeks ago," Wolf offered.

The ranger sat up and leaned closer. "Where?"

"Near Civil, a day's ride east, on the Canadian River. He's too lazy to have gone far."

"I appreciate the information. Can you tell me how to find Civil?"

"I'll do even better. I'll take you there."

"Good enough."

Kincaid poured himself another slug of whiskey and leaned back against his saddle. Stretching out on the ground, his back to the fire and the other man, Wolf eased into a light sleep. He woke up just as dawn painted a sliver of light on the horizon.

The ranger was already moving around, his horse groomed and waiting to be saddled. Considering how much whiskey the man had put away, Wolf guessed Ranger Kincaid didn't sleep much. The reddish stubble on his jaw made him look older than he had last night.

As Wolf rolled to his feet, Kit dropped a few twigs on the fire and stirred it to life. "There'll be coffee before long."

"Thanks." Wolf walked away into the brush a few yards to answer nature's call and circled around to check on Scarlett. She nickered a greeting as he smoothed his hand down her long neck. "We've got a long day ahead, girl. Best eat while you can." Leaving the horse to it, he returned to the fire.

Kincaid was on his knees, scratching landmarks in the dirt with a stick. "We're about here."

"You don't want to ride with me?"

Kincaid studied the land. "No offense, but I do better on my own."

Wolf accepted the stick and scratched a jagged gouge in the

dirt. "This is the Canadian. The best place to join it is here, about five miles beyond White Creek." He added the landmark. "You'll cross a few other streams, but you'll know the White. The creek bottom is covered in white rock."

Kincaid nodded, studying the developing map. "Which direction after I cross the White?"

"Head north. When you get to the Canadian, turn east. One long day in the saddle will get you there in time for supper." Wolf tossed the stick into the fire. "You can get a room and two hot meals a day at the rooming house, but the food is… Let's just say Mrs. Dorsey means well." He shuddered. "Truthfully, her cooking is enough to make a confirmed bachelor go looking for a wife."

The ranger laughed, low rumble of sound. "I understand." Kincaid pushed to his feet and stood still for a few seconds, favoring his right leg and swaying like a sapling in a breeze. "Anyone in particular I should ask for help?"

"Sheriff Freeman and Harvard Browning. He owns the saloon," he clarified. "Lizzie…" he started, then changed his mind.

"Lizzie," Kincaid prompted.

Wolf stood. "Never mind. She can't help." If Lizzie heard him say that, she'd throw every shoe and boot in the house at his head, followed by a sharp knife, but he didn't want to send this man to Lizzie. He didn't want her to be tempted. The realization shamed him, but he couldn't help the way he felt. Wolf wanted her for himself.

Somewhere in the last several weeks, alone with only his thoughts, he'd realized Lizzie was his match in every way. Every dream, every need, every fantasy, she was right there with him. She brought him laughter, joy and contentment, things he never thought to have again.

For the first time since that awful day when his beautiful Emily died in his arms, he had a reason to go on living. And he wasn't giving her up.

CHAPTER TWENTY-ONE

Lizzie stomped out of the small, whitewashed house, barely resisting the urge to slam the door behind her. "Five weeks," she hissed. For the better part of five long weeks she'd poked needles through cloth, adding silly ruffles to chemises, making dresses and bonnets and useless little bags you couldn't even hide a proper revolver in. And for what? Trying to make her into a lady was like trying to teach a pig to dance. You might manage a few stumbling steps, but what was the point?

She wandered through Civil, muttering to herself.

"Is anything the matter, Miss Sutter?" Willouby Carruthers lunged forward and grabbed for her elbow as she tripped on her skirt hem.

"Not a thing," she snarled. "Just trying to avoid having to wash all this dang fool fabric."

"It is a lovely frock," he gushed, steering her around a steaming pile of horse dung. "Most becoming. Will you be wearing it to the July Fourth social?"

Lizzie stared at him, confused. "The what?"

"Civil's annual basket social," he explained. "It's held every year on the Fourth of July."

"Stands to reason it'd be every year if it's an annual event."

Carruthers blushed. "Well, of course. Foolish of me." He glanced away, giving Lizzie a close-up view of his Adam's apple bobbing up and down his throat with every nervous swallow. "The town council decided to combine the celebration of our founding with that of our country's independence. Quite frugal of them, don't you agree?"

"Frugal," she sniped. "Figures."

"You don't approve, Miss Sutter?"

"Not for me to approve, Mr. Carruthers. I'm only visiting."

"Yes. Quite." He looked away again. "Will you?"

Lizzie concentrated on crossing the street before glancing his way. "Will I what?"

Carruthers stopped so fast, Lizzie almost pitched face first into the dust. Her skirt swooped forward and tangled around his legs, making him blush like a schoolboy caught admiring his barely-there whiskers in the water trough.

"Pardon me, Miss S-Sutter." He doffed his hat, tucked it between the two of them like a shield and proceeded to crush the brim in both hands. "If I may, uh, may be so bold. I wonder." He swallowed and she watched that manly lump pop up from his high starched collar and disappear again. "May I, uh, that is, uh, would you c-consider—"

Lizzie glowered at him. "Spit it out, Carruthers. I've got places to be."

Carruthers cleared his throat and pulled at his collar with one long, bony finger. "If your card is not full, would you do me the honor of granting me a dance, Miss Sutter?"

The words poured out in such a rush Lizzie had to play them back through in her head to figure out what the man said. "Dance? Now?"

"No, no. At the, uh, that is," he stammered. She glared at him until he stopped and took a breath. Before she could interject, he started talking fast. "I realize a woman of your beauty and skill will be in great demand, but would you do me the great honor of granting me a dance at the social? Perhaps the reel?" His voice rose with each syllable until he squeaked out the last as he ran out of air.

"Sure. Fine." She stepped around Carruthers and started down the wooden sidewalk.

"Th-thank you, Miss Sutter," the schoolmaster called after her. "I look forward to the event with great anticipation."

She slapped at the air in a farewell wave and strode away, aiming for home.

"Home," she huffed. She didn't have a home. Nice as Hannah was, Lizzie was still a guest. Home certainly wasn't in San Francisco, where the woman who'd given birth to her waited anxiously, if her letter was to be believed. "When mules preach," Lizzie grumbled as she stomped through the front door of Hannah's home and down the hall to her bedroom.

She couldn't even call Wolf's house home, though she'd thought, for a while there—

"Stop it!" She ripped her bonnet from her head and threw it on the bed. "Damnation!"

"Miss Lizzie?" Cal appeared in the doorway. "Is there somethin' wrong?"

She spun toward the door. "What are you doing here? You're supposed to be in school." But she'd run into Carruthers in the street.

"Nuh-uh. School's done. No more Mr. Carruthers for the whole summer." Cal danced a jig around the rug by the bed and threw himself backward onto the mattress. "And only four more days until my birthday."

Lizzie swatted his boots off the quilt. "You think I'm going to forget?"

"Nope." Cal rolled his head back and forth, squirming closer to the pillows.

"Then why do you remind me at least six times every day?" His mischievous grin had her smiling back. She held out a hand and tugged him to his feet. "Go change and meet me in the garden. Just because school's out doesn't mean the work is done. We have potatoes to dig."

"Okay, but I hope you know which ones are potatoes and which ones are weeds."

"Hey," she ruffled his hair. "It's not my fault. How was I supposed to know which was which?"

"Good thing Mrs. Weaver got there before you pulled them all out of the ground." Cal's laughter rippled behind him as he dashed away.

For the rest of the afternoon, while Hannah was at Millicent's finishing the hem of Lizzie's latest dress, she and Cal worked their way up and down the neat rows of vegetables, digging up potatoes, gathering corn and beans, and pulling the weeds they were sure of. As the sun sank toward the horizon, Lizzie followed Cal inside with a brimming bowl of snap peas.

"I think we have enough for dinner." Cal eyed the growing piles of ripe vegetables on the kitchen table.

"And then some," Lizzie agreed, astonished at the amount they'd picked. "I guess we'll be canning tomorrow."

"And that's only three days before my birthday," the boy teased. Lizzie threw a green bean at him. He dodged the missile with a laugh, then grew serious. "Do you think Pa will be back in time for my birthday?"

"He promised, didn't he?" Cal's nod was half-hearted. "He's not going to miss your birthday."

The boy picked a twig out of the bowl of peas and set to peeling the bark off with his fingernail. "When's your birthday, Miss Lizzie?"

"I don't know." She thought back, trying to recall if her mother had ever bothered to commemorate the day, but couldn't dredge up a single memory. "It's sometime in the summer, I suppose, since I can't recall ever celebrating it with my family, and that's when my father would have been at sea. The Captain—that's my grandfather—the Captain never bothered with things like birthdays."

Calvin stared at her, wide-eyed and slack-jawed. "Ain't it written down somewhere?"

Lizzie shrugged, and concentrated on sorting vegetables. Any that were overly ripe would have to be used first. "Probably back East somewhere. But who'd care?"

"I do! And you should." His forehead creased as he thought hard about something. Suddenly, he grinned. "I know. You can share my birthday. Pa's is in the winter and that's too far away. I'll go tell Mrs. Weaver it's your birthday, too, and she'll make sure you have—"

"Calvin, no." Lizzie snagged his arm as he went to run past.

272 ♥ Tracy Garrett

"This is *your* special day."

"But I want it to be yours, too. Please?"

The pleading in Cal's blue eyes did her in and Lizzie flopped into a chair. She knew he was playing her like a fiddle, but she couldn't resist. She always crumbled in the face of sweetness. Good thing she and Wolf hadn't managed to start a family while she was living that dream. Of course, it was doubtful a child of hers would turn out the least bit sweet. "Oh, all right. I'd be honored to share your birthday, Calvin."

Lizzie watched him run down the hall and out the front door, feet running before he ever touched dirt, in a hurry to spread the news. Yet another thing about her that wasn't true. Lizzie plucked at a loose thread on her apron. First, the home that wasn't hers; now, an invented birthday.

With a loud sigh, she went to find Hannah's recipe book, 'cause sure as shootin' she was going to have to bake a cake for the social. The damned thing had to be perfect, too, or Millicent Freeman would never let her live it down. And to top it off, she had to spend the whole day dressed up like a fool female. And dance with Willouby Carruthers. Would it never end?

CHAPTER TWENTY-TWO

July 4, 1890

He was going to be late.

Wolf urged his horse up the hill overlooking his cabin, the midday sun hot on his face. Chasing that herd of deer he'd practically ridden into had taken him the wrong direction, until it was too late to finish the trip home. He'd been in the saddle since before first light, but he still wouldn't make it back in time to take Lizzie and Calvin into town before the social started, like he'd promised. And Lizzie would be disappointed that he'd broken his promise to be home in time for...

He hauled back on Scarlett's reins and brought her to a halt. Lizzie. Not Emily. He'd forgotten. For one blessed minute, he'd forgotten. Replaced Emily. No. Not replaced. Never that.

Wolf dropped the reins and covered his face with his scarred hands, hands Emily never liked to have against her soft skin for very long, though Lizzie didn't seem to mind. Scarlett wandered forward a few steps before stopping to nuzzle at some sweet grass.

He took one shuddering breath, trying to hold back, then gave up the fight. Tears ran freely, washing away the last of the grief, the regrets. Lizzie was right. Even if he'd been near the cabin that horrible day, he might not have been able to stop what happened. And life—his son's life—had to move on.

He lifted the reins and steered Scarlett to the primrose-blanketed spot under the lone cottonwood tree on the hill. It was time to say goodbye. He dismounted and stood for a long time, breathing in the silence, the faint fragrance of primroses.

Lizzie and Cal must have kept them watered.

Of all the women he might have imagined falling for, he would never have come up with Lizzie Sutter. She was nothing like Emily, yet she was perfect for him. He wanted to get to the cabin and tell her. But he had something to finish first.

"I'm sorry I wasn't there to save you, Emily. You and Amanda. I promised your daddy I'd keep you safe, and I failed. That's something I'll have to live with for the rest of my days. But Calvin is going to be fine. So am I. And it's time we get on with living. Rest in peace, honey."

As the weight lifted from his heart, he turned for home, for the future. For Lizzie.

From the top of the hill, the house looked quiet in the afternoon light. Nothing moved save a few clouds too thin to offer respite from the blazing summer sun. He glanced toward the corral and felt the past wash over him in a cold wave.

The horses weren't in the corral. His breath backed up. Nothing moved. No smoke, no— Nothing. Just like before. Wolf staggered under the weight of terror. Whistling for Scarlett, he vaulted into the saddle and kicked the horse into a reckless gallop down the slope.

"Lizzie? Calvin!"

He slammed through the front door, but the room was empty. Panic stole what air was left in his lungs. "Lizzie!"

"They ain't here."

He spun toward the voice, drawing and cocking his revolver. "Where are they?"

Zeke Williams stumbled backward and fell down the porch stairs.

"Where the hell is my family?"

"I-in town. Harvard moved them to Civil the same day you left and hired me to keep an eye on the horses 'til you got back."

The haze of panic-born fury eased a little. Wolf pointed his revolve at the dirt beyond Zeke's head. "Why?"

"Somethin' Black Jack Hayes said, I gathered. I didn't ask too many questions and Mr. Browning, well, he didn't offer too many details. Just hired me and sent me out here."

Wolf shook with the need to break something. He breathed through the urge. Once he regained a bit of control, he holstered his weapon. "My apologies, Zeke." He crossed the porch and offered the man a hand up. "I guess I wasn't thinking."

"Understandable. Been there myself."

Surprised that the man had shared even that much about his past, Wolf coaxed Scarlett close enough to snag her reins.

Zeke Williams was a mystery to everyone in Civil. He'd shown up one winter, haggard and more dead than alive. His gift with animals garnered the respect, if not trust, of enough of the townsfolk that he stuck around, did odd jobs to feed himself and keep up a steady supply of whiskey. But he didn't become a part of the community. And he never talked about his past.

"Any idea where Miss Sutter and my boy are staying?"

"With Mrs. Weaver, I think they said. But Mr. Browning, he'll know fer sure. Want to see your horses?"

Wolf followed him around behind the barn to a temporary rope corral, and stopped so fast Scarlett nearly knocked him off his feet. "Where did you find Blackhorse?"

Zeke grinned wide enough to show off the gaps where his teeth should have been. "This pretty girl came wanderin' up a couple of weeks ago, looking confused and hungry. I saw your mark and knew she belonged, so I groomed her good and set about fattening her up some." The little black mare came at Zeke's whistle and pushed her head into his chest, looking for attention.

Wolf checked her over. "I'm glad to have her back." He ran a gentle hand down each leg. The horse was strong and healthy. "You did a good job on her."

"She let me do whatever was needed, as long as there was a scoop of grain waiting." He cackled with delight when the horse tossed her head in agreement.

"Why did you put up the temporary corral?" Wolf set to work stripping gear from Scarlett and Smoke. The packhorse was so tired he didn't even flick an ear at the attention. "I've been meaning to build one over here, but there hasn't been time."

"The horses had about trampled the grass to nothin' in the other one, so I moved them over here a few days ago." Zeke patted Blackhorse once more before sending her across the corral with a gentle slap to the rump. "Figured to give the turf a chance to recover some. Been tossing water on it and it's coming along perty good."

"You watered the flowers, too?" Wolf motioned toward the primroses with his chin.

"Yep. They sure do smell nice."

Wolf led Scarlett and his pack horse inside the temporary corral and Dandelion wandered over and snuffled his hand, looking for a treat. "Spoiled the horses, too, I see."

Zeke laughed, a whiskey-rough sound. "Most likely. Can't seem to resist them big eyes."

Wolf thought of a particular pair of dark eyes he was helpless to resist. "I understand completely."

"You best get a move on if you want to get to the social afore the food's all gone." When Wolf reached for Scarlett's saddle, Zeke waved him off. "Go on. I'll take care of the horses. There's pelts in that bundle, there, I reckon. I'll see they get laid out proper. Got nothing but time right now, anyway." He clucked his tongue when Scarlett shied from him. "Easy, pretty lady. Nothin' around here's gonna hurt you none."

In spite of Zeke's protest, Wolf started untying the bundles from the pack saddle. "Aren't you going to the social?"

The crack of laughter sounded a little forced to Wolf's ear. "Nobody wants the likes of me to show up."

"I do." Wolf stated the simple truth. "And I'm sure Lizzie and Browning do, too." For a second, he would have sworn tears sparkled in the man's rheumy eyes.

"I appreciate that, Richards. I truly do." He turned back to work, ending the discussion. "I'll finish up here. You get on to town 'fore you worry those waiting for you. I'll have Big Red saddled and waiting for you, whenever you're ready."

Not wanting to embarrass the man, Wolf thanked him and went to clean up. When he stepped into the silent house, a piece of paper on the floor caught his attention. The wind must have swept it off the table when he opened the door. He squinted at the words and moved closer to the door for more light. The handwriting was angular and tough to read, just like the woman who'd written the note.

> *You were right and I was wrong. Black Jack knows I'm here and I won't risk Cal. We're heading into Civil. I'm sorry you had to find the place empty again.*
> *L.*

Wolf rolled his shoulders, easing the tension of the past half hour and a few of the kinks of weeks on the trail. Those he loved were as safe as they could be until he reached them—which would be a long time coming if he didn't get a move on.

Setting the paper aside, Wolf went to the trough, pumped it full, stripped down to his altogether, and cleaned a month's worth of dust and grime and sweat from his skin. Dripping water onto his bare feet, he drained and refilled the trough, snatched up his boots and dirty clothes, and strode for the house.

Twenty minutes later, dressed in his Sunday pants, a clean white shirt and black string tie, with his hat dusted and boots buffed, he climbed into the saddle and headed for Civil. By the sun, he guessed the time to be around four o'clock. The social started an hour ago. Lizzie was not going to be happy.

• ♥ •

When he hadn't shown by noon, Lizzie was sure something

was wrong. She waited two more hours, trying to put the finishing touches to the cake she'd baked while watching the second hand hitch its way around the face of the grandfather clock in Hannah's kitchen. Finally, her patience ran out and she threw down the icing-coated knife in disgust.

She'd done her best, but the birthday cake was hideous. The three layers looked even, but somewhere along the way, the center of the cake had collapsed. It took most of a second batch of icing to fill the hole to level. Snatching a few wildflowers from the jar on the table, she tied them together with a bit of string and stuck them into the icing-filled gorge, then carefully packed the cake into the basket Hannah had loaned her.

Another one sat off to one side, stuffed full of roasted rabbit and molasses beans. Along with her biscuits, and a jar of Hannah's chokeberry jam, some man would at least be full when he finished eating the picnic she'd packed.

"Aren't you dressed yet?" Hannah bustled into the kitchen. "If you're late, Millicent will never let you hear the end of it." She shooed Lizzie toward her bedroom. "Come on. We have to hurry."

"I'm going out to search for Wolf, not put on some fancy dress," she argued, while Hannah kept herding her down the hall.

"No, you are not. You are getting dressed and taking your basket to the schoolhouse. Besides," she reasoned while untying Lizzie's apron. "You don't even know where to begin looking."

"I'll check the house first." Though, if he wasn't there, she didn't have a clue where she'd go next.

"That would be a waste of time since Zeke will tell him where you are. If Cain said he'd be here, he will be. Mind your hair, now."

Earlier, Hannah had spent an hour fixing her hair, piling it into a fluffy arrangement on the back of her head and roping it into submission with several long ribbons. At least most of it had stayed in place.

Carefully stripping off her icing-spattered shirtwaist, Lizzie poured water into the wash basin. "Why'd you call him Cain?"

"That's his name. Cain Tobias Richards. He earned the nickname Wolf because he was so talented a tracker and hunter."

"I guess you've known him a while." The thought that Hannah could claim Wolf's attention based on years of shared history made her a little ill.

"I knew Emily much longer." Hannah turned her away from the mirror and began fastening buttons on the bright yellow dress. "We were girls together at an army fort back east. Then her father received his promotion and they moved west to take over his command and my family returned to Baltimore. When my husband and children died…" She fell silent, but kept buttoning Lizzie into the dress. "My parents were gone by then and I had no reason to remain where I was, so I moved to Civil to be near Emily. There. All done."

As Hannah left to finish getting ready, Lizzie stared at her reflection in amazement. Fifteen minutes was all they'd taken to clean her up and layer on the pounds of fabric a woman was required to wear in this town. Fifteen minutes. And she hardly recognized herself.

Turning one way then the other, she had to admit she looked—feminine. But would Wolf like what he saw? And what would she do if he didn't?

"Maybe this isn't a good idea," she muttered as she fussed with the lace on her sleeves. "I could just send the baskets with Hannah and stay home." Then she wouldn't make a fool of herself, strutting around in front of the whole town dressed up like a sun-colored peacock.

What if she poisoned someone with her food? Or forgot the steps to the dance Carruthers was so looking forward to? She might trample his toes and maim him for life. When she'd just about convinced herself that staying home was the only way to be sure she didn't kill someone, she heard Hannah humming in the next room.

For some reason, the woman was actually looking forward to the celebration. And after all the time Hannah and the others had spent on her, Lizzie knew she couldn't back out. With a soft moan of fear, she pressed a hand to her belly where the few bites of lunch she'd managed threatened to make a reappearance.

"This is silly, Elizabeth Ann," she whispered. What was she so afraid of? It was just a bunch of people getting together to eat and dance. If she fell on her face, what did it matter?

Staring out the window toward the south—toward Wolf's home—she forced herself to face the truth: she was scared to find out what Wolf would think of this new Lizzie. She was so in love with him that she'd spent a month changing herself into the kind of woman he wanted, the kind he'd married before. What if it wasn't enough? What if, after all she'd gone through, he still didn't want her for a wife? Then what?

The bitter taste of failure filled her, bringing tears to her eyes—and making her mad.

So what if he didn't want her? She'd be no worse off than when she came to this stupid little town. She would just head for San Francisco, like she'd planned.

Tucking the brightly painted finger top she'd whittled for Cal's birthday present into the reticule that matched her dress, Lizzie stuffed a little two-shot derringer into her skirt pocket. It was too small to do much good, but it was the only thing Mercer had that wouldn't be obvious. Satisfied Millicent wouldn't spot it, Lizzie yanked open her bedroom door and stomped to the parlor to wait on Harvard. "If I ain't good enough, so be it." As she flung herself into a chair, a flash of yellow in the mirror caught her attention. Disoriented, Lizzie slowly rose to face her reflection.

She really did look like a female. The corset Millicent insisted she wear gave her curves she hadn't known were there. The dress she'd sewn, with the help of every female in town, made her feel—well—pretty. Feminine. Like a real woman.

Butterflies took wing in her stomach, making her nervous all over again. Lizzie took as deep a breath as the corset allowed and smoothed her skirt into place. And wrung her hands until her finger joints popped under the pressure.

And paced to the window and back. And around again. On her third round, the rap on the door scared her half to death.

Pressing her hand over her pounding heart, she went to answer the knock. "Damnation! Did you have to go and frighten a year..." She trailed off when all Harvard did was stare.

Self-conscious, Lizzie patted at her hair and tugged at the lace around her collar. "Do I look ridiculous? I do, don't I?" She laced her fingers together to keep from fussing with her skirt again. "Tell me the truth."

Harvard swept his hat from his head. The late afternoon sun glinted off his burnished gold hair. He really was a handsome cuss and, as a saloon owner, they might be well suited. But he wasn't Wolf.

"Miss Sutter, you look amazing. Absolutely—" He stepped inside and walked a slow circle around her. "Amazing."

"Doesn't she?" Hannah joined them, helping Lizzie with her bonnet and shawl. "Here, take your basket, Lizzie." Catching up her own, Hannah led the way out the door.

Picking up the last basket containing the dreadful birthday cake, Harvard offered Lizzie his arm and a roguish grin. "Richards won't know what hit him."

• ♥ •

Wolf only paused long enough to turn his horse over to Malcolm Douglas at the livery. Flipping an extra two bits to the man to unsaddle and groom the gelding, he strode back into the sunshine, knowing his horse would be well cared for.

He could hear the fiddlers warming up by the time he joined the crowd at the schoolhouse. He greeted friends as he made his way past the tables loaded down with baskets of food waiting to be auctioned off, but he hadn't yet spotted Cal or Lizzie.

"Richards! Over here."

Wolf joined Harvard in the shade of a big tree.

"I wondered when you'd arrive. Cal has been watching for you since daybreak."

"Pa! You made it." Calvin came running around the school-house, loose shirttails fanning the hot afternoon air behind him. Wolf snagged the flying body and spun his son in a circle, hugging him close.

"I promised I'd be here, didn't I?"

"That's what Miss Lizzie said, that you gave your word and you'd keep it no matter what. And. You. Did!" He huffed out the words as Wolf gave him another squeeze.

Wolf dropped Cal on his feet and ruffled his hair. "I do my best, son. Happy birthday, Cal." With a flourish, he held out the new book he'd bartered from a cowboy at the last trading post he'd visited.

"Thanks, Pa. I've never read this one."

"That's why I got it for you." He ruffled his son's hair.

"Miss Lizzie gave me this." He pulled a brightly painted toy from his pocket. "She whittled it and painted it and everything."

Wolf glanced around to see if anyone was close enough to hear Cal's slip. "That's really nice, Cal. Where is Mister Sutter? I haven't seen him yet."

Cal's grin widened and he nudged Harvard, as if the two shared a secret. "Oh, he's around back, I imagine." Before Wolf could question him further, one of the other boys called Cal back to their game of hoops.

"What was that all—"

"You haven't seen the decorations around the park, have you? Millicent and the celebration committee have outdone themselves." Harvard strolled away, ignoring Wolf's question.

Something was definitely going on.

The half-acre of flat, open land behind the schoolhouse had been transformed. A large plank floor had been assembled for the dancing, with a raised platform at one end currently occupied by two men Wolf didn't recognize, tuning their fiddles, Mr.

Petersen holding a long saw across his knees, and Sheriff Freeman, who always had the job of calling the dances and controlling the raucous basket auction. The entire area was edged with a railing made of freshly cut tree branches wrapped in red, white, and blue bunting, befitting the day.

Wolf accepted the glass of punch Audelia Mercer insisted he try and followed Harvard around the structure. He spotted Calvin in the middle of a knot of boys, but he still couldn't find Lizzie. He wanted to see her, needed to know how she'd fared being in town under Millicent's watchful eye for a more than a month.

Folks took their places as the fiddlers struck up a lively reel. Carruthers strutted by, his collar so stiff he couldn't turn his head to his partner, a lovely woman Wolf didn't recognize. The man looked dumbstruck with awe. Who would have thought the schoolmaster would have snagged a woman in this little town? As the dance got underway, Wolf watched the couple parade past, the woman watching her feet carefully as if she wasn't quite sure of her steps. Something about her seemed familiar, but he was certain they'd never met.

"Who is that with Carruthers?"

Harvard grinned at him. "You know her."

"I don't. A man doesn't forget a woman that beautiful."

Harvard threw back his head and laughed like a braying mule. "This evening is going to be entertaining." He slapped Wolf on the shoulder. "Excuse me. This is my dance."

As the music changed to a waltz, Harvard relieved Carruthers of his partner, took the woman in his arms and started moving. Her sunny yellow skirt flared as they turned and the setting sun made her hair glimmering with all the colors of autumn. Just like Lizzie's. Where was the woman, anyway?

As Wolf watched the couple, something Harvard said that made his dance partner laugh, and the sound hit him like a punch to his gut.

That was Lizzie!

• ♥ •

Lizzie knew the moment Wolf came around the school-house. Her gaze drank him in, reassuring herself he was no worse for wear. But the longer he went without breaking into the dance, or even acting like her saw her, she went from joy to disappointment to simmering anger. When she stumbled into Willouby for the third time, she forced herself to concentrate on what she was doing. There'd be plenty of time to give the infuriating man a piece of her mind after the dance was done.

The instant the fiddles stopped, she started around Car-ruthers, barely acknowledging his thanks for the dance. She'd just reached the edge of the crowd when the music started and Harvard caught her hand.

"I believe this is my dance."

"Just a minute. I need to go tell Richards—"

"Later, my dear. Let him stew a while longer."

His words slowed her headlong rush enough for him to take her in his arms. "What are you talking about?"

"He didn't recognize you, Lizzie. He asked me who the beauty was dancing with our Willouby."

"You're lying!"

Harvard ignored her interruption. "When I told him you two were acquainted, he also accused me of lying. Said he'd never forget meeting a woman as beautiful as you."

Lizzie was dumbfounded. She studied Harvard for a long, si-lent moment. "You're serious." She couldn't stop the grin from spreading. Wolf thought she was beautiful. Just as quickly, it faded. He thought *this* Lizzie was beautiful, this parody of a real woman. Not the real her at all.

She needed to leave. Now, before she did something foolish like give in to the tears burning in her eyes.

"Lizzie?" Harvard tightened his hold, almost as if he knew she was about to bolt. "What is it?"

"He likes what he sees now." She felt miserable. "This isn't the real me."

The lines of concern on Harvard's forehead smoothed. "Lizzie, he was enraptured long before he saw you dressed so beautifully."

"He was?"

"Of course. How could he resist you?" Harvard turned her in three sweeping circles before rejoining the line of dancers. "About now he's realizing with whom I'm dancing. Let's give him something to be jealous about, shall we?" With a quick grin his only warning, he spun her around, making her laugh.

Oh, how that idea appealed. Pasting on a brilliant smile, she lifted her chin. "I think that's a fine idea, Mister Browning."

As the waltz ended, Sheriff Freeman called on the women to gather near the stage where all the food baskets were placed. Lizzie tried to move hers to the back, out of sight, but the sheriff spotted her and took the basket from her.

"Remember, all the money we raise will be used to expand the school and buy more slates, since Mr. Carruthers assures me our young people are working so hard, they're wearing out those we have.

"Absolutely correct, Sheriff," Willouby piped up. "They are indeed becoming quite brittle with all the erasing."

As laughter rippled through the crowd, Freeman hefted Lizzie's basket. "Let's start right here. Who'll give me the first bid for this container of delights?"

Willouby Carruthers jumped in with his bid, followed by one or two others. Lizzie started when she heard Wolf join the bidding. Harvard upped the ante and Carruthers immediately offered more.

"There's nothing in there worth the kind of money you boys are promising." Everyone in the room laughed, causing her to blush even more.

Sheriff Freeman quieted the crowd. "Now that we know whose basket it is, will anyone top Mister Carruthers's bid?"

"I'm happy to." Wolf pinned Lizzie with a stare that made her shiver in anticipation—and not of the food.

Then another man joined the bidding. "I believe I will, Sheriff." Black Jack Hayes stepped out of the crowd. The hatred in his eyes made her blood run cold. Without hesitation, Wolf moved to stand between Lizzie and the danger Black Jack presented.

Harvard quickly increased the bid, as did Carruthers. Finally, mercifully, Millicent called a halt.

"Mr. Freeman?"

"Yes, Mrs. Freeman?"

"We could be here all night, the way the gentlemen are strutting and posturing. Close the bidding and move on."

"Yes, Mrs. Freeman." He banged the gavel to the crowd's amusement. "Sold to Mister Carruthers for five dollars and two bits. Come and collect your prize and your dinner partner, Willouby."

• ♥ •

Once the food was consumed, along with a piece of the icing-laden, though surprisingly tasty birthday cake, Carruthers gazed at Lizzie and sighed in what she supposed was meant to convey infatuation. "You are…amazing. Truly amazing, Miss Sutter. Not only accomplished in the kitchen, but lovely as a flower."

She snorted. "Don't ruin a pleasant meal by lying."

His brows came together in confusion. "You doubt the sincerity of my compliment?"

Lizzie thought of the look on Wolf's face when he'd recognized her. "Let's just say I've seen myself in a mirror, and I'm nothing much to look at."

"I must disagree, Miss Sutter. Every word I said is truth. I don't understand why you felt it necessary to masquerade as a male, though I'm sure your reasons were sound, but I, for one, am very glad to have been graced with a glimpse of your true nature."

Lizzie just stared at the man, unable to make sense of the flowery words he'd uttered. "Come on. They're starting up the music again."

For the next set, Lizzie was again partnered first by Carruthers. As the dancing came to a stop, she sighed and let her shoulders slump. She really wanted to escape this crush of people and be alone to think. But she'd promised, so she straightened and glanced to the line of men to see whose boots were in jeopardy this time. The smile she'd plastered on her lips slid away as her gaze collided with Wolf's.

"Miss Sutter." As the fiddlers started up, he inclined his head, took her hands and led her into the dance. Her heart started pounding and her head swam with every sashay. He was here. And she was dancing with him. A lifetime's worth of girlish dreams spilled into her heart as he held her, turned her out and pulled her close again. His eyes glittered, and she thought he was glad to see her. But she certainly didn't imagine the way his fingers caressed her arm as he released her and stepped back to make way for her next partner.

Her heart bumped once with joy and what she knew was a silly smile curved her lips. He *was* glad to see her! Still grinning like an idiot, she glanced toward her new partner—and stumbled to a halt. Black Jack Hayes waited.

As Hayes released his current partner and headed for Lizzie, she recoiled and tripped over the hem of her dress. Wolf caught her elbow to steady her. "Stay away from her, Hayes." Before Black Jack could respond, from across the dance floor Calvin howled in pain. "Leave me alone." Lizzie spun toward the sound and saw one of Black Jack Hayes's goons standing near Cal. Wolf spotted him at the same moment. "Go stand with Hannah," he growled, then stalked across the room toward his son as Harvard closed in from the other side.

Hannah grabbed Lizzie's hand. "This isn't going to end well."

"I'm going to level the odds." Lizzie shoved up her sleeves, preparing to dive into the fray.

"No need, Elizabeth. I'll handle it." Millicent sailed past, heading for the knot of men surrounding Calvin. From the corner of her vision, Lizzie could see the sheriff striding to catch up. As the music ground to a halt, Lizzie could hear Hayes's goon hollering about not having touched the stupid kid. Wolf stiffened, seeming to grow taller, broader, before her eyes.

Lizzie didn't want to stay put like some well-trained pup. She wanted to wade into the middle of the fight and knock some sense into Wolf—and just beat on Hayes. But Hannah held her back, hissing some fool thing about not distracting Wolf, so she subsided, seething with unspent fury.

"We'll have no more of that, gentlemen." Millicent Freeman strode into the center of the melee. "This is a party, not a brawl." She arched that eyebrow and glared at each offending male in turn. "You will behave or you will leave." No one argued, which wasn't a surprise, considering the sheriff stood at her shoulder. After several tense seconds, Millicent turned to the fiddlers. "Let's begin the reel again, shall we?"

Slowly at first, then with more speed as Millicent turned her glare across the crowd, people resumed their places, shuffling Lizzie along with them. She watched until Hayes and his men disappeared around the schoolhouse before turning to find Calvin stepping into the spot opposite her. When she met his gaze, he winked.

Why, the little schemer. Had he started the fight on purpose, to keep her from dancing with Black Jack Hayes? She stared at him, but he only looked back in wide-eyed innocence. When the music started, Cal grabbed her hand and jumped into the reel with enthusiasm. He didn't know all the steps and neither did she, but with Hannah on her left and Millicent's niece on the right, both calling out the steps and turns, they kept up with the others.

They made it almost to the end before Cal's feet tangled with hers and they both went down, howling with laughter. Lizzie remembered at the last second to tuck her feet under her skirt, which kept her demure and unexposed—and unable to get off the floor unaided. Wolf and Harvard each took an arm and lifted her to her feet. When she stumbled on her hem, Wolf took the brunt of the impact. Her lungs refused to work, and her heart took off in a full gallop.

Finally. That was the only word that formed in her muddled brain. She was finally in his arms.

"Walk with me, Miss Sutter."

Though it wasn't really a question, Lizzie nodded, properly thanked a giggling Calvin for the dance, and accepted the arm Wolf offered to escort her off the dance platform. If anyone stopped them, Lizzie thought she'd happily commit murder.

Once they'd gained the relative privacy of the trees, Wolf turned to her—and dragged her into his arms. The kiss tasted of all the loneliness she'd felt and the spice of the man she loved.

His hands stroked up and down her back, rifling over the tiny buttons. The sensation sent ripples of pleasure through her. As he roamed lower, she leaned into him, soaking up his heat. She let her fingers climb his chest and twirled the ends of Wolf's string tie.

"You clean up nice, Mr. Richards."

"And you…" He pressed a kiss to her temple. "I didn't recognize you, Lizzie. You look beautiful tonight."

She tried not to read anything into his words, but it was hard to ignore the stab of uncertainty.

"What's this?" Wolf traced his thumb over the derringer in her skirt pocket.

"I feel naked without some kind of weapon." *And why the hell did that word make her blush now?*

"What other surprises do you have hidden under this pretty dress?" He brushed the backs of his fingers along the top of her bodice. He only touched fabric, but her breasts tingled as if he'd brushed them. Then his hands wandered lower and he stopped. A wicked grin lit his face and his eyes glowed with intent. Before she could protest, he wrapped his fingers around her ribs and pressed, lifting her pale flesh until she nearly came out of her corset. "Beautiful."

Wolf leaned down to brush his lips over the exposed skin and Lizzie stabbed her fingers into his hair to hold him closer. "I don't think—"

"That's right," he breathed against her. "Don't."

Lizzie sucked in air, suddenly afraid she might embarrass herself by fainting, when the click of a gun being cocked froze them both in place.

"Turn around and face me, Richards! We have unfinished business. And keep your hands where I can see them or I'll make your boy an orphan."

Wolf lifted his hands from Lizzie and turned to face Black Jack, staying between her and Black Jack. When she took a step to the right, he moved with her, keeping her on his right and a bit behind, blocking her shot. It took her only an instant to realize he was keeping her gun hand hidden from Black Jack. That he trusted her judgment—and her aim—warmed her more than all his kisses ever could.

"Spit it out, Hayes." Wolf stood tall and strong, a mountain between her and danger. Keeping her movements small so she wouldn't attract attention, Lizzie eased her revolver from her pocket. As Black Jack spoke, she pulled back the hammer and readied the little gun. The accuracy wasn't good beyond fifteen or twenty feet, which meant she had to hit with the first shot. After that, Black Jack would have them both dead to rights.

"You may as well come out where I can see you, *Miss* Sutter."

Concealing the gun in the folds of her skirt she stepped into view and watched for her opportunity. Gathering her courage, she sneered at Hayes. "I'll thank you not to use that tone of voice when addressing me." If she could goad him into losing his temper, letting his attention wander for just a moment... That's all she'd need to rid the world of one Black Jack Hayes.

"Why's that, Sutter? Because you're a *lady*?"

The contempt he loaded into that one word set a match to

her temper, but the sound of people coming their way and the laughter of a group of people broke through the tense silence.

"This isn't over, Richards." He turned to leave, then suddenly spun back and fired. Instantly, Wolf knocked Lizzie to the ground, spoiling her shot.

A woman in the group screamed, voiced were raised in fear and concern. The shouts from a couple of men followed Black Jack into the woods, giving Wolf a chance to pull Lizzie to her feet. "Are you all right?"

"Other than having a mountain fall on me, I'm fine. Why'd you do that? I had a bead on his head!"

"There were other people coming in from that way."

"I wouldn't have missed!"

Still, his point was proven when a mass of folks poured into the tiny clearing from all sides.

"What happened?"

"Are you hurt?"

"Someone get the sheriff."

"I'm right here." Sheriff Freeman parted the crowd and made his way to Wolf and Lizzie. "Neither of you are bleeding, are you?"

Wolf shook his head.

"Neither is Hayes, unfortunately," Lizzie spat out.

"Figured it was him." He pointed to four men. "Saddle horses and gather your weapons. I got a telegram from the Texas Rangers about Hayes. We'll go after him. He's disturbed my peace one too many times."

"Tonight?" one of them protested.

"One hour!" The sheriff turned to leave, taking most of those gathered around with him. When it quieted again, only Harvard and Hannah remained.

"We should go, too," Harvard cautioned. "No need to separate yourself from the crowd and make it easy for Hayes."

Without a word, Wolf took Lizzie's hand and tucked it into the crook of his elbow. As he led her back to the light of the lanterns around the schoolhouse, Lizzie stared at her hand, so dark against his white shirt. Not delicate. Not ladylike. Not perfect. Certainly not the hand of a woman Wolf Richards might want to marry. "Damnation," she whispered.

• ♥ •

By the light in Hannah's little parlor, Lizzie surveyed the damage done to her dress. "It's ruined," she lamented.

"It's only a dress, Lizzie." Hannah looked Lizzie up and down, her concern obvious. "Black Jack didn't hurt you, did he?"

"Don't insult me." Lizzie shook out the back of her skirt. "That gambler couldn't hit the side of a barn if he was standing a yard away."

"I was so worried." Satisfied Lizzie wasn't hiding anything, Hannah went to the mirror on the far wall to remove her hat. "What an evening." She plopped onto the settee and rubbed her hands together in glee. "We haven't had this much excitement in years. Oh, who am I kidding? The social has *never* been so much fun." She giggled. "When the men started fighting over your basket, I thought Millicent was going to have apoplexy."

Only half-listening to Hannah's gushing, Lizzie checked over her derringer. Satisfied she was as prepared for trouble as possible, Lizzie stuffed the gun back into her pocket and went to peek out between the window curtains.

She shaded her eyes against the light in the room. Would Wolf take Cal to Harvard's for tonight? Or were they heading for the ranch? She squinted into the darkness, hoping to catch a glimpse of him, but there were too many people milling around out there for her to be sure.

"I'm sure he's fine, Lizzie."

She stiffened, but didn't glance at Hannah. "Who?"

Hannah snorted. "Who, indeed. You don't think anyone was fooled, do you?"

Lizzie dropped the curtain and stumbled back a step, dumbfounded. Did the whole town know how she felt about Wolf?

"Oh, I'm just teasing you. Don't fret so. I doubt anyone else noticed. I figured it out right away, but I was expecting it." She pulled the pins out of her hair and let the blonde mass unravel into her lap. "I mean, you've dropped a few hints, and the way you blushed when he claimed you to dance…"

Lizzie knew she'd been found out. "You don't think Richards noticed, do you?" Part of her hoped he had, the other half was appalled at the notion. She was no good at this female stuff.

"He might figure it out if he thinks about it." Hannah jumped when a heavy hand knocked on the front door, then giggled. "That didn't take long at all. Good night."

Before Lizzie could ask her what she meant, Hannah closed her bedroom door and the pounding on the door started up again. The owner of that fist was going to get a piece of her mind. She was not in the mood for company.

Lizzie stomped down the hall and flung open the front door. "What the he—" The expletive died on her lips. Wolf didn't wait for an invitation. He pushed into the house, backing her up, step by step, until he could shove the door closed.

"You shouldn't be here," she managed, backing away from him, all the way into the sitting room. Suddenly realizing she was giving ground without a fight, she planted her feet. "What do you want?"

CHAPTER TWENTY-THREE

Wolf paced the tiny room, feeling like a caged animal. He avoided looking at Lizzie, not sure what he might say if she asked what was wrong. On his fourth trip around the room, she ran out of patience with him. "Just forget I asked. Show yourself out."

As she spun around to leave, Wolf stepped in front of her. "I want to get one thing straight."

"What?" Lizzie crossed her arms over her breasts, plumping them and grabbing his attention. "I'm listening."

He grabbed her by the shoulders, yanked her close and fused his lips to hers. Her sputtered objection became a moan deep in her throat. She pounded her fists once on his chest then gathered his shirt in her fingers. When he eased up a little and teased her lips with his tongue, she slid her hands around his neck, grabbed fistfuls of hair for balance, and rose on her toes to kiss him back.

Wolf dragged her closer, molding her to his rock-hard center. His tongue stabbed past her lips and tangled with hers, challenging her to a sensual duel she didn't refuse.

Minutes passed. Maybe hours. Wolf finally forced himself to let her go, dipping in for one last kiss before putting some space between them. Lizzie's eyes were slow to open and their slumberous midnight blue depths nearly pulled him under again.

"Why'd you stop?" She licked her lips as if trying to get at every last bit of his taste.

Wolf's body tightened painfully. He gritted his teeth to keep from taking her up on her unconscious offer. "I had no right to come in here and... I apologize." He rubbed the back of his neck, trying to loosen the stiffness there. Too bad Lizzie couldn't work out the stiffness a little farther south.

"I wish you wouldn't." She walked closer, until her skirt wrapped around his legs and her breasts pressed into his chest. "Apologize, that is."

She grabbed his head, her nails biting into his scalp, and pulled him down to meet her. Her lips captured his and his good intentions went up in smoke.

The sound of laughter floated in through the open window. Wolf thrust her away and went to the far side of the room. "Stay over there," he ordered when she started to follow. "Someone might see."

Lizzie blinked, as if coming out of a trance. "What?" She glanced toward the window, confused. Her shoulders stiffened when she realized what he meant. "Damnation," she muttered.

"I won't argue with that." He wiped his palms down his face and willed his body to cool. "I should go."

"No," she objected. "I mean, please don't. We're adults. Surely we can be in the same room, carry on a conversation."

Wolf studied the furniture. Everything looked too small and too close together. "Not in this room, we can't."

"Then let's go out on the porch. There are at least a dozen chaperones still out and about, so we'll have to keep our hands to ourselves."

Wolf snagged his hat from the chair and nearly pushed her out the door. The hot summer day had left behind a warm night, and the air felt like silk on his exposed skin. The thought made him look at Lizzie. He remembered her beautiful skin, luminous in the moonlight, so soft and pale next to his hands. Wolf stroked a strand of dark hair off her cheek. "Carruthers was right, you know. You are amazing."

"I'm not," she insisted. "This is just a bunch of fabric. It's not me."

"Good evening, Miss Sutter. Mr. Richards." People crowded

up the walk to the base of the stairs.

"We wanted to stop by and check on you." A woman Lizzie barely knew took the lead. "You weren't injured in any way by that terrible ordeal, were you?"

"No, we're fine, Mrs. Stephens," Wolf took the lead. "But I know Miss Sutter appreciates your concern."

"Yes," Lizzie blurted. "I appreciate it. Thank you."

"Well, if you need anything," another offered. "Anything at all, you just ask, ya hear?"

"We will check on you again tomorrow, my dear."

As they wandered away, Lizzie stared into the darkness. "That was Audelia Mercer."

"And the preacher and his wife, and the Johnsons. Mercer must be with the posse."

"They really seem to care about me." Amazement colored Lizzie's voice.

Wolf turned Lizzie to face him. "Of course they do. You're a member of this community now. A lot more folks stopped me on my way over here and asked me to convey their concern."

She elbowed him in the ribs. "So why didn't you?"

"I hadn't gotten around to it, yet." He lifted her chin with a gentle touch and kissed the tip of her nose. "I got close to you and everything went straight out of my head."

"Like what?"

He grinned. "Are you fishing for a compliment?"

"Hell, no," she snapped, and spun away.

"Now, take it easy, woman." He tugged her back to his side and urged her into the shadows. He didn't need anyone seeing them and ruining her reputation. The moment they were out of sight, he tugged her off balance and into his arms.

"Finally," she sighed when he released her hands. "I thought we'd never get back to that."

Her hands were moving before he could respond, stroking places that were bound to get them in trouble. "Cut that out, woman." Wolf gathered both her hands into his and waited until she looked at him. The desire darkening her eyes nearly made him forget what he wanted to say.

"First, I'm sorry I was late getting back. I was even more successful than I expected." He stroked a thumb across the back of her hand, needing to feel her soft skin again. "I had to take the time to build a travois to haul everything out of the mountains. Then I detoured to a couple of trading posts to sell what I could."

"That's wonderful, Wolf. You and Cal will be fine now. I'm certain of it."

"You will be, too."

She shook her head. "You don't need to pay me. Zeke did what I was supposed to do. Pay him."

"That's not what I mean."

Elegant eyebrows gathered over her confused gaze. "I don't understand."

He leaned close to catch a bit more of her scent. "You are so beautiful, Lizzie. I couldn't believe it was you—"

She wrenched out of his hold. "I understand. Please don't say it."

"Wait a minute." Wolf followed her to the porch. "Let me finish."

"No. I can't bear to hear you say the words. If I'm not good enough as I am—"

"Let me finish, Lizzie."

"Richards!"

Wolf hissed a curse at the interruption. "What do you want, Browning?"

"The sheriff is requesting your presence. He wants you to join the posse going after Hayes and his men."

"I'm not joining any posse. I just got home."

"That's what I told Sheriff Freeman, but he'd still like to have your input. You know Hayes better than anyone."

Wolf studied Lizzie for a long moment, but couldn't decipher the look in her eyes. "Fine, I'll tell him what I can, then we're heading home. Where's my son?"

Lizzie flinched away when he reached for her hand.

"Cal is with the Fischers. He's invited to stay the night."

"That's not necessary. Lizzie, I'll be back in Civil in a few days and pick up what supplies we need and some money I'm owed."

"You should stay in town, at least for tonight." Harvard checked the shadows before continuing. "Black Jack was making a lot of noise about finishing what you started."

Wolf stared. "I didn't start anything."

Harvard waved away his concern. "I know, and so does the rest of the town, Wolf, but that won't stop Hayes. You have to take Cal's safety into consideration."

"The safety of my son and Lizzie is all I'm concerned with," Wolf interrupted, anger obvious in his voice.

"Then stay. There's no good reason to stake yourself out as bait on your homestead."

Wolf shook his head. "I promised Zeke I'd be back tonight. He's watched my horses long enough. Cal and I will be fine."

"Zeke will manage one more night, Wolf. It isn't worth the risk. Please. Stay here."

"Fine," Wolf gave in. "You make sense. I'll go tell Cal after I talk to the sheriff."

"Miss Sutter, do you wish to ride with the posse?" Harvard studied Lizzie's face as he asked. "Sheriff Freeman said you'd be welcome."

For a moment, Lizzie was tempted. "No. It's a waste of time. Hayes will go to ground, like the snake he is, and choose his next moment carefully."

"I can't argue with your reasoning," Harvard agreed.

Wolf stroked a hand down Lizzie's arm to capture her hand. "I'll be back in the morning. There are things we need to discuss." The sadness, the resignation in her eyes, troubled him.

Lizzie nodded, but he wasn't reassured. *Later*, he told himself. He had other matters to attend to. "Where's the sheriff?"

"He said they would gather in the schoolhouse, since the lanterns are still lit."

Tipping his hat to Lizzie, Wolf strode down the walk and turned toward the schoolhouse.

Harvard watched Lizzie as Wolf disappeared from sight. "He's a lucky man, Elizabeth. I only hope he realizes it."

"But which *me* does he want to see over his breakfast table?" she whispered.

CHAPTER TWENTY-FOUR

Lizzie looked haggard when she stepped into the mercantile, dressed in a pretty calico nearly the color of her eyes. Wolf turned his back on the supplies piled up and ready to be loaded, just so he could watch her walk toward him.

"I was about to come and call on you, Miss Sutter."

She stopped three steps away. "I could change. If you want me to."

"What?" Wolf set down the cartridges he held. "Change how?"

"I know I'm not much of a female, but I can learn." Tears glittered in her eyes, giving them the look of precious gems.

"Lizzie, I don't want…"

The bell over the door jingled as Black Jack Hayes stepped inside.

"Well, if it isn't Richards *and* Miss Sutter. I'm glad to find you both here."

Lizzie stumbled when Wolf pushed her out of the way. He only hoped she'd duck when the shooting started, because the only way Hayes was leaving the store today was in a coffin.

"You really are as stupid as I thought," she taunted Hayes. "The whole town is looking for you."

"I have a bit of unfinished business with Richards." Hayes stood calmly, his arms relaxed, as if he wasn't facing a noose.

"Get it done, Hayes."

"If you'd just sold me your property when I asked, Richards, all of this could have been avoided. But no, you have to hold on to that patch of dirt like it's the only spot those useless horses can be grazed."

"What could have been avoided?" Certainty settled like a stone in Wolf's gut.

"It was a shame, what happened to Emily. She was loyal to you, I'll grant that. It would have been better if she'd accepted their offer."

"*You* sent them?" The pain in his heart threatened to take him to his knees.

"The Harrisons? Of course I did. I needed the land, they needed... Well, they took what they wanted, didn't they?"

Wolf's pistol made a whisper of sound as he drew on Hayes. "You evil son of a bitch!"

Black Jack laughed, making no move to draw his gun. "You won't shoot me, not if I don't draw on you. I'm only sorry I wasn't there when the Harrisons arrived. I'd have been first in line to enjoy her."

Wolf's finger tightened on the trigger. Finally, Emily and Amanda would rest in peace.

"Wolf, don't!" Lizzie pleaded. "He's not worth what it will cost you."

"He deserves to die." His voice shook. The rage filling him, spilling over, didn't surprise him. The loss of control did. He never lost control...except with Lizzie.

"I won't argue that." She moved closer to Wolf, staying on his left side to leave him a clear shot. "But you don't need to be the one. Let the law sort this out. The Rangers will take care of him if the sheriff doesn't. You don't need any more ghosts haunting your dreams."

Wolf savored the fear that crept into Black Jack's eyes at the mention of the Rangers. But could he let another exact revenge for Emily and Amanda, again? A man was supposed to protect his family. The truth washed through him on a wave of relief. Lizzie and Cal were his family now, and he needed to think of their future. Together. "You're right, honey. The sheriff can handle this."

"Which I'm happy to do." Sheriff Freeman came in the back way, his gun trained on Hayes, making enough noise to wake the dead—and to keep from getting shot. "A Texas Ranger rode back into town last night with Hayes's two gunnies tied to their saddles. They started talking when they realized keeping silent meant they'd be hanging, too." The sheriff glanced at Wolf. "Keep him covered, if you don't mind." The sheriff holstered his pistol and approached Hayes, staying out of Wolf's line of fire. "Hands up and turn around, nice and slow. If you so much as flinch, Richards has my blessing to put a bullet through your tiny black excuse of a heart."

Hayes must have seen the hope in Wolf's eyes. Raising his hands, he allowed Sheriff Freeman to handcuff him and relieve him of the pearl-handled revolver at his waist.

"Hey!" Lizzie studied the revolver then aimed a glare at Hayes. "That's mine, you thief."

"That means I can add attacking Miss Sutter to the charges that ranger already has on you." Freeman seemed pleased at the thought.

Lizzie started toward Hayes. "There'd better be another one, or I swear I'll—"

"It's probably in his saddle bags outside," Sheriff Freeman interrupted. "You'll need to come by the jail and identify them, Miss Sutter."

"Check his boots, Sheriff," Wolf interrupted. "He carries a Bowie knife in each, plus a single shot behind his belt buckle."

"Guess I'll have to strip him when we get to the jail house." Once the sheriff had relieved Black Jack of every weapon he could find, Freeman led a trussed-up Hayes out the door and past the crowd of onlookers. "Someone bring his gear to the jail and take his horse to the livery."

Wolf pointed his weapon at the floor and eased the hammer forward, his focus still on Hayes. "He deserves hanging."

"No doubt," Lizzie agreed, "but that isn't for you to decide. Let the law take care of it."

After holstering his revolver, Wolf snagged Lizzie's hands. "Why, Lizzie?"

"You didn't need to bring Black Jack to justice. It was time to let the sheriff do what had to be done."

Wolf tugged her closer, smoothed a hand the length of her braid. "I don't care about that. Why would you offer to change for me?"

She looked away, studied the floor. "I…" She leaned into his touch for a moment before putting a little more space between them. "You want a perfect woman for your wife. I know I can never be as good as Emily, but I'll try—"

"No." He turned Lizzie to face him, framing her face with his hands. "I'm not looking for another Emily. I loved her and I suppose a part of me always will. She gave me my son. But she's gone. And there's this other woman I know." He kissed the tip of her nose. "She dresses like a man, shoots better than I do, and her language would make a sailor blush. And she's perfect for me, just the way she is." He brushed a kiss on Lizzie's forehead, her eyelids, her lips. "In fact, there's only one thing I would change."

Lizzie's eyes drifted open, her gaze suspicious. "What would that be?"

"Your last name." Wolf eased away to look her in the eyes so she never doubted that she was exactly who he wanted. "Will you marry me, Elizabeth Ann Sutter? Make us a family again. Build your tomorrows here, with me."

Her eyes reflected her shock. "Did Millicent tell you my full name?"

Wolf's shout of laughter echoed through the store. Lizzie didn't join in.

"You really want to marry me?"

She sounded so unsure, he couldn't tease her anymore. "I really do." Wolf kissed her, a gentle caress.

"No more bird's nest hats and fancy hair," she warned.

He kissed her again, harder. "Agreed. Now and then, though, would you wear a corset under your union suit?" Wolf brushed a fingertip along her jaw and down her throat to where her buttons began and leaned close to her ear. "Just so I can take it off you?"

Lizzie grabbed a handful of his hair and tugged his lips to hers. "You've got yourself a bargain, Richards."

The bell over the door tinkled cheerfully as some fool started inside. With a snarl, Lizzie drew Wolf's revolver and shot the bell clean off the doorframe, without looking around. Carruthers's scream of terror could be heard before the door slammed shut.

Wolf broke their kiss, laughing. "One thing's for certain—life with you will never be boring."

"Count on it," she agreed, and wrapped her arms around his shoulders to pick up where they left off.

About the Author

Award-winning author Tracy Garrett has always loved to disappear into the worlds created within the pages of a book. An accomplished musician, Tracy merged her need for creativity, her love of history, and her passion for reading when she began writing western historical romance. Tracy resides in Missouri with her husband and their furry kid, Wrigley.

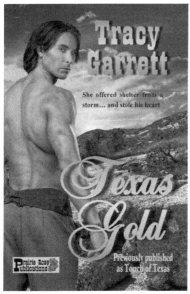

TEXAS GOLD

Texas Ranger Jake McCain is hot on the trail of a band of murderous outlaws when they ambush him and leave him for dead. A candle in a faraway window shines dimly in the night, and with his last ounce of strength, he makes his way through a blinding snowstorm to a solitary cabin and blessed shelter where he can heal.

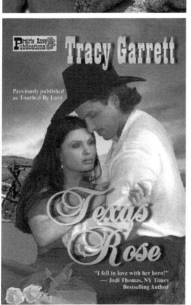

TEXAS ROSE

Texas, 1847~

A PROMISE MADE…

A loner with a heart of ice and nerves of steel. A dangerous, fast gun for hire. Jaret Walker has only his honor and the reputation he's built for himself to call his own. When a promise sends him to isolated Two Roses Ranch and Isabel Bennett, the woman he's come to protect, all he can think of is making her his—in every way. But she's the kind of woman a man like him can never have—for he's a man with a past that haunts him, and has no future to share.

76527524R00171

Made in the USA
Columbia, SC
10 September 2017